THE EYES IN THE DARK

TALES OF CROW #1

CHRIS WARD

AMMFA
PUBLISHING

ALSO BY CHRIS WARD

Head of Words
The Man Who Built the World
Saving the Day
Ugly Thirteen

The Fire Planets Saga

Fire Fight
Fire Storm
Fire Rage
Fire Flare
Fire Hunt

The Endinfinium series

Benjamin Forrest and the School at the End of the World
Benjamin Forrest and the Bay of Paper Dragons
Benjamin Forrest and the Lost City of the Ghouls
Benjamin Forrest and the Curse of the Miscreants
Benjamin Forrest and the Rise of the Pure Blood

The Tube Riders series

Underground
Exile
Revenge
In the Shadow of London
Genesis: The Rise of the Governor

The Tales of Crow series

The Eyes in the Dark
The Castle of Nightmares
The Puppeteer King
The Circus of Machinations
The Dark Master of Dogs

AUTHOR'S NOTE

The Eyes in the Dark is a horror-thriller set in Japan. It's laced with a tracing of dark humour, and a little suspension of belief will help with its enjoyment. In terms of context, assume the characters are speaking in Japanese unless otherwise noted, even though the dialogue intentionally uses a lot of British and American slang. This was inspired by the wonderfully colourful English subtitles you get for some Japanese teen movies, but just assume the characters are using their native language equivalent.

In addition, any Japanese words or terminology are noted in *italics*. Prices are usually noted in yen, and in general a good conversion is 100yen = $1.

While the book is conceived as the first of an ongoing series, it is very much a standalone story and can be read as one.

I hope you will enjoy my little book about crazy happenings up in the Japanese mountains. Now, if you're ready, strap yourselves in for the ride…

PROLOGUE

WOODEN KNEES TAKES A WALK

THE CLACKING BRANCHES of the leafless trees beat out the kind of tune that the old man the local kids called Wooden Knees might have made if, before he followed his father inevitably into rice farming, he had decided to take up tap-dancing instead. As it was, Masanori Kojima paused, put his hands on the accursed parts of his body, and looked up at the grey sky with something like trepidation.

It was a little late in the year, but he knew a stand of red pine deep in the woods where he'd been claiming the sparse crop of *matsutake* mushrooms as his own since he was barely more than a sapling himself. None of the other farmers knew its location, but the fungi he could sell for as much as twenty thousand yen apiece came late in the year because of the orientation of the hill. No one ever thought to search once the snow had begun to fall. While he despised the taste of the nasty, musty little things himself, the profits from his secret crop would keep old Wooden Knees drunk for the rest of the winter.

But the weather was turning. It was December the sixth, as the calendar read, but closer to New Year by the look of the sky, almost groaning above him as it ached to dump its load of accumulated moisture down upon his head. Masanori glanced upslope towards the last crest before he reached his secret spot, wondering whether it might be better to cut his losses and run. Getting caught out here in heavy snow didn't bear thinking about.

For a few minutes he stood in contemplation, staring upslope for a while, then looking back the way he had come, through a skeletal glade of leafless trees, the brown curls of their shed skin heaping up on either side of the trail he had made with his heavy boots and heavier bag. He could be home and stretched out under his heated table in a couple of hours, a glass of *sake* in front of him and some quiz show playing on the television. But if he soldiered on for just another hour there could be a basket of money sitting inside the front door.

In the end it came down to simple economics. This was almost certainly his last foraging trip of the year. A good crop now and he could rest easy for the winter. His mouth curled up in a thin, wrinkly sneer as he considered the other uses for the money.

'A reward,' he muttered, in that reedy whine that ended conversations quickly. 'A little reward for my efforts.'

He'd make this one count, put in an extra half an hour to really go over the ground, then splash out on one of the younger girls who hung around at the end of the shopping arcade late on Saturday nights. The younger ones wouldn't touch an old bag of bones like him unless he could pay way over the going rate, but even the prettiest girls had their price, and perhaps if he took a trip to the pharmacy beforehand he could get something that would make him able to do a little more than just leer as they took their clothes off. *Yes,* he thought, *it's time for old Wooden Knees to do some proper knocking.*

Feeling a little bulb of arousal bouncing around down in his pants, he slung his bag back over his shoulder and started up towards the rise.

His legs started to shake and his knees to knock together long before he reached the crest of the hill, but, huffing and puffing like an old steam locomotive, he finally made it, leaning against a tall sapling to catch his breath. The stand of pine was just ahead; hopefully with it several dozen litres of *sake* and a couple of lustful nights reliving his youth.

He started off, stumping through the trees towards a large boulder poking out of the ground that marked the edge of the red pines. Just beyond it, also benefiting from the prolonged warmth of the hillside's westward-facing orientation, was a thicket of bamboo. It stretched around the area of pine, a natural barricade, making this the only way in.

Spotting a small hump in the undergrowth at the foot of the nearest pine, Masanori grunted in satisfaction, dropped his bag down on the rock, and got down on his knees to brush away the pine needles and humus beneath.

The flat head of a *matsutake* mushroom peered up at him. 'Huh,' old Wooden Knees muttered. 'A hand job and a litre of *sake* to wash it down with. Good start.'

As he cupped a hand underneath it to work it out of the ground, something moved in the undergrowth to his left.

Masanori froze. A bear, maybe? It was rare that Japanese brown bears attacked hikers unless they were suckling young, but breeding season came in the spring and the summer had been plentiful, so unless it had some kind of disease…

Behind him came the crunch of a footfall, lighter than a bear but too heavy for a deer. Masanori let out a slow breath. Could someone have followed him? He cursed under his breath. 'If that's one of you fuckers…'

A sudden zipping sound, like a jacket being undone in a hurry, came from just beyond his shoulder. His head jerked around, his vision blurring as his old eyes took a moment to catch up, then something heavy and black was swinging towards him out of a background of bare forest. Like black wings it seemed to open out to fill his whole world, then something was closing over his head, drawing in around his neck. Masanori scrabbled at his face and tried to roll backwards, but strong hands on his back shoved him forward, his knees knocking together with that familiar wooden clump.

He pushed his hands down on the grainy turf and started to rise.

Something heavy struck the back of his head and his senses switched off like the last electric bulb in a dark hallway.

His knees seemed far too close to his face. As he came to, Masanori realised he was clutching his legs to his chest and pushed them away, stretching out the old muscles in his back as he peered into the gloom around him.

He felt floorboards under his feet; the absence of a breeze suggested he was inside. Groaning, he pushed himself up into a sitting position. His eyes slowly adjusted to reveal the insides of a single-roomed log cabin. There appeared to be no windows and only a single night-light in the ceiling, pushing back the darkness with a dim, orange hue. A tiny red LED light flickered alongside it.

Behind him was a wall, so he leaned back against it, pulling his knees up in front of him again. Directly opposite was a closed door. He lifted a hand and touched the back of his head, immediately withdrawing his hand as pain shuddered through him. Gingerly touching it again, he found no blood but a thick, meaty lump.

'Where am I?' he shouted. 'Someone let me out!'

In answer, there was a click and the door swung open, letting in a chill wind that swirled and wrapped itself around him. Masanori gasped and tried to shrivel up into the wall, but the door stayed open. After a few seconds he climbed to his feet, hobbled across and tried to close it, but it was stuck firm.

He peered out into the gloom and saw the shifting shadows that were the nearest trees of the forest outside. He felt a great sinking feeling that this was some sort of a game. Few people in the town liked him, but Masanori didn't much care. He didn't make trouble, or spread gossip, or screw people over. He just did what he did with a sneer instead of a smile.

It was also quite clear that he couldn't stay here. A cabin in the woods where the doors opened of their own accord ... nope. Not his idea of a good time.

If whoever had jumped him and left him here wanted him dead, he would be dead already. Whatever sick kind of a joke this was, it was clearly meant to rattle him. 'Won't get the better of me, you bastards,' he muttered. 'When I find out who's behind this there'll be trouble.'

He leaned out into the dark. The grey cloud had departed to reveal a partial moon smiling down on him, giving him just enough light to see. Glancing to the right, he could make out a shadowy ridgeline some way above him. So, they'd taken him down into the valley. The stupid fools. Masanori knew this forest better than he knew the varicose veins on his thighs. It was dark and it was cold, but he was hardy inside the battered suit age had left him with. It was only a mile or so downhill towards where he had left his little truck. The key was inside the rim of the front right tire, waiting for him. The angle of the moon told him it was past midnight, but in a couple of hours he could be home having a hot bath.

And in the morning he'd start figuring out who was behind this.

Masanori lurched out into the dark.

He'd gone no more than a few feet when he heard a rustling sound over the wind, and a deeper, thicker sound that could only be...

A pair of shining crimson lights appeared through the trees ahead of him, bobbing at a height that was above his head. Masanori didn't stop to consider the impossibility of it. He turned and rushed back towards the cabin as something huge and fearsome charged out of the trees.

He was within a couple of feet of the door when it slammed shut on him. He heard something whirring and looked up to see a blinking LED light just above the door. Then it was gone as something thick and sharp and furry gripped his legs and wrenched him backwards.

He didn't see the bear's teeth as they closed over his waist, because his eyes were shut against the pain, but he felt the sensation of one body becoming two as the creature separated his chest from his hips, and for a moment he felt a strange sense of weightlessness. Then the pain washed over him like a *tsunami*, and the snarling, ripping claws and the glowing crimson eyes became Masanori Kojima's last memory.

PART ONE

CLOUDS ROLL IN

1

THE STUDENTS ARRIVE AT BRITISH HEIGHTS

THE BUS STOPPED on the corner of the winding mountain road. To their right the forested hillside rose steeply upwards; to their left it dropped away, pencil-straight pine trees poking out of sparse undergrowth, branches already laden with early season snow. The driver and Kirahara-sensei were getting off, pointing and talking in loud voices about something in front of them on the road. Jun Matsumoto leaned back in his seat, sighed, and tried not to think about Akane. He could hear her voice near the back of the bus, telling that meathead clown Ogiwara to stop doing whatever he kept trying to do. Beside Jun in the third row seat, Kaede reached out and pulled his hand towards her thigh. He went through the motions as he always did, running his fingers over her soft, pliable skin, wishing he felt the same desire as all the other boys, especially knowing firsthand how quick she was to take off her clothes.

'I hope I'm rooming with Michiko,' Kaede whispered into his ear. 'I can pass her off easily. Then we can be alone.'

Jun forced a smile. 'I can't wait,' he said.

Kaede's face turned sour, her narrow eyes bunching forward into a frown, her lips curling up. She had one of those faces that drew boys like a magnet, bitter and unforgiving, but knowing … so, so knowing. Yet Jun, who had seen the other side of that sneering smile, knew what lay there, and it was nothing. She was a good lay, but once the sex was over … their relationship was hollow, empty. She had nothing to talk about, no opinions on anything other than who was hip right now in the gossip magazines, which pop star was cheating on which actress.

'What's that supposed to mean?' she spat at him. 'You not interested all of a sudden?'

'It's been a long journey. I'm just tired, that's all.'

Kaede glared at him a moment longer. 'You better not be tired later. Long journeys have an effect on me too. And if you aren't interested, Jun—'

Kirahara-sensei was back on the bus and tapping on the microphone for attention. 'Sorry about that,' the teacher said. 'We'll be continuing on now.'

He put the microphone down and started whispering to the driver again as the bus pulled off, steering out and around whatever had caused them to stop.

'Fucking hell!' shouted Ogiwara from the back of the bus, thumping on the window. 'Look at that! The whole fucking mountain is about to come down!'

'Ogiwara, that's enough!' Kirahara-sensei shouted into the microphone, causing a boom of feedback that made the students groan and cover their ears. 'Sit down.'

'Sir, we're all going to die!'

Ogiwara's fellow judo club members, taking up the back two rows of the bus, joined in with his Satanic laughter, thumping the armrests and stamping their feet like a crowd of hungry monkeys.

'Sit down, boy!'

'What's he shouting about?' Kaede said, leaning over Jun's front to peer out of the window as they moved around the obstruction. Jun found himself staring down her cleavage at the mounds of two pert breasts. Trying not to stare, he turned towards the window.

A huge rent in the tarmac ran right down the middle of the road. It looked like an earthquake fissure, but up here in the mountains it was much more dangerous. The bus had been winding its way up the twisting and turning mountain roads for what felt like hours, and they had seen several scree slopes dipping away from the road, held up by walls of thick concrete. When the rain got into the earth and froze in the winter, great sections of the hillsides could just slew away. Every year there was something on the news about some mountain village or other that had been wiped off the face of the earth by a rushing wave of mud and vegetation.

The crack was subsidence.

Kaede's hand was on his thigh, just inches from his crotch. He didn't feel remotely aroused, which made it lucky she was more interested in the situation outside. *Break up with her,* a little voice whispered to him. *You don't even get along. Do it now and save yourself the trouble of doing it later.*

'Look,' she said. 'There are no cones, nothing. It must have just happened.'

The bus rounded a corner, leaving the huge crack in the road behind them. A collective sigh of relief went up from the judo boys in the back, and several began to laugh. Within moments, they were making macho remarks and crude puns about cracks and crevasses and filling holes, while the girls whined at them to shut up. Jun looked back between the seats to see Akane roll her eyes at something Ogiwara had just said.

When he turned back, Kaede was glaring at him. 'What are you looking at? Something more interesting than me?'

'No, nothing.'

She shrugged and twisted around to face the front. 'Good.'

Jun suppressed a sigh and looked out of the window.

Twenty minutes later the bus crested a rise and a lumpy line of snow-covered hills appeared in front of them as the road flattened out. A sign reading BRITISH HEIGHTS appeared on their left, and the driver swung them in through a cast iron gate and down a long, wide avenue between several Medieval-style British buildings. Three or four storeys tall, they were all wooden-framed with overhanging eaves and ornate doors and windows. The students began to *um* and *ah* as they passed a building that resembled a castle, complete with a cannon outside standing in a few inches of snow, and a tumbledown church on the other. Jun knew from the guide leaflet each student had received that it was all fake—bought in England, dismantled and shipped over before being rebuilt up here in the Japan Alps—but the look of authenticity was impressive. Glancing up at a wood-framed building that looked similar to pictures he'd seen of Shakespeare's birthplace, Jun couldn't help but wonder how romantic the rooms might be … except he was sharing a twin with Ogiwara. He wouldn't even be able to toss one off in peace.

The bus turned a corner, drove past a large Christmas tree sitting on a traffic island in the middle of the cobblestone road, and pulled up in a courtyard outside another building that looked like a castle. A main turret in front of them housed the entrance, with two-storey arms reaching around to encircle them on either side.

Kirahara-sensei stood up, the microphone in his hands. 'We have arrived,' he said. 'Take your bags and head into reception, straight up the stairs there.'

Kaede's hand had found its way into Jun's, and he found himself jerked into the aisle, right in front of Akane, with Ogiwara pushing her from behind. Akane gave him one quick look with those lovely oval eyes, her mouth opening slightly as if to sigh, then she looked down at her feet as she waited for him to move.

'Come on, lovebirds, hurry up,' Ogiwara laughed. 'You can do some porking later. Let the rest of us get off the bus first.'

Jun glared at him but kept his mouth shut. He had despised Ogiwara even before Akane had fallen leave of her senses and taken up with him, but the other boy outweighed him by several kilograms and was captain of the judo team. Picking a fight now—or indeed at any time—was an especially bad idea, particularly as they had to spend the next three nights in each other's company.

A wide set of stone steps led up to the main entrance, a Medieval-style stone arch with Japan's Rising Sun flag fluttering alongside the Union Jack above it. As they started up, a rotund middle-aged Western man with receding hair, a red-tipped nose, glowing cheeks, and comically large fluffy white sideburns came bursting out of the doors, strode to the top of the steps and spread his arms wide.

'Welcome, welcome! Welcome, friends! Welcome to British Heights!'

Kirahara-sensei led the students up the stairs as the bus drove off to park in a corner of the courtyard. 'We are from Kagawa Commercial High School,' the teacher said, in passable English that was good enough to draw whoops of surprise from several of the boys. 'My name is Kirahara Makoto. It's nice to meet you.'

'Rutherford Forbes,' the blustery man said, scooping up Kirahara-sensei's hand in two hairy, liver-spotted paws of his own and shaking it like a dog ragging a beloved toy. 'I am the owner of British Heights. Its founder, its beacon, its architect.'

Jun knew the words but the meaning was starting to lose itself. Kaede was hanging on to him with one hand and sniggering into the other, so he tried to glance back towards Akane, but she had her back to him in the middle of a group of other girls. He sighed and looked back at Forbes, who looked like an out-of-costume alcoholic Santa Claus as he huffed and puffed his way through a conversation which, from the confused frown on Kirahara-sensei's face, had already out-Englished their teacher.

A few minutes of formalities later, they found themselves crowded into an ornate reception area, all wood-paneling and intricate carving, the walls adorned with old paintings of British countryside scenes. A sweet-smelling log fire burned in a wide grate opposite a more modern reception desk, while at the back of the entrance room a wide staircase wound up past a mock stained glass window to the floor above. A large chandelier that looked plastic, and lights set into alcoves on the wall, left everything in a dim, twilight glow. Clearly a mixture of authentic British artifacts and carefully designed modern fittings, Jun had to look at the PCs on the reception desk to remind himself that he hadn't stepped back into some Olde Worlde Britain.

'It's romantic,' Kaede whispered in his ear. 'If you steal me some flowers from somewhere I might be nice to you later.'

He nodded, thankful that he didn't have to reply as a man came out from behind the reception desk and called them to order, this time in a language Jun could understand.

'Welcome to British Heights,' he said in Japanese. 'My name is Tomoya Mitsui. We hope you will enjoy your stay here and get the chance to practice your English with the foreign staff.' A collective groan went up from the group, causing Kirahara-sensei to snap at them for silence.

'English sucks!' one of the boys near the back shouted, drawing an angry frown from the teacher.

'You can leave your luggage here,' Mitsui continued. 'In the main hall down the corridor you will be formally welcomed and then watch a video presentation. After that you will be assigned to your rooms.'

Jun glanced around as the students trailed Kirahara-sensei down the corridor towards an open door at the end. The owner had disappeared. At the other end of the corridor a tall, lithe Japanese woman stepped out of a doorway, glanced up as she crossed the hall, and disappeared into another. Jun frowned. She had seemed vaguely familiar.

'…FOUNDED in 1995, British Heights has been the only place for students looking for a deeply cultural experience in the middle of the Japan Alps for almost two decades. Every dormitory building represents a different period in British history, from the early 14th through to the 17th century, while the Grand Mansion is an authentic representation of an 18th century British stately home, with all furnishings and contents shipped from Britain. Beyond our living British history, our classes take in numerous aspects of British culture, from cooking scones to Shakespearian language. Here at British Heights we hope you will find all of your dreams fulfilled…'

The voice on the video droned on and on. Jun, sitting near the back, tried to concentrate on the pictures flicking past on the projector screen, but all he could think about was being somewhere else. With someone else.

Akane was sitting in the second row, between a couple of her girlfriends. Ogiwara was with the meatheads over on the left. Kaede was playing with her phone under the desk, scowling as she failed to pick up any signal.

'It's like, where the hell doesn't haven't a phone mast these days?' she muttered. 'Like, where the hell are we? Africa?'

'The Japan Alps,' Jun whispered.

'Yeah, I know that.'

'Everything all right back there?' came a voice from the front of the hall, and Jun looked up to see one of the foreign staff teachers staring in their direction.

'Um, yes, fine thank you,' Jun answered in his best English. Beside him, Kaede's cheeks had reddened. A few rows in front of him, Akane briefly looked back then turned away again. Jun gave the teacher a regretful smile and allowed a dirty wave of embarrassment to wash over him.

AN HOUR later the students had been allocated their rooms and Jun found himself sitting on the edge of his bed, looking through an explanation booklet about British Heights while a shirtless Yohei Ogiwara flexed his muscular arms in front of the big desk mirror on one wall of their room.

'I expect you want me to dish the dirt,' Ogiwara said, not turning around.

'What?'

'About how Akane is in the sack?'

Jun groaned. 'No.'

Ogiwara turned around. 'Come on, Matsumoto,' he said, a smug grin on his face. 'You must want to know! You can't have lived next door to her for your whole life and not wondered?'

'Shut up.'

Ogiwara throw back his head and gave an exaggerated snort of laughter. 'You're so transparent, Matsumoto. Everyone knows that.'

'What's that supposed to mean?'

Ogiwara turned and gave him a smirk. 'I'll let you figure it out.'

Before Jun could reply, Ogiwara grabbed a shirt from his bag and pulled it over his head. 'Hurry up, won't you? We're late for class.'

THE GROUPS for the classes were mixed, so Jun was spared the company of either Kaede or Ogiwara. According to his map, his class was in the upstairs lounge room of the dormitory nearest to the main entrance, named Elizabeth I. The ground was icy and a light snow had begun to fall, so he pulled his jacket around him, ducked his head, and soldiered on. Jun hated the stuff, but luckily his town rarely had more than a light scattering once or twice each winter. Why did they have to come here? The rest of his grade had taken a trip down to Kochi on Shikoku Island. That city had palm trees. Even though it was December, they were probably still going to the beach.

Jun, having not had a chance to go since they arrived, ducked into the toilet just inside the main door as the other students filed up the stairs. He sat down for a few moments, then checked his hair in the mirror. He looked like he hadn't slept for a week. He picked at a spot on his forehead and rubbed his eyes.

Outside in the corridor, a bell chimed. 'Shit,' he muttered, and hurried for the door.

The door opened into a flurry of flying papers and a curse of frustration. Jun stared as the fluttering sheets came to rest in a circle around him, then looked up into Akane's angry face.

'Be careful, Jun!'

'I'm sorry,' he muttered, leaning down to scoop them up, shuffling them into some kind of order. 'I didn't see you there.'

'You weren't looking.'

Akane sighed. Jun held out her sheets of paper and she put them into her bag. 'I'm sharing a room with Ogiwara,' he said, not able to meet her eyes.

'How nice for you. I bet you have lots to talk about, sharing notes and all that.'

'He hasn't said anything about you.'

Akane rolled her eyes. Jun wanted to reach out and touch her, to pull her into his arms.

'Don't lie to me. I know what he's like. He's an asshole.'

Jun couldn't hold himself back. 'Then why are you with him?'

Akane shrugged. 'Why are you with Kaede? Oh, I forgot. Everyone knows why you're with her. The same reason anyone gets with Kaede.'

'It's not like that. She's … deeper than anyone realises.'

Akane rolled her eyes. 'I don't care about you and your pervert fantasies.'

Jun blushed. 'I didn't mean that! I meant–'

'Save it.'

Jun sighed. *Why am I defending her? I'm defending a girl I don't like to a girl I do. What's wrong with me? Why can't I just say it?*

'If you must know, Ogiwara and me have broken up. I got a little tired of his childishness and the idiots he hangs around with.'

Jun frowned. 'It didn't sound like you'd broken up.'

'Oh, so you *were* talking about me?'

'No! I mean, *he* was. I was just trying to get ready for whatever stupid class it is I'm late for.'

Akane sighed again. She lifted a hand as if she was about to say something important, then she let it drop to her side. 'Look, Jun. I'm sorry, but you're right. We're both late for class.'

Before Jun could reply, she turned and hurried off down the corridor, slipping through the door and skipping down the road towards the next building. He watched her until she was out of sight, then put both hands up on the nearest wall and went to headbutt it, stopping just a couple of centimetres short.

He'd grown up on the other side of a three-foot wall from her. He'd seen her grow from a dorky, gap-toothed kid obsessed with the piano into a talented young woman who could break hearts with a single glance. That she seemed to seek out the biggest goons in school to date was irrelevant; at times her choice in men was akin to charity, but nothing could hide the truth: Akane Yamaguchi was a woman to be desired and swooned over.

Jun, who had spent his childhood pushing her off slides, putting bugs down the back of her shirt, and slamming mud pies into her hair, had come into that knowledge in the final year of junior high school. He had spent the three years since trying to convince himself otherwise, that the messy-haired, muddy little kid with whom he had played with train sets and hunted for butterflies was in actual fact the only person he could ever imagine himself being with.

Why can't I just tell her? This time he did thump his head against the wall. He winced, rubbed his forehead, and headed off to find his class.

2

THE BAND TAKES A WRONG TURN

Ken Okamoto slammed a fist down on the hood of the van. He held it there a moment, his eyes squeezed shut, letting the violent surge pass. One day it would take him over like a puppeteer shoving a gloved hand up into his cloth ass, but for now he felt it subside. He opened his eyes and looked up at Bee, standing nearby, his long pale face and huge, almond-shaped eyes watching him with a wide-eyed innocence, like a little kid watching his brother beat a puppy to death.

'I don't know,' Bee said slowly, his strange, echoing voice muted by being outside. 'I don't know at all.'

Ken glared at him a moment, then let his gaze drop. After all, it wasn't Bee's fault that O-Remo was a raging junkie. Nothing was Bee's fault; it never had been and never would; he was just the bass player after all, and bass players were designed by their very nature to be the ghosts of rock bands, forever in the shadows, neither claiming nor rejecting the adulation and the fame as it came, bloomed, and faded. They were merely a background, a cardboard cutout of a stable scene behind a nativity play. While Ken and Dai fought and battled alongside O-Remo as he faced up—and usually lost—to his personal demons, Bee was just a silken sheet draped over everything, soaking up the blood as it was spilt.

Dai came running around the side of the gas station, shaking his head. Big, muscular and square-jawed, it was impossible for Dai to ever look concerned, but the eternal look of concentration on his face had cracked a little. One curl of gelled hair was sticking up, and his eyes scanned the forest across the road.

'He's in the can,' he said.

'I thought we checked there?'

'The ladies.'

Ken sighed. 'I guess we should have thought of that. What's he doing?'

'What do you think? I don't know where he got it, but he has some stuff.'

'Did you flush it?'

Dai shook his head. 'He tried to scratch out my eyes.'

Ken slammed his fist back down on the van's hood, and this time his rage bloomed. He punched the scratched bodywork over and over until the side of his fist ached. It was lucky tomorrow was a day off, as his hand would probably now be too bruised to play.

'Fuck him. Fuck him!'

'All right, calm down. Not like it's anything new, is it?'

'He promised.'

Dai grinned. 'And like you don't break promises, Ken? Like there aren't a hundred girls out there who you've lied to?'

Ken scowled. 'Lying to girls won't break up our band. Taking a junkie lead singer on the road might.'

'Hey! Where's the party, comrades?'

They all looked up as O-Remo Takahashi, charismatic lead singer of doom metal titans Plastic Black Butterfly, came prancing around the side of the gas station, his arms spread wide, a huge grin on his anorexic, pockmarked face. Despite the cold he was wearing just a t-shirt and skintight trousers under a thin cloak that looked stolen from the set of a vampire movie. His face had once been angularly beautiful, but the drugs had turned graceful curves into sharp, irregular contours that made him look like a robot trying to burst out of a net of human skin. At the age of thirty-six, the looks that had once soaked the panties of stadiums full of screaming girls were just a memory.

As, Ken reflected sourly, were a lot of things.

O-Remo laughed, aimed a couple of mock punches at Dai's stomach, fired a finger-pistol at Bee's face, and clapped Ken on the shoulder. 'You fill her up ready? Let's hit the road, boys.'

'Where did you find it?' Ken muttered, feeling deflated, as he often did beneath O-Remo's natural star power. 'You said you were clean.'

'I don't know what you're talking about, my old friend. I was just powdering my nose. And a fine nose it is, wouldn't you agree? Not a single minute of surgery.'

Ken sighed. 'Get in the van and let's get out of here.'

Dai was the designated driver, Ken the navigator. O-Remo usually took up a casual observer's position from the sofa-bed wedged into the space behind the front seats. They had cut a hole in the awning separating the front from the back compartment for him to see out, although within a few minutes of the van setting off he was usually asleep. Further back, behind the sofa which doubled as a buffer for their gear in the event of a crash, Bee sat on a beanbag in the middle of a miniature New York skyline of amplifiers, mike stands, drums, and guitar cases. That he preferred to sit in the dark and peer into the screen of whatever electronic device was this month's toy of fancy was one reason for the extreme pallor of his skin. The other, of course, was the make-up. They were a doom metal band after all.

'The sat-nav says left,' Ken said.

'Are you sure? The last sign said Toyama straight on.'

'It's probably a quicker route.'

Dai peered out of the van's windscreen towards a rising highland area to their right. He frowned. 'Maybe, I guess. I haven't changed the tires to the winter ones yet, though.'

Ken shrugged. 'It's not that cold. I imagine we'll be out of the mountains before the roads ice over again. It's only a couple of hours.'

'If you say so.'

Dai turned them off the main road, following the little mountain road as it wound up towards the distant peaks of the Japanese Alps, first through dry rice fields dusted with a light covering of snow, then into stands of pine that gradually drew in around them. The road began to head up, and twenty minutes later the verges were twenty centimetres deep in snow as the pines leaned over the van, cutting off the sunlight.

'I'm not so sure about this,' Dai said, adding 'Shit!' as the van bumped into a pothole.

'Watch out, fool!' O-Remo shouted. 'I'm trying to get a little shut-eye before tonight's show.'

Ken turned to glare at him, but the singer had already lain back down on the sofa, skinny hands behind his thin, scrawny neck.

We should have broken up years ago, he thought, giving a small shake of his head, and it would be hard for any of them to argue with his logic. They should have put themselves down like a two-legged, diseased dog, ended the misery. The days of arenas and playing the Budokan, the finest venue in the country, weren't coming back, and while they could make a steady living driving around the country in their van, playing to three hundred people every night in forgotten little towns, the shadow of their former success hung heavy over their shoulders, like a thundercloud forever waiting to douse their fading fire. They weren't getting any younger, and, much as it pained Ken to admit it, they weren't getting any better. Perhaps it was preferable to let it go, get a job in a convenience store or some part-time work teaching guitar to kids, and quietly reminisce on cool autumn evenings about the days when they had ruled the land.

'Road is getting worse,' Dai said. 'Perhaps we should turn back.'

Ken ran a couple of fingers over the sat-nav's touch-screen, widening out the map. He peered at a thin line winding up, flattening out a bit, and then winding back down.

'I'd say it's as far to go on as it is to go back. We've made our choice.'

'Who set the sat-nav? I always take the major roads.'

'Thought you boys might like the scenic route,' O-Remo laughed, his voice slightly slurred as the drugs began to wear off.

'You dumb bastard. It might not look far, but these kinds of roads are often more trouble than they're worth.'

'Shit! Look at that!'

Dai was pointing out into the road ahead. A huge crack had opened up down the length of the asphalt, at least six inches wide, splitting the road in two like a cracked crust of bread.

'Um, I think we'd better go around.'

Dai groaned and pointed at the dashboard. 'The fuel's going down. I thought you filled it up?'

Ken grimaced. 'Just enough to get us to Toyama,' he said.

O-Remo laughed again. 'Scrimping on fuel again, were you?' he said, his voice nasally, his words bookended by two bloody sniffs. 'Just like the good old days, huh?'

Ken closed his eyes, feeling that familiar rush of blood. He thought about saying something back, but it was better to stay quiet. O-Remo was unpredictable at the best of times; high, he was as random as the free prize draws at the 7-Eleven.

'There's a third option,' came Bee's voice. The bassist was standing over O-Remo's sofa, so pale against the darkness of the back of the van that he looked almost translucent. Ken shivered. Bee's eyes were huge and alien, flicking from his, to Dai, to O-Remo and back again.

'What option?'

He held up his tablet. That satellite navigation system of yours is so old this van was built around it. When you all started to catfight I had a look at the map on my tablet. There is no road ahead. It's been closed for five years. The only way is back the way we came and then north up around to the coast. However, there's a storm coming in. We passed some kind of study village a kilometre back, so I suggest we overnight there, see if we can get some fuel or even get our van fixed if they have a mechanic.'

'But we'll have to cancel the gig,' Dai protested. 'What about the fans?'

Bee rolled his huge eyes. They seemed to take a few seconds to come around again. 'The last email from the promoter said we'd sold thirty-seven tickets. I'm pretty sure it won't end our career any more than the last three years has been doing.'

'But I was going to meet someone!'

Ken sighed. 'Can't you just toss one off like the rest of us for once?'

Dai said nothing. He thumped a hand against the dashboard and jerked the van into reverse, spinning them backwards so fast Ken gasped as he thought for a moment that they would smash straight through the low, rusty crash barrier and plummet down into the ravine below. Bee looked unconcerned and O-Remo just laughed.

'You never know, there might be some hot doom metal fans at this place,' Ken said.

'Fat fucking chance,' Dai muttered. 'There's hardly any left in the whole country. We should have broken this band up years ago.'

'No one's stopping you,' O-Remo said. 'Drummers are like persimmon trees. You don't notice how many there are until winter comes along and strips away the leaves. And then they're everywhere. And they all look the same.'

'Shut the fuck up,' Dai said.

Bee disappeared back in among the equipment and the others lapsed into silence. A few minutes later they came to the small turning on their left, almost hidden by overhanging foliage. Dai turned the truck into the thin lane and ahead of them appeared an ornate corrugated steel gate announcing BRITISH HEIGHTS.

'Oh, Jesus,' Dai muttered. 'I hate the fucking British. All they listen to is whiny indie shit and pop crap.'

The others were quiet as Dai steered the van down a little street with mock Medieval buildings lining both sides. He reached a small roundabout with a Christmas tree tied up with fairy lights on a little central island, and took the first left turn up to a large castle-like structure with a car park at the front.

'I'll go in,' Ken said, just wanting to get away from the others. 'Stay here. I'll see what they say.'

He climbed out of the van and went up a set of steps to a main entrance. Inside, a Japanese girl and a couple of blonde-haired foreigners were sitting behind a reception desk. The foreigners stared at him glumly, but the girl, whose nametag identified her as MIKA, offered him a nice smile.

'Can I help you, sir?'

'We lost our way,' Ken said. 'We were supposed to be in Toyama tonight but our van has a fuel leak and we heard there's a heavy storm coming in. Do you have rooms or something? And ideally a mechanic who could have a look at our van?'

Mika smiled. 'Of course. She pushed a tariff card across the desk towards him. 'These are our hotel rates. Three meals are included.'

Ken glanced down the list. It wasn't cheap, but it was just for one night. There were singles, twins and even quad rooms available, but the last thing he felt like right now was spending any more time with the others. He had a credit card, and he could charge it to the band account. It might or might not ever get paid off, but at least he could forget about it for a while.

'Four singles, please. Just for tonight. We'll be moving on in the morning.'

'Certainly.' She tapped away on the computer while the two foreigners just stared at him. After a few seconds she looked up. 'And we do have an onsite mechanic who can have a look at your vehicle. There will be a small fee, of course.'

'No problem.'

Mika handed him four keys. 'These are for your rooms. You're all in the Lord Winchester building. Desmond will show you to your rooms.'

She said something in English to one of the foreigners, and a dorky kid of about eighteen stood up. 'This way,' he said in English, leading Ken back out into the car park.

The others had climbed out of the van. Dai was looking eagerly towards an annex building on the edge of the Grand Mansion titled The British Arms. A sign displaying a picture of a frothing beer mug stood outside. O-Remo was scratching at his face, while Bee stood silently and still beside him, like a wraith.

'You can leave your van here,' Desmond said in thickly accented Australian English which Ken could only just understand. Then he waved at them to follow as he headed off towards one of the buildings.

They had just got inside, and Desmond was showing them to a quartet of antique but comfortable-looking rooms, when Ken heard a gaggle of laughter coming from a set of stairs that led up to the second floor. He turned around, his eyes widening as a cluster of schoolgirls came skipping down the staircase towards them.

'Oh my,' Dai muttered beside him.

One or two of the girls looked up, and a flash of recognition crossed their faces. Then they were being bundled out of the door by others coming down the stairs behind them.

Ken nodded slowly. Perhaps it wouldn't be such a bad thing to be stuck up here for a day or two. Once, high school girls had been their bread and butter, filling the halls and the live houses, and often later their beds, as their popularity grew.

They hadn't appealed to the nice types. Nice girls didn't like their kind of music. They appealed to the girls hanging on by a thread to respectable society, the girls destined to become hostesses, disillusioned waitresses in titty bars, factory floor workers, and *pachinko* parlour cashiers. The disaffected youth.

And Ken had seen plenty of disaffection coming down the stairs. Bad girls stood out a mile—they wore too much makeup, their skirts were rolled up higher than school policy allowed, their shirt buttons were undone, they wore rings and earrings, their hair was tinted with dye.

Beside him, Dai was smiling.

'I hope that pub's open late,' the drummer said. 'I think we're going to enjoy staying here after all.'

3

KARIN REMEMBERS HER PAST

KARIN KOBAYASHI ROLLED over in bed, reaching out a hand to caress the sheets. She touched a wet patch where Rutherford had been lying and hastily withdrew her hand. She rolled back over, pulled the duvet down and hooked her arms over it, staring up at the ornate ceiling.

What happened to me?

Her body ached and her vagina still tingled from the sex. Rutherford had gone, throwing some clothes on and hurrying downstairs as a bus group showed up a little earlier than expected, leaving her alone in the Queen's Bedroom, a mock-country home-styled room which was usually opened as a museum for guests. Today though, it was off limits—closed for "renovation"—as Rutherford was feeling a little kinky.

She had discovered with Rutherford that foreign penises were only uniformly large in the porn industry, but what he lacked in size he made up for in effort, making use of his fingers and his tongue like some fifteen-year-old getting laid for the first time, doing just enough to satisfy her, making her forget for a few minutes that she was screwing someone more than double her age, who had probably never been attractive.

Unfortunately, looks weren't everything.

She closed her eyes, dreaming of how she might utilise his money to revive her career once they were married. She could probably afford to finance a comeback album, pay for some good reviews in the press, maybe land a TV appearance or two. She was only thirty. She wasn't quite past her best yet.

Where did it all go wrong?

She had danced her heart out. Trying not to puff as her heart raced, Karin stood in line as the tall man with the slicked-back hair strode up and down in front of them. Some of the other girls were making eye contact, offering little smiles, one or two even winking, the little tramps. Karin just kept her eyes down, not daring to suggest anything. It would be or it would not be.

'You,' he said to a girl three down from her, and in a burst of giggling and excitement the girl jumped out of the line and ran over to the crowd of waiting parents and friends. A middle-aged woman with a weathered version of the same face swept her up in a hug, spinning her around.

Karin didn't even dare to sigh. The girl was not the best looking, not even the best dancer. Karin's hopes rose.

Six more times he picked girls out of the lineup of thirty. As their chances of selection become slimmer, so the euphoria of the selected grew. The seventh girl gave a high-pitched scream worthy of a horror movie victim and actually fell to her knees, slapping at the ground. The tall man gave a *humph* and moved on.

Karin was beginning to despair. At sixteen, she still had time for other chances, other auditions for other singing troupes. But this was the big one. Girls Chorus was already established as an arena act; if she made the cut as a junior member she had a ready-made staircase up to stardom in front of her.

'And ... you.'

Karin barely dared to look up, but the well-shined leather shoes had stopped in front of her, pointing in her direction. One foot tapped impatiently.

Karin looked up over immaculately pressed Ralph Lauren slacks and a Versace smoking jacket to a chiseled face with cold eyes and a tight, thin-lipped mouth. He was frowning slightly like a teacher about to admonish a student.

'Thank you, sir,' was all she could say as she took a single step forward.

Immediately there was chaos, as the girls not chosen exploded into dramatic displays of grief and failure, crying, shouting, wrapping each other up in hugs. Karin stood quietly, glancing up at the crowd of caring mothers and fathers, sisters and brothers, wishing that just one of her family might have come.

Only her boyfriend, Hiro, stood there, a smile on his face that had forced itself through the cloud of uncertainty. He put out his arms to embrace her as she walked slowly over, but she saw his thoughts in his eyes. They were over. He had come because he loved her and supported her, but they both knew that in the event that she was chosen—how unlikely she had thought it would be!—their relationship was dead. Hiro, captain of the baseball team at their school in Kanazawa, would have to wave goodbye as she moved down to Tokyo to spend the last two years of her high school days in a special stage school. They might play the game of a distance relationship for a while, but it wouldn't last.

'Well done, Karin,' Hiro said, finally wrapping his arms around her. 'I'm so proud of you.'

'Thanks,' she said into his shoulder, feeling a mixture of disbelief and regret. 'I can't believe I did it.'

'I always knew you would. I can't wait to see you up on stage performing,' he said. 'You'll be on the TV and everything. I can tell people, "There's my girl".'

She smiled, but it was sad, full of pain. Hiro was a nice guy, better than she was worth. But even if it wasn't for the distance that would now open up a void between them, the very nature of her future would stamp their relationship out.

The first rule for all the girls in Girls Chorus was the simplest: no boyfriends.

SHE CLIMBED out of bed and pulled on her clothes. The showers in the Queen's Bedroom were ornamental, so she would have to go back to Rutherford's suite to clean herself up. She pulled on her dress, brushed out a few creases and went over to the window, peering out on the courtyard below.

A bus had parked up in a corner of the car park, alongside it a shabby van with a faded logo on the side. From this distance Karin couldn't read it, but the colours were vaguely familiar. Between the buildings at the bottom of a gradual slope away from the main hall, the distant peaks and hills of the Alps were visible, already coated in snow. White stripes like lines of paint angled down the hillsides through the trees, and if she squinted she could just about make out a few moving dots that were skiers and snowboarders.

Karin scowled. She hated winter and everything that was associated it. She would never have left Tokyo if it hadn't been for the scandal.

She made her way down the corridor and through a door at the end. The Queen's Bedroom suite, together with the King's Bedroom and a vast study, made up most of the second floor. One door opened out on to the classrooms and a gymnasium on the second floor of the west wing, while the other way exited through a stairway that led down to the Grand Mansion's main dining hall.

Karin took the stairs down to the first floor and went into the swimming pool changing rooms. In winter the pool was hardly ever used, so she liked to have a swim on her own, partly to wash Rutherford off her and partly to keep in shape—if she ever did make a successful comeback she would have to look the part. Rutherford might be a doughy, balding mess, but his money was made and banked. Hers was still out there waiting for her, and unlike a businessman, in the entertainment industry you couldn't earn it behind closed doors.

She opened her private locker and changed into her swimming costume. Seeing herself in a floor to ceiling mirror, she couldn't help but smile in approval. Thirty years old and she looked as good as at any time during her career. She had a tight, lithe figure and bright, seductive gaze that could grace any magazine cover across the land. It was just that in Japan, public betrayals ran deep.

Swimming had always been part of her training regime. At the studios in Shinjuku there had been a twenty-five-metre pool which the girls used regularly to loosen up and stretch out their muscles before a hard day of dance training.

Karin pulled herself effortlessly through the water, counting up lap after lap until after she had reached fifty she pulled herself up onto the side to take a break. Her body tingled with exertion, the muscles in her shoulders and back aching more than they might once have. She ran a hand through her hair and peered out at the courtyard.

'What the…?'

Four men were walking across the courtyard toward the van that was parked up alongside the bus. One of them went to the back door and pulled it open, revealing a bank of guitar amplifiers inside.

Karin dropped back into the water, peering over the edge to watch. At this distance they would never recognise her; her hair was slicked to her scalp and the floor-to-ceiling windows facing the outside were steamed up.

'What are you lot doing here?' she whispered, as O-Remo turned around, his eyes scanning the buildings of the complex, as he might once have done when faced by a baying arena crowd.

She couldn't help but smile. They'd broken up years ago, but she still had a little fondness for the singer.

After all, they'd once been engaged to be married.

4

JUN DREAMS OF AKANE

IT WAS A BEAUTIFUL SPRING DAY. Jun's family and Akane's family had piled into their cars and driven down to the hot spring town of Kamiko Onsen, where they had a picnic under the blooming *sakura* trees in the grounds of an old castle. While their mothers gossiped and their fathers drank cheap beers and talked about baseball, Jun and Akane ran off to explore.

Even at ten years old, Akane was a faster runner than Jun, skipping up the steps and along the wooden paths while Jun panted and puffed as he tried to follow. It was always the case; while he hadn't wanted to admit it, he had also followed Akane into music by pestering his parents to get him an electric guitar for his tenth birthday. While he couldn't do more than slap at the strings in discordant aspiration, he had immediately adapted to the lifestyle of a practicing musician: days and long evenings sitting in a darkened room, only moving to eat, sleep, and go to school. Akane's legs were as active in gym class as her fingers were on the piano keys, so when she finally came to a stop inside a little glade, she was barely out of breath. Jun bent double, trying to force air into his aching lungs while Akane laughed and patted him on the back.

'Oh, Jun, you're such a slowcoach,' she teased him.

'I let you win,' he gasped.

'Oh, that was a race, was it?'

And off she dashed. Jun groaned, then staggered off in pursuit.

She didn't go far, just into the corner made by two crumbling walls that had once been part of an outer castle keep. The castle proper would have been wooden and was long gone, but the walls were made of stones the size of Jun's chest. He sat down beside Akane, eyeing the walls nervously, as if they would defy their years of immovability to come crashing down and ruin his afternoon. Akane, as if picking up on his nervousness, patted his arm.

'Don't worry, Jun!'

'Why did you come up here?'

Akane lay back on the patchy grass and tucked her hands behind her head. 'Do you wonder much, Jun?'

'About what?'

'About the future. What's going to happen to us?'

'What do you mean?'

'When we're old, silly. When we're really old, like our parents.'

'What do you mean?'

Akane laughed. 'Isn't there anything else you can say? Is your head full of bricks, Jun Matsumoto?'

'I ... I...'

'How many children will we have? Will you work for the government office or will you be bright enough to become a teacher? Will I be a member of the PTA?'

Jun knew that Akane wouldn't accept another fobbed off non-answer. So he took a deep breath, and said, 'We'll have five children. I'll definitely get a job as a teacher, probably science. You'll work part-time teaching piano, although when you do recitals at the culture hall you'll earn more than you do in an average month. You'll be a member of the PTA too. In fact, you'll be chairman.'

'Chair*woman*.' Akane laughed. 'I love you, Jun. You're my best friend, and one day you'll be my husband too.'

Jun blushed. 'Shut up!' he heard his mouth say. 'That's disgusting.'

Akane just giggled quietly to herself.

They stayed there for a while. Jun always found Akane's wild assertions disconcerting, but he'd learned to just brush them off as fantasy. Her mother often lambasted her for making her own piano interpretations of popular songs, because she had an overactive imagination.

He guessed it just went with the territory.

JUN JERKED awake to find Ogiwara slapping at his stomach with a wet hand towel, a twisted smirk on his face.

'Wakey wakey, sleepyhead,' he laughed. 'Guess who's in trouble for missing second class? You dopey goon. I didn't want to tell Kirahara but you were supposed to be sitting next to me. I kindly volunteered to go and get you, but you looked so peaceful that I let you sleep. I told Kirahara you'd run off somewhere.'

Jun sat up and rubbed his head. He wanted to shout back at

Ogiwara, but the lingering memory of the dream was still fresh in his mind, and he felt like Ogiwara was shouting at him from the other side of a pane of glass.

That had been such a good day, so peaceful, so relaxing. What had happened after that?

Jun groaned. He remembered now.

'What's the matter, Matsumoto? Having a wet dream again?'

Jun felt a thread inside him snap. He stood up and shoved Ogiwara back against the door. 'Why don't you shut your mouth? I know Akane dumped you—'

Jun felt his arm twisting away from him and then the room was spinning as Ogiwara shoved him face down onto the bed. A knee pressed into his back and Ogiwara's breath tickled his ear.

'Try that again and I'll do you,' he said quietly. 'And for what it's worth, she didn't dump me, we broke up.'

Jun, hearing the failure in Ogiwara's voice, couldn't help but laugh. Ogiwara scowled and pressed down harder on Jun's back, but Jun cried out and a moment later a hard rap sounded on the door.

'What's going on in there?'

Ogiwara snapped back upright, pulling Jun up with him as Kirahara-sensei opened the door.

'Matsumoto was just having a little trouble getting dressed,' Ogiwara said, snapping a military salute at Kirahara-sensei, which made the teacher scowl. 'I was just helping him.'

'Out,' Kirahara-sensei said, flicking a thumb back over his shoulder. Ogiwara hurried for the door.

Kirahara-sensei turned on Jun, who was brushing himself down. 'Why did you miss the last class?' he asked. 'You're here for your own benefit. Not mine, not anyone else's. You're here to do something different and refreshing, not just waste everyone's time. Especially not your own.'

'I'm sorry, I fell asleep.'

'Ogiwara said he couldn't find you.'

Jun shrugged. 'The guy's a clown. He probably looked in the wrong room. It was a long journey, and that first class was kind of boring … I only lay down for a moment during the break, but I must have nodded off.'

Kirahara-sensei sighed. 'I'll let it go, Jun, but make sure you show up for classes. Continual bad behaviour will count towards your final report.'

Jun felt his anger rising. 'What does it matter? You know I've got nothing to look forward to when I leave this goddamn school. I'll be making lunchboxes in some factory or working in a convenience store. What's the point?'

Kirahara-sensei smiled. 'Well, Jun,' he said, 'if that's all you've got to look forward to, you'd better get enjoying this school trip while you still can. Next class is British sports, isn't it? I played cricket once. Stupid game. Far too many rules. Hurry up now.'

As Kirahara-sensei went out, Jun sighed again. In a sense his teacher was right, but that didn't make things any easier to deal with. But it wasn't the thoughts of his post-school career that were bothering him. He had been thinking about what happened later that summer, when both he and Akane were ten years old. Even now, almost eight years later, he didn't like to think about it, but whenever he looked at Akane he was forced to remember. That was part of what had pushed them apart, but more so was the affect those events had had on her – turning a bright young girl with a love of piano into a dark, brooding teenager who rarely smiled and slept with bad boys as a form of passive rebellion.

Jun shook his head, grabbed his bag, and headed for class.

O-REMO FINDS THE LOOKOUT

'HEY, bartender! I'll have three more of these!' Dai said, holding up the pint glass. 'He turned to Ken, sitting on a stool beside him in the quaint, British-style pub. 'One thing I do love about the British,' he said, 'is the way they drink out of big glasses. None of these little schooners like we're used to. It's just a shame their beer's so piss-weak. You have to drink fifteen glasses of it just to get drunk.'

'Remember that gig we did in London?' Ken said with a wistful smile. 'On that showcase tour for the record company? We didn't expect anyone to actually show up for a bunch of Japanese metal bands so we all got tanked beforehand. And the place was packed!'

'Yeah, and do you remember the state of the toilets? Jesus Christ.' Dai slapped his knee. 'I guess that's the consequence of having crappy beer.'

As if on cue, the bartender brought three full pints of Bass and put them down on the countertop. Dai held out a note. 'Fucking expensive in here, isn't it?' he muttered to the others as the bartender went off to get his change. 'I guess that's what happens when you have to ship the booze to the top of a mountain.'

'At least they have some,' Ken said. 'We could be stranded here with nothing to do but listen to O-Remo talk codshit.'

'Where is he?' Dai said.

'He went for a ramble.'

'A what? Like *a walk?*'

'In the forest. On the nature trail around the site.'

'You mean he's gone to shoot up where he's sure there aren't any cameras?'

Ken nodded. 'That's about it.'

'And talking of being missing, where's all the high school pussy? What happened to that army of chicks we saw earlier?'

'They're students, Daichi,' said Bee, standing quietly off to the side, holding his pint in two hands in front of his chest as if it was a baby someone had impolitely left him with. 'It might have slipped your attention, but we're in a pub. Our country's licensing laws are relevant even here, on the top of a mountain.'

Daichi grinned. 'They have to come out and play at some point.'

'Don't get your hopes up.'

Ken grinned. 'And they're probably in some stupid cultural class right now, like gingerbread making.'

Dai sniggered. 'Or how to suck at soccer.'

Bee rolled his huge eyes. 'Or how to absolutely rule at classic rock.'

'Don't be ridiculous, you moron,' Dai said. 'If they were doing that, we'd have heard them.'

O-REMO CRIED out as he slipped on the snow, but he managed to grab a nearby branch just before he crashed down onto the slushy earth.

'Phew.'

He moved on, stepping over the lumps of fallen branches and rocks covered by a few inches of wet snow. The path angled away from the main complex of British Heights, heading towards a lookout point a few hundred metres distant. Around him a snow-covered forest floor stretched away. Behind him through the trees was the back of the dining hall, but in front the trees sloped gently away to the left as the path meandered along the top of the rise.

Every few seconds O-Remo nervously glanced back over his shoulder, looked left and right, stopped and listened. There were bears in the woods, so the sign said, but O-Remo wasn't worried about them. There were too many people around in the study centre for his liking. He had been about to spike up in the dorm when a group of kids had come prancing down the stairs right next to his room. The doors only had the flimsiest of locks and if one of the kids happened to burst in and see him...

Well, it would be the end of their career.

The band was merely in a short-lived slump. O-Remo knew without any doubt that within a year or two they'd be playing arenas again. He'd be dating actresses and he might even get around to kicking his junk habit.

For now, though, the less people who saw the better.

Plus, always one for adventures, he found the idea of shooting up in a forest quite exciting. Find a nice view, jab that spike, maybe even write a song.

He turned past a thicket of dead vines and saw the lookout point up ahead of him, at the bottom of a slight slope that rose up again to a small peak. It was a wooden hut, about the size of their van, and it looked out on a panoramic view of the Japanese Alps. O-Remo gasped.

'Well, how delightful.'

He headed down the slope and up into the little shelter. It had an open window space on one side for viewing the mountains and wasn't exactly draft-proof, but it was dry inside and there was a wooden bench for him to sit on. He pulled out his pipe and the little bag of goodness he'd bought from a mate of a mate in Tokyo a couple of days before, and loaded it up.

It might have surprised the others to know that he had been quite the student of Japanese geography as a boy. There in front of him he recognised the flat, bowl-shaped peak of Takeyama, the spiky head of Goryu, and behind it the twin peaks of Kashima with the needle of Yari-ga-take, the second tallest mountain in Japan at 3192 metres, poking up behind the others further to the south. From where he sat, an immense alpine valley stretched away in both directions, a patchwork of lumpy, forested hills and crystal, ice-covered lakes. There was nothing to suggest humans had ever made it here, as if British Heights and the lookout point were the very vanguard of civilization.

Except that down there in the valley, perhaps five kilometres away, was a square shape. O-Remo frowned. Perhaps it was a concrete dam or a buttress erected against an unstable slope. Evening was drawing in, draping everything in a grey hue, so he couldn't be quite sure what he was looking at. Plus, he was starting to get that wonderful little buzz.

Despite the smack dancing its little jig through his veins, O-Remo was getting chilly. He'd brought a thick duffel jacket and was encapsulated in a hat, a neck-warmer and thermal underclothes, but when the sun went down the temperatures dropped quickly in the mountains, and with a looming dark smudge heading in from the north it was unlikely the sun would be showing itself again for a while.

He stood up, and headed back toward the Grand Mansion. He didn't have to guess where he would find the others. If they couldn't play music there was very little they were interested in other than drinking and girls, in whichever order came first.

The pub was in a mock-15th century farmhouse at the end of the east wing of the Grand Mansion, so when he reached the main loop of the nature trail he turned left towards the pub rather than taking the other fork which he had come by, heading slightly downhill again, around behind the dining hall, the souvenir shop, and the pub. It angled out a little, back towards the ridgeline, skirting around several buildings behind the Grand Mansion that were roped off and labeled with signs reading STAFF ONLY.

Spotting a narrow alley between two of the buildings that would save him a few hundred metres of walking through slush, O-Remo climbed over the rope barrier and waded through a pile of heaped snow until he reached a cleared section of concrete path that encircled the nearest of the staff buildings. With the gloom now thickening and the temperature beginning to dip below freezing, the concrete had iced over, so he stepped gingerly across it towards the front of the building.

He had just reached the corner when a door opened not ten feet away and a woman stepped out. Dressed in a long winter jacket and with her hair tucked into a woolly hat, she looked like an elegant snow queen as she closed the door and stepped neatly down a set of steps. As she reached the bottom, the sound of an engine being revved came from the courtyard outside the Grand Mansion. O-Remo and the woman both turned to look at it, and when O-Remo saw her face he shrank back out of sight.

What the hell was Karin Kobayashi doing here?

Ten years ago they had been the darling couple of the media, but he hadn't seen her since she'd jilted him at the altar on their wedding day. Of course, he'd heard about her since. He'd followed her fall from singing star into public disgrace with a bitter sense of satisfaction, but he'd heard nothing about her for years.

Karin tucked her hands into her pockets and stepped out across the street, heading for the Grand Mansion. *I need to talk to her,* he thought, pushing away from the wall and starting to follow.

The world turned upside down as he cartwheeled over, one foot catching on a loose piece of stone, the other slipping on a patch of ice as he tried to correct himself. He tumbled forwards, bounced down a couple of stone steps, and came to rest in a heap in a little hollow cut out of the slope. He heard Karin stop and call out, but he kept his head down in the shadows, out of sight. After a few seconds the sound of her shoes began to move away.

O-Remo stood up and brushed himself down. Darkness had descended quickly, and Karin was just a silhouette as she climbed the steps and went through the main door into the reception area.

Suddenly he didn't feel like going to the pub to meet the others. He wanted to be alone in his room for a while.

His side, just below his ribs, was aching from the fall. He patted himself there, and gasped. Muttering curses to himself, he thrust a hand into his pocket and pulled out the two broken pieces of his pipe. The little bag of his stuff had burst, and he dropped to his knees to scoop up the granules where they had fallen.

'Shit, oh shit, oh shit…'

He pushed what he could salvage back into the remains of the plastic bag and put it into his jeans pocket. His heart had begun to race, the fear of running out of stuff on top of a mountain with no way to get more … but it was okay, he had just enough to get him through until tomorrow and they would be in Toyama by then, where he knew someone who could sort him out. And he didn't need his pipe – he was adept at making things on the fly if he had to. It would be harder to hide … but ten years as an on and off junkie had made him pretty resourceful.

Cursing his luck, he hurried off towards his room.

RUTHERFORD FORBES NODDED SLOWLY as he watched the footage of the junkie former rock star on the CCTV screen. All around him, a bank of TV monitors displayed almost every part of the complex.

'Hmm … this one could be interesting,' he said, tugging on a saggy lump of fat hanging from his chin. He turned to the man sitting with his back turned, bony shoulders hunched forward over a computer screen. 'Professor, do you think we could arrange for this one to get … startled?'

The hunched figure in the white coat didn't turn around. Forbes winced at the ghastly rustling sound as the professor's head nodded up and down in affirmation.

'A pleasure…'

6

PREPARATIONS FOR DINNER

'HAVEN'T you wondered why there are no other students here?' Ogiwara said, leaning close to Akane. She grimaced and arched her head away, but Ogiwara wasn't about to be put off. 'Seriously? It's weird, don't you think? While I personally believe these lessons suck giant rat's balls, I can see how they'd be popular for nerds.'

'Just leave me alone.'

He grinned. 'Why?'

'We broke up.'

Ogiwara sneered and leaned closer to her ear. 'We break up when I say we break up. Got that?'

'Everything all right back there?' the teacher, a tall, bearded Australian whose nametag identified him as MATT asked in English. 'Do you have something to share, Mr—' Matt leaned closer, squinting at Ogiwara's name tag, '—Ogiwara Yohei?'

'Go eat out a minke whale's pussy, you upside-down country tosspot,' Ogiwara said in rapid fire Japanese that made the class burst into laughter.

'Excuse me?'

'I'm fine, thank you. And you?' Ogiwara said. The class erupted again.

Matt gave a slight shake of his head and returned to the front of the class. 'Well, if you have anything to add, please feel free,' he said, turning back. 'And now, for our next activity…'

Akane groaned as Matt put her into a group with Ogiwara and two of his judo club minions, Shin Nakamura and Riki Mishima. As they played some stupid board game, Nakamura spent more time leaning around the side of the table to look at her legs than rolling his dice, while Mishima and Ogiwara traded stupid jokes like two kids at playschool.

'Seriously, though, don't you think it's weird that there are not more students here?'

'It's nearly Christmas,' Akane said. 'It's winter. What do you expect? I bet it's packed in summer.'

'Exactly,' Ogiwara said. 'It's near Christmas. There should be loads of people here. I hope there's turkey on the menu tonight. I want some proper English food, goddamn it. If all we get is spaghetti and fried chicken I'm going to toss a plate of it all over one of the stupid foreigners they have working here.'

'Oh, just shut up.'

Nakamura sniggered. Ogiwara looked at him and grinned. 'And by the way, are you going to dress up as one of those cute little Santa's helpers for me this year? You know, my Christmas present? Mishima said they sell maple syrup in that stupid gift shop. Perhaps I could get some and pour it all over you.'

'You're a disgusting pervert. You have a dick the size of a needle, but even that's much bigger than your brain.'

This time Nakamura and Mishima sniggered at Ogiwara, who glared at them until they shut up. He turned back to Akane. 'And how big is Matsumoto's dick, then? So small it's practically inside out?'

'Shut up.'

'Come on, you must know.'

A hand fell on Ogiwara's shoulder. 'It's big enough,' Kaede said, giving Akane a snide grin. 'You morons still playing in the sandpit, are you?'

'What do you want?'

'Just found out something that might interest you. Ever heard of Plastic Black Butterfly?'

Ogiwara frowned. Mishima looked up in surprise. Nakamura gave Akane's legs one last glance, then turned his attention to trying to see down Kaede's top.

'Yeah, course I've heard of them,' Ogiwara said. 'I downloaded one of their CDs for free, but it was shit so I deleted it.'

'Yeah, me too,' Mishima said.

'And me,' Nakamura said. 'But Ogiwara said it was shit, so I deleted it.'

'Shut up, you dumb tool.'

Kaede leaned down towards him. 'They're only fucking here,' she said.

'What?'

'Their van's up in the courtyard. At least it's got their logo on the side. I guess it could be some shit covers band, I don't know.'

Akane stared. What a bizarre coincidence. Plastic Black Butterfly was Jun's favorite band.

———

'Is that turkey ready yet?'

Ron looked up and stared. 'What? I can't speak Japanese.'

The girl pouted and planted delicate hands on her hips. 'I spoke English. Is that turkey ready?'

'Oh.' Ron glanced up at the oven. His eyes widened as he noticed the temperature setting. He'd put it to 150 centigrade for four hours. Wasn't that what it had said on the packaging? Or was it 250? Or two hours of one and two hours of the other?

He looked back at the girl. He'd only been in Japan a couple of weeks. If he screwed up perhaps he'd get deported. It was only a turkey, it would be fine, surely…

'It's ready,' he said.

She smiled. 'Great. Let's get it carved up for dinner.'

As she walked away, Ron pulled on a pair of oven gloves, took the turkey tray out, and put it down on a countertop. It was steaming and looked baked on the outside, but the little thermometer pushed into its centre hadn't popped out yet. After a moment's hesitation, Ron gave it a little tug. Turkey juices dripped off its pointed end as it slid out of the bird. He nodded in satisfaction. Juices meant it must have cooked okay. He smiled and reached for a carving knife.

It would be fine. Tonight's Christmas dinner would be one the guests would never forget.

———

'And this is how you hold a knife and fork…'

Jun sighed. Sitting at the back of the lecture hall, he gazed forlornly at Akane's back as the teacher on the podium talked them through dining etiquette with the help of a slideshow that was so overly jovial it was almost sarcastic. Down near the front, Ogiwara's minions had descended into a chorus of mockery, whooping and jeering as the teacher manfully battled through his presentation. Over to Jun's left, Kirahara-sensei was peering at a clipboard, the only sign of his embarrassment a slight grimace and a frown.

'So, enjoy your meal!' intoned the teacher, breathing an audible sigh as the students jumped up in a rush and headed for the exit. Jun noticed Kaede leaning close to Ogiwara's ear, but rather than feel any jealousy he only felt a sense of relief. Perhaps if they paired off

—and no one would doubt they suited each other—Jun might be able to patch things up with Akane.

'Hey.'

She was standing right beside him, those lovely eyes looking up at his. If only she could have smiled, she would have looked perfect. A needle twisted inside his gut at the sight of her, the pain evident on her face. How he would have loved to take that pain away.

'Hi. How … are you?'

She shrugged. 'I thought you might be interested. It's what all the others are talking about. That band you like, Plastic Black Butterfly … they're here.'

Jun stared. 'Huh? What on earth do you mean?'

'Jun, their van is outside, parked up beside our bus. Don't ask me why they're here … but they are.'

'My favorite band…'

'I thought you'd be interested.'

'Thanks for telling me. Have you seen them around? Perhaps I might get an autograph or something.'

Akane gave a brief smile. 'I'll tell you if I see them.'

Then, before he could reply, she had turned and headed down towards the front of the lecture room, where a couple of her friends were waiting. One of them, Natsumi, looked up at him and gave a small shake of her head.

'Come on, Jun,' Kirahara-sensei said, gathering up his clipboard and stuffing it into a briefcase, 'let's go eat before the judo lot get all the food.'

7

DINNER IS SERVED

RON SMILED PROUDLY as he carried out the carved turkey and set it down on the buffet table, the centerpiece between all the spaghetti, fried chicken, rice salad, and mini hamburgers. It looked great. He'd had to hide a couple of pieces that were a little redder than he would have liked underneath a small side-salad garnish, but none of the students would take more than a couple of pieces each, and that wouldn't do any harm, would it?

No, it would be fine. Ron twisted the platter a little so the meat was facing outwards at its best angle, nodded with satisfaction, and headed back into the kitchen to bring the next dish.

Working in Japan was turning out pretty well.

'ONLY TAKE WHAT YOU CAN EAT,' the waitress, whose name was Janine, intoned in patronisingly slow English as she stood in front of the long trestle table. 'We like to see clean plates here. And when you're done, please take your plates to the kitchen.' She grinned, ignoring a chorus of groans. 'And now … you may begin.' Her additional, 'Enjoy your meal,' was all but lost beneath the sound of scraping chairs. The students leapt up *en masse* and rushed for the buffet tables.

Huffing out her cheeks, Janine marched over to the new kid, Ron, who was standing by the entrance to the kitchens with a thin smile on his face, watching the rabble of students as they piled their plates with food.

'Like bloody vultures, aren't they?' she said under her breath. While she doubted any of the students would understand, some of the Japanese staff spoke English, and unlike the foreigners, who were all on three-month working holiday visas, they were company loyal. 'Bad lot, these, so I heard. Some special class of messed-up kids.'

Ron shrugged. 'They're no more unruly than the kids at my school were,' he said.

'This is Japan. They're usually a lot more polite. This lot, though ... bloody animals. Look at them scoffing all the food! All that turkey's gone already.'

Ron smiled. 'So it is,' he said. 'I guess they must love British traditions.'

'Love being greedy, more like,' Janine replied with another huff. 'You catching the minibus down into town tonight? Some of the staff are organizing a little Christmas party.'

'Sounds great,' he replied.

* * *

STANDING at the back of the line, Jun heard Akane groan a few places in front of him. When he reached the buffet table, he saw the platter labeled TURKEY was already empty. As he picked up a couple of hamburgers and dumped them on his plate, a blonde-haired young foreigner only a couple of years older than himself came and picked up the empty turkey platter, gave it a satisfied smile, and carried it out into the kitchen. Jun waited a couple of minutes, but when the young man came back he replaced the empty space with another plate of meatball spaghetti. *So much for British Christmas dinner,* Jun thought. *Perhaps I'll get lucky tomorrow night.*

As he carried his plate back to the table, the main door opened and Kaede came in, followed by Ogiwara. Both were grinning. Both had flecks of snow in their hair. Kirahara-sensei stood up and immediately began to admonish them for being late. Kaede fluttered her eyelids and smiled coyly at the teacher, while Ogiwara did his usual thing of staring at the ceiling in exasperation until the berating was over.

Dinner, in the absence of any turkey, was a boring affair. Jun ate three bowls of rice and a couple of pieces of smoked salmon, but his appetite was gone. Akane sat opposite him, engaging in occasional banal conversation with her girlfriends, but she seemed to have gone even further into her shell than usual.

Ogiwara, a few seats down, was now berating Nakamura and some of his other judo mates for gorging on turkey, leaving him none. 'After all the things I've done for you clowns ... I'll never show you pictures of my girlfriends again!'

Akane's head shot up. She glared at Ogiwara for long seconds, then looked back down at her plate.

IT WAS LATER that same summer. Akane, ten years old, was waiting patiently outside the front door of her piano school for her mother to pick her up. She waited and waited as the evening got darker and the streetlights came on, until finally the teacher came outside to ask her what was wrong.

'My mother is two hours late,' she said.

'Perhaps she's got stuck in traffic.'

Akane shrugged. 'Perhaps,' she agreed, but the smile had gone.

An office worker, driving home after a work party, four times over the legal alcohol limit, ran a red light at eighty kilometres per hour. Akane's mother had turned right into his path.

The hospital said she died instantly. That was something.

Her father, sick with grief, hung himself three months later. Never a strong man, he saw his wife in his daughter's wide eyes, and his own suffering in Akane's sullen face.

Her grandparents became her parents, but the darkness became her guardian, and her best friend, Jun, became a reminder of all that had gone wrong.

8

O-REMO MEETS A STRANGER

'WHERE THE HELL IS HE NOW?' Dai said, standing outside the pub with Ken as Bee strode up the road towards them, shaking his head.

'He's not in his room.'

'Fuck him, then. Let's just go to dinner.'

The three of them headed for the dining hall. There only seemed to be one school group staying at British Heights, which Ken could see was a disappointment to Dai. It meant less options. Still, there were probably more people here than had been showing up at their gigs for the last two years. Perhaps they should stage an impromptu concert.

Except their lead singer was missing.

Ken was actually starting to worry. If O-Remo got too high, took leave of his senses and wandered off, he could get lost out in the snow, which was beginning to dump, blanketing everything. The weather had really turned, and while an onsite mechanic had fixed their fuel leak, he wondered whether it would even be possible to leave.

Still, they had credit cards. And the Christmas tree standing in the lobby outside the dinning hall promised special Christmas food.

Ken, who could count on one hand how many times in his life he'd eaten turkey, was very much looking forward to a few slices.

Dai pushed through the doors into the hall. They were met by a fat waitress whose nametag identified her as JANINE. With a wonderfully fake smile, she pointed them towards a table laid out for four people on the far side of the room.

As they followed her towards it, Ken noticed how a hush descended on the group of high school students. There were roughly twenty, and now every single head was turned in his direction.

Several mouths hung agape, while one or two of the girls were unconsciously fiddling with their hair. Ken smiled. It didn't surprise him to see a massive grin on Dai's face.

'Dinner is buffet-style,' Janine told them in English. 'You can eat as much as you want. Unfortunately the turkey has all gone.'

'Greedy fucking students,' Dai said, after she had left them alone. 'At least some of them are decent looking. Do you think they're wondering where our lead singer is?'

'I think everyone's wondering that,' Ken said. 'Not least of all us.'

'He could be dead,' Bee added. 'He could have shot up in the forest and now be lying under a growing snowdrift. Do we replace him or break up?'

Dai clapped him on the shoulder. 'I think we stop worrying about it for now and eat, before those students finish everything off.'

SHE HAS to be here somewhere.

O-Remo had checked all of the rooms he could find, but Karin was still proving elusive. After hiding his stuff under his mattress he had gone back to the Grand Mansion to look for her. He'd found himself wandering through room after room of mock Medieval charm, from a chapel to a library to a pantry complete with plastic food. Tacked on to the end of the living museum were modern facilities, a swimming pool and weights room on the lower floor, a gymnasium and a youth club-styled recreation room on the second, complete with video games, a pool table, and a couple of pinball machines.

The whole building was almost deserted. There were a couple of staff on reception, but everyone else seemed to be in the dining hall. Of course it was entirely possible that Karin was in one of the dormitory buildings, or the other study centre near the main gate, but the snow was heavy now and he was convinced she was in here somewhere.

He had found one locked door. He knew, almost beyond certainty, that she was behind it.

Peering through the keyhole, it appeared to be some kind of mock stately home suite. He could only see a corridor, but it was wide and lined with ornately carved coffee tables topped by expensive-looking vases and sculptures. Paintings in large dusty frames hung between intricate windows flanked by thick drape curtains.

Several doors led off the corridor. She was in one of them, he knew it.

'AND THE WINNER of this year's bestselling single goes to … Girls Chorus!'

Karin jumped up along with the rest of her bandmates, whooping with delight, pulling each other into hugs and punching fists into the air. In reality, they'd known their single had to be close, but to have that final confirmation at the end-of-year music industry awards, that they—*they*—had done it, had the bestselling single of the year and a place in the records books … it was almost too good to be true.

It was Karin, the designated group leader, who was required to make a speech. As she stood up on a stage not nearly as big as many she had danced on, a microphone in front of her and a hushed crowd of five thousand industry professionals and other artists watching every flicker of emotion on a large screen behind the stage, the words came slowly at first.

'This is the greatest honour … in our wildest dreams we never thought we'd stand before you like we do today, with the bestselling single of the year. It really is a dream come true. First of all, I'd like to thank … my sisters in the band.' Cheers, group hugs, tears. 'And I'd like to thank my family, for always supporting me. And my…' She paused, Hiro's face flashing into her mind like a misplaced firework, temporarily blinding her. He'd made it more difficult than she had wanted, crying in her arms at Shinjuku station as she said goodbye for the last time. *No boyfriends is the rule, and even if I could … it just wouldn't work. We're too far apart.*

He had thought she meant distance, she had meant in life. He was on a career path to a simple life as a train conductor or ticket officer, she had the world at her feet.

'…and I'd like to thank our manager, Banba-sensei.' Her eyes picked him out of the crowd, where he was nodding slowly, his arms folded, a grim, stern look on his face as if he had written this line for her. 'You have given us everything. You have been a mentor to us, and … a father figure when we needed help. Without you there would be no Girls Chorus.'

The crowd erupted into applause. After a few moments for the other girls to say a couple of brief thank yous, they filed back to their seats. Banba-sensei gave her a quick wink as she sat back down, and for a moment she caught a glimpse of the human behind the public mask. Dread flooded through her. She had never known just how tenuous their fame would be, how easily they could be dropped or kicked out of the band, to disappear back into obscurity. As leader of the group she had more power because of her visibility, but she knew three of the other girls regularly shared his bed to ensure their continuing involvement.

The money wasn't even that good. Livewire Entertainment Ltd, the company under which Banba-sensei ran his stables of boy and girl-groups, took seventy percent of everything, even external work such as TV commercials. If her expense account was withdrawn she would barely be able to cover the rent for her modest apartment in the Tokyo Docklands. The contract had offered slave wages in return for a dream, but what choice did she have? What choice did any of them have? If she could get out while the group was on top she had a chance of a solo career or even TV or film work, but she was contracted to make three more albums. There was no telling how successful they might or might not be after the three to four years it would take for those records to be made.

At the after-show party, Karin played her part, entertaining record company bigwigs and TV producers with the smile that shone from the covers of a dozen magazines each week, but her mind was elsewhere, torn with indecision. Did she have the nerve to quit the group, to risk years of legal wrangles in order to take her freedom back?

At times, being a member of Girls Chorus felt little different to being a prisoner on day release. She had barely a day off a month, was driven everywhere by a Livewire Entertainment Ltd chauffeur, rarely had five minutes where she wasn't in either the company of the other girls or the management. It was stifling. Two girls had quit a year before, but two junior members, already in the public eye, had merely been promoted to the main group through a public vote, filling the vacated spaces without fuss. You never quit a band when you worked under Livewire Entertainment. You *graduated*. Your passing from the group was celebrated at a contractually binding farewell concert, and twenty thousand fans would wave you goodbye as you faded into obscurity.

The girls, for all their fame, were tools. The only real winners were Banba-sensei and his financiers.

She'd spent three years on a treadmill of touring, recording, and fashion shoots. She was exhausted. She was surrounded by people almost twenty-four hours of the day, but she was so desperately lonely.

She wanted out.

SHE OPENED her eyes and looked down to see the bald crown of Forbes's head bouncing up and down between her thighs. He liked to screw her at least twice a day, and he had some pills he took that gave him the libido of a teenager. Still, it didn't change anything. He wasn't a teenager. He was a sixty-seven-year-old balding, overweight, British businessman with more money than the Japanese government. He repulsed her, but the wilderness years had made her accustomed to revulsion. And it wasn't so bad really. All she had to do was put up with a few grunts and a bit of sweat and it was over for another few hours.

As he lapped at her like a dehydrated cow drinking from a trough, she closed her eyes, thought about some of her better lovers, and wondered how long it would be before he got tired and gave up trying to make her orgasm.

***

SNOW WAS DUMPING all around him as O-Remo tried to get a foothold on the slippery wall to push himself a few more inches up the drainpipe. The building was only two floors, so why did it look so damn high?

He'd managed it once. The back wall of the building had several vestibules protruding from it, with drainpipes on each corner. He had managed to shimmy up one, but the light he had seen had turned out to be a standing lamp sitting alone in an empty room. The next room along, though, had a brighter light in it, and he was sure he had finally found her.

O-Remo wished he had brought his stash with him. Just to smell it now, to hold it in his hand, would give him the comfort to push on, to see through the window above him and find out what Karin was doing here at British Heights.

'Oh, shit!'

His shoe slipped on a crust of ice and he fell backwards, landing in the snow that was now about fifteen centimetres deep. Relief that he didn't have his stash washed over him, but he really felt like giving up on his detective mission and going back to his room.

One more try, he promised himself.

He rolled over, wiping snow out of his face, and climbed back to his feet. He glanced left and right along the gloomy back of the building, wondering if there was an easier way up, a ladder that just happened to be leaning against the wall nearby, or even just a coil of rope. But there was nothing, only a——

O-Remo's head jerked back around, his heart thundering.

There, back in the trees, about twenty metres away, a bird thing was standing with its head cocked, watching him.

The only light on the edge of the forest came from the windows above him, so his eyes could be mistaken. Then of course, there was the snow, which was falling so thickly that it would cover his eyes in a few seconds as he tried to look. But there was definitely something there, a strange, feathery creature that stood with its head cocked, beady eyes watching him above a long, curved beak.

'Huh? What the hell?'

It looked like a bird. It should have been a bird, but it couldn't have been, because it wasn't in a tree or even near a branch, *it was standing in the middle of the path,* watching him, its head about five feet off the ground. A thin, pinched face, small eyes that seemed to reflect the light from the window above him. *Rather like a cat's,* he thought. *Knowing, intelligent.*

Predatory.

He blinked, and the bird thing had gone. The snowfall was getting heavier and heavier, bringing with it a dense fog, and O-Remo could barely see his hands in front of his face.

Suddenly he really didn't want to be out here anymore, in the twilight shadows behind the Grand Mansion, a long, long way from any way to get inside, with the snowfall getting worse.

And something out here with him.

He'd had hallucinations on smack before. They were more like strange, waking dreams, but he'd never really feared them. He gained a new perception on things, and the band, whether the others would admit it or not, had got some great material out of his drug binges. But this ... this was different.

The snowfall eased for a moment, and the trees reappeared, but the bird thing had gone. Perhaps he was just tired, or sick, or it was the drugs after all. He grimaced and turned away, glancing back up at the window one last time. If Karin was up there, she would have to wait.

Time to get out of here.

He looked down at his feet, and there it was crouched beneath him, spindly arms wrapped around its bony knees, its hideous half-human, half-crow face peering up at him. The mouth-beak opened as it cocked its head, and the beady eyes blinked.

'A penny for your thoughts?' it said, in a thin, reedy voice.

O-Remo screamed and fell backwards in the snow, flapping at the cold, white drifts like a drowning man lost at sea. He rolled over and over across a gentle embankment, managed to get to his knees and began to crawl away around the back of the building, panting hard, gasping for breath. He didn't dare look back, but he heard a high-pitched, cackling laugh.

'Help me,' he moaned, unable to find the strength to cry out. 'Help me...!'

It was coming after him, and he would die tonight, out here in the snow. There would be no more tours, no more gold records, no more drugs or sex with groupies, no reconciliation with Karin, the love of his life. It was over, he would die out here, very soon.

He could hear a rustling at his shoulder, and was sure it was bearing down on him as he stumbled to his feet, staggering along the base of the Grand Mansion, one hand on the wall for support. He twisted his ankle in a snow-covered drain, fell and cracked his knee, and for a second thought about giving up. Then he took another step forward and stumbled against what looked like a fire door. It swung inwards, depositing him on a thin, worn carpet amidst a flurry of snow.

O-Remo turned and shoved the door shut, not thinking about why it might have been open in the first place. There was no lock that he could see, but he pushed himself to his feet and staggered away from the little vestibule into a wider corridor. His hands left bloody prints on the wall, and though he couldn't remember how he had hurt himself, the sight of his own blood finally found his voice.

'Help *me!*' he screamed at the top of his lungs. He'd rarely put on such a vocal performance at a show, but as he collapsed to the ground, he heard footsteps running towards him, and he prayed-prayed-*prayed* that it wasn't the bird-man-thing come to drag him back into the snow and the dark woods beyond.

THE SCREAM CAME from outside the window just as Forbes groaned and ejaculated inside her. Karin, her legs aching from his hollow, desperate thrusts but her body feeling no sense of pleasure at all, frowned.

'Was I that good?' Forbes gasped breathlessly in Japanese, slumping down on the bed beside her, his grey chest hair slicked against his saggy man-tits. His tiny penis popped out of her and flopped over on its side like a dying worm.

'It wasn't me,' Karin said, looking away from him. 'It came from outside.'

'Oh, really? Perhaps it's those high school kids messing about in the snow.'

'Wouldn't they be having dinner around about now?'

Forbes huffed. 'I guess they might.'

From somewhere below them on the second floor came the muffled clump of a door closing, followed a few seconds later by the sound of screams.

Forbes sighed. 'Oh dear,' he said. 'Sounds like someone's got themselves into a spot of bother that will no doubt require managerial attention. I'm afraid I'm going to have to leave you for a while, my love.'

As Forbes climbed up from the bed and pulled his clothes on, Karin lay back on the bed, stunned.

She knew that voice, of course she did. She'd heard those screams in dozens of arenas all across Japan, watching from the side of the stage as Plastic Black Butterfly tamed another rabid crowd of teenagers.

It was O-Remo.

9

———

BAD TURKEY AND A MONSTER IN
THE WOODS

NAKAMURA COUGHED and dropped his plates on to the floor as a scream of 'Help me!' came from the hall outside the dining room.

'You dumbass,' Ogiwara said. 'You got sauce on my trousers. I've got half a mind to make you eat a fistful of piss-stained snow for that.'

'Didn't you hear that?' Nakamura said.

'Some kid playing around,' Ogiwara replied. 'Who gives a crap?'

'In case you haven't noticed, we're the only kids here. There are no other school groups. Just us and a bunch of staff.'

'And that shit rock band.'

'Yeah, and three of them.'

'One of them's getting up,' Nakamura said, coughing again.

'Stop your stupid coughing! If I get sick because of you, I'll kick your ass.'

'Sorry, I just feel kind of strange.'

'Must be the air pressure. I've never seen so much snow.'

Nakamura didn't reply. He was watching the table where the big, muscular drummer and the weird bass player with the abnormally large eyes were sitting, as the good-looking one who played lead guitar went running out into the hall.

'You don't think that scream came from their singer? No one's seen him here but there were four places set at the table. You know there were those rumours, don't you? That he had a drug problem, which was why their last three albums failed. Perhaps this place is also a reform centre.'

'Shut up, you idiot. I don't care what some stupid rock band is doing. They suck. I might go over and tell them that right now.'

He glanced back at the other students. Several of the girls, including Kaede, were staring at the band with obvious adulation. It made him sick. He spat on to the floor.

'Ogiwara! You dirty boy!'

Ogiwara grinned. 'Sorry, Sensei. I had a frog in my throat.'

'Clean that up! And help Nakamura pick up his broken dishes. The staff shouldn't have to pick up your mess.'

'Yes, sir...'

As Kirahara-sensei stalked off, Ogiwara turned back to Nakamura. 'I don't know about you, but there's definitely something funny going on about this place. I think we should check it out.'

KEN FOUND O-Remo slumped in a leather armchair in the reception area, blood dribbling down the side of his face from a cut on his forehead, one leg hooked up over the thick armrest as if he'd been blown there by the wind. His chest rose and fell in great choking shudders, while his fingers played nervously with the metal studs along the chair's seams. A pale-faced Japanese receptionist stood nearby, holding out a small towel, while behind her a tall foreign girl fumbled with a first aid kit.

'What happened?' Ken said, squatting down beside his singer.

'Outside ... outside, I saw this thing.'

'What on earth were you doing outside?'

'Walking.'

Ken rolled his eyes. O-Remo had that look about him, that look that said he'd been using. 'Are you sure you saw what you saw?'

'It was this bird thing...'

A chuckle came from behind them. Ken looked up to see Rutherford Forbes, the owner of British Heights, standing at the foot of the wide staircase leading up to the museum rooms on the upper level. Ken knew Forbes by reputation; he had his fingers in industries all across Japan, even a couple of record companies. He was the very definition of the "Man" their band had tried to stick it to. He found himself scowling.

'What?' he said, looking up at the billionaire just as the man zipped up his trousers. 'What's the matter?'

'He saw our resident ghost,' Forbes said in decent Japanese, a layer of mirth beneath his words. 'Professor Crow, we call him. Something of a local legend, he is.' He turned to O-Remo. 'Looked a bit like a spindly man with a bird's face, did he?'

O-Remo nodded. 'It was hideous.'

Forbes gave a wide grin. 'Been a while since the last sighting, so congratulations. You've joined an elite club.'

'What are you talking about?'

'His visits are, of course, infrequent. Limited to those of a ... certain disposition.'

'What is that supposed to mean?' Ken said.

Forbes gave him a wide, shit-eating grin. 'Professor Crow tends to appear to people in bad weather, when the air pressure is heavy, and night has fallen. There have been four or five sightings over the last ten or twelve years. He's quite a local celebrity. In the summer, teams of hikers go out looking for him.'

'So he exists?'

Forbes laughed. 'As much as the abominable snowman exists. Or the Loch Ness Monster. But the existence of those are backed up by hard facts, don't you know? Depending on whom you ask.' He winked. Ken felt the urge to punch him.

'He was right there!' O-Remo shouted, holding his hands out in front of him. Squatted at my feet. He spoke to me ... he said ... he said...'

'What did he say, young man?'

O-Remo shook his head. 'I can't remember.'

'"A penny for your thoughts?"'

O-Remo started screaming again. Forbes chuckled.

'It was definitely him, then. Do you have a troubled mind, young man? The Professor always seems to appear to those with a few ... issues ... to contend with.'

O-Remo was a weeping mess. Ken patted him on the shoulder. 'Come on, bro. Take it easy.'

Forbes looked at Ken. 'I think your friend needs a good night's sleep. We can take him back to his room.'

O-Remo jumped up. 'No! I'm not going back out there! That thing is still out there!'

Forbes wore a pained expression on his flabby, rosy-cheeked face. 'Look ... okay. We can put him in the King's Bedroom for tonight. That's upstairs.' He waved two of the receptionists forward, and in English told them: 'Escort this young man up to the King's Bedroom and make him comfortable. Give him these.' He handed over two tablets. 'And ... lock him in. It's for his own benefit.'

As the two young ladies took one of O-Remo's arms each and led him up the stairs, Ken wondered how much he was supposed to have understood. Forbes perhaps didn't realise the amount of English music Plastic Black Butterfly listened to on the road while their crusty old van limped from one dive to another, and how it had made Ken's listening comprehension in particular extremely good. *Maybe I'm just paranoid,* Ken thought. *A couple of sleeping pills and a night away from the smack won't do O-Remo any harm.*

Or it might make him go cold turkey, but I guess we'll worry about that if and when it happens. Out loud, he muttered, 'At least someone gets some turkey. Bastard students.'

He took one last look at O-Remo's limping feet as the two receptionists helped him up the stairs, then he headed back to the dining hall. He hadn't finished eating yet.

———

MOVING out of the way as the guitarist strode past them, Ogiwara pulled Nakamura close. 'Did you hear that? There's some fucking monster in the woods. Man, we have to go look for it. Perhaps we can catch it and sell it.'

'You're crazy. There must be two foot of snow outside. I'm not going out in that unless I have to. Let's go and play some pool up in that common room on the second floor.'

Ogiwara shrugged. 'You're a pussy, but all right. Let's go see if some of the girls want to come.' As Nakamura groaned and clutched at his stomach, Ogiwara added, 'And just go and take a dump, for God's sake.'

———

BACK IN THE DINING ROOM, Kirahara-sensei was telling the few remaining students who hadn't disappeared in all the commotion that they could have some free time before bed. Jun glanced up at Akane, who had barely eaten anything while those around her had gorged themselves. He offered her a smile, but she just looked at him for a moment then looked down at her plate, at an assortment of leftover spaghetti, potato croquettes, lumps of teriyaki chicken, and a scattering of rice. She ran a finger up and down her fork as if it was an old friend, then put it down at the side of her plate.

'Okay, so you know what you have to do for tomorrow, don't you?' Kirahara-sensei was saying while most of the remaining students ignored him. 'I want one side of your notebooks written about the classes that you had today. You can hand them in to me before breakfast. Until tomorrow, you can have free time to do as you wish. There's a pool and a gym on the first floor, and a recreation room on the second. You can also use the lounges in your dormitory buildings. The shop is open until eight, and you can buy soft drinks in the pub until nine. You may have noticed that it's snowing quite a bit outside. Feel free to go and mess about in it, but dress warmly and don't go away from the centre—'

'Because there's a monster in the woods!' shouted Ogiwara, coming in through the door to the dining room and doing a crude Frankenstein impression before leaning in and pretending to bite

Kirahara-sensei's neck. The teacher flapped a hand to shoo him away as Ogiwara danced out of range, grunting with laughter.

Kirahara-sensei sighed as most of the students followed Ogiwara's lead and burst out laughing. Even Akane offered a brief smile. Jun just rolled his eyes.

'So, off you go,' Kirahara-sensei said. 'But, you know, watch out for Ogiwara's monster.'

More laughter, followed by a grinding of chairs as the rest of the students stood up. Jun scowled as a couple of coughing students pushed past him. He looked for Akane, but she had gone. He sighed and turned to leave, then felt a hand on his arm.

'Hey.'

Kaede pouted at him. 'I heard you were telling Ogiwara about us.'

'What? That clown. I didn't say anything—'

'You liar. You only went with me so you could tell your stupid friends about me. You're a prick, Jun Matsumoto, and you're dumped.'

Jun stared at her. There was a hint of a smile on Kaede's lips as she stalked off, almost as though she'd come to a natural conclusion about their relationship and had used the first excuse she could find. The result made him happy, but the delivery made him feel like a piece of crap. Shoulders slumped, he trailed after her, the last student to leave the dining hall. As he reached the door, he glanced back. The band had gone, and the only people left in the dining hall were the waiting staff as they cleared away the leftover food.

'It's going to be a bitch to get down the mountain in this snow,' Janine said to Ron, as they stood around in the reception area, waiting for the staff bus. 'I'm surprised they didn't cancel it tonight.'

Ron nodded. 'What's the plan?' he asked.

Janine grinned. 'We'll get hammered at an all-you-can-drink bar, then we'll go to karaoke. Have you tried that yet?'

'Not yet.'

'It's awesome.' Janine grinned. 'There's a hotel in town where we've booked some rooms. We'll split the costs between us, then get the minibus shuttle back up in the morning.' She gave him a nudge in the ribs. 'So who knows what might happen after karaoke?'

Ron gave her a weak grin. After all the beautiful, slim Japanese women he'd seen around since he arrived in the country, the thought of sleeping with an overweight, spotty Australian didn't really appeal to him. Perhaps if he got drunk enough it wouldn't be so bad…

'There's the bus,' Janine said, as the sound of an engine came from outside. 'Sucks for all the people who have to work tonight.'

'Are there many?' Ron asked.

'There's only one school group in, plus a handful of private guests, so I think just one on reception and a couple in the pub. Sucks for them, but they might be able to drink a couple of sneaky vodkas while they work.'

'Do the Japanese do that?'

'Who fucking cares? It's time to party!'

10

BAD THINGS BEGIN TO HAPPEN

SOME OF THE boys had gone up to the gymnasium to play
badminton. A few of the girls were taking a dip in the pool, and the
rest were either in the common room upstairs or messing around out
in the snow. Jun sat in the recreation room on the first floor, a British
lifestyle magazine open on one knee, his iPhone on the sofa beside
him, but with no signal display. At a table on the other side of the
room, Kirahara-sensei sat with one knee folded over the other,
flicking through a book on old British furniture.

'Don't you want to go off and play with your friends?' Kirahara-
sensei asked after a few minutes.

'No. They aren't my friends.'

'Come on, Matsumoto, I don't know why you think everyone
hates you. I think it's more a case of them not really caring either
way. Kids don't have the patience to make friends like adults do.
You're either outgoing and put yourself out there, or you get
ignored.'

'I never said that everyone hates me. For the most part they don't
want to hang around with me, but that's different.'

'And why's that? Don't you have a girlfriend?'

'I did. We broke up.'

'Oh, how awful. When was that? Haven't you got over it
by now?'

'About ten minutes ago.'

'Oh.'

'She was a skank anyway.'

Kirahara-sensei raised an eyebrow. 'You shouldn't describe
someone that way, Jun. Especially not to a teacher. The
academically correct term is "misunderstood".'

Jun smiled. Kirahara-sensei's lip lifted in a slight smirk, then he turned back to his book.

'Sensei,' Jun said, 'do you like music?'

Kirahara-sensei looked up again. 'What kind of question is that, Jun? Of course I like music.'

Jun grimaced. 'Do you like … rock?'

Kirahara-sensei closed the book and put it back on a rack next to his chair. He folded his arms and cocked his head. 'You mean, do I like black metal, like your band plays, and like that band that's staying here plays—what is it, Plastic Black Butterfly?'

Jun felt himself blushing. 'Um, yes. But I guess you're not interested.'

Kirahara-sensei smiled. 'Keep it a secret, eh? I have their first four CDs. I have the first album on limited edition picture vinyl. It's numbered.'

Jun leaned forward, his eyes narrowing. 'What number do you have?'

Kirahara-sensei also leaned forward, matching Jun's gaze, unblinking. '667. They were all numbered the same. It was kind of like a joke, that they were one better than the devil or something.'

Jun grinned. 'Sir, you're actually cool.'

'Don't tell anyone, eh. Believe me, I could tell you a thing or two about black metal. When I was eighteen I went to Scandinavia for a month. I spent practically every night at either a gig or a rock club. By the end my ears were fucked.'

As Kirahara-sensei sat back, laughing, Jun gaped. 'Sir…'

'I even got laid with this Finnish goth skank—I mean, this misunderstood girl.' He smiled. 'Keep it to yourself, eh. You can tell the other kids I listen to enka and all that other grandma shit. Appearances, and all that.'

Jun nodded. 'Sure.'

Kirahara-sensei stood up. 'Well, I'd better go and check on the rest of them.'

Jun watched him head out of the relaxation room and wander down the long, straight corridor, past the reception area and out of a door at the end. It led to the pub. Jun smiled. He picked up his phone again, wanting to do anything other than read the stupid magazine on his lap, but it still wasn't picking up any signal.

Snow was piling up on the window panes outside. At least two feet of it had fallen in the last couple of hours, and it was showing no signs of abating. Jun couldn't understand why some of the boys were out making snowmen: they'd be buried as soon as they were finished. Still, kids did what kids did.

He glowered at his phone for a few seconds, wishing for a single bar of reception. His band, Shock Tact Ticks, which he had formed with three kids from another school, had recorded and released a single on the Internet a couple of weeks ago. Checking for sales had become an obsession ever since Jun had seen the first one pop up an hour after the song had gone live. Since then they'd sold thirty-five, and Jun clung to the chance of a viral hit like a one-armed man hanging on to a rope dangling beneath a helicopter. His band wasn't the best in the world—not even in their part of town—but interest from someone in the business was the only thing that might keep him out of packing lunchboxes for office workers for the rest of his life.

But the signal remained dead.

Might as well go get some sleep. Breakfast is at seven.

He stood up, shoved his phone into his pocket, and put the magazine back into the rack beside the window.

As he turned back towards the entrance to the recreation room, the door that led through to the gym and swimming pool changing rooms burst open. Akane's friend Natsumi staggered out, soaking wet, dressed only in a skimpy swimsuit that left nothing to the imagination. Jun started to look away out of politeness, then Natsumi jerked forward and vomited all over the recreation room carpet.

Jun saw bits of mushroom, carrot, and even half an undigested potato floating in the soup that began to soak into the floor. As she doubled over again, he took a step back to avoid a fine spray of bile that splattered across his shoes.

'Jun, help her!' Akane screamed, barging through the door and grabbing Natsumi by the shoulders. 'She just threw up in the pool. Mika and Yoshimi are also sick. I've got to go back in and help them.'

She levered Natsumi down onto a couch, then turned and dashed back through the changing room doors. Jun took a tentative step closer, only for Natsumi to lean forward and start choking up more bile. Akane's friend was on the cheerleading team, and had the kind of body that would grace any pop singer. Jun felt repulsed though as she retched and coughed, strings of saliva dangling from her mouth.

'Are you all right?' he asked, and she gave a barely perceptible shake of the head. 'Water,' she croaked.

The command stirred Jun into action. There was a water dispenser on one side of the recreation room, so he ran over and filled a paper cup for her. She nodded without looking up, gulped it back, then promptly threw it up all over his chest.

'Oh, Jesus.'

'Sorry…'

'Jun!' Akane screamed as the door burst open again. Akane staggered through with another girl huddled against her. 'Take her!'

Akane shoved the girl forward, and she stumbled into Jun's arms. Akane turned and headed back through the changing room doors.

The seriousness of the situation seemed to finally kick in like the first bass drum beat after a bridge section. Jun helped the girl down on to the couch beside Natsumi. He recognised her now as she leaned back, the wet strands of hair falling away from her vomit-covered face.

Rena, another cheerleader, a bad girl, but not in Kaede's league. He couldn't say he'd spoken to her more than twice. He remembered picking up a book for her in the corridor once. The only thanks he had got was a roll of the eyes as if he'd been trying to hit on her, then she had stalked off to class.

'Sit still. I'll get you both some towels.'

He hurried off to the equipment rental booth. There were no staff members around so he went into a stockroom in the back and returned with a stack of towels. He was just draping them around the girls' shoulders when Akane pushed through the door again.

'Jun! Help me!'

She was dragging the third girl by the arms. Jun ran to help her, taking hold of the girl's legs and helping Akane carry her to an empty sofa. The girl's swimsuit was stained with vomit, and her head was lolling from side to side. Her eyes were closed, and she was mumbling something incomprehensible under her breath.

'Jun, they're all sick! Get help!'

'Where?'

'Anywhere! Kirahara! The staff!'

'Okay.' He ran out of the recreation room and sprinted down the corridor to the reception desk. A Japanese girl with the name card MIKA was sitting behind a computer, a frown on her face. She looked up as Jun skidded to a stop in front of her.

'Some of the girls are sick,' he gasped.

Alarm registered across Mika's face. 'We have a first aid kit,' she said. 'Or some aspirin if they need it.'

'They're vomiting! One of them is nearly unconscious!'

'Oh, right. I'll call Mr. Forbes.'

'Quickly!'

Jun hurried on down the corridor, pushed through a door that let to an outdoor covered walkway along the length of the east wing. The snowfall was so thick as to leave the outside world a wall of blindness. Drifts of fluffy powder three feet high pushed across half of the walkway like the froth on a spring tide, and Jun pressed himself against the wall to get around it, his feet slipping and sliding where some of it had turned to slush under the walkway lights.

When he pushed through the door to the pub he found Kirahara-sensei, a Japanese barman, and two members of Plastic Black Butterfly tending to two boys and a girl who were sitting back against the wall, their clothes stained with vomit.

'There are three sick girls in the recreation room,' Jun shouted.

Kirahara-sensei looked up. 'I think we have a problem here,' he said.

WHEN JUN GOT BACK the Grand Mansion, Akane had managed to pull some clothes on to the girls, but two of them now looked barely conscious. Only Natsumi was properly awake, and her eyes darted around with confusion in between fits of retching.

'It's happened to some of the others too,' Jun said. 'Over in the pub.'

'What are we going to do?'

Jun looked up at the sound of running footsteps. Rutherford Forbes, esteemed owner of British Heights, was hurrying down the corridor towards them, his belly bouncing up and down as Mika from reception jogged along behind him.

'What's going on?' he asked in Japanese.

'They're sick,' Jun said. 'It must be something they ate.'

Forbes rounded on him. 'Then why aren't you sick, boy? Nothing wrong with the food here. Perhaps it was something you had on the way.'

'We all brought lunch from home.'

'Well, something else then!'

'What do we do with them?' Akane said. 'They're going to die!'

Forbes flapped a hand at her as if swatting her words out of the air. 'Don't be stupid, you brainless twit. They'll be fine. They just need some antibiotics or something. Let's get them to reception and—'

'Help!'

Ogiwara came rushing out on to the corridor from the stairs to the second floor. He bounced off the opposite wall, a spray of vomit following him as Nakamura staggered down the steps in his wake. Nakamura groaned, bent double, and vomited again, this time on the plush, antique carpet.

'Jesus Christ, you idiot, that carpet costs a fortune to clean!' Forbes shouted. 'Can't you use a bag or something?'

'There are two more passed out upstairs,' Ogiwara gasped. 'One of them is definitely going to die. Mishima gave him mouth to mouth and he just got a faceful of puke, the fucking spaz.'

'Shut up, you dumb prick!' Akane shouted. 'This is serious!'

'Suck my dick, bitch,' Ogiwara shouted back. 'Oh, you already did.'

'Fuck off!'

'Children!' Forbes boomed. 'Can we cooperate here, before the reputation of my fine establishment is ruined by a bunch of idiot misfits like you lot? Let's get the sick students to the reception area and I'll arrange for them to be taken down to the hospital in the town.'

'There's three feet of snow outside!' Jun shouted.

'We have chains on the tyres,' Forbes said, with the air of a snow ranger talking to someone who's never seen snow. 'We just don't have much space.'

One by one, Jun and Akane helped the girls up the steps to the reception area, where they lined them up on one of the sofas. Mika moved among them, wiping the vomit off their faces with a damp cloth. Jun then rushed off to help Kirahara-sensei while Akane ran upstairs.

Fifteen minutes later, the reception area looked like a scene from a zombie movie, as twelve vomit-caked high school students lay around in various states of consciousness. Of the students, only Jun, Akane, Ogiwara, and Mishima were healthy. No one had seen Kaede since dinner.

'We have to get them down to the hospital,' Kirahara-sensei said to Forbes.

The owner of British Heights nodded reluctantly. 'One of my staff has gone to get our winter snowmobile. It has caterpillar treads, so the snow should be no issue. It's limited for space, though. The students not displaying any symptoms should stay here.'

Kirahara-sensei kicked out at a wooden hat stand, knocking it to the ground.

'What if they get sick in an hour or two? It's food poisoning! It might not kick in until later.'

Forbes puffed out fat red cheeks. 'Do you mind? That's expensive.' He turned to Jun and the others who weren't sick. 'What did or didn't you eat that might have caused this to happen to them? I refuse to believe it was our food here, it is prepared with the highest—'

'The turkey,' Jun said. 'I got there too late. So did Akane.'

'I don't know what you're talking about—'

'Neither did I,' Kirahara-sensei said. 'I was at the back with these two.'

Ogiwara nodded. 'And I was outside checking out that band's van with Kaede. So—wherever she is—she must be fine too.'

'What about you?' Kirahara-sensei asked Mishima.

'I was, um, taking a crap.'

Kirahara-sensei nodded. 'So, something was wrong with the turkey. Mr. Forbes, this is a serious problem. If any one of these students is to die—'

The groan of an engine came from just outside the main entrance. Jun wiped the condensation off a window and peered out to see what looked like a bulldozer, minus the front blade, sitting outside. The snow was so deep it appeared to be sinking.

'Okay, let's get them loaded up,' Forbes said, as the man Jun remembered from the bar came running up through the snowdrifts on the entrance steps.

Kirahara-sensei came over to Jun and the others. 'I don't need to tell you we have a serious situation here.' He looked at each in turn until they all nodded. 'I don't want to leave you up here, but as Mr. Forbes said, there's not enough room in that vehicle to take those who aren't sick. There's only just room for myself. I don't want to leave you, but it's my duty to go with the sick students and ensure they get proper medical care. What I need from the rest of you in the meantime is some maturity and cooperation.' Again, he looked from one to the other until each of them nodded. 'No infighting, no petty squabbles. In fact, as none of you ate that turkey you should be fine. As should Kaede, wherever she is. I suggest you go to your rooms, have a shower and get a good night's sleep. You'll be perfectly safe here.'

Ogiwara, a frown on his big, sloping brow, leaned forward. 'Um, Sensei … what about the monster that guy saw in the woods?'

Kirahara-sensei's face turned red, and for a moment Jun thought his teacher would explode. Then, very quietly, he turned to Ogiwara and said, 'I suggest you keep your room door shut. Perhaps even put your suitcase up against it. That should deal with the sucker.'

Ogiwara gulped. No one else dared to speak. Kirahara-sensei looked around the faces once more, then nodded to himself. 'Now, if you could all help get your sick classmates into that snowmobile, it would be much appreciated.'

They worked two people to a student. Between Jun, Akane, Ogiwara, Mishima, and the two members of staff that were still on duty, they managed to get the students down the steps and into the back of the snowmobile within ten minutes. Jun wished the members of Plastic Black Butterfly had come to help, but Kirahara-sensei had said they'd gone off looking for their own bandmates, two of whom had vanished. It didn't appear that either of them were sick, just missing.

The whole time, Forbes stood by the front door, holding it open for the others with a look of frustration on his face, as if the whole episode were nothing worse than a group of messy builders tramping in and out of his house carrying handfuls of bricks.

Finally, the last student was loaded into the snowmobile, its windows already steamed up with the breath of a dozen sick students. Kirahara-sensei, caked in so much snow he looked like an Arctic explorer, came up to the main entrance, where the others had gathered.

'We're heading down now,' he said. 'Just remember, you're representing your school. I hope to be back up here in the morning, and I expect to find all of you attending your classes as expected.' He glanced around the group again. 'But … thank you for your help. This is not an ideal situation, but I can assure you, they'll all be fine once they see a doctor.'

'Natsumi was puking up blood,' Akane muttered.

'It was probably spaghetti sauce,' Ogiwara said, and this time Kirahara-sensei actually nodded. 'Let's hope that's all it was,' he said. 'Now, I'll call in to the centre's landline as soon as I know anything. You all have phones in your rooms, so you can be contacted.'

'You'd better go, Sensei,' Jun said.

Kirahara-sensei nodded again. He looked at Rutherford Forbes, still standing inside the door, and for a moment his expression soured. 'Take care,' he said to the students, and headed back down the steps to the waiting snowmobile.

They stood and watched the snowmobile trundling away in the snow, moving so slowly as it paused to make a turn that it looked like it had stopped altogether.

'That piece of shit's never going to make it,' Ogiwara muttered. 'They'll all freeze to death out there in the snow. They'll be found in the morning turned into ice.'

'Just be quiet,' Akane said.

Jun felt something pressing against his palm. After a moment he realised it was Akane's hand. He gave it a squeeze, but she didn't look at him. Her eyes stared straight ahead, out of the little window into the snow, following the tracks of the snowmobile that had now trundled out of sight, taking most of their friends away.

As Jun watched, the snow began to fill in the tracks, as if they were never there.

11

———

BEE FREAKS OUT

'So where do you think Dai's gone?'

Bee shrugged, but didn't answer.

'Are you all right?'

'Yes.'

'You don't sound it.'

Bee didn't answer. Ken fell silent, and with Bee trailing along behind him he headed back towards their dormitory building. Luckily, it wasn't far from the Grand Mansion, so they were able to get most of the way under the covered walkway of the west wing, and then beneath the overhang of the adjacent building, but there was a section of around fifty metres where they had no choice but to wade through the deepening snow.

As soon as they stepped out into the blizzard, Bee gave a little gasp.

'Are you sure you're all right?'

'Just a little claustrophobic.'

Ken frowned. Bee was more than a little claustrophobic. After just one tour across Europe they'd never played overseas again; the bass player couldn't handle air travel. When the band had been successful enough to dictate its own security terms, they'd been able to slip him enough sedatives to get him through the flights, but once their popularity and their entourage began to decline—at the same time that O-Remo's reputation began to burgeon—travel became far more complicated, and after one particularly painful incident on a short internal flight, they'd gone back to travelling by van.

Ken reached the porch of their building and turned back to look for his bandmate. Bee was standing halfway across the snow-covered road, buried up to his waist, staring off into space. His arms were held out at his sides, and with the snow falling all around him he looked like a zombified incarnation of Jesus, in his white shirt and with his long, straight hair.

'Bee!'

'Can't … move.'

'Shit.' Ken waded back out into the snow and gripped his bandmate around the waist, wrestling him forward. Bee moved one tentative step, then another. 'Come on, damn it. You'll freeze to death.'

'Death … is … everywhere.'

'Shut the fuck up.'

Ken glanced up at Bee's eyes, and saw the terrible glazed look that he hated so much. On stage it happened sometimes, when Bee drifted off to another place, only his hands remaining rooted in the music they were playing, his mind elsewhere. Back in the early days, when they'd all been happy recreationals together, Bee had scared the crap out of them on many a drunken, drugged-up early morning with the weird, otherworldly ramblings he used to come out with.

'It's coming,' Bee whispered, leaning into Ken's ear.

Ken almost threw him down in the snow and left him behind. He shivered from his toes to his neck, and not because of the freezing cold and the snow. His whole mind seemed to be shivering.

'I can feel it coming closer,' Bee whispered again. 'But it's just the start, Ken. It's … just … the start.'

'Shut u—'

A screech cut through the suffocating press of the blizzard, like the sound of glass being scraped across metal in some factory construction project gone wrong. Ken gasped and looked around him. Something shifted in the snow just a few metres away, but the blizzard was too heavy for him to make out more than just a silhouette that might not have even been there at all. He dragged Bee forward onto the porch steps of their dormitory, and bustled him through the door into the warm interior. He pulled the door shut behind them and pushed up the latch just as something shadowy darted past the door.

'Just let it in,' Bee mumbled. 'Let it in and let's finish this. Resistance only leads to suffering.'

'Keep going,' Ken said, pushing Bee through the second door into the main first floor corridor. The kitchens were to their right, the lower floor's bedrooms up a couple of steps to their left, with the toilets and shower room at the far end. Across from them, a staircase led up to the second floor, a lounge room, and another row of guest rooms.

Inside the comforting heat of an air-conditioned guest

dormitory building, Ken's heart rate began to slow, the panic that had overcome him out in the snow gently subsiding like the last chord of a song. Bee stood beside him, eyes slowly coming back into focus, his head topped with a triangle of snow that would have been hilarious in other circumstances. Ken reached up and swiped it off the top of Bee's head, then brushed down the bassist's clothes.

'I'll be retiring to my room,' Bee said. 'I have something I can take to help me sleep. Do you want one?'

Ken shook his head. 'No, I'm good.'

'Okay.'

Bee walked up the corridor and turned into a room a couple of doors down. The two intervening rooms were silent. O-Remo was locked in the King's Bedroom in the Grand Mansion, but Dai was still missing. The drummer had told them he had forgotten something and disappeared out into the snow. None of them had seen him since.

Dai, with stacked shoulders and thick arms from years of pounding the drums, could take care of himself better than any of the rest of them. If he managed to avoid getting lost in the forest he'd be fine.

Still, that thing…

Ken had barely got a look at it. Just a shadow, shifting in the dark, but it had been tall and thin, as O-Remo had said, and that sound had been something inhuman.

As he heard the rattle of the door behind him, he had a sudden urge to be behind a lock. He rushed into his room and pulled the door shut. The latch was flimsy and could be easily broken, but he attached it anyway, then pulled one of the two twin beds across in front of it. Turning back to the window, he stared in horror at what he hoped were just shadows and drifts of snow, not eyes peering in through the foggy glass. He pinched his eyes shut, and pulled the curtains across before he could look too closely.

Then he sat down on his bed and wiped the sweat off his hands.

An air-conditioner hidden inside a wooden cabinet hummed softly beneath the window. The room was comfortably warm at least, although Ken's teeth were chattering. In the corner of his room was his guitar case. All of the rest of their equipment was in the back of the van, but Ken never let his guitar out of sight. It was a crutch that had got him through a lot of stressful times, and he had never forgotten the debt he owed it. More than one woman had walked out of his life due to feeling second best, but when you played lead guitar in a nationally famous band, there was always another waiting. At least there had been.

He picked up the case and turned it over in his hands. It felt strange, unfamiliar. It took him a few seconds to figure out what should have been obvious.

It was too light.

With shaking hands he flicked up the latches and pulled the lid open, staring in horror at the empty space inside.

His prized instrument was gone.

DAI HAD SPOTTED the opportunity at the end of the hall on the second floor. When you went somewhere new it always paid to explore a little, because you never knew what little nuggets of interest you might find. Leaving the boys to go 'look for something', rather than use the toilets in the pub, he had headed along the east covered walkway beside the dining hall and back into the Grand Mansion. Then, after relieving himself, he went for a little stroll.

The girl was sitting on a chair, one finely formed leg crossed over the other, tapping into a smartphone with a look of frustration on her face. She had straight jet-black hair to just below her shoulders, fake eyelashes that seemed to flutter as if a little motor had been installed into her forehead, and pouty lips that looked like they rarely did anything else. He recognised the type easily: she had that world-hates-me-and-I'm-pissed-about-it look that made her a perfect target.

'No reception?' he said, ambling up to her. 'There's a fucking surprise, up here in the middle of buttcrack nowhere.'

She looked up and a sour look flashed across her face. *It's the drummer from that band no one likes anymore,* that look said. It set him at an immediate disadvantage, but it was merely a perception he had to replace with one more appropriate.

'The fucking retard driving our van made a wrong turn,' he said, neglecting to mention that he was the man in question. 'Ended up here. Fucking moron.'

This time she smiled. There was nothing this girl liked more than criticism of others. 'What a dick,' she said.

'Honestly, we thought about leaving him in the snow, but we make the douchebag carry all our gear while we sit around and get pissed. Can't be dealing with that shit ourselves, you know.'

'Right,' she said. 'So I suppose you have to put up with him. And you ended up here.'

'And the fucking pub shuts at eleven.'

She looked at her watch. 'It's almost nine. You don't have much more time. Why aren't you in there now?'

He smiled the smile that had opened a thousand pairs of legs. 'Because I don't like drinking with the same dickhead that got us stuck up here in this storm. Looking at his ugly mug makes everything taste bad.' *Now to cast the line.* 'Don't worry, I have all the booze in my room that anyone could want. I took the liberty of stocking up.'

Her eyes flicked across his broad chest and over the muscles that bulged through his shirt. While not big compared to most Western drummers, Dai considered the tight t-shirt to be the essential fashion accessory. Clothes a size too small made what meat you had stand out. If you had a beer gut it was counter-productive, but he didn't have to worry about that just yet. Not selling many CDs meant he got plenty of exercise behind the kit on their seemingly endless tours through the dives of the country.

'This place sucks,' she said, looked up at him. 'It would probably make it easier to deal with if I had a drink or two.'

Dai nodded slowly. Her eyes watched him, unblinking. She had taken the bait and was now rolling the hook back and forth across her tongue.

'Let's go,' he said.

He led her down the stairs, out under the west wing's covered walkway. When they reached the steps leading down, now thigh deep in snow, Dai turned back to her. She was glaring at the snow as if it had done her a personal slight, her nose wrinkled, her eyes narrowed. He felt that familiar gnawing sensation in his gut, that he *needed* to get with this girl, and *needed* to do it *now*.

'Okay,' he said. 'You can either start wading through this shit fucking Arctic storm and risk getting those rather lovely thighs of yours frostbitten, or you can let me carry you.'

She held his gaze again. 'I thought you'd never ask.'

Dai smiled. He leaned over and let her leapfrog up onto his back. He wrapped his hands under her legs, loving the way they shivered beneath his touch, and stepped out into the snow.

He'd never had to give someone a piggyback through a snowdrift before. He made it halfway back to his dormitory building doing a kind of high-kneed frog walk, before slipping over on a patch of hidden ice and upending them both in the snow. One moment they were standing straight, the next he was covered in a dense blanket of powder, and the girl was thrashing around in the snow beneath him.

As he dragged her back upright, he waited for the slap, or the accusation, or the berating. He was used to women shouting at him and had a number of strategies to either re-rail his intentions or make a hasty exit. It would be a disappointment to lose her when he'd been so close, but these things happened. Just like drumming, there would be another day.

When he found her arms wrapping around his neck and her lips pressed against his, his mind went blank. This was one situation he couldn't ever remember being in.

'Get me the fuck inside your room, and I'll let you warm me up,' the girl said, and as Dai lifted her up, this time wrapping her legs around him from the front. 'I'm tired of all this cold. I want something warm, and I want a lot of it.'

Dai smiled. Feeling his arousal rising and the way she shifted to accommodate it, he realised he'd never even asked her name.

THE FIRST TIME was the best. She said she was eighteen, but he'd been with women ten years older than him, veteran groupies who spent more time in the beds of minor rock stars than in their own, who hadn't known the tricks she did. He guessed the Internet must be as useful for women as it was for men.

By the time she'd quite literally fucked him across the room, he was ready for a rest. The girl though, full of the vitality of a teenager still early in her sexual life adventure, sat with her head propped up on the back of her hand, gazing at him with predatory eyes.

'That the best you've got?' she asked.

'Sweetheart ... after the drive I had today...'

'I thought you said some retard was driving,' she said with a smirk.

'Yeah, I meant as in ... as a passenger ... um...'

'Kaede.'

'Yeah, that's it.'

'So, I'll ask you again, is that the best you've got?'

The upper half of his body felt drained and ready for bed, but the lower half thought otherwise. Before he could answer, Kaede had slipped a hand into his pants and was helping him wake back up.

'So,' he gasped, a few minutes later, 'are you going to tell your friends you got laid with the drummer of Plastic Black Butterfly?'

Kaede, now straddling him, working herself back and forth, shook her head. 'No. I'll tell them you were with some better band. Practically anyone would do. Even the house drummer for some shitty variety television show would be preferable.' She grinned and patted his chest. 'It's all about appearances, you see.'

Dai grinned and rolled her off him, turning her around on the bed so she faced the window, on all fours. He stood on the floor and lined himself up behind her. 'I have something to show you,' he said. 'I think you'll agree when I'm done that not all of our songs suck.'

'Prove it.'

'I'm going to play you one of my favorite rhythms.' He gripped her buttocks and slid himself into her, loving the way she moaned.

He couldn't play anything complicated, because while it was easy to replicate the bass drum rhythm, he only had two buttocks available to combine as the kick, snare, toms, and cymbals. But, using Kaede's body as his kit, he made a good show of it.

Four minutes into the song, Kaede's breath was coming in little gasps as Dai surged towards the growing crescendo. It was an old party trick that had got him mentioned on several dedicated groupie websites, and even in one published book. He was known in the industry as the drummer who could fuck in rhythm, and it was a title he was proud of. As he entered the last few bars of the song, he was sure he could hear Ken's frantically strummed guitar chords over the top, although they sounded oddly dulled, as if the instrument was being played unplugged behind glass—

As Dai heard Kaede groan, reaching orgasm at the same time as he did, he looked up at the window where the curtains were pulled back, and saw a hideous birdlike face tapping its beak against the glass, the sound of a guitar chord coming from the instrument it held in its arms.

It looked like a man in some nightmarish Halloween costume, and for a moment Dai felt the urge to laugh. Then the creature let out a hideous high-pitched screech that rattled the glass in its ancient frame. Kaede looked up and screamed. Dai pulled his flaccid dick out of her and fell back across the bed, rolling onto the floor as the girl tumbled down on top of him.

The window imploded with a crash of glass and the scream came again, filling the room. Dai slapped his hands over his ears, and squeezed his eyes shut. The world seemed to fill with a smacking, smarting pain. Then he felt something small and hard club him just over the ear, and realised the girl was slapping him across the face.

'We have to get out of here!' she screamed.

Dai groaned and tried to sit up, but the girl was sitting on his chest, crushing the air out of him. He shoved her aside, feeling an immediate chill from the open window. He had felt only pleasure a minute before, but he now felt exposed and terrified.

He looked up and saw a thin, bony arm, with talons where fingers should have been, reaching in through the window. The claws scraped across what was left of the glass, and a feeling like a dead man's fingers ran down the back of his spine.

12

CREAKS AND GROANS ON THE
MOUNTAIN ROAD

THE SNOW WAS SO THICK it was like the snowmobile was driving into a shoal of constantly moving albino fish, darting away from the vehicle's dim headlights as they dipped and rose over the drifts of snow piling up on the road.

In the back, the groans of the still-conscious students made a dying chorus. Kirahara-sensei leaned forward and peered out of the windscreen at something he thought might resemble blindness. Only the occasional sight of a tree or a hedgerow in their peripheral lights reminded him that they were actually on a road.

'Is it much further?' he asked the driver, the young man who had been working behind the pub bar.

The man shook his head and shrugged. 'Your guess is as good as mine. This is insane. I've never seen a storm like this. It snows hard up here every year, but it's rare to maintain this intensity for this long.'

Kirahara-sensei glanced back towards the students. He was happy that he couldn't see them in the dark of the back seats; that way he could pretend the groans belonged to more than just three or four, that they were all likely to make it to the hospital safely and wake up tomorrow in a warm bed.

The truth was that it looked like several would never make it.

'An hour?' he asked, trying to remember how long it had taken them to get up to British Heights just that morning.

The driver gave a frustrated grimace. 'Look, I don't know. Maybe, if the roads going down are clearer. They're a little more sheltered by the trees, so there's a chance we'll make better progress then. This thing will only go twenty kilometres an hour and its ten to the nearest town. We're not off the crest of the headland yet.'

Kirahara-sensei tried to think about the other students he had left behind to take his mind off those in the back. Matsumoto was a decent kid, if misguided. He just needed a little more self-worth. He seemed to be fighting against feelings that didn't really exist, and it would ruin him. Ogiwara was a lost cause. The kid had a brain, but he was hell bent on wasting it. He was the prefectural judo champion, which was quite an achievement, but he'd failed in the first round of the national finals last year and that had been his last chance. If he was able to focus himself long enough to get into a college he might be able to take it up again, but otherwise he was destined for a production line somewhere.

Mishima was a decent kid, but a follower. He had no initiative, no drive of his own. Kaede Maruyama was what she was, a playgirl. She had future hostess written all over her, but at least hostess jobs paid well.

Akane Yamaguchi … she was the interesting one. Freakishly talented but plagued by tragedy, the poor girl didn't really know whether she was coming or going. She spent way too much time hanging around with lowlifes and not enough with nice boys like Matsumoto, who complimented her well. *They would make a nice couple*, Kirahara-sensei thought, *if they could only get over what happened.* Still, they were young, he figured. There was time.

The snowmobile pitched forward. Kirahara-sensei grabbed the dash to stop himself headbutting it, and heard the students shifting around in the back.

'We've started the descent,' the driver said. 'Hang on. This looks like it could be a bit bumpy.'

'What about the students?'

'They're strapped in, aren't they? I'll go as carefully as I can, but this isn't easy.'

Kirahara-sensei watched with nervous apprehension as the trees closed in, high up on the embankment to the left of them, sloping away steeply into a ravine to the right. Snow was piled erratically depending on the angle of the wind and the cover of the trees, and at times the snowmobile seemed to rise up so high on one side as it dug its way over a drift that he thought they might just go tumbling down into the valley.

The snowmobile's engine whined and then they came to a stop, idling in the road. Kirahara-sensei looked across at the driver and saw a bead of sweat running down the young man's face.

'Why did you stop?' he asked. 'Come on, get us moving again. What are you waiting for?'

The driver turned towards him, his face ashen. 'Don't you hear it?' he said, so quietly that Kirahara-sensei could barely hear him. 'Don't you hear it coming?'

'What? Damn it, man, talk to me.'

'That rumbling noise.'

Kirahara cocked his head. The young man was right; there was something. A low growling … like an angry dog, or an approaching train…

'What is it?'

The look of hopelessness in the young man's face chilled Kirahara-sensei to the core, as if someone had dropped his heart into a bucket of ice.

'Landslide.'

Then the roar was everywhere, filling the air around them, and the snowmobile became a rolling, tumbling, bouncing thing as a wave of trees, snow, and earth came rushing down on top of it. Kirahara-sensei screamed, but there seemed to be no sound as the hillside's battle cry drowned out everything.

13

JUN FINDS AKANE

'So what do we do now?' Ogiwara said, hands on hips.

'We should—'

'Shut up, Matsumoto. I wasn't asking you.'

'The games room is open until eleven,' Mika said, sounding like the welcome video they had watched in the main hall. 'The pool will close at half past ten.'

'Shut up. I wasn't asking you either.'

At Ogiwara's tone, the girl shrank away, disappearing back behind her desk.

'Ogiwara, you're a real—'

Ogiwara stepped forward. 'Not another word, Matsumoto.' He turned to Akane. 'Perhaps we should retire to a room somewhere?'

'Get lost, you pig.'

Ogiwara glanced at Mishima, rolled his eyes, and started to laugh. He took a step forward, but Akane just stalked off down the corridor, back towards the dining hall. Ogiwara began to follow, but Jun stepped in front of him.

'Leave her alone.'

'This could end badly for you, Matsumoto.'

Jun didn't move. 'Leave her alone,' he repeated.

Ogiwara clenched a fist and swung it, pulling it short just in front of Jun's face. Jun tried not to flinch. 'We're not done yet,' Ogiwara said through gritted teeth.

They stared at each other for a moment, then Ogiwara started to laugh again. He turned back to Mishima, who was standing back by the door, shifting from foot to foot.

'Come on, Mishima,' he said. 'Since you're not a pussy like the rest of them, what say we go gatecrash the snooker room upstairs and have ourselves a couple of games?'

Mishima gave a nervous laugh. 'Okay, let's go.'

Jun watched them reach the stairs at the end and climb up out of sight. Several dark stains on the carpet seemed to jump out at him, a reminder of what had happened. Behind him, Mika was busying herself with wiping the vomit from one of the sofas.

Jun turned around, looking for Akane, but she had disappeared. He knew she wasn't going to get sick, but he didn't want her to be on her own, so he trotted off down the corridor to look for her.

Outside, the snow was still pelting down. Jun briefly wondered what had happened to Kaede, because no one had seen her since just after dinner, but if she had been with Ogiwara then she wouldn't have got sick. Probably she was making trouble somewhere for someone.

Leading off the corridor were several rooms. Jun tried a couple of doors, and found himself peering into the dark interiors of classrooms decked out in classical British stylings: high-backed, ornate wooden chairs, wide, heavy-looking tables, and framed prints of old hunting scenes and country landscapes hanging from the walls. He wished he could appreciate the detail and the beauty of British Heights, but he was too worried about Akane.

At the end of the corridor, a wide double door on the left opened on to the lecture theatre where they had sat through the orientation video. On the right was the glass-framed door into the dining hall. Just in front of it were two more entrances, one leading outside to the covered walkway down the east wing that led to the pub and the shop, and the other heading upstairs to the second floor.

The lecture room was locked. Jun glanced through the outside door, looking for Akane's footprints. The snow drifting in through the open side was untouched, so she hadn't gone that way. The dining hall was also locked, leaving just the stairs.

Jun hurried up, past more framed paintings on the walls, around a curve in the staircase where a window looked out on the wide courtyard below. He paused for a moment. Their bus was still there, buried in snow above its wheel arches. Alongside it was Plastic Black Butterfly's van. He wondered what had happened to them too; the lights of the pub were still on so they were likely finding comfort in a few drinks. Outside the pub, lights that had been hung in the trees to light the place up like a fairground were dulled beneath a coating of snow.

Is it ever going to stop?

He ignored a sign marked PRIVATE to push through the door at the top of the stairs, and found himself in the museum area, modeled on an old British manor house. The wide corridor led right along the top of the north wing of the Grand Mansion. In the middle was a staircase that came out in reception. Nearest to Jun were two rooms labeled King's Bedroom and Queen's Bedroom. Both were locked. On the other side of the staircase, two doors were labeled Library and Study. Jun gave a wry smile. He felt like a player in a giant game of Cluedo.

Who committed the murders? Who murdered all those kids?

Jun pushed the voice out of his mind. 'No one murdered them,' he muttered. 'They're all still alive.'

'Is that what you think?'

Jun jumped, for a moment thinking the voice was still in his head. He spun around and found Akane standing behind him, the door to the library just clicking shut.

'They'll all be fine,' he said. He reached out for her hand, but she pulled it away.

'No, they won't,' she said, her voice empty, hollow. 'You saw them. They're all going to die long before they make it to a hospital.'

'Akane…'

'There are no happy endings, Jun. You know that.'

He started to reply, but she turned and disappeared through the library door, closing it behind her. Jun took a deep breath, trying to think of something that might make her feel better, then went in after her.

He found himself in a room right out of 18th Century Britain. The library and the study—adjoining through a wide archway— were filled wall to ceiling with musty leather-bound books. A series of antique desks, sofas and easy chairs were scattered about the room. Akane was sitting behind a desk in one corner, one leg crossed over the other, an old dial telephone in front of her and a feather-pen in a holder on the other. When Jun approached, the light from a dim lamp behind her illuminated a large map of ancient Britain pressed under a pane of glass. Akane had one hand resting on a book called *The Book of the Home 1921 1st Edition*, while a newspaper dated just a few days before looked a little out of place beside the telephone.

'It's pretty, isn't it?' she said.

'This place? It gives me the creeps. I could quite imagine Ogiwara's monsters after coming in here.'

Akane sighed. 'Please don't talk about that … moron. That was a mistake and I don't want to think about it.'

'I'm sorry.'

Akane sighed and leaned back in the chair. She put her legs up on the table. 'I feel like a foreign diplomat,' she said. 'Could you imagine me as a diplomat, Jun?'

He smiled. 'I think you'd be a great one,' he said.

She nodded. 'Anything to get out of this country.'

'I know what you mean.'

Akane's head jerked up. 'Do you, Jun? Do you really? After all, everything's fine and dandy for you, isn't it?'

'That's not fair.'

'Why isn't it?'

She sighed again. She uncrossed her legs and leaned forward, propping her chin on her hands. She was so naturally beautiful that he couldn't look away, but those dark, knowledgeable eyes were not the same as the happy-go-lucky youthful eyes they had once been. Too much tar had been poured into the river of Akane's life, poisoning the water that had once flowed pure and clear.

'You're a wannabe, Jun. You want to have problems so you can lament to the world about them. You go out of your way to be disliked, and you upset people because then you have a reason to be miserable. It's a choice. That's one reason I can't stand you anymore.'

Her words were like a knife cutting across his throat. 'That's not fair.'

'You don't understand, Jun,' she said. 'You don't know what it feels like to be scarred. To be scarred inside.'

He sat down across from her. 'I can't change things.'

'You can appreciate what you have. You have parents that love you and care for you. You have … parents.'

He slammed a fist down on the table. 'It wasn't my fault. I didn't ask to be there that day!'

Akane sighed and looked away, back towards the window behind her.

'I know, Jun. But you were.'

HE HAD LEFT his history textbook at Akane's house the night before. Jun, thirteen years old, in the first grade of junior high school, had an assignment due the next day. Akane had piano practice, but she wouldn't mind him stopping by. It was Thursday, so there would likely be no one home, but Jun knew where the spare key to the house was kept, in a drawer inside the garage.

The night before they had been studying in her room. As always, Jun had felt a little disconcerted with the shrine of photographs to her mother which watched him from a noticeboard above her desk, but it was impossible for him to understand the feelings she was going through. Losing her mother had broken her heart, but Akane was burying herself in studying and her piano practice. Four nights a week she went to a local piano school, where she stayed for three or even four hours, just practicing. Sometimes, she said, if she knew her father would be drunk again, she didn't want to come home.

The sky was spitting rain as he approached their street, a small suburban cul-de-sac with his own house facing the main road and Akane's house tucked in around the corner. Hers was a pretty little two-storey house, made of prefab plastic in a Norwegian style, with high windows and a tall, pointed roof. It had been reformed just two years before, and her mother had kept it spotless. Now the grass had grown up on the little front lawn, and a couple of bags of beer cans and *sake* bottles stood outside the front door. There was no car in the drive—it had been wrecked in the accident that had killed her mother, and Akane's father had vowed never to step inside one again —but Jun was surprised to see Akane's father's bicycle lying on its side just in front of the garage door.

On the surface her father had coped admirably well with her mother's death, continuing to get up each day and go to his company job, but while he had always liked a drink, now he liked half a bottle pretty regularly. Most nights he brought home some packaged *bento* from the supermarket for Akane and himself, then drank himself to sleep in front of the television. He would always exchange pleasantries with Jun, but as soon as the bottle opened the words dried up, and Jun often heard him crying downstairs in the living room while they studied upstairs together. Jun had once made the suggestion that they study at his house, but Akane had got angry at the idea of leaving her father alone, and he had never mentioned it again.

The bike, despite a kick rest, was lying on its side as if thrown down. Jun glanced up at the window of his own bedroom in the house next door and really wanted to just go home. Something was wrong.

There were two entrances to the garage, a wide door for the car at the front which was always locked, and a small door at the back for a person, down a thin alleyway between their two houses. Jun opened the latch of the little gate at the front and made his way down along the side of the garage. Akane's back garden was in a similar state to the front. There was no Western-style lawn, just some ornamental pines and maples growing between several large stones. The little patio outside the door was overrun with weeds though, and the windows were grimy. Jun wished he could help more, but Akane always turned a blind eye to the gradual decay of her home, and any mention of it would bring vitriol forth in a flood.

The back door to the garage was slightly ajar. Jun's legs trembled, and in that instant he realised it was cowardice that would make him step through that door. Bravery would be to turn and walk away, but the fear of not knowing would make him push that door open at the same time as others banged shut forever. He was too afraid to walk away.

The single bulb inside the garage was on, but a long shadow hung over the entrance, parting the light like two curtains drawn back. In the centre something large hung from the ceiling, something black and rectangular, stock still like a giant sleeping bat.

Akane's dad had put on one of his daughter's hooded tops and zipped it up. The yellow electric cord that he had looped over a hook that might have once hung up a drill or an electric saw poked out from the side of the hood covering his face like a line of twirled-up police tape. On the ground, tipped over on its side, was a kitchen chair with a single broken leg. The broken piece had been sawn almost all the way through. A workbench where the deed had been done was set up inside the front door, a little halo of sawdust spreading out around it.

From the stench and the puddle beneath him, Akane's father had shit and pissed himself. His face, puffy from asphyxiation but pale and blue from rigor mortis, looked down on Jun at a crooked angle, his dead eyes staring blankly into Jun's own. That gaze said a thousand things; it was accusatory, regretful, and compassionate at the same time.

Jun's legs fell out from under him. He hit the ground hard, his head striking the hard concrete of the garage floor, knocking him out.

When he came to a few seconds later, he had rolled over away from the dangling corpse, facing the back wall. It took him a few seconds to realise what had happened, what he had discovered, but the fear of seeing those dead eyes gazing on him for one more second made something break in his mind. He pulled his knees up to his chest, squeezed his eyes shut, and waited for it all to go away.

That was how Akane found them both, more than an hour later. Her father hanging dead, her best friend curled up in a whimpering ball on the ground.

It didn't matter that Jun had nothing to do with it, or that it appeared her father had left work at lunchtime and been dead for several hours at the time of Jun's discovery. None of that mattered. He had been there. He had been at the scene of her father's suicide, and she would forever associate the horror of that moment with her best friend's face.

14

THE BOY WHO BUILT ROBOTS

RUTHERFORD FORBES PULLED the steel door shut behind him and pulled down the security bar. None of those damn kids had seen him slip away, but he'd had a terrible sense of foreboding about such heavy snow.

'Professor, where the hell have you been?'

The spindly man in the white jacket seated at the computer terminal didn't turn around, but Forbes heard a watery chuckle.

'Just having a little fun, sire,' he said in a reedy, pinched voice. 'Just playing a few games in the snow.'

'Damn it, Professor, how close did you get to that singer?'

'Hahaha, I put the wind right up his shirt, sire.'

Forbes looked up at the monitor screens. 'Are they all settling down for the night?'

The Professor stabbed a few keys and the screens flickered through a variety of different views. 'We've lost a couple of the outdoor cameras,' the professor said. 'Methinks you need to change the wiring, hmm?'

'Don't mock me, you fool.'

'Charmed, sire. Well, your special guest is sleeping in the King's Bedroom, and your even specialer guest is partaking in forty or forty-five winks in the Queen's Bedroom … two of those kids are playing snooker, and, um, drinking stolen Johnny Walker…'

'Those thieving little bastards. I'll have their school billed for this.'

The professor chuckled. 'Two others, the pretty glum girl and the pretty glum boy, are having a little lover's tiff in the study. How … antiquated.'

'And the others?'

The professor flicked through a few screens. 'No idea. Probably asleep. It's after ten thirty, time for bed, sire!'

'Yes, yes.'

'And ... oh, look!' The professor pressed a switch and a view of the lounge room of Stewart House appeared. The muscular one from the band and a young girl – presumably the unaccounted for one – were huddled together under a handful of blankets on one of the sofas.

'What the hell are they doing?'

The professor cackled. 'Nerves be a little frayed, one suggests,' he said.

Forbes glowered. 'Professor Crow ... what did you do? We agreed on the singer, only.'

Professor Crow pushed back his chair and spun round. Forbes gasped. He never got used to the professor's hideously deformed face. The sneering bottom lip beneath the hardened beaklike nose, the downy feathers that covered his cheeks, the black beads of his eyes...

'I gave them a little ... serenade.'

The professor threw back his head and screeched. Forbes slammed his hands over his ears, turned away and went back through the steel door, and up a staircase towards the Grand Mansion of British Heights, situated on the surface two flights of stairs above him. Even as he reached the door that opened out into the back of a cleaning cupboard, Professor Crow's screeching laughter drew like fingernails across his eardrums.

THE OLD CHINESE woman had something she wanted him to see. She tugged at his arm and he let her lead him into the warren of back alleys off Daonung's main street, into a pungent stench of boiled tofu and cooking chicken offal. Rutherford wrinkled his nose and grimaced, trying not to cough as the rich aroma of cooking food engulfed him.

He glanced back at the road as it receded behind him, replaced by the crumbling walls of doorless shacks, but Rutherford felt no fear despite his obviously expensive clothes, or that he was the only Westerner in this town. He smiled at the sight of one of his factory's uniforms hung up to dry in the glassless window of a shack, and smiled politely when a couple of people came to shake his hand.

Was this what it was like to be a rock star? A politician? A demi-god, even?

The school he had built educated the poor children who would grow up to work in his factory for pay far above the local average.

They would grow up healthy, drinking the clean water the wells he had drilled provided, work hard, and spend their excess money in the revitalised shops in the town square. Rutherford had nothing to do with any other local businesses, but a few carefully placed bribes in the local government had ensured no other outside corporations could set up shop in the town, meaning the money stayed in the community. Rutherford Forbes, the enigmatic British businessman, was hailed as a saviour.

Daonung's mayor had wanted to erect a statue of Rutherford in the town square as a thank you for dragging the town out of abject poverty, but Rutherford had declined with thanks. On his visits he simply enjoyed eating and drinking as he chose, and taking the occasional pretty Chinese girl to his bed.

Daonung was one of three towns in Sichuan Province which Rutherford had taken under his control. He liked to visit them all at least once a year, just to check on things. He especially liked to get out among the people. He spoke no more than a few words of Chinese, but that personal touch made him more than just a distant benefactor, it made him one of them.

'Come, come,' the old woman said, pulling on his arm. 'Please ... I show.'

Rutherford had no pressing engagements until the following day. A girl named Fu Shi was waiting for him back at the modest villa he had built on the town's outskirts, with a warm smile and a firm body, but he'd taken his fill of her once today already. He liked to mingle with his workers, and many of them lived in the little warrens of shacks either side of the single main street.

Rutherford smiled as the woman led him past an outdoor toilet and shower block that looked lifted from a European campsite and deposited here in rural China. It was another one of his touches. Provide for one's flock, and one's flock will provide for you.

At a piece of cowhide hanging down over a shack entrance, the woman paused. She turned to Rutherford and took hold of both his hands. He was no more than five foot ten inches, but she seemed tiny in comparison, peering up at him out of a sundried face.

'Inside,' she said.

'Sure, let's go.'

He started to turn towards the door, but the woman held on with a grip that was surprisingly strong. When he turned back to her, she let go of his hands and held her fingers up over her face.

'Here ... no look,' she said. With the other hand she pointed at her temple. 'Here ... look.'

Rutherford frowned. Look with his mind but not with his eyes, is that what she was saying? What on earth was she about to show him?

She gripped his hands again and nodded. When he copied her nod, she muttered, 'Okay,' then turned and went inside, pushing the hide door aside for him to follow.

Inside, the woman's home was as poverty-stricken as he had expected. Just a couple of shreds of dirty carpet covered a floor that was part earth, part concrete. A cable hung across the ceiling, allowing the woman's home to have crude electric lighting. Rutherford, who ensured the local council received enough money to ignore the obvious theft lines connected to the electricity wires, admired the people's ingenuity. In adversity they had found ways to cope, and he liked that in a potential workforce. It was one reason he had come to poor Sichuan to set up his factories, rather than a more industrialised province.

'In,' the woman said, pointing at another cowhide door leading to a separate room. 'In … here.' She pointed to her face and her temple again, repeating the same action as she had outside. Only when Forbes nodded and told her 'Okay,' did she pull back the covering and let him step inside.

Something crunched underfoot, and Forbes lifted his shoe to reveal a silvery glinting man about the size of his palm, its square head now detached from its body. He frowned and nudged it aside with his foot, looking up at the treasure trove he now found himself in.

The room looked like an electronics closet. Bits of wiring and pieces of metal covered the floor, while heaped in the corners were crude electronic contraptions built out of others. Rutherford recognised circuit boards and old computers, video players, and even the shells of a couple of televisions.

Sitting on a stool in the middle of the tiny room, bent over something, was a child with a big mop of brown hair. Dressed in what Rutherford could only describe as sacking, the kid was muttering to himself as he fiddled with his latest creation.

'What's he doing?' Rutherford asked the woman.

'He build,' she said. 'Kurou! Kurou! Show … he.'

The boy let out a whiny cackle that sounded like a squeaky bicycle chain. Rutherford winced, but the woman looked up at him and jabbed a finger into her temple again.

Something small shifted in the dark, moving along the ground in short, jerky movements. It looked like a crude doll fashioned out of bits of metal. No more than six inches high, it took a few faltering steps towards Rutherford. When it got to within about a foot of him, the boy clapped a hand on the edge of the stool, and the tiny man jumped eight inches in the air and spun around. Then it began walking back towards its creator.

Rutherford gasped. The boy was making robots.

'How old is he?'

'Five.'

Rutherford gasped. 'Are you sure?'

The woman nodded. She pointed to her temple again. 'Here … strong,' she whispered.

'Let me have a look at you.' Rutherford stepped forward, reaching for the boy.

'No!' the woman screamed.

Only as his hand fell on the boy's shoulder did Rutherford realise the child didn't have a mob of brown hair, he was wearing a sacking hood over his head. He pulled it off before the woman could stop him.

The boy jerked and fell of the stool, twisting around. The single dim bulb in the room pushed the shadows back from his face.

Rutherford squeezed his eyes shut and looked away. He understood the gestures now.

The boy—if he could be called that—was a monster. His nose, fused with his upper lip, was long and hooked, calcified, and his protruding bottom lip made him look like a remarkably ugly bird. His eyes were beady little dots peering out of a feather-covered face. His hands, pressed across his chest, were barely more than talons.

'What the fuck are you?' Rutherford whispered.

'Kurou,' the woman whispered. 'My … boy.'

Rutherford nodded. 'Kurou,' he said slowly. '*Crow.*'

The boy was so ugly he was painful to look at. He was the kind of monster that would have been drowned at birth in years gone by, a monstrosity created out of mutated genes or radiation or both. He had a face that would grace darkened rooms and nightmares for the rest of his life. He was, without doubt, an abomination.

But he was also a genius.

15

JUN TALKS TO AKANE

'IT WASN'T MY FAULT,' Jun said from where he was slouched on an armchair in the corner behind the door, one leg up over the armrest, his hands behind his head. He stared across the study, at the window and the snow still falling outside. An ancient clock on the wall told him it was five minutes past midnight. 'I just found him, and I froze. I couldn't have stopped it. No one could have.'

Akane, lying on her side on a sofa behind him, sighed. 'I know, Jun. But you were there. When I came home from piano practice and I couldn't find him, I went into the garage and you were there. I can't separate you. When I remember his face I think of you.'

'Can't you try?'

'I have tried.' She shook her head. 'I lost everything that was beautiful in my life. I lost my mother, and my father, and my best friend.'

'I'm still here.'

'Not to me, Jun. Not that same boy that I used to play with in the park, who used to help me with my homework. That boy is gone. Or if not gone, then ... soured. Can't you understand that?' Akane rolled over on the sofa and pressed her forehead against the old, faded plush. 'If you hadn't been there, you might have been the crutch that could have helped me through it all. I could have still seen the old memories in your face.'

Jun wanted to scream. It was like trying to break through a steel door when he had the key in his hand. 'All you have to do is look forward,' he said. 'Stop looking back.'

She didn't reply at first. Jun stared at the old books on the shelves: a hundred million words of advice but not one line that could help him.

'I can't,' she said. 'What is there to look forward to? My grandparents are in their eighties. They'll be gone soon. I'm an only child. I'll be alone in the world. It won't matter who I play piano for, the people I want to listen won't be there.'

Jun said nothing. It seemed there was no getting through to her. He was just thankful that she was still in the same room, that after so long she was talking to him. It wasn't exactly progressing as he would like, but it was better than the silence, better than watching her with other guys.

'Why Ogiwara?' he said at last.

The sofa creaked as Akane stiffened. 'What?'

Jun smiled. 'I mean, we go to a school generally populated by fuckwits. I gather that you've been hanging around with those types because you don't want to think about your past, but … I mean, did you have to pick the biggest fuckwit of all? There are plenty in the lower ranks that would have been just as unfulfilling.'

Akane gave a welcome laugh. 'Nothing by halves,' she said. 'But yeah, he's a clown.'

'He's the biggest clown in the school. The guy is an absolute, bon-a-fide tit.'

'He's good looking.'

'Mr. Kirahara is good-looking. You're not banging him!'

Akane slapped the back of the couch. 'Shut up, that's disgusting!'

'I bet you're thinking about it now. I bet you can't get it out of your head.'

'What, Ogiwara and Sensei?'

It was Jun's turn to laugh. 'Yeah, you've got me.' He shifted around on the chair to look at her. 'He's actually pretty cool, you know. He was telling me about how he was into metal, and that he once went to Scandinavia.'

'Huh. Who'd have thought it?'

'Yeah, I was kind of surprised.'

Akane stood up. She came around the couch and pushed Jun's leg down off the armrest. Then, giving him a reluctant look, she sat down beside him.

'Hey.'

'Hey.'

She didn't look at him at first, just stared straight ahead, her hands in her lap and her back rigid like a girl at convent school awaiting confirmation.

'I'm scared, Jun.'

He reached out a tentative arm and put it around her shoulders. For a moment she resisted, then she relaxed and leaned in against him. 'Yeah, me too,' he said.

'Don't think this changes anything.'

'I won't.'

'It's getting cold though. I'm cold, Jun. And tired.'

'We should go back to our rooms.'

'No! I can't. I can't move. I want to stay here, with you.'

Jun nodded. 'Okay,' he said. 'Everything will be all right, you know. We'll wake up tomorrow, all the staff will be back, and we'll have to go to some stupid class at nine o'clock to learn how to write in old world English or something. The snow will probably have stopped and Kirahara-sensei will have come back with all the others. They'll probably be a bit pale, but they'll be fine.'

Akane said nothing. Her eyes were closed, and she was breathing softly against his chest. Jun looked around. She was right, it was starting to get cold. There was a heater not far from them but the light had blinked off. It was probably on a timer. He lowered her back into the chair and went to look, but it had no manual controls.

He didn't want to leave her alone, but he had little choice. There was nothing in the room that could cover them, and the thought of going outside in the snow to return to their rooms filled him with dread. In the hall, the main lights had switched off, leaving just a handful of emergency lights at regular intervals in the ceiling.

The stairs down to the reception area were totally dark. Jun considered going back for Akane and taking her downstairs. There was a fireplace opposite the reception, although it had been unlit earlier. If they could get a fire going, perhaps they could warm up a bit. Still, a strange foreboding feeling hung in the air like damp, and he didn't want to leave the safety of the library. He knew the two ornamental bedrooms were locked, so he could find nothing to help him there … but perhaps towels from the recreation room?

Again, he didn't want to leave Akane alone while he went down to look. Frowning, he went over to the window to look out on the courtyard below. He pushed the curtains aside and looked out. A couple of streetlights cast a dull glow over the snowy world below. Beyond them, the illuminations outside the pub had switched off, but Jun could see that the snow had finally stopped. That was something at least.

He started to turn away, then looked up. Of course, the curtains! There were none in the study or library, which meant the single-pane windows would let the cold in quickly, but out here in the hallway each window had thick drapes. Jun pulled up a chair, climbed up on its seat and began to unpick the nearest ones. They were old and dusty, but they were thick and at least ten feet long.

Ten minutes later two of them lay in a heap at his feet. As he picked them up in his arms, straining under the weight, he glanced back out at the courtyard one more time, and froze as he saw a thin figure wading through the snow, moving across the buried road between the dormitory buildings and the pub. Jun couldn't recognise the figure over the distance, but he watched until the person had disappeared out of sight behind the pub, probably heading to where Jun had seen the staff quarters to be on the map.

A tingle ran down Jun's spine. Sure, it was likely just a member of staff—a janitor, perhaps—out doing his nightly rounds despite the snow, but there was something about the figure that made him uneasy.

Something he didn't like at all.

16

THE COLD SETS IN

OGIWARA SMASHED THE CUE BALL, grunting as it bounced up off the green baize, struck the red ball side on, and trickled over to the cushion to where it settled. The red ball moved a few inches towards the pocket and came to rest against the pink.

'Piece of shit stupid game,' Ogiwara said, making the motion of breaking his snooker cue over his knee. 'Typical of the stupid English to invent something so hard. All of their games are stupid and hard, have you noticed that? Cricket, snooker, golf … they're all stupid games and ridiculously hard. They should have invented something like soccer, which is easy.'

'They did invent soccer,' Mishima said.

'Shut up, no they didn't. It was the Americans.' Ogiwara lifted the bottle of Johnny Walker and took a swig, coughing most of it up over the table. 'Ah, I don't know how anyone can drink this piss.'

He passed it to Mishima, who took a sniff and put it back on the bar. An assortment of bottles stood on the shiny surface beside them: Smirnoff, Don Perignon, Bacardi, Suntory Whiskey, Jamesons. They'd tried them all, but while they'd managed to get pretty drunk, none of the drinks had much appeal to their teenage drinking tastes.

'I tell you want we need,' Ogiwara said.

'What?'

Ogiwara tossed the snooker cue on to the table. 'Beer.'

'Yeah? Where are we going to get beer from?'

'The pub, you moron.'

'But the pub'll be shut by now.' Mishima peered down at his watch. 'It shut at eleven, but students weren't allowed in after nine.

It's half twelve now. I don't know about you, but I'm getting pretty tired.'

'Don't be such a pussy. Come on, let's go break in and have ourselves a party. Perhaps we can take some to Kaede's room and have a bit of fun.'

'Yeah?'

'Well, you can film me while I bone her.'

'Oh, great. What if she's got sick?'

'Then you can do her.'

Mishima frowned and shrugged as Ogiwara pulled his jacket off a chair and swung it over his shoulders. 'Cheap bastards have turned the heating off. You notice that?'

'Yeah. Probably an automatic system or something.'

'Automatic systems are stupid.' Ogiwara twisted the metal handle of the heavy snooker room door, but it didn't budge. 'Huh? What the hell? Some motherfucker has locked it!'

'Shut up, man. What do you mean?'

Ogiwara pumped the handle and tugged the door. It didn't budge, so he pushed a shoulder against it, just in case it opened outwards and in his drunkenness he'd forgotten.

It still didn't budge.

'That's it, you crazy madhouse of motherfuckers...'

Ogiwara went over to the snooker table and grabbed a handful of balls. One at a time he flung them at the door. Mishima winced at each heavy thud, but Ogiwara wasn't done. He grabbed a snooker cue, dug the tip into the green felt, and ripped a line up the centre of the table.

'Oh, man, you shouldn't have done that,' Mishima said. 'Remember what they said in class earlier, about how much it cost to replace?'

Ogiwara stared at him. 'You think I'm done? I'm just getting started.'

He grabbed the bottle of Johnny Walker and slammed it down on the snooker table. Mishima jumped back as the bottle shattered and bronze-coloured liquid soaked into the cloth, turning it a shade of greenish brown.

'Fuckers,' Ogiwara muttered. He took the cue over his knee and made to break it, but he just winced as his knee slammed into the flexible wood. Instead, he propped it against the edge of the table and stamped on it gracelessly until it finally cracked and snapped. Ogiwara jerked the two ends until it broke in two, then he flung them away across the room.

'That'll show them,' Mishima said.

Ogiwara, breathing heavily, slammed his palm down on the snooker table. 'What do we do now?' he said. 'The door's locked.

There's that tiny window on the back wall, but we're on the second floor.'

'We can't go out there tonight,' Mishima said. 'Who knows how bad the snow is. We might drown if there's enough of it piled up outside.'

'Or break our fucking necks.'

'If we wait until morning at least we'll be able to see what's going on.'

Ogiwara slapped the table again. 'God damn it.'

Both fell silent. Mishima started to tidy up the mess on the snooker table, but after a glare from Ogiwara he stopped. Instead, he made a show of taking a swig from the Smirnoff bottle, but winced and spat the vodka out on the floor.

Behind the little bar in the snooker room was a small stock room. Ogiwara went inside and found a sink with running water. There was a stack of fresh tea towels beside it, so he carried them back into the snooker room and dumped them down on the bar.

'You gonna clean up?

Ogiwara shook his head. 'Tie one round your head.'

'Why? I'll look like some construction worker.'

'Just do it. It's getting cold. We're going to freeze our tits off.'

Mishima scrunched up his face as if he was going to cry. Ogiwara groaned. The last thing he needed was a crybaby on his hands. 'We need to keep our asses warm,' he said. 'These walls look pretty thick but it's going to get cold.'

'Yeah, man. This sucks.'

Aside from the tea towels, the only thing they could find to act as a blanket were the thin plastic covers for each of the two snooker tables. They split the tea towels, wrapping them around their necks and hands like scarves and gloves. Ogiwara took one bench and Mishima took another. They wrapped themselves up in the plastic snooker table covers like human butterfly larvae and lay down, but even as Ogiwara tried to get comfortable, he could feel the air temperature dropping. The bench had a thin cushion, but it wasn't even half the thickness of a futon and the wood dug into his shoulder.

'Are you asleep yet?' Mishima asked.

'Shut up. I'm trying.'

'I'm cold.'

'Drink some more whiskey.'

'We'd be warmer if we lay side by side.'

Ogiwara scowled. 'You think I'm some gay bastard? I'd rather freeze to death than lie next to you.'

The minutes ticked by. Mishima started to snore. Ogiwara shifted and rolled over, feeling a little shiver as the shifting of the plastic sheet sent a chilly draft racing down his body. He tried to sleep, but it was no good.

He got up and went over to Mishima's bench. The other boy stirred as Ogiwara put a hand on his shoulder and shook him awake.

'If you ever tell a soul about this, I'll gut you,' Ogiwara said, pushing Mishima back against the wall and lying down beside him. 'And if you get a boner I swear I'll hack it off with a rusty saw and cauterise it with a cigarette.'

'Sure, whatever you say,' Mishima yawned.

Pressed together like two spring onions in a plastic packet, it wasn't much warmer. Ogiwara still shivered, feeling a small press of heat from Mishima against his back, but not enough to push the cold away. He pulled his knees up and wrapped his arms around them, ducking his head down, the tea towel tied over his eyes. Ogiwara had a jacket, so his upper body was fairly snug, but his legs and arms and face all felt the bitter chill of the cooling air.

I'll get you, he thought, as the spirits he had drunk allowed his weariness to fight through the cold and drag him down towards sleep. *Whoever locked that door, I'll find you and I'll cut your damn throat.*

'ARE WE SAFE?' Kaede whispered.

Dai, wrapped in a duvet they had stolen from a second floor bedroom, stared at the barricade of chairs and tables they had piled up against the back of the lounge door. It looked well enough fortified to at least give them a warning if someone tried to break through, but he was more concerned about the windows. There was nothing they could do except draw all the curtains and hope that the thing they had seen couldn't climb well enough to make it to the second floor.

It had been Kaede's forward thinking to grab some stuff from an upstairs bedroom before barricading themselves in. Naked, they had crouched by the lounge door, waiting for the thing to come up the stairs, until they had both been shivering wrecks. Aware they would probably die anyway, after a few more minutes with no sound or sign of the bird thing, Dai had watched the stairs while Kaede slipped into the nearest bedroom and grabbed whatever she could. They now wore a toweling bathrobe each and had several pillows, duvets, and blankets. As well as several tables for study, the lounge had three sofas. Two were now pushed against the door, holding up the table that was jammed under the door handle. They were sitting on the third.

'It must have gone by now,' Dai said. 'I'm not keen to go and check though.'

'What was it?'

Dai shook his head. 'The more I think about it, the more I think it had to have been some sort of sick joke. We're all fucked up and nervous after what happened to your friends, and our minds are playing tricks on us. Yeah, something smashed the window, and yeah, it had Ken's guitar, but what if it was just some asshole in a mask? One of those foreign tossers they have working here or even one of your mates?'

'Crap,' Kaede said. 'No way that was a mask.'

'No way to know unless we go looking for it.'

'I'm not going down there!'

'I guess that settles it then.'

'Perhaps it was of your bandmates. What about that weird bass player?'

Dai shook his head. 'I'll accept that he's weird, but he's not that type. Trust me. I've spent the best part of my life sitting next to that asshole. He likes to run his mouth about weird conspiracy shit, but he's not the type to dress up and start climbing in dormitory windows. Whatever that thing was, it lives out there somewhere.'

'What about your singer?'

'O-Remo? He's locked up in the Grand Mansion over there after freaking out. I'm starting to believe he saw something, though. He always manages to find something to get himself high, so we tend to take what he says with a large-ass bag of salt.'

Kaede sighed and leaned against Dai's chest. He looked down at her, unable to stop himself feeling aroused. There was some monster bird thing out there in the snow, possibly even downstairs, but he had a hot eighteen-year-old leaning against him in nothing but a bathrobe. And, he already knew what she could do when she took it off.

'What say we find some way to put that thing out of our minds?' he said.

Kaede looked up at him, those lovely eyelids fluttering. 'I thought you were never going to ask,' she said.

JUN LOWERED the folded heap of curtains over Akane's sleeping form and tucked it in around her as best he could. Then, so as not to frighten her when she woke, he pulled the armchair a little further away and sat down on it, pulling his knees up under him to keep out the cold. He then wrapped the last curtain around himself until only his face was poking out.

The thick velvet drapes were surprisingly warm. Every time he shifted a little draft would whistle down through the folds, but if he didn't move his body slowly began to heat up. He stared at Akane as he listened to her slow breathing. He wanted to go to her and hold her, but he didn't want to push her any further. She'd opened up to him more than she had in years. For the first time in as long as he could remember there was the chance their friendship might be rekindled.

Outside, the snow had begun to fall again, but it was lighter than before. Jun wondered whether Kirahara-sensei and the sick students were okay, or whether they'd been trapped by the snow. It didn't bear thinking about.

Perhaps, in the morning, everything would be okay again.

17

———

HELL BREAKS OUT

KIRAHARA-SENSEI OPENED his eyes to a blinding light and a loud humming noise. Under his body everything was hard and icy cold, but the pain across his back and shoulders was enough to make the likelihood of lying in snow unimportant.

Am I dead? he wondered. *Is this what it feels like?*

His eyes began to adjust. He turned his head because his body wouldn't respond, and gasped at the sight of a bloody, twisted body lying beside him, partially covered in snow.

'Oh, Natsumi, oh no…'

Her clothes were red and stiff with frozen blood. One arm lay a few feet away from her body, covered in red frost.

The snowmobile lay behind her, upside down and with the roof ripped off, impaled on a broken tree like a piece of *yakitori*. Other snow-covered shapes were scattered all around, some hanging out of the remains of the snowmobile, others lying further away as if thrown there in the crash.

The treads of the snowmobile were still, its lights were off.

So what's going on? Where are the lights and the noise coming from?

He tried to roll over but his body failed to respond. He couldn't feel his hands or his feet, and there was only a hollow gnawing feeling coming from his stomach. The nearest light was coming from behind him. Rocking his shoulder from side to side he managed to swivel around, and what he saw both surprised and alarmed him.

The hillside behind him had partially collapsed, mounds of snow-covered fresh earth with trees sticking out like breadsticks in a stew. Through a gap in two large heaps of rocky soil he saw an opening, a dark cave like a mine entrance, only with lights blinking far back in the dark. Once buried under the hillside, it had been exposed by the landside. As Kirahara-sensei watched, something huge and dark appeared far back up inside the cave and disappeared into a side tunnel.

It had been black or dark brown, and huge. Walking on all fours with a kind of languid grace.

'Oh my, they should be hibernating by now...'

A scream came from the trees back in the direction of the snowmobile. He jerked his head and managed to get himself into a sitting position in time to see a student stagger out of the trees and collapse into the snow. It was Nakamura, one of Ogiwara's judo mates. The boy looked pale and drawn as he bent forward and vomited on to the ground.

Behind him came a huge growl out of the trees.

'Run, boy!' Kirahara-sensei tried to shout, but his voice came out in a barely audible croak. The boy took a few steps closer, then stopped, staring down at Kirahara-sensei.

'Oh my god, Sensei...'

'What is it, boy? What—'

Kirahara-sensei looked down at his body and gasped. His legs were missing at the knees, the bloody stumps crusted over with frozen blood, around them deep gashes that looked like teeth marks.

'How—how—how...'

Even now, seeing the remains of his legs, the pain wouldn't come. Either the cold was a remarkable anesthetic, or his nerves were destroyed.

Or he was losing him mind.

'It'll be okay, Sensei...'

Something huge and dark stepped out of the trees and swiped a massive paw at Nakamura, ripping open his back like fingernails through old newspapers. Nakamura screamed, but he was helpless as the creature dragged him away into the trees.

As another growl came from behind him, so close he could practically smell the creature's breath, Kirahara-sensei closed his eyes and hoped that, whatever it was, it would kill him quick.

PART TWO

SNOWBOUND

18

PROFESSOR CROW SURVEYS THE
DAMAGE

BEING up before sunrise suited Kurou. He looked out of his small window in the tower room on top of the Grand Mansion's roof and peered up at the sky, a featureless, deep winter blue that would lighten gradually as the sun rose above the mountain peaks to the east. So, the storm had cleared out, but it wasn't all good news. There was more snow forecast for this evening, but at least the rest of the British Heights staff could enjoy what looked like being a pleasant morning. Kurou rarely went out during the day, only if he had to or if he was on official business, which was not often. He wasn't the most personable of Rutherford Forbes's many hundreds of staff.

He left the window and peered into the little hand mirror at parts of his face. It was about the size of his palm but he had smeared grease around the outside, leaving only a keyhole about a centimetre across. Under the beady little eyes, in which the slightly lighter brown of the irises could only been seen from real close up, the leathery, reptilian skin was bagged and bruised. He was tired from his exploits of the night before, but, as usual when Forbes let him out to play, he had got carried away. Forbes was as pissed as a queen with a bee up her breeches now, but spreading a little of the fear he saw whenever he was faced with his own reflection cheered Kurou up considerably. Forbes would get over it. Kurou would be grounded for a few weeks, but sooner or later he'd be let out again, when Forbes wanted to sell a few more tickets for the ghost hunting tours.

His aerie, as he thought of it, had three hundred and sixty degree views of the surrounding area. Running in a line from the south-east to the north-east, the Japan Alps ploughed an immense furrow up through the fabric of the land, dipping away and rising again to the highland area where Forbes had built British Heights. A hundred kilometres to the north, on a clear day Kurou's sharp eyes could pick out the glittering swell of the Japan Sea. To the west the highland rose again into some minor peaks where ski runs cut arcing swathes through the trees, before dropping down into the flatland of Nagano City. To the south, the highland dropped down towards the Tokyo basin. To the south-east, on some days he could see the rising cone of Mount Fuji.

Kurou, standing back at the window now, sighed. How he longed to fly like his ancestors might once have—his true ancestors, not the ones who raised him—up over the trees and the lakes, soaring on the wind without a care in the world…

He turned away, back towards the table where a tray of breakfast waited for him, delivered by one of Forbes's underlings in a dumbwaiter that also serviced the Queen's Bedroom on the second floor. It was a selection of the usual dog food that the guests got, sloppy eggs, soggy cereal, microwaved sausages, and a bowl of yesterday's rice for good measure. The staff, most of whom were rotated every three months, didn't know about his existence beyond the legend that Forbes advertised on the website. They didn't ask questions of who they were sending food up to at 6 a.m. every morning because they weren't paid enough to care.

Today's food looked even stodgier and less fresh than usual. Kurou arched his head over it and sniffed it with the long, calcified nose that Forbes and many who saw him thought of as a beak. It had a distinctly old scent. Probably all of it was yesterday's leftovers, reheated. He guessed the kitchens must be understaffed.

He shoveled the food down his throat and replaced the tray in the dumbwaiter. Then he went over to what looked like a cupboard door in the wall but was actually the entrance to a spiraling metal staircase that descended through the middle of one of the Grand Mansion's thick corner walls to the subterranean command centre, which was of course off limits to the centre's guests.

With a cackling chuckle, he climbed up onto the vigorously polished banister and slid all the way to the bottom, crashing off at the last turn and landing in a heap on a large, foul-smelling beanbag that had been breaking his fall every morning for almost a decade.

He stood up and brushed himself off, then made his way down the dim brick corridor to the laboratory.

A wall of flatscreen television monitors set into one wall displayed a rotating series of huge, wall-sized eye-camera videos. Currently playing was an hour-long montage of an eagle's view as it soared above the Sierra Nevada mountains in California, gliding, ducking and wheeling, spinning down towards the earth and pulling away again, soaring back up into the sky. Kurou gave the best smile his thin, barely movable mouth could achieve, and pulled up a chair at his workstation.

Three state-of-the-art computer monitors and their tiny touch-screen keyboards made a semi-circle around him. It was here that Kurou connected with the world. He logged on to one computer and began replying to a message from the previous evening that his little escapades out in the snow had left hanging, while logging on to several news and media websites with the other. On the third he loaded up the security systems for British Heights and ran a quick inventory check.

Flicking his gaze from one screen to the other at a speed few would be able to comprehend, Kurou completed a number of business deals for Forbes's companies while trolling Youtube videos and several dozen random forum sites at the same time. On a couple of robotics sites he was a moderator and a senior member, while on others he was a nuisance. With a compartmentalised mind that could drift from insanely talented scientist to teenage prankster to cool deal broker in the blink of an eye, Kurou was adept at dealing with a number of different tasks at once. With one hand and occasional cursive glances he set up a multi-million dollar arms deal with a South East Asian government, while with the other he arranged a date at a coffee shop with a pretty girl from New Orleans who had fallen for one of his dozens of fake dating site accounts. It would suck for her to be stood up, but the alternative—that he might actually show up—was far worse.

His eyes paused for a moment on the inventory of British Heights. While he didn't care much for the place – it was just a cover for Forbes's more illustrious pursuits and provided a number of loopholes to work and trade out of Japan – it did amuse him. He had as good an eye for culture as anyone.

There were problems. Brought on by the freakish snowfall, there had been a landside on the south-eastern approach road, meaning there was currently no way up to the centre. There was an old forest track, but that was no good until the snow melted in the spring. The centre's Internet was down—his own was through a high-calibre satellite link encrypted to be accessible only through his secure servers—and the staff was reduced to a skeleton crew, just one receptionist and two other Japanese staff to cover the restaurant, the shop, and the pub between them. Not that they would be needed—the guest roster had been greatly reduced by whatever fool had undercooked yesterday's turkey. Besides the staff, there were just five students, four members of that formerly famous rock band, Forbes's little lady friend, and the great red-cheeked bastion of wealth himself.

Oh, and Kurou, but he existed in the dark corridors between fear and consciousness, so he didn't count.

Satisfied that things were suitably chaotic, Kurou switched over the screen to a view of the day job—and stared as a scene of chaos appeared on the display in front of him. Alarmed, he keyed in a few commands and his display wall switched from the eagle's camera view to a shot of snowy, forested carnage. Bodies lay half buried in the snow, torn apart. He typed a couple of commands and a 3D map appeared on the screen. Kurou zoomed in on the industrial complex that extended beneath the innocent ground on which British Heights stood, miles of interconnected laboratories, computer labs, and testing facilities. At one end were the enclosures. As Kurou zoomed in further, he saw a flashing red light against one of the walls.

There had been a breach.

He switched back to the video mode and cycled through the views of a few internal security cameras. Beside a few hurrying scientists, the views were of rooms and empty corridors.

He frowned as best his feathery forehead would allow. This was very bad, very bad indeed.

The landslide had ripped off one of the outer walls. The test subjects had got out, and were now roaming around somewhere in the forest.

Kurou leaned back and gave an ear-splitting screech. Part of him wanted to howl in frustration that he would now have to authorise a cowboy mission to trap the test subjects before they found a population centre and caused untold amounts of damage.

And part of him—the creator part, the scientist, the *father*—wanted to sit back and watch to see what happened.

He rubbed the hard lumps that looked more like a bird's talons than human hands together with glee.

19

MORNING HAS BROKEN …
EVERYTHING

JUN LIFTED his head to see rays of cold sunlight streaming in through the windows of the study, hanging dust curtains over the old desk. He sat up and rubbed his neck. It was sore from the way he had been lying with his head jammed into the crutch of the chair, his knees pressed up against his chest. His hands and arms had a deep, ingrained chill, but the heating had come back on, and as he rubbed them they began to warm.

Akane was lying on the sofa behind him, snoring softly beneath a pile of curtains, only the top of her head and one shoe poking out. Jun smiled. He reached over and brushed a strand of hair back from her face. She looked so peaceful, and he'd hate to wake her. Instead, leaving her to sleep, he made his way out into the corridor and looked out of the window from where he had borrowed the curtains onto the courtyard outside.

A clear sky hung above the vehicles buried in the snow. As the morning had brought warmer temperatures he saw how the snow had began to sag, depressions appearing across it as it thickened and settled. Unless it was cleared, when the air cooled this evening the entire centre would be encrusted in a layer of ice.

There was no sign of any people. He ventured down the stairs and found the reception desk unattended, although the smell of food was drifting up the corridor from the dining hall. The front entrance was unlocked, so he went outside and stood looking down on the courtyard, a blanket of white with the lumps of two buried vehicles in one corner. The wind had caused the snow to drift, and at the top of the stairs, outside the overhanging roof, it was nearly up to his waist.

Everything was silent and still. No breeze, and no sign of

activity: no tracks in the snow, no passage cleared by a snowplow. It was as if they had been abandoned, left alone.

The early morning sun warmed his face, but Jun found it difficult to dispel a deep sense of uneasiness. The horrors of the previous night still cut deep, the sound of sick, screaming students still rung in his ears. Despite the obvious beauty of the fallen snow, there were too many unanswered questions out there for him to feel any sense of ease.

He waded down the steps towards the courtyard, the snow up to his knees. It was white and fluffy, and despite his past misgivings about the stuff, he found himself smiling. It was nearly Christmas, after all.

Jun went back up the steps. As he headed for the stairs he heard a little gasp of fright and looked up to see the receptionist from the previous night, Mika, standing behind the desk. Her eyes were bagged and her hair a little out of place, the crisp business suit and layer of makeup hiding a hard, troubled night.

'Oh, good morning,' she said, her duty forcing a smile on to her face. 'I trust you slept okay? How was your room?'

'Never made it,' Jun said. 'I bunked down upstairs with another friend.'

The girl's veneer of professionalism dropped away. 'I'm sorry to hear that,' she said. 'Things fell apart a little last night, didn't they?'

Jun sighed. 'I guess you could say that.'

The girl smiled and went back behind the desk. She lifted a telephone and tapped the receiver. Frowning, she looked up again and said, 'Our phones are out and our Internet connection is down. We haven't heard from your teacher or your friends. I'm sorry. Hopefully the connection will be restored later today.'

'Can we get down to the town today? Those of us that are left would rather just go home, I think,' Jun said, but as the words came out he wasn't sure he believed them. Saitama and home was back to his no-future schooling, and back to Akane hating him. The idea of being snowed in for a few days was growing more and more appealing.

'We get heavy snow most years,' Mika said with a hopeful smile. 'Usually the staff would be outside clearing it, but most of them went down to the town last night. There was a bit of a Christmas party for the foreigners. They were supposed to be coming back this morning, but so far we've not seen them.'

'Where's your manager?' Jun said, immediately feeling a little silly, like a kid acting at grown-up.

'Mr. Forbes?' she shook her head. 'I don't know. Probably in his private apartments.'

'Which are?'

'In an annex to the staff quarters. But visiting them is forbidden.'

'I'm not staff,' Jun said. 'I'm a paying customer.'

'Well, I can lodge your complaint and then ask Mr. Forbes to contact you about it when he's free.'

'Isn't he free now?'

'I don't know. The internal phone connections are also down.'

Jun nodded. He left her to her work and headed back up the stairs. When he entered the study, Akane had got up and was standing by the window, looking out at the high embankment that rose up behind the Grand Mansion towards the forest beyond.

'Oh, there you are,' she said. 'I wondered where you'd gone.'

'I just went to see what was going on,' he said. 'I found a receptionist downstairs, but she didn't know anything. All the phone lines are down. It looks like we're stranded up here until they get a plow in.'

Akane didn't look round. She stared out at the snow, a soft smile on her face.

'It looks so pretty, doesn't it?'

He came to stand beside her. 'It looks cold.'

'It's so untouched, Jun. So perfect.'

'I smelt food cooking,' he said. 'It's just after seven, and on the schedule breakfast was at seven fifteen. There might not be many people here, but it looks like they're sticking to the schedule. Do you want to go down?'

'I want to go outside,' Akane said. 'I want to walk in the snow for a bit.'

'Oh. Okay.'

Akane led Jun downstairs. In the reception area, Mika was able to find a couple of pairs of snow boots for them to wear, but warned them against going too far, especially as more bad weather was forecast. While Jun nodded politely to the receptionist's words of warning, Akane stared out of the window with a glazed look in her eyes.

They went out through the side door beside the dining hall. Through the window, Jun saw that five places had been set up for breakfast beside a laminated sign with their school's name on it, but Akane had no interest in eating. She led him down past the shop to where a break in the buildings before the pub and the staff quarters behind it gave access out to the nature trail that encircled the whole complex. Jun recognised the spot where he had seen the figure the night before, but if there had been tracks in the snow they had long since been covered. Looking up at the dark windows of the staff quarters though, he couldn't help wondering who might be watching.

Akane took his hand and led him through the knee-deep snow, her boots leaving trenches for him to step in. The snow was slushy underfoot, and Jun hoped that with enough sun it might melt off the roads and paths. It was a long way back to the town, but it was mostly downhill. There would be less snow the lower their altitude got, and Jun wasn't against the idea of making a hike for it.

No, another voice reminded him. *Just let it play out. What have you got waiting for you except all the stuff you wanted to get away from?*

It was romanticism versus logic. The sensible part of him knew that being stuck up on a mountaintop with no access to the outside world couldn't possibly be a good thing, while the romantic part of him thought it was wonderful. Alone in a snowy resort with Akane, cut off from the rest of the world…

'There's the trail,' she said from beside him, and he must have jumped because a smile broke out on her face. 'What are you scared of, Jun? Nothing to worry about out here.'

'If you say so. What about that thing that was seen last night?'

Akane rolled her eyes. 'A monster seen by a recovering drug addict on a snowy night after he'd had God knows what? Yeah, right. And anyway, it's the daytime. Monsters only come out at night, everyone knows that.' She threw him a smirk.

'Why are you so cheerful? I feel like I spent the night sleeping on a hard concrete floor. My neck is killing me.'

She smiled again. She had the most beautiful smile. It had been missing far too long.

'I guess I just feel a little more relaxed than usual,' she said. 'Perhaps solitude suits me.'

'But what about me? I'm here too.'

'Yes,' she said. 'You are.'

She lapsed back into silence as she led him up a gentle slope and into the trees. The trail was hidden beneath the snow, but its route easily followed because it was marked on one side by a yellow rope fence that poked up out of the drifts that had blown across the path.

Jun glanced nervously at the snowy forest stretching away in front of them as they crested the rise and Akane started down a meandering path towards a lookout building in the distance.

'Oh, wow, let's go down there,' she said. 'Look at the view!'

She let go of his hand and hurried down the slope in an awkward frog-walk that made Jun smile. If there hadn't been so much snow, she might have skipped, he thought.

She was already up inside the lookout when Jun reached it, peering out of a wide opening at the view of mountains and lakes stretching away into the valley below them.

'Wow,' he muttered. Saitama was all high rises and grey streets. The only mountain Jun had ever really seen had been the distant snowcapped peak of Mount Fuji, visible on clear days from parts of Tokyo. From where they stood the hillside dropped away into a deep valley, then rose again into foothills that surrounded a line of mountains stretching away in both directions.

'Isn't it wonderful?' Akane had taken his hand again, but it was more like a mother leading her child as she leaned forward to look out, not looking back at him. 'It goes on forever.'

'Yeah,' he agreed. 'It's nice.'

'There's nothing down there. I can't see any roads or anything. No houses. It's completely untouched.'

'I guess it's pretty uninhabitable.'

'I wish there was a telescope here or something,' Akane said. 'I'd love to have a closer look at that bear down there.'

Jun started. 'What bear?'

She pointed. 'Down there, just on our side of that frozen lake. You can see it moving.'

'That's not—'

It couldn't be. The moving shape was at least a kilometre distant, but looked to be about the size of a car. Asiatic black bears were native to the Japan Alps, but they ought to be hibernating now.

'I wonder what it's doing?'

Jun felt a knot forming in his stomach. 'I don't know, but I have a bad feeling about this. The signs said to watch out for bears, so I think we should perhaps go back.'

'Don't be silly, it's miles away.'

He grimaced. 'Yeah, *that* one is. What if there are more?'

'Shouldn't they be … what is it? Sleeping right now?'

'Hibernating. Yeah, they should. Perhaps it's hungry.'

He watched the shape moving through the trees with a growing sense of trepidation. It had to be a bear. He could see the way its legs lifted and fell, the way its head hung low to the grown as it walked. Every so often it paused to investigate the trunk of a tree or something buried in the snow. Its head would swing from side to side, it would nozzle at something, or it would squat back on to its haunches to reach up into a tree's lower branches.

A big Asiatic bear weighed around a hundred kilograms and could kill a human, but at this distance a bear that size would be little more than a brown dot. This one was clearly visible, right down to the flattened triangles of its ears.

Its size was something Jun didn't want to think about.

'We really should be getting back,' he said, reaching out to take hold of her hand.

This time Akane looked back. Something glittered across her eyes and she frowned. 'That's not a normal bear, is it?'

He shook his head. 'No,' he said.

20

A MEETING UPSTAIRS

Banba-sensei delivered the news to Karin with croissants for breakfast.

'We're graduating you from Girls Chorus,' he said, putting the plate down in front of her. The bathrobe hung open to his waist, only a loosely tied cord hiding his modesty.

'What do you mean?'

'You're leaving the band.'

"Graduation" was a blanket term for kicking out the girls who'd outstayed their welcome to bring in fresh blood. There could be any reason: a class of personalities, a girl had fallen pregnant, pissed off the management, or simply gotten too famous within the group to undermine the puppeteers pulling the strings. It was written into every girl's contract that any intention to leave the band would be carried out with the full graduation ceremony—which, depending on the popularity of the member in question—could involve a tearful farewell concert tour, a TV show special, an advertising campaign, even an honourary CD single release. What wasn't allowed—unless a girl had the best lawyers in the land—was to just leave.

The wonderfully gullible public bought it every time. The cat fights and backroom squabbles over money manifested into group hugs and teary goodbye interviews, because if they broke with contractual protocol they would never get a job in the entertainment industry again.

'I don't want to leave,' she said automatically. She'd thought about it a thousand times and even though leaving was the one thing she was desperate to do, fear of the unknown was even more terrifying than the oppression of being a dancing, underpaid mannequin for an entertainment company.

'You've grown too big for the group, Karin,' he said, going to stand behind her and rubbing her shoulders. One hand started to slip down her top, and she gritted her teeth for the few seconds it took him to entertain himself. It had been his bed that had got her to where she was, leader of the group, face of dozens of ad campaigns, and in a position where she'd been strong enough to force rule changes in the structure of the system. She only stayed with him once every couple of weeks, but it was enough to sour what little enjoyment she still felt in the band.

And of course, there was the guilt.

Her relationship—the first officially sanctioned one for any Girls Chorus member—with O-Remo Takahashi, charismatic singer with rising metal titans Plastic Black Butterfly, had been the catalyst for the end. They had become media darlings, adorning dozens of print pages and hundreds of websites every week. Plastic Black Butterfly was selling out the same arenas that Girls Chorus was playing as part of a Livewire Entertainment showcase tour.

But the management didn't like it, so the axe had finally fallen.

'What happens now?' she asked, the food suddenly unappetizing, as Banba-sensei went back around the table and sat down.

'You still have one more album in your contract,' he said, not looking up. 'There will be a farewell concert, of course, either at the Budokan or Saitama Super Arena. You're popular. We could fill both. After that we'll put out a solo record.'

She would miss the other girls—most of them—and she would miss the adoration from the fans, the packages delivered to the company in her name, the soft toys and the love letters and the homemade gifts. The chances of a transition to a successful solo career were not high; it happened, but more often than not it was a case of diminishing returns; one decent solo album followed by a succession of failures or a branch out into another media career that would never be as lucrative. There was that girl from that massive group a few years ago. Within a year she was starring in increasingly unsuccessful horror movies, before even that avenue dried up. The last time Karin had seen her, it had been as the presenter for a daytime cable shopping channel.

Karin had the advantage, being the obvious star of the group. It was one reason for her graduation, so that Banba-sensei could seize back control before Karin got too vocal in the press about their working conditions or salaries. Her place in his bed was expendable; she was just one of a line-up of eager girls prepared to do whatever it took to get on stage.

'I'm thankful for everything you've done for me,' she said slowly, staring at her plate. 'I'm sure the graduation will be a great success.'

'Of course it will,' he said, smiling. 'How could it not be?'

And then things started to go wrong.

THE CONCERT WAS AN UNBRIDLED SUCCESS. Twenty thousand crying fans crammed into Saitama Super Arena to watch Karin Kobayashi's graduation from Girls Chorus. Almost the same number waited outside, watching on giant TV monitors. The scene in the backroom was like something out of a refugee hospital. Everyone was shouting and crying. The other girls in the band— who got on rather better than any of them might have anticipated— talked of mutiny. Hearing about Karin's graduation only days before the concert, they talked of quitting en masse, reforming under a different name and hiring their own songwriters.

It was a nice gesture, but it was futile. Deep down they all knew who pulled the strings, and talking up their comradeship was merely an acknowledgement of support. Karin would be fine. The rest of the band would be fine. In six months everyone would have moved on.

Karin cried herself to sleep that night, and even with O-Remo beside her, talking of their impending marriage and making those little jokes that she loved so much, she was inconsolable. A major chapter of her life was over, even if she felt able to breathe properly for the first time in years.

Under Banba-sensei's guidance she got to work on a solo album. Now out of the band, she could fully embrace her relationship with O-Remo. Banba-sensei's bed became a thing of the past, and their relationship returned to being solely professional. There was no talk of a further contract, but her popularity with the fans of Girls Chorus meant that one solo album at least – and its accompanying tour – would recoup all of Livewire Entertainment's costs and set her up for the next couple of years. And if it did really well – hitting the Oricon Top Five – record companies would be clambering over each other to sign her up, even if Livewire preferred more malleable artists on their books.

And then, heading home from a brief tour of Indonesia with Plastic Black Butterfly, O-Remo tried to carry a little black bag through customs at Narita International Airport.

O-REMO WAS SHIVERING when he woke up, even though he could

hear the hum of the air-conditioner. He rolled over in the huge double bed and gripped the pillow, his fingers clenching tight to try to hold off the shakes. It was a mild withdrawal because his recent use had been infrequent, but it was enough to gnaw at his insides like a giant insect, eating its way out of his stomach. It would get worse over the course of the day, but if he could survive until they got down to Toyama this evening he knew a man who could sort him out.

He climbed out of bed, and the memories of the night before returned. The bird thing out in the snow, crouched at his feet, taunting him.

He fell to his knees, his cheeks burning, and vomited on the floor. As he coughed and retched, he saw blood on his hands where he had scrabbled to get into the building. For a moment he couldn't even remember why he'd been outside in the snow.

'Karin…'

The word came out as a croak. She was here somewhere, in this building.

She had left him at the altar, and his life had never been the same. He had a simple question for her, one he needed to ask, had needed to ask for six years.

Why?

There was the obvious answer, of course, the crutch she had leaned on when she spoke to the press, but they had reviled her anyway, ruining her career.

He'd meant to throw out the stash before he boarded the plane, but he'd woken up late and just forgotten. He'd got through with larger amounts before, but customs had been sharper than usual that day.

His lawyers got him off with a suspended sentence, a slap on the wrists. His passport had been revoked for two years, and there were a number of countries that would no longer allow him entry, even now, six years later. Not that it mattered; by the time he'd been busted Bee had started to freak out on flights anyway and as for the profits, touring overseas had never been worthwhile.

He often got blamed for the band's sudden decline, but that was bullshit. The *Method in the Madness* album had bombed—taking their whole career with it—because it had sucked.

Ken, so often a factory of crunching riffs, had been misfiring for that one. The follow up, *Plastic Machine Pain*, had been better—much better, in fact—but the rot had set in, and the slide had begun. Still, singing was what O-Remo did. There was nothing else. The day the band broke up would be the day he put a bullet into his head.

If he could find one.

He gripped his temples, trying to ignore the throbbing, and

thought back to the previous night. He had seen a light on in one of the second floor windows and tried to climb up, that was it. He'd been a little high, but not enough to really impair his judgment. The bird thing he'd seen had been real. What it was, he didn't know, but it was out there somewhere, and Karin was in here.

He went to the door and tried the handle, but it was locked. Instead, he went to the window and peered out at the snow. From the second floor window he could see the trail he had taken into the woods yesterday, winding its way through the trees on the other side of a snow-covered tennis court.

He had very little memory of why he had ended up in this bedroom. He remembered Ken half carrying him and dumping him on this bed. Ken must have locked him inside.

He went back to the door and pounded on it, shouting Ken's name. His knuckles ached from cracking against the hard, cold wood, so he started to kick instead.

'Let me out!'

No answer came. O-Remo turned away from the door, looking around the room. With ancient dressers and ornate chests of drawers lining a room of antique chairs and tables, glass chess sets and stuffed birds, it could have been lifted from the British Museum, where they'd gone once on a day off during their short European tour. As he stared at all the ancient fittings and stuffy reminders of an age of upper-class snobbery, something snapped.

Screaming in rage, he grabbed the nearest dining table chair and smashed it into a large mirror over an ornately carved dresser with stag's hooves for feet. As the glass shattered, he gripped the dresser edge and pulled it forward, spilling glass all over the floor. Next, he ripped an ivory dial telephone off a table top and flung it against the wall, where it broke into pieces. Then he heaved a chess set over and pulled a bookshelf down from the wall.

He didn't notice that what he thought was a closet door had opened, and a face was peering through the opening, until he lifted a lamp over his shoulder and readied to throw it.

'O-Remo?'

He paused with the lamp in his arms like a Roman gladiator about to throw a spear. The large, bright eyes he had once drowned in stared at him out of a familiar if slightly older face, her skin still pale, still flawless. She was wearing a thin lace nightgown that left little to the imagination, and memories of the sweet nights they had spent together flickered through his mind like a flipbook of pleasant photographs.

(*'I got this vid on mail order from the US,' Dai said. 'Let's have a watch on Bee's laptop.'*)

(*'Ah, no, man, that can't be her…'*)

(His hands cover his face as tears burst like sun flares from his eyes)
'Karin...'

For a moment time froze. O-Remo stared at the woman who had jilted him at the altar, and Karin stared at the man she had loved enough to ruin her career. Then lights came on, and the credits rolled. Karin screamed, slammed the door, and ran.

It took O-Remo a few seconds to register that she had gone. Then his feet were moving, bursting through the doorway into a more feminine version of the room he had slept in, still ornate and gorgeous in a musty, otherworldly kind of way, but with a more petite dresser, prettier, more colourful furnishings, pictures of beautiful landscapes on the walls instead of hunting parties and sailing ships.

A large door on the other side of the room was swinging closed. O-Remo's feet propelled him forward, but by the time he had reached the corridor outside she had vanished. He ran to the door at the end that opened on to the second-floor classrooms, but there was no sound of footsteps, so he retraced his steps and went down the stairs to the reception area, where a girl he vaguely remembered being present the night before was peering at a computer screen with a look of frustration on her face.

'Did you see her?' he asked.

'Who, sir?'

'Karin. Karin Kobayashi.'

'Oh, her? Mr. Forbes's lady-friend? No, I'm sorry, I haven't seen her since yesterday.'

O-Remo staggered as her words sank in. She couldn't be. It just wasn't possible.

He gripped his temples and sank to his knees, screaming.

21

TROUBLE FOR THE BAND

Ken slept better than he thought he would. When he woke up to see seven a.m. on the little digital clock beside his bed, he didn't immediately remember that his guitar had been missing. When he sat up though, it was leaning against the wardrobe, with the case propped open beside it.

He gasped and kicked at the sheets, scrabbling up the bed until his back pressed against the wall, but whoever had stolen and then returned the guitar in the night was nowhere in the room. He thought about that shadowy figure he'd seen out in the snow and shrugged it off. It had to have been Dai.

But how had he got into the room?

Ken flinched as a creak came from the door, and saw it was standing open a couple of inches, swaying slowly back and forth. He jumped up from the bed and clenched a fist as he made his way to the door, wondering what he would do if someone was really out there. The corridor, though, was empty.

He was sure he had pulled one of the beds across in front of the door, but it was back in its original position, pushed up against the wall. He looked down at the floor, but there were no scratch marks where the bed frame's wooden legs had scraped across the wooden boards. Whoever had replaced the bed in its original position had done so by lifting it up.

Taking another look into the corridor, he walked down to the dormitory's front entrance and stepped out into the snow. If there had been an intruder, the tracks had long ago been buried, but there weren't even any depressions in the snow that could indicate old footprints. It had to have been someone from inside the building, and since Bee had come in with him, that left Dai. He was sure there were no other guests.

He went back up to his room, and seeing no reason not to, grabbed some fresh clothes and went to take a shower. He was thankful for the lock on the door this time, and thankful for the fresh aspect the jet of hot water gave him.

Dai had probably picked up one of those high school girls and wanted to serenade her with some bullshit to get her pants off. Knowing Ken's guitar would be in his room when all the other gear was stuck in the back of the van, he had decided to borrow it, hoping Ken would have stayed at the pub and not noticed. Then, finding Ken asleep and the room barricaded, he had…

No. He hadn't just slipped inside, because those beds were heavy. If he'd pushed the door Ken would have heard the bed scraping across the floor.

Ken dried himself off and went back to his room. He stared at the bed for a few moments, then went out and knocked on Dai's door, trying to resist the urge to storm in shouting. To his surprise, the door swung open. It hadn't even been latched.

Ken stepped inside and stared.

The window hung open, several panes just jagged teeth of glass shards, the rest of them in pieces on the floor. The bed was a mess, the sheets damp with the kind of stains Dai always seemed to find in whatever town they had a show, and Ken could guess what had happened. Something had broken in, surprising Dai and his new friend.

Feeling a growing sense of trepidation, he walked to the window, pushed it open and peered out.

The snow had drifted deep up against the windows. Below Dai's window were a mess of half buried footprints, and he now knew how whatever or whoever it was had got into his room and taken his guitar.

The same mess of footprints were under his own window.

'It played us a fucking song,' came a voice from behind him, and Ken spun, his heart leaping into his throat, but it was just Dai, dressed in a bathrobe, with a young girl beside him in similar attire, holding his hand. 'That motherfucker played us a goddamn song and then tried to come in.'

Ken didn't reply. He remembered the shadow he had seen out in the snow. 'We'd better find Bee,' he said.

But when he knocked on Bee's door it swung open silently, also unlocked.

Ken stepped inside, followed by Dai and the girl.

Bee's bed was untouched and the room was empty. Of Bee or his things there was no sign.

THERE WAS nothing much they could do except carry on. Ken waited in the corridor as Dai got dressed and then together they went over to the adjacent dormitory building and waited for the girl, Kaede, to throw on some clothes. Dai was much changed; ordinarily he would have been bragging about his conquest the moment the girl was out of earshot, but as she went into her room he just stood in silence beside Ken and stared off into space. Neither spoke. Neither had anything much to say.

They headed up to the dining hall and found places set out for breakfast. There was only a small table of bread rolls, some rice, and some cornflakes. Only one cook was visible in the kitchen, and the waitress was the same girl who had been on reception the night before. She looked flustered and out of place, her apron failing to hide the business suit she wore underneath.

There were five places laid out for Kaede's high school and four for the band. None of the other students were present, and O-Remo and Bee were also absent, so Ken, Dai and Kaede sat down together. They grimaced with embarrassment as the single waitress recited a poor speech in English about breakfast customs and about waiting their turn, when there was hardly any food or guests.

As they ate quietly, with their conversation limited to occasional humourless jokes or remarks on the weather, Ken glanced around, looking for any hint to what was going on and what had happened to the rest of the guests and staff.

It was obvious the students hadn't returned, but if the receptionist was being forced to double up as a waitress it meant that most of the staff were missing too. He had figured they stayed onsite overnight, but perhaps they'd gone down to the local town and been stranded by the blizzard.

He looked up as Kaede pulled out her mobile phone and held it up into the air. 'Nothing,' the girl said. 'This stupid place is a reception black spot.'

'It must have Wi-Fi,' Dai said. 'That's done by satellite. A few trees and hills won't stop that.'

'I've tried it,' she said. 'Nothing. It's almost as if it's been blocked.'

Ken was just thinking about asking when the waitress approached.

'Sorry to bother you,' she said, 'But if you have a minute after breakfast, one of your party is in a bit of distress.'

Ken raised an eyebrow. 'Which one?'

'Mr. Remo. He's sitting behind reception now. He had a headache so I gave him some aspirin.'

Ken nodded. 'Thanks.' As the waitress left, he looked at Dai. 'He's not got a headache,' he said.

'Yeah. We need to get him out of here.'

'What's the matter with him?' the girl asked.

'Nothing you need to worry yourself with.'

'Is he on smack?'

'Keep your voice down.'

'Go fuck yourself.'

Sighing, Ken got up and left, heading for the reception. As he left through the dining hall he glanced back to see Dai and Kaede with their heads together, laughing and joking. He shrugged. It was Dai's usual way. He'd be happy with her for a couple of days, then he'd can her and they'd move on. The snotty-faced cow could bask in the glory of fucking a former rock star for a little while, but she'd be shoved back into the ranks of the down-and-outs before long.

Isn't that the paradox? Isn't that where we are now? a little voice chided him.

Perhaps it was time to go into TV music production, Ken wondered, as he headed down the corridor. It had none of the buzz and you didn't get the chicks, but the money was good and the work was steady. It would mean abandoning the others, of course. O-Remo had nothing outside the band except a steady decline into drug addiction, but at least Dai was good enough to get session work. Bee would probably join a cult or something.

Ken was the musical powerhouse of the band, the one with the theory knowledge and the classical training. He'd be okay, but quitting the band would be severing the final thread of his dream … to play a round of arenas one last time.

O-Remo was lying on a sofa in the plush office behind the reception desk, staring at a TV with the sound down low. A newscaster was talking into the camera while some war footage on a dusty Middle-Eastern street played on a screen behind him.

'Are you all right?'

'She's here,' O-Remo said, without looking up.

'Who?'

'Karin?'

'What? What the hell are you talking about?'

'Karin's here. I haven't seen her—well not in person—in six years, yet she shows up here of all places, and even worse, she's banging that old British man. I could cut his throat right now.'

'Forbes? The manager? Did we just step into a TV drama or something?'

O-Remo sat up on the couch and fixed Ken with a glare. 'This is not a joke,' he said.

Ken nodded. He noticed the slight shake in O-Remo's arms and wondered how long the singer could hold it together. In some ways, this experience—Karin aside—might do him good. It might give him a chance to clean up.

'Have you eaten anything?'

'No. I'm not hungry.'

'They're serving breakfast.'

'I'm not hungry.'

Ken sat down beside him and stared at the TV, which was now interviewing an old Japanese man outside a ramshackle house. 'Look, just eat something, then hopefully we can get off this mountain by lunchtime. They'll have to send a plow through at some point.'

'No.'

'What?'

O-Remo was staring at the screen. He lifted his finger and pointed. 'That looks familiar, doesn't it?'

Ken turned to look. The picture was now showing an aerial view of a huge landslip. As he watched, another huge mess of snowy trees and earth came crashing down, obliterating the trees below it, leaving a brown-grey stain down the middle of the hillside. Underneath the picture, text was scrolling across the screen.

'That's the approach road, isn't it?' O-Remo said, voice rising. 'That's the way we came in, isn't it?'

Ken nodded. 'I think it is. Damn, I wonder if those students made it down okay. Nothing on the news about any casualties.'

'It was the only way in, wasn't it?'

'On Bee's map, yeah.'

'Good.'

'Huh?'

O-Remo jumped up. 'This is the chance I need,' he proclaimed, raising one arm in the air as if he was on stage. 'This is fate, Ken,' he said, slamming a fist against his heart. 'We're trapped! We're trapped up here! Just us ... and her.' He smiled, and Ken tried to ignore the way O-Remo's eyelids were fluttering as if he he'd got a fly stuck under them.

Before Ken could reply, O-Remo turned and sprinted out through the door, almost knocking over the receptionist as she came behind the desk, the waitress's apron now gone.

'Everything all right?' she asked.

Ken just shrugged. He pointed at the screen. 'News reports just came in. The access road has been destroyed by a landslide caused by the heavy snow. Looks like we're trapped here until they can find another way in or send up a helicopter.'

The girl's dutiful smile dropped. 'Oh my.'

Ken smiled. 'I guess we'll have to just make do. Don't have a boyfriend, do you?'

'Well, I—'

'That's a joke. What I do hope is that this place has lots of supplies.'

'We have plenty of food. It's not uncommon to get snowed in, although they can usually get a plow up within a day or so. Excuse me, I'd better try to find Mr. Forbes.'

Ken followed her out, casting a longing eye over her back as she hurried away down the corridor. So, they were stuck here. He'd been thinking to start shoveling out their van, but guessed there was no point now. They had to sit here and wait for help.

Just us … and her.

A little tingle passed down Ken's back as he remembered the broken window in Dai's room, the footprints outside his own, and O-Remo's desperate screams.

And that thing out there in the woods.

We need a band meeting, Ken thought. *If only I can get them all to stop running off for five minutes.*

He went back to the dining hall, looking for Dai, but even he and the girl had disappeared. He looked up at the clock on the wall, which read seven thirty, and wondered if it was too early to get a drink in the pub.

22

SECRET NEGOTIATIONS

KUROU FROWNED at the body lying on the ground below him. The man's shredded uniform marked him as a member of maintenance, but his head was missing and his ID had been torn away too. It was the second body he had seen, but there would be more the closer he got to the complex. He hurried down the corridor, wondering what kind of design flaw had made Forbes build them big enough for the creatures to get into. He guessed they hadn't expected the test subjects to grow so huge. The overwhelming success of their program was one of the reasons for Forbes's incredible wealth: he'd already received payment for the first shipment, due in two years' time. Nine of the terrifying things for a secretive North Asian nation, with an option on up to a hundred more, depending on demand and the success of the first group.

He reached the end of the corridor and passed through the remains of a door into a laboratory. It looked like a bomb site; almost nothing was recognizable besides a few human limbs and the remains of some microscopes. The immense power of the landslip had torn the front end off the facility, upsetting the power inside and destroying enough walls to allow the creatures to get out. Of course, after years of testing, they had turned on their captors at the earliest opportunity. They'd run rampant through the powerless facility, smashing through doors and walls and killing everyone they could find.

And then they'd gone looking elsewhere.

Kurou turned a corner and found himself confronted with a mangled wound of a corridor filled with soil and rubble. He nodded, satisfied. The charges he had detonated in the hillside above the facility had covered it off again from prying outside eyes. While he had his own agenda of course, he was still Forbes's employee, and often protecting Forbes's best interests also protected his own. Keeping a lid on what they did in caverns buried in the hillside below British Heights was of paramount importance.

With the secrecy of the facility restored, Kurou's only problem now was how to hide its prized assets from the outside world. Rather difficult, considering the creatures he had designed to kill as efficiently and brutally as possible were now wandering about in the forest.

The easiest way to catch an animal was with bait. As he headed back towards British Heights, Kurou considered what he could use.

RUTHERFORD FORBES LOOKED like he had blown a fuse. His hair, usually pushing out from beneath a layer of gel or grease, had broken free, and was bunching above his head like clouds of smoke. In fact, with his face a deep crimson red, Kurou thought he looked rather like a volcano set to explode.

'What are you laughing for?' Forbes said, as soon as Kurou entered the control room. 'Take that damn smirk off your ugly face and turn away from me.'

Kurou gave an amused birdlike squawk and sat down at his desk, putting his feet up on the table, his legs crossed over. 'Some problems solved, some unsolved,' he said.

'Professor, what the hell happened last night? How serious is it, and what are our options now?'

'The snow must have caused a landslip,' Kurou said. 'It was unprecedented, of course, but the animal enclosures were built rather too close to the hillside to be safe. The slippage sheered off a section of the compound, cutting the power and exposing our laboratories to the outside world. Luckily, I've since hidden our facility again by detonating some explosive charges I had placed further up the hillside just in case something like this might one day happen.'

'And the animals?'

Kurou gave the best smile his beaklike face could achieve. 'Wandering around in the woods. They killed everyone in the compound that I could see, and I assume they've gone looking for more food.' He shrugged. 'You know, as they were designed to do.'

Forbes swung a punch at Kurou, who kicked back on the table, the wheeled chair spinning him out of range.

'Fuck. This is not a laughing matter, you dumb fool.'

'Oh, but it is. Aren't you just a little interested, sire? After all, we could count this as a live experiment, couldn't we? All we need to do is throw them some bait.'

'We'll be discovered. We need to arrange to leave the country as soon as possible.'

'Sir, we can't even get out of British Heights until the snow clears.'

'We must arrange for a helicopter.'

'Don't you think it would be suspicious, sire, for the owner of British Heights to leave his guests and staff behind? This is Japan. It's not easy for you to leave the country unnoticed.'

Forbes scowled. 'Do you not have a way of stopping the creatures by remote?'

Kurou shook his head. 'Unfortunately, the damage caused to the compound has severed our electrical systems. I'm working on getting them running again, but it could be several hours.'

Forbes nodded, and inwardly Kurou gave a brief smile. His mastery of the system was expected, but so was his loyalty. It was a grave mistake.

'You should do your best to put the minds of your guests at ease,' Kurou said. 'It might be safer to have them airlifted out of the centre. Then we can draw the creatures here and trap them before they cause further damage.'

'How?'

Kurou reached out and patted Forbes's shoulder with one taloned hand. 'Leave that up to me, sire. You know I have all the answers, don't you?'

FORBES LEFT Professor Crow and stalked back upstairs. He muttered obscenities under his breath but all he wanted to do was scream. If the contents of his underground laboratory were discovered by the authorities his whole business empire might be threatened. Huge bribes had secured him the land on which British Heights had been built, and still more had turned eyes away from the construction work. Not just the complex on the surface but the tunnels below ground. For fifteen years his business had been in operation, British Heights acting as a perfect cover for the movement of large sums of money in and out of Japan, but the real wealth lay beneath the snowy forest, in the laboratories Professor Crow and his team maintained.

THE CALL CAME out of nowhere.

Working out of China, Forbes Enterprises had developed twin industries in industrial robotics for the manufacturing industry and genetic manipulation designed to increase meat yields in cattle for the food industry. His scientists came from all over the globe, but the heavy lifting was done by the people of the villages he took over. At the helm of it all was the enigmatic Professor Crow, a scientific genius who was never seen in public and heralded an almost mythical status. Both arms of the business were booming, and only forty-three years old, Rutherford Forbes, billionaire, was one of the most eligible bachelors on the planet. Marriage to his work left no room for anything other than bed companions, but Forbes maintained a public image as a one-man economic powerhouse. Now, though, boredom was setting in. The money was stacking up and the business was running itself, but Forbes wasn't content to just swallow up smaller companies like a tsunami chewing up fishing boats, he wanted to innovate, to take the technology he and Professor Crow had developed to a new level.

The phone call gave him that chance.

A private plane picked him up, his destination an uninhabited island in the South China Sea. In a remote hunting lodge, he met and talked with a group of men whom he knew only by reputation. There, his destiny was revealed.

'If you can build a giant cow, what else can you build?' spat the spokesman, a sour-faced Asian man with cold, grey eyes.

Forbes looked around the room, from the fine whiskey in a decanter between him and his interviewers, to the military caps worn by two of the three men. The third, much younger, wore his hair slicked back and had a simple black suit, not unlike a schoolboy's uniform. He stayed silent throughout, just listening with quiet intention as the two military officials slipped from English to their native language and back again.

'We have a long border, you understand,' the first man said again. 'Maintaining a guard is a costly expense. What we require is something that can roam free, yet obey its duty when necessary. A guard dog, if you like.'

Forbes nodded. 'I can do that.'

'It needs to be something capable of surviving harsh winters, and living in mountainous terrain. Something omnivorous, for food at times might prove scarce.'

'Simple.'

'What kind of time frame can you give us?'

Forbes considered. The genetic manipulation alone would take years, then there was the breeding and rearing of the animals in sufficient quantities.

'You are thinking long term, I presume?' he said. 'I can do nothing within five years.'

'Of course. Our nation will stand forever. And we hope that its guard dogs, when delivered, will stand alongside it.'

'Fifteen years,' Forbes said. 'I will require part payment for the initial shipment up front, and will in return provide details of all development procedures, prototypes, tests carried out, and an ongoing update on general progress and a constant reevaluation of the timeframe in which delivery can be made.' He leaned forward. 'I assure you, gentlemen, you have come to the right person.'

The first man turned to the others and for a few minutes they conversed quietly in their native language. Finally, the first man turned back. He stuck out a hand halfway across the table and stood up.

'Done,' he said.

With a large grin, Forbes stood up and shook the man's hand.

23

JUN AND AKANE RECONCILE

THE DINING HALL was deserted when Jun and Akane got back into the Grand Mansion. Jun was feeling hungry, but Akane didn't want anything, so they went back out into the snow and headed for Akane's dormitory.

'What I really want is a bath,' she said. 'Can you wait outside for me, though? I'm a little scared to be alone right now.'

Jun shrugged. 'Sure. But have you got anything to eat?'

Akane smiled. 'I have some chocolate.'

'I guess that'll have to do.'

Akane went into the building first, but Jun bumped into the back of her as she stopped dead just inside the entrance. 'What's that noise?' she asked.

Jun listened. The sound of gasping moans was coming from Akane's room, along with the creak of straining wood. He smiled. 'At a guess … I'd say that was Kaede. Who might be in there with her … I guess you'll have to find out.'

Akane's eyes hardened. 'Damn that girl. All this crap and all she cares about is getting laid. I don't care what she does, but I want my clean clothes and they're in that room.'

Before Jun could say anything, Akane marched up to the door and shoved it open. The weak latch, secured from the inside, popped off the door with a sharp crack.

Kaede and someone else screamed, and Jun heard the thud of bare feet landing on a wooden floor.

A moment later Akane came back out, pulling her little pink suitcase along behind her. She closed the door, raised an eyebrow at Jun, and said, 'Let's go. I think they're done being disturbed for today. Wow, you should have seen them jump.'

They went outside and waded across the snow-covered street towards Jun's dormitory, Jun holding Akane's case in his arms.

'Who was it?' he asked, when they were inside.

'The drummer from that band,' she said. 'They were proper going at it, but when they saw me you'd think they'd seen a ghost. Kaede literally pissed herself. It was disgusting.'

'Really?'

'Yeah. I probably should have knocked.' She smiled. 'He had a good body but his dick was kind of small.'

'I really didn't need to know that.'

Her smiled vanished. 'You screwed her, didn't you?'

Jun sighed. There was no point pretending. He'd never been an item with Akane anyway, but for some reason he felt like an asshole. 'Yeah, he said. 'She's not exactly a girl for waiting.'

Akane nodded as if she'd just found out her mother had died all over again. 'She was cheating on you, you know. People talk. She was pretty much passed around the judo changing rooms. Ogiwara is the only one I know of who's never been there, and that's only because I kept tabs on him.'

Jun knocked on his door but no one answered. He pushed the door open and found both beds still made. There was no sign of Ogiwara.

'If it's confession time, can I ask?' he said, sitting down on the bed. 'I've confessed to you.'

'Why do you want to know? It's not like we've ever been a couple.'

He shrugged. 'I guess I just do. I hate that chump. I want to hear that you've never screwed him.'

'So it's okay for you to bang Kaede but I'm supposed to be some virginal maiden in a white dress, is that it?'

Jun smiled. 'Something like that.'

She sat down beside him and rested a hand on his knee. 'Well, since we're confessing, yeah. I did. Twice.' She looked up at him and raised an eyebrow. 'If it makes you feel better, he was crap. He has a ridiculously small dick and he has no idea how to use even that. You'd think something so small would have a pretty short instruction manual, but he clearly hadn't read it.'

Jun grinned. 'That does make me feel better.'

Akane sighed. 'I don't know what stories you've heard, Jun, but he wasn't the only one. Much as you might like it, I'm no angel. I might not have the body count of someone like Kaede, but I'm not the bastion of purity and innocence you might want.'

'Can I ask why?'

'Escape,' she said, without hesitation. 'Everything I do reminds me of what happened. Everything. Every spare minute when my mind isn't occupied brings those memories back. And the memories live on in everything I used to love. Piano … you.'

Jun turned towards her. Akane's eyes were filled with tears and she looked a mess. Her hair was sticking up in clumps and her make-up was blotching from not being removed the night before.

'You're the most beautiful girl I've ever known,' he blurted suddenly, the words feeling lumpy on his tongue. 'I've never loved anyone else but you.'

'Jun…'

Before he could chicken out, he reached across and grabbed her arm, pulling her towards him. As he searched for her lips she tried to duck away, and instead they bumped heads. Jun fell back on the bed, his hands over his forehead and his eyes squeezed shut against the pain. Beyond the darkness of his eyes he heard Akane sobbing.

'Jun.'

He didn't open his eyes. 'I'm sorry. I'm just freaked out.'

'Jun!'

He opened his eyes, and there was Akane's face, right above him, her eyes so close he could see the way lumps of eyeliner had clumped up in her lashes. Her eyes were watering, but whether it was from their clash of heads or tears—or both—he didn't know.

She leaned down and kissed him.

He pulled her close, wrapping his arms around her. They rolled over on the bed, Jun's hands searching for her body, pulling off her clothes and tossing them onto the floor. Akane's fingers clamped over the back of his head, digging into his scalp, her legs reaching around him. Kaede hadn't been his first, and as the singer in a rock band he'd never found it hard to attract good-looking girls, but he had never wanted anyone like he wanted Akane right now. Life's harsh realities had taught him that expecting happy endings was a direct route to heartache and suffering, but if there was a *one* in his life then it was the girl in his arms. He kissed her with an intensity he'd never kissed anyone before, and he let his body release all of its desperate passion on her.

An hour later, exhausted, they lay beside each other on Jun's bed, facing the ceiling. Jun had one arm around Akane's neck, and she had one hand resting on his stomach. They hadn't spoken since they had first kissed. Jun was terrified of spoiling the moment and bringing them both bumping back to reality. He couldn't guess what Akane might be thinking. Less than twelve hours ago he had been her most hated person on earth.

'Perhaps we could get jobs up here,' she said suddenly. 'I could work in the kitchens and you could … I don't know, dig snow and rake leaves?'

'Thanks.' He smiled. 'Well, it does look like they're pretty understaffed.'

'I don't want to go back,' she said. 'I like it here. It's a bit cold and a bit creepy … but it's kind of nice.' She turned to look at him. 'Peaceful.'

'I was thinking the same thing. If we go back—'

He didn't get a chance to finish. A crackling sound came from out in the corridor, causing both of them to jump up. Jun wrapped his arms around Akane and they backed away, terrified of what was about to happen, only for a little cough to introduce a speech through an old, tinny public address system.

'Good morning, dear guests … this is Rutherford Forbes, owner of British Heights. You may be aware that we seem to have suffered from a few minor problems in the last twenty-four hours, but rest assured that your stay will be back on track as soon as is humanly possible. In the meantime, I would like to ask all guests to please assemble in the dining hall at approximately eleven thirty. There you will be given a full explanation—as far as we know it—on everything that has happened and what will happen next. I look forward to seeing you then.'

The public address system clicked off. Jun looked at Akane. 'Sounds ominous,' he said.

Akane raised an eyebrow. 'Eleven thirty, it said?'

'Yeah.'

She smiled and reached out a hand. 'It's only just gone nine. What are we going to do until then, Jun?'

24

TROUBLE FOR FORBES

SHE IGNORED Banba-sensei's calls for as long as she could, but after four days she gave in. She didn't need him to tell her what she already knew—her contract had been cancelled. In the wake of O-Remo's drug bust and her subsequently jilting him at the altar, her solo album had bombed. No longer the starlet former lead singer with Girls Chorus, she was the washed up former lover of a drug-addled failed rock star.

Her career was in freefall, but Banba-sensei said he had one last case to make to her.

She met him in a late-night restaurant in Shinjuku. He was late; she was already a little drunk when he arrived, sitting at a corner table in the dim room with a candle flickering in front of her, picking at some pickles and soy beans.

'What I have for you is work that will be distributed outside of Japan,' he told her, almost before he had made himself comfortable. 'It's all I can do for you, I'm afraid. There's no contract, but there's plenty of work available and the money is excellent, comparable to what you were earning before. You're still young, Karin.'

She mulled over his words as he ordered food, and then rather presumptively a bottle of champagne. 'I need you to know that I'm doing this as a favour,' he continued, popping the champagne and pouring it into two glasses. I could just as easily set you adrift, watch you waste your life in hostess bars or on crappy cable TV shows paying convenience store wages. You're not going to like this, but at the end of the day it's just work. And it's lucrative.'

When he told her she scoffed, threw her champagne over him, and stormed out, but his words lingered on: *It's just work.*

After two more days of ignoring his calls, she opened an email and glanced over the figures he was quoting. Five thousand US dollars for a day's work, under an assumed name, and in productions which Banba-sensei assured her would only be distributed outside of Japan. He even insisted on writing that into each contract that she signed.

The first time was in a seedy love hotel in Shibuya with two big, muscular American guys who were clearly old hands in the trade. For two hours she was passed back and forth like a piece of candy while three men operated one still camera, one handheld camera, and a boom. While one of the male actors was working on her she could closer her eyes and imagine it was just regular sex, but then one of the cameramen would shout 'cut!', tell her to change position, and the whole thing would start over again. It was seedy, emotionless, and degrading, but she was five thousand dollars richer at the end of the day, and her involvement was over as soon as they considered she'd been screwed senseless enough times to get a decent take.

She went home and cried herself to sleep.

Two weeks later, she called up Banba-sensei and arranged for another contract.

IT WASN'T hard to get good at it. Her looks had got her into Girls Chorus in the first place, and the years of dance training had kept her body tight. The worst thing she had to swallow was her pride.

She quickly became in demand for the "foreigner on Japanese" market in the US and Europe, and turned down five contracts for every one she accepted. Her fees quickly doubled, and soon, with just a couple of days of work a week she was earning as much as she ever had in Girls Chorus. Yet something was eating away at her, and it wasn't just the endless succession of increasingly faceless men with whom she had to get intimate on camera.

Each time she took off her clothes and did whatever she was told to do, a little piece of her soul was stripped away. She found herself increasingly angry, lashing out at people for no reason, and one day she woke up and looked into the mirror and hated what was staring back at her. The bright-eyed innocent young girl who'd dreamed of being adored by thousands of people had become a hard-eyed woman closing in on her thirties, a glorified prostitute staring down a barrel at a bleak and unwelcoming future, waiting for someone to pull the trigger.

Out of the blue, her high school sweetheart, Hiro, called her up and invited her out to dinner. She'd been at her lowest ebb for weeks, barely getting up long enough to switch on her apartment's lights unless she had to go out and work. She lay around in bed, watching TV, pretending she couldn't remember the scent of a hundred grunting men all over her body.

The phone buzzed on the bedside table and she snatched it up, expecting Banba-sensei or some other contractor looking for her to take another job, but the number was unrecognised. Only her mother had it, so she clicked ANSWER and said, 'Hello?'

'Hey, Karin, it's me. Hiro.'

Her heart skipped a beat. 'Hiro?'

'Yeah. I'm sorry to call you up like this. Your mother gave me your number.'

'Oh … um, how are you?'

'I'm fine. Listen, next week I'm going to be in Tokyo for a couple of days on a work training thing. I was just wondering if you'd be interested in meeting for lunch? It would be great to catch up.'

The clouds seemed to part before her, revealing a clear blue sky where before there had been only grey. She smiled, feeling genuinely happy for the first time in months.

'Sure, that would be great.'

Hiro suggested a place not far from Kichijoji. It was a nice neighbourhood, one that always calmed her. It was a good suggestion. She agreed and hung up.

When the day came around it was an effort to find something decent to wear. Her wardrobe was a mixture of odd dresses from her years on stage and dress-down stuff, jeans and t-shirts. In the end she managed to find a relatively subtle frock that she had once worn to an awards ceremony. She wore black jeans underneath and a t-shirt over it. As she twirled in the mirror she thought she looked pretty good, almost like in the old days.

It was a cool spring morning when she got off the JR line at Kichijoji and strolled up past the quaint art galleries and cafes towards the restaurant where they had arranged to meet. Much as she knew it was folly, she still remembered the fondness she had felt for Hiro, and although a thousand lives now separated them she wondered if she might feel a little of the old attraction. Would he have changed? Would he still be the strong young lad with whom she had shared her first kiss, or would he have bulked out and lost all his hair?

Her heart was making little butterflies in her chest as she entered the restaurant, a pretty little Italian with trestles in the windows and framed pictures of European spices on the walls.

She recognised Hiro instantly. He was sitting at a table near the back wall. He had barely changed. His hair was still cropped short, almost to his scalp, and his jawline was still firm. Beneath the suit he wore, his body looked strong and lean.

'Hello, Hiro,' she said, pulling out a chair and sitting down.

'Karin.' He gave her a smile. 'You look so lovely. Would you like a drink?'

He ordered a beer for himself and an orange juice for her. As the waitress left, Karin shifted in her seat, feeling awkward. 'I thought I'd never see you again,' she said.

'It's strange how things turn out,' he said, as the waitress returned with their orders and set them down on the table. 'I followed your career. I have all your Girls Chorus CDs and your solo one. I was so proud. I brought something for you.'

'As Hiro leaned down to take something out of his bag, Karin frowned. Something had been wrong with his words—

Was…

Hiro tossed a DVD case onto the table top. Karin stared down in horror at a picture of herself, sitting with her legs open, her modesty protected only by a towel, while a muscular Western man sat behind her, his hands cupping her breasts. She was pouting at the camera as he licked at her neck.

'Thanks for making me a laughing stock. The boys in the office loved this one.'

Karin barely noticed the beer as Hiro stood up and threw it over her. Even as the sticky liquid got into her eyes, her vision was fixed on the DVD box, the title written in Japanese katakana.

Banba-sensei had promised her no one would know. It appeared he had broken his promise.

As Hiro's heavy footsteps marched out of the restaurant, Karin began to cry.

JUN WOULDN'T LET Akane's hand out of his as they made their way to the dining hall for the meeting called by Rutherford Forbes. He wasn't sure how many people would show up, but it was a surprise to see just the owner himself, Mika from reception, an old woman he assumed was the cook, a young man he had seen opening up the gift shop, two members of Plastic Black Butterfly, and Kaede standing beside them. She stuck her tongue out at him, then rolled it across her lips, a gesture which he couldn't be sure meant whether she was happy to see him or not. He chose to stare at the huge Christmas tree set up beside the entrance, as if perhaps believing in Santa Claus might solve all their problems.

There was no sign of Ogiwara or Mishima, nor of Bee or O-

Remo. While Jun could imagine that his classmates were up to no good, he couldn't start to guess what had happened to the other two members of the band.

Forbes, too, seemed a little put out by the poor turnout as he climbed onto a low stage at one end of the dining hall and gave a little cough into a microphone. He surveyed the nearly nonexistent crowd with a dissatisfied frown, like an unpopular comedian surveying a ragtag audience.

'Thank you for coming,' he said in clear, well practiced Japanese. 'I guess that your companions are all enjoying the wonderful facilities we have here at British Heights, as well they might in such circumstances. Please feel free to pass on to them what I am about to say.' He paused and cleared his throat. 'I'm afraid its not particularly good news, but there is no need to panic. Unfortunately, due to last night's unexpectedly heavy snowfall, there has been a landslide just to the south of here. Part of the access road to British Heights has been destroyed, so for the time being there's no road route back down into the valley.'

'What about our friends?' Jun called out.

Forbes sighed. 'We've had no word from them, I'm afraid. All our telephones are down and our Internet signal is being blocked, we believe, by approaching weather systems. Rest assured, I'll let you know as soon as I hear anything. I'm sure they're all fine.'

Kaede started to sob into Dai's shoulder. Ken just sighed. Akane stared at Forbes and Jun bit his tongue against a stream of curse words that threatened to spill out.

'The good news is that from today onwards, for as long as you're all stuck here, there will be no charge for your room or board. All facilities will also be free. However, some of them may not be operated due to staff shortages. We do understand, however, that we can't just expect you to sit around.'

Both members of the band rolled their eyes. Beside Jun, Akane smirked. 'You'd hope so,' she muttered.

'I do have a favour to ask, though,' Forbes continued. 'We are hoping that by this afternoon a rescue helicopter will be dispatched to begin airlifting you all down to the local town. We can't expect you to stay up here, although we are well provisioned. However, we need somewhere for the helicopter to land, so we'd like you all to lend a hand in clearing the snow from the courtyard outside the Grand Mansion to create a makeshift landing pad.'

Dai groaned. 'You're a cheeky bastard,' he called. 'You going to be paying us for this?'

Forbes shifted uncomfortably. 'I'm afraid that we have limited manpower. If the helicopter is unable to land, you could be stuck up here for several days. The weather forecast says the snow will close in again this evening.' He cleared his throat. 'I do appreciate your cooperation in all this. Snow shovels can be found in the janitor's cupboard next to reception. Now, if there are no questions, I'd like to thank you for your time and efforts, and apologise one more time.'

As Forbes got down off the stage, the two band members and Kaede wandered over to Jun and Akane. Jun felt Akane's fingers tighten over his as Kaede looked him up and down.

'Hey,' Ken said.

For a while Jun had forgotten that Plastic Black Butterfly was one of his all-time favourite bands, and that the lead guitarist and the drummer—by far the two coolest members of the band, in his humble opinion—were standing in front of him, looking as pissed off as he felt. One of them was even banging his ex-girlfriend.

He opened his mouth to speak, but no words would come out.

'He has all your CDs,' Akane blurted. 'And until he thought it was kind of lame to have posters of your band on his wall, his bedroom was so dark you could have set it on fire and still not been able to see anything. When he saw you at Summer Sonic in Tokyo four years ago he kept his wristband on for three months. When he was twelve, he told me that if he ever had a daughter, he would name her Butterfly—'

'All right, shut up!' Jun interrupted.

Akane grinned. 'Guys, meet your greatest fan.'

'Charmed,' Dai said. 'Are you friends with Kaede?'

As Kaede pouted, Akane said, 'She's his girlfriend.'

'Oh.'

'But since he loves you so much he's probably quite proud of her.'

Kaede aimed a slap at Akane. 'Shut up, you bitch.'

'Tramp.'

'Whore.'

Ken put up a hand. 'Okay, ladies! Since this is the winter equivalent of getting stuck on a desert island, let's not go *Battle Royale* on ourselves. Let's go and shovel some snow, shall we?'

As Dai led Kaede towards the door, Ken fell into step beside Jun and Akane.

'Summer Sonic, yeah? I remember that one. Probably the last big show we ever did.'

'You were awesome.'

'Thanks.'

'And for what it's worth, your last album was badass, even if it only sold three copies. I own two.'

Ken laughed. 'Cheers, kid. You play?'

'Yeah. A bit of guitar, but mostly vocals. I've got a band.'

'Yeah?'

'Yeah.'

'Name?'

Jun gave a bashful smile, feeling his cheeks redden. 'Shock Tact Ticks. We put out a song called *Sledgehammer Carrion Bulldozer.*'

Ken raised an eyebrow. 'Are you serious? I've got that song. It's magnificent.'

Jun's mouth dropped open. Beside him, Akane started to laugh. 'Dude, are you fucking serious?'

Ken clapped a hand on Jun's shoulder. 'Kid, Plastic Black Butterfly might not be on the crest of the rock wave anymore, but I do my best to keep up with what's current. I heard about that song from a producer mate. He makes a point of hunting for new bands. He says he listens to so much worthless crap that every time he finds a gem it sticks out. He said when he heard your song on some streaming site he fell out of his chair.'

'You're just saying that.'

'What I'm saying is you're good, kid.' Ken smiled. 'Unfortunately, that might not be enough, but you can be safe in the knowledge that this guitar player wished he'd written that song.'

Jun nodded but said nothing. Coming to terms with something so frighteningly awesome would take time. His favourite guitarist liked a song he had written. It was the stuff of dreams.

'That's awesome,' he said at last.

'I told you we should just stay here,' Akane said. 'Cool stuff seems to happen up here.'

Ken laughed. 'I wish I could say the same. Unfortunately, the longer we're up here the more concerts we'll miss and the more money we won't make. Plus, the isolation isn't good for a bassist with claustrophobia issues and a singer with a dependency problem.'

'Where are they?'

Ken shrugged. 'Your guess is as good as mine.'

'Aren't you worried? They might be out there in the snow.'

Dai looked back. 'Bee might be out there in the snow. That spacehead is probably building a treehouse for all we know, in which to await an alien visitation. O-Remo is probably hiding in a closet somewhere.'

'I tell you what, kid,' Ken said. 'If you give us a hand to dig out our truck so we can unload a bit of gear, I'll see if they'll let us set it up in the pub over there and we can have a bit of a jam.'

Jun stared. 'Are you serious?'

'Yeah, why not.'

Akane nudged him. Jun shook the stars out of his vision and looked at her. She was holding out a bright red snow shovel. It was probably unused; the blade had not so much as a scratch.

'Time to get busy, fanboy.'
'Um, thanks.'

IT WAS clear from the look on his face that Rutherford Forbes was having a very bad day. He was sitting at his large work desk by the window of his office overlooking the forest to the west, the mountain peaks just visible through the trees. Karin had never seen him do any real work there; mostly he just read the newspapers he received via mail order from the UK, or sometimes messed about on the Internet. As a result, his desk was cluttered with trinkets and other junk which on good days she found amusing and on bad days irritating. He had one of those endless pendulum things made out of metal balls, which clicked away for hours every time he set it going. He had a Rubik's Cube she had never seen him touch, the blue squares making a T with red on one side and green on the other. He had a few little pictures and carvings from across the world: an elephant from Africa, a tiny oil painting of a quaint village street from Greece. And he had one of those rubber stress balls, forever resting inside a large marble ashtray he had bought in Peru. She had never seen him touch it, until today.

He was crouched forward, staring out of the window, crushing the blue and pink ball between his fingers until the plastic bulged. His face was set into a grimace, and as he first turned towards her, his thinly-haired scalp flushed bright red, she was reminded of Jack Nicholson in *The Shining*. He looked maddened, borderline insane.

'What's the matter?' she asked, closing the door behind her. 'I heard about the problems with the students, and I know the snow was unexpected—'

'What do you know about problems, you stupid whore?' he spat at her, little drops of spittle actually spraying out across the room. 'So easy to solve everything when you all have to do is lie on your back.'

Although Karin was taken aback by the unusual viciousness of his tone, it was not the first time. He'd never struck her, but she'd seen the worst storms of his temper, and the best course of action was always to give him some space. She wondered if perhaps today she might be able to bend it to her advantage.

'Oh, Rutherford, I'm sorry,' she said. 'It's insensitive of me to trivialise everything. Is there something I can do to help?'

He looked uncertain for a moment, and she knew the storm had broken. Perhaps with women from his own country he might have expected an argument, but she was more adept at pacifying him.

'You don't understand,' he said sullenly, tossing the stress ball away behind him. 'This is very bad, very bad … for business.'

She thought he had been about to say something else, catching himself just in time. He was obviously still in shock after so many of the students were taken ill. There would certainly be an investigation, and if one happened to die it could have massive repercussions. British Heights was only the tip of the iceberg of his wealth, but what she knew of the rest of his businesses was that they were overseas and she had no intention of leaving Japan. She wasn't marrying him to be his wife.

'What are you going to do?'

He shrugged. 'I had to reassure them that things would be sorted out. I arranged a meeting of all the guests in the dining hall, but there was very little I could say or do. Of course, due to the snow we've only got a skeleton staff, and with the collapse of the road—'

'What?'

'You didn't see the news?'

She shook her head.

'The access road was destroyed in a landslip caused by the adverse weather conditions. That road is the only way up here during winter, so we're stuck. Our phone lines are down and the Internet reception is being blocked by something, so we're stuck waiting and hoping for the rescue workers to send in a helicopter.'

'How long could that take?'

Forbes shrugged. 'How long is a piece of string?'

Karin nodded. It was no wonder he was so worked up. At the knowledge that the road was gone she felt her own claustrophobia closing in, wrapping itself around her. She had never been a fan of the snow, and now it seemed all encompassing, a blind spot on her life. She could only hope that rescue workers could get up to them as quickly as possible, otherwise she might start to go crazy.

'I'll go and take a swim,' she said. 'Perhaps you should join me. It might help you take your mind off things.'

Something in Forbes's face changed. He looked her up and down, then his blotchy, dough-ball of a face offered her a lecherous smile. 'That … you could do yourself, my dear,' he said, reaching down and unbuttoning his trousers. 'Come here, won't you?'

Years ago it would have disgusted her, but Karin had done far worse in the name of coin since her musical career had coughed its last breath and died. Every cell of Forbes's disgusting old body repulsed her, but five years in the porn industry had taught her how to fake things extremely well.

She raised an eyebrow, licked her lips, and kneeled down.

A few moments later, Forbes began to groan. Karin closed her eyes, and dreamed of the money she would have when they were married.

25

ESCAPE FROM THE SNOOKER ROOM

'Okay, up you go. Can you see a way down?'

From where he stood up on the window ledge, Mishima shook his head. 'No. But I might be able to get onto the roof. There's some guttering that I can grab.'

'Do it then, but hurry up. I want to get the hell out of here.'

Mishima squeezed himself out through the small window and vanished. Ogiwara stared. Then Mishima's face appeared, leaning over from above.

'It's easy, come on.'

Ogiwara climbed up onto the stack of chairs they had made. It trembled a little under his feet, but he gripped the window ledge to hold himself steady and levered himself up until the bottom edge of the wooden frame was taking his weight.

Outside, a snowy embankment rose sharply below him, leveled out, and became fenced-in tennis courts. Beyond them was the forest, and beyond that were the bumps of the highland hills further to the south. Everything was coated in a thick carpet of snow. Ogiwara scowled.

Mishima had been right. They were fifteen metres off the ground, but there was no way down from here. However, the outer window ledge was at least fifty centimetres wide and offered an easy stepping stone to clamber up onto the roof which was just above them. Mishima had cleared the snow off the ledge, and Ogiwara grabbed the edge of a piece of corrugated guttering and hauled himself up.

'Nice view,' Mishima said, pointing across the roof to where the peaks of the Japan Alps rose in the distance. 'You can see for miles.'

'Shut up, you clown. Let's find a way down off this godforsaken roof so I can sort Matsumoto out once and for all.'

'How do you know it was Matsumoto who locked us in?'

Ogiwara punched Mishima's arm, making the other boy flinch. 'Who else would it have been? That weasel must have pinched the key from reception. I'm going to smash his face in.'

The snow on the flat roof came up to their knees. It was fresh and untouched, although the morning sun had begun to help it settle, making it a chore to wade through. They went across to the front of the building, looking for a way down, but there was just a sheer drop down onto the courtyard, so instead they turned west and hiked along the top of the building towards where a single room appeared to be sticking up out of the roof, just to the west of the main entrance.

'That looks like it could be a janitor's room or something,' Ogiwara said. 'We'll break in, beat the crap out of the old toad for not clearing the snow, and then go downstairs and batter Matsumoto.'

Mishima sniggered. 'Cool.'

'And then I'll find my girl and get some action.' He grinned. 'You can go and have a wank in your room.'

'Shut up.'

'You shut up!'

When they finally made it to the protruding room, they discovered it was a lot bigger than it had looked from further away across the roof, and was actually two rooms stacked on top of each other. They couldn't see into the upper room, but the lower room looked like a self-contained living-dining area, complete with bookshelves, tables and chairs and a three-piece suite. Ogiwara leaned against the window and peered in, but the room was empty. He banged on the glass; it was surprisingly thick. Without anything to break it, they had no way to get in.

'Looks like a little love nest,' Ogiwara said. 'Probably where that owner guy brings his prostitutes. If I can find the way up I'll bring Akane up here so I can bang her while I watch the sunset.'

'Awesome.'

'Shut up, you loser. Hurry up and find me a way in.'

If there was a way into the room from the roof, they couldn't find it, but exploring near the back of the Grand Mansion, Mishima spotted a maintenance ladder fixed to the wall and waved Ogiwara over.

It looked an incredibly long way down. 'We'll rock scissors paper for who goes first,' Ogiwara said, then proceeded to play a hooked c-shape with his hand. When Mishima looked aghast, Ogiwara grinned. 'Tiger's claw. Beats everything. Screw you, loser. Over you go.'

Mishima scowled. 'You're such a cheat,' he said.

'Cheats have the hottest girlfriends. Losers have their wrists.' He gave Mishima a little shove. 'Come on, hurry up. I'm getting hungry. Make sure you clear off all the ice. I don't want to fall.'

Mishima grimaced as he climbed over onto the top of the ladder, but once he was on it he descended quickly. Ogiwara, feeling a little nervous himself, followed him down.

'Right,' he said, as he jumped off onto the ground. 'Let's find Matsumoto and give him a hiding.'

26

GAMES IN THE SNOW

O-Remo had no intention of leaving the Grand Mansion until the roads were cleared and the band could get away with Karin kidnapped and locked in the back—he hadn't yet figured out how to execute that part of his plan—but within a few minutes of leaving the reception area, as he wandered through the corridors, ducking into and out of rooms in search of some sign of her, the itchiness under his skin began to return.

He knew what it meant, of course, but he was no longer thinking straight. He needed a hit or he'd start to get worse. All he needed was a little hit.

He'd dropped most of his stash on the path out in the snow, but there was still a little bit left in his room. It would be enough to sort him out until they could get down to Toyama. If they didn't make it down by nightfall, though, he'd be in trouble. He didn't want to think about that.

He went down to the recreation room and slipped out of the door on to the covered west walkway. The wind had been blowing from that direction, meaning that while the east walkway was buried under drifts of snow, the west was almost clear. O-Remo crept along it, glancing frequently back over his shoulder as if the bird thing might appear again. Even though the sky was as blue as a mountain pond and the sun was shining brightly over the top of the buildings, the thought of seeing that thing made his stomach churn. He was beginning to doubt himself again, unsure whether he'd really seen it, or whether he'd been suffering some sort of drug-induced hallucination.

You didn't hallucinate on heroin. Anyone who knew anything about substances would tell you that. But O-Remo had dipped his fingers into enough mind-altering pies over his career to have left some pretty nasty stuff kicking about in his body. Who knew what was inside him, just waiting for a trigger? He'd read all the stories about bad acid trips, about people never being quite the same again, and wondered whether the bird thing might have been a figment of his chemically enhanced imagination. The more time that passed, the more possible it seemed.

His room in the dormitory building looked as he had left it. The bed was untouched, and his case still stood under the window. He sat down on the bed, trying to remember where he had hidden his remaining stash, then with scrabbling hands he pushed the mattress back and stuffed his hand underneath, imagining his hand closing over the little bag of goodness that would get him through the rest of the day.

It came away empty.

Panicking, O-Remo stood up and threw the mattress back. Then, at the sight of nothing but the springs of the bed, he got down on his side and pushed himself underneath, hands windmilling across the floor, looking for where it might have fallen.

For more than two minutes he scrabbled like someone suffering a seizure, then he managed to control himself enough to realise the horrible truth.

It was gone.

He sat up and pushed himself back against the wall, wrapping his hands around his knees, trying to stop shaking. Suddenly the room seemed incredibly cold. His heart was skipping in his chest, unsure what rhythm to choose. It wasn't just the need for a fix that was screwing with him, it was the fear of being unable to find one. He'd been to enough therapy sessions to know that withdrawal was as much in the mind as it was to do with the chemical dependency of his body, but when he was in the grip of it, that knowledge made no difference. The need overcame everything.

Someone had been in here and taken what was left of his stash. There was no other explanation. Perhaps it had been a cleaner, but why would they have been looking under his bed? He hadn't slept in it. It hadn't needed to be made.

His eyes fixed on something in the middle of the floor, just in front of the door, something that had got caught in the thread of the rug that lay across the end of the bed and was poking up, swaying slightly in a draft coming up through a gap in two of the floorboards. O-Remo didn't want his eyes to focus but eventually the tiny thin object seemed to ease into clarity of its own accord.

A feather.

He scrabbled at the bed and managed to push himself up. With his legs becoming more and more uncertain underneath him, he stumbled towards the door, slipped and fell to his knees, then scrambled back to his feet again.

He managed to get through the hall and push through the doors to the outside, where he collapsed in the snow, breathing hard. He grabbed a handful of it and shoved it into his face in an attempt to clear his mind, but too much bad stuff was floating through there now.

That bastard thing he had seen out in the snow had taken his stash. That bastard bird thing was following him, tormenting him. Whatever it was, it was sadistic, like a playground bully picking on a handicapped kid.

'Whatever you are, I'll kill you,' he whispered, wishing his hands would stop shaking. All he could think about was smashing a baseball bat into that evil thing's ugly face. Whatever it was, if it could exist and if it could get into his room and steal his stuff, it could die.

He struggled back to his feet and looked around. First things first. He had to get himself sorted out. Then he would hunt that motherfucker down and kill it. Without a hit though, he could barely walk.

He had dropped his stash outside the building behind the pub. He had seen Karin in there. What if she was there now? He winced, scratching at his neck, feeling something like ants running across his skin. It was just the junk, he knew. It was calling for him. Finding Karin had become a lower priority, but what if she had some stuff? She'd never done any, but she'd taken it off him from time to time when he was trying to quit. She wouldn't have thrown it away, would she? What if it was in her pocket, or in a drawer in her apartment somewhere?

O-Remo didn't care that the paranoia in him was taking over his thoughts. He was so desperate that the wildest possibility became a thread of hope to cling to. He staggered off into the snow.

The staff quarters loomed up in front of him. The door had a keypad lock on it, but someone had left it propped open with a snow shovel. O-Remo slipped inside, scanning the mailboxes on the bottom floor for Karin's name. Ben, Steven, Lizzie, Amanda … neither Karin's nor Forbes's name were there, but across the top of the other four boxes was a larger box with tape across it. An unoccupied apartment or one owned by management, who had their post delivered to the front office? O-Remo started up.

Between the second and third floors was a longer set of stairs, with only a single door at the top, as if this part of the building had been made intentionally separate from the rest. O-Remo crept up to the door and leaned an ear against it, but heard nothing from inside.

Very carefully he took hold of the handle and turned it, hearing a soft click next to his ear.

Unlocked, he eased the door inwards and peered inside. The room looked like a cluttered office, with a few filing cabinets against the wall, a leather sofa which looked like it had taken a lot of use, and a wide desk topped with all manner of nick-nacks…

…and in front of it, a bloated, blotchy-skinned Englishman with his hands gripping the desk at his sides as his neck arched back, his mouth expelling a little gasp of pleasure, his belt undone and his trousers around his ankles…

…and on her knees in front of him, the woman O-Remo had loved loved *loved*, who had jilted him at the altar on their wedding day and disappeared into both physical and media obscurity, the woman for whom he would have given up everything and gone running to the ends of the earth—

Her head bobbed up and down, wet juicy sounds coming from her mouth, the same sounds that had made O-Remo rant and rave when the video came up on Bee's computer tablet that time—

'Nooooo!' he screamed, barging into the room, rushing forward and barreling into them, pulling Karin's head away from something slick and wet, shoving her aside as the fat foreigner squealed like a little pig and his manhood swung through the air like a blunt, floppy sword … O-Remo grabbed the nearest object he could find, a metal pendulum thing—similar to one he had seen on the desk of that sour-faced executive at Dogswill Records, their current record label, as he told the band that their new album would be their last—and he jerked it up off the desk and swung it around in a wide arc towards Forbes's ugly, flushed face.

'Security!' Forbes squealed, punching a fat red button halfway up the wall as the pendulum thing spanked him across the right cheek and he grunted and spun, a podgy roll of fat as he triple-axled to the floor.

'Get out!' someone else screamed, and O-Remo turned to see Karin glaring at him, a wet and sticky film around her mouth which she wiped away with a swipe of her sleeve. 'Get the fuck out of here!'

'Come with me!' O-Remo screamed back, grabbing her hand and dragging her towards the door as Forbes crawled towards them like a fat sow nosing towards its trough, snuffling and trying to speak through blood dribbling from his nose.

'Shut up, you idiot!' Karin shouted, but O-Remo grabbed her around the waist and literally lifted her out through the door. She had never weighed much, and she seemed lighter than usual. No longer able to pay for roadies, the band had taken to lugging their own gear at gigs, something that had paid off across O-Remo's shoulders and back.

The stairs seemed to escalate around him as he found himself on the ground floor and carrying her out into the snow, even as she screamed and protested in his arms.

'I'll never let you go again!' he cried, shoving his face into her hair as she struggled to get out of his grip. 'I'm sorry! I'm sorry for everything! We should have been together!'

'Get off me, you drugged-up asshole!' she shouted, kicking out at him, but a blue mist had descended over his eyes and he could no longer feel anything other than the gentle wrap of the cool, dry winter air.

He had to get her away somewhere where he could talk to her, but nowhere in the complex was safe, not now that Forbes had called for security. It didn't matter that O-Remo had seen no more than a skeleton staff and that unless the security were hidden away somewhere then the blaring of an alarm would be filling an empty room. He dragged her out into the snow behind the staff quarters, manhandling her over the low rope on to the nature trail like a wrestler attempting a slam through.

The lookout. It was the only place that was suitable. It was romantic with its nice view. She would forget her anger and melt into his arms. Then he could ask her if she had any stuff and they would both be all right.

'Let me go! Remo, let me go back!'

'No, no, Karin! I need to talk to you.'

'I don't want to talk to you! I don't even know why you're here!'

'We got lost—'

'I don't care!'

'Just listen to me. I need your help.'

She stopped struggling. O-Remo relaxed his grip, but still kept hold of her arms as he pulled her along through the snow, both of them stumbling and knocking into low branches that flicked snow all over them.

'What? What do you need? Are you using again? You know that's why, don't you?'

He shook his head. 'That's not why. You loved me.'

'I tried to love you,' she said. 'I couldn't.'

'You're a liar!'

Karin sighed. 'I got paid to fake it, Remo,' she said. 'I got paid very well and I got good at it. My whole life has been a lie, so you're on the mark there.'

'Don't be stupid. We could have been happy.'

'We could never have been happy!'

He reached the foot of the lookout cabin and pulled her up the steps into the shadowy interior. 'What we had was special, Karin. Why did you leave me? Why didn't you show up that day?'

She took hold of his arms and looked up into his eyes. 'Because I couldn't live with myself for what I'd done to you. What I'd done behind your back with other men.'

O-Remo stared. 'What do you mean? Who?'

Karin reached up and grabbed his face, pulling him towards her. 'The woman you wanted me to be never existed!' she shouted. 'I tried to be her, I really did, but I couldn't be anyone other than myself. All I've ever cared about was being famous, and that meant doing whatever I needed to do. Why the hell do you think I'm here?'

O-Remo felt a white bolt of heat flash through his brain. Everything seemed to haze over and he pushed her away from him, wanting to get away. 'You liar!' he screamed, twisting around, trying to turn his back to her and run, but suddenly he was staring out at empty space and then he was tumbling forward, slipping through the open window of the lookout and falling forward into the snow. As it buried him upside down to his waist he heard an icy slewing sound and then he felt himself moving forward, slipping down the slope. The sky appeared for a moment and trees flashed by on either side, little more than a fuzzy brown blur.

Caught in some kind of mini-avalanche, he could do nothing other than let the snow take him. He flapped his arms like a drowning man fighting for the surface, but the snow was too heavy and moving too fast. As the avalanche tumbled him over and over, he felt his leg collide with a tree, hold its own for a moment and then give way, but the searing pain was hidden behind the terror until he suddenly came to an abrupt stop.

It took a few moments for his spinning mind to catch up and his vision to clear. When the world came to a complete halt he found the snowy forest to be rather serene, utterly silent and still.

Then he shifted his position, and pain exploded in his leg.

He could only expel a weak gasp, the pain taking his breath away. He twisted his head and saw the top of his knee poking out of the snow. There was no sign of the rest of his leg, but a red crescent had bloomed out around it like the petals of an ice flower.

The slightest movement caused lances of pain to shoot up his thigh. He twisted his head and saw a messy gash in the otherwise pristine snow of the steep hillside above him. He couldn't see the lookout, but it had to be somewhere up there. It was a long way up, but he could already feel the snow beginning to chill his skin through his clothes. Looking up between the snow-covered trees, there was no sign of the sun. Even at this relatively early time of the day, this valley had already fallen into shadow and the temperature would continue to drop.

Karin was still up there, wasn't she? Or had she fallen too? No, she'd been behind him, back in the lookout. She'd go for help, wouldn't she?

O-Remo clenched his fingers over snow and flung it away from him. How long would help take? With his knee and the cold he wouldn't last long.

He could still feel the draw of the junk. His arms and hands were shaking from the onset of the withdrawals, and his throat felt parched and dry. He wanted to shut his eyes and die, but the urge wouldn't let him. Karin was up there too, and their conversation wasn't finished.

The task facing him was near impossible, but he had no choice. Somehow he had to get back up the hillside to the lookout.

27

CONFRONTATIONS AND RESCUE PLANS

FROM BEHIND A STEAMED-UP window on the second floor, Ogiwara and Mishima watched as Jun, Akane, and the others got to work digging out the courtyard below.

'We'll get him,' Ogiwara said. 'As soon as he's alone. God, did you see that?'

'What?'

'The way he touched Akane's arm. Thinks he has a chance there with my girlfriend. I'll show him. You just watch me.'

Mishima nodded. 'Cool,' he said.

'Do you have any idea how much I like it,' Jun said, standing his spade up in the snow and turning to Akane, 'when you look at me like you've been looking at me this morning?'

She raised an eyebrow as she heaved a load of snow on to the pile by the edge of the courtyard that they had been making together. 'Enjoy it while it lasts.'

'Don't say it like that.'

'I was joking.'

'I know, but every time I see you look up I worry that you might start looking at me like you used to.'

'Don't talk about it.'

Jun turned away and hefted another spadeful of snow. 'Sorry, but—'

'Jun!'

They lapsed into silence. As he shoveled the snow, Jun looked back up at the Grand Mansion. They had managed to clear a path a couple of metres wide from the main entrance all the way down to the courtyard gates. Dai and Ken were working on making a circle in the centre wide enough for a helicopter to land, while Kaede was at the bottom of the steps, stabbing irritably at the snow with her spade as if hoping it would shift of its own accord.

'It would help if they had a snow-clearing machine or something,' Akane said at last. 'There must be one somewhere.'

'I reckon so,' Jun said. 'I'm pretty convinced they've only got us doing this to stop us complaining.'

'And we'll be so starving by the time they serve up yesterday's leftovers again for lunch that we won't care.'

'Be nice if Kaede helped a bit more,' Jun said. 'We might finish before it gets dark.'

Akane's eyes were like daggers. 'Getting bored of my company?'

'No, nothing like that—'

The main entrance of the Grand Mansion burst open and the young man from the pub came running down the steps. He dashed along the path they had cleared and then veered left across the snow towards the staff accommodations behind the pub, pushing through the door and running up the stairs.

'What was that all about?' Akane said.

Jun jabbed his spade down into the snow. 'I don't know, but let's go and find out.

Akane trailed along behind him as they headed after the young man. Glancing back, Jun saw Dai and Ken following too. Kaede had retreated to the warmth of the reception area.

As he reached the entrance to the staff quarters, Jun saw the door had clicked shut, leaving no way in. He stood there awkwardly for a moment, wondering what to do, then through a foggy window saw the young man helping Rutherford Forbes down the stairs. As the young man pushed open the door, Jun held it for them to come out.

Forbes looked disheveled and unkempt, his clothing creased and his shirt untucked. A large gash on one cheek had dribbled blood down onto his shirt collar. He flapped his hands as the young man helped him out the door.

'You!' he shouted at Ken and Dai. 'Get out of my resort!'

'What's going on?'

'That bastard singer of yours attacked me. He's kidnapped my girlfriend. Find him, find her, and get out!'

Ken looked confused, glancing at his bandmate then at Jun and Akane, but Dai stepped forward, his fist clenched. 'Shut your mouth, old man, or I'll shut it for you.'

'You bastards, you'll do time for this.'

Dai took another step forward. The young man didn't seem keen to put himself between the burly drummer and his boss, while Ken had a look on his face that suggested he wished he was elsewhere. To Jun's surprise, it was Akane who stepped forward, getting between Dai and Forbes.

'Shut the hell up, the lot of you!'

'Don't you speak to me like that—'

Akane slapped Forbes across the face, her palm landing with a meaty crack. She wiped the blood off her hand without looking down, her eyes fixed on the owner of British Heights.

'Which way did they go?' Jun said.

Akane rolled her eyes. 'I think it's pretty obvious from the tracks, don't you?' She pointed at the scuffed, damaged snow leading towards the natural trail. 'Let's go find them.'

Akane took the lead with Jun and the band just behind him. At the rear, Forbes hung back with the young man from the pub, muttering and complaining about his wet shoes. Akane set a sharp pace, marching through the snow like a hunter trailing wounded prey, and Jun had to hurry to keep up. They had barely gone a hundred yards when Jun saw a woman staggering towards them. She was inappropriately dressed in just a light top and jeans, and her hair was a mess of twigs and snow. When she saw them she stopped and waved her hands over her head.

'Help me! He fell!'

Before Jun could react, Ken and Dai were pushing past him, striding through the snow towards the woman.

'Where is he?' Ken shouted.

'The lookout,' she gasped. 'We argued ... he slipped, and the snow—oh god, the snow...'

Ken shoved past her, Dai close on his heels. As Jun reached the woman he thought she looked familiar from somewhere, a washed-up TV celebrity from his childhood, perhaps. She had one of those faces that was *too* pretty, that looked like it had been cut out of a magazine, yet at the same time there was a weariness in her eyes that suggested her life was a rollercoaster that had taken one last turn into an unstoppable freefall.

'Jun, did you see her?' Akane said as the woman passed them. 'That was Karin Kobayashi.'

'Who? That name ... I've heard that name...'

'Girls Chorus, Jun. My cousin has all their CDs.'

'O-Remo's ex-girlfriend,' Jun said, remembering. 'I never really cared much about their personal lives, but I remember something about her running out on him. I read about it on Wikipedia.'

'After she graduated from the band her solo career flopped,' Akane said. 'I heard that she'd got into porn, but she kind of went off the radar after their relationship ended. So my cousin said, anyway. I always thought they were shit.'

'What's she doing here?'

Akane shrugged. 'No idea.'

'Feels like we've stepped into some Korean drama or something,' Jun said, smiling.

Akane laughed. 'Please don't tell me you watch those.'

'No, but my mother—' He stopped. 'Sorry.'

Akane shrugged. 'Forget it.'

They had reached the lookout. Ken and Dai were inside, peering down the slope as Jun and Akane came up behind them.

'Fucking snow is too warm to stick,' Dai said, punching the wooden wall of the lookout. 'The sun bakes it, then the cold freezes it, and it slips off. Do you think he's alive down there?'

'One way to find out.' Ken cupped his hands over his mouth and shouted, '*O-Remo!*'

An echo was the only response. He tried again, this time with Jun and Dai joining in. Akane stood and watched, frowning.

'Can't hear anything,' Dai said.

'Your ears must be as screwed as mine,' Ken said. 'Of course we can't hear him.'

'I can!' Akane blurted. 'There!'

Jun cocked his head. It could have been the wind, or it could have been the gentle settling of the snow, but he thought he heard a faint, '*Help me!*' drifting up from the valley.

'We've got to get down there and get him,' Dai said. 'We'll need ropes and maybe digging gear. We have to get him before dark or he has no chance.'

'Where is he?' came the angry voice of Rutherford Forbes as he barrelled up into the lookout and pushed the others aside. 'Where's that bastard? I'll string him up for this.'

Dai turned and knocked Forbes to his knees with a heavy punch to the cheek. 'Shut up, you fat old turd.'

'You'll regret this!' Forbes wailed as Ken dragged him back up. 'I'll make sure you get put away!'

'Shh,' Ken said, wrapping a hand over Forbes's mouth. 'Just be quiet now. Dai's not in the mood for putting up with your whining. Just be thankful that I'm here.' He marched Forbes back to the steps of the lookout. 'Now, be a good man and go back and find us some ropes. We have a rescue to perform.'

As Forbes stumbled off back up the path, muttering obscenities under his breath, Dai turned to Akane. 'Sorry about that,' he said. 'I hope I didn't get blood on your clothes.'

Akane smiled. 'No, I think I'm okay.'

Dai nodded. 'I bet you kids didn't expect this when you signed up for this trip, did you?'

Jun laughed. 'I guess it beats learning English. Now, how are we going to find—'

His words were cut off as a huge roar echoed out across the valley. As the sound reverberated and then died away, the four of them looked at each other. No one said a word for several seconds. Jun was afraid to breathe.

'I'd guess that wasn't O-Remo,' Ken said, in a voice that was barely above a whisper.

Jun looked back up towards British Heights, but Rutherford Forbes had disappeared. 'Was that a bear?'

'If it was,' Dai said, 'I really don't want to meet it.'

28

FUN AND GAMES IN THE FOREST

KAEDE HAD no interest in messing about in the snow any longer than she had to. As soon as she saw the others wandering off towards the staff quarters after the man had come running out, she went inside where it was warm.

In the reception area, Mika had got a fire going. Kaede sat down for a while, but after a few minutes of staring aimlessly at the flames, she got up. Mika was sitting at the reception desk, trying to look busy. As Kaede wandered over the receptionist looked up and gave an apologetic smile.

'What time's lunch?' Kaede said.

'I'm sorry?'

'Not much else to do up here except eat, is there?'

Mika's cheeks flushed. 'I'm sorry about all this.'

'Whatever.'

'You could take a swim or view the rooms upstairs.'

Kaede shrugged. 'I hate water and I hate old things. They smell bad.'

'Well, there are some magazines in the recreation area.'

Kaede rolled her eyes, but it was better than nothing. She waved a dismissive hand at Mika like someone shooing away a pigeon, and went to find something to do.

In the recreation room she found a bunch of fashion magazines, but they were months out of date and the only articles of interest she'd already read before. She still couldn't get any reception on her phone and the computers in the recreation room wouldn't connect to the Internet.

She would have seriously considered making a hike for it if she didn't hate snow, hate forests, if the road hadn't collapsed, and if she actually knew where they were. There was nothing to do to pass the time other than screw the drummer from that crappy rock band, except that now he'd run off to be a hero even that seemed out of the question.

Frustrated and bored, she went upstairs. She found nothing much to look at except a bunch of old rooms with dirty, dusty furnishings, so she headed down the west wing towards the gymnasium, wondering if she could at least find a TV that was working or even a box of DVDs. It was that or slit her wrists, she figured. There was only so much boredom any human could take.

In one room, which contained lines of wooden benches, she found a TV, but the only signal was a worthless fuzz and there were no DVDs anywhere. She banged her hands on the screen and screamed as loud as she could, but it made no difference.

There were two other rooms on the west wing before the gymnasium. As Kaede came out of the TV room, she saw the door to the next room standing a little ajar. A strange knocking sound was coming from inside.

She had grown up in Saitama, and while there wasn't a lot of crime there or elsewhere in Japan, there was enough that she felt cautious enough to consider running away. However, she felt so close to dropping dead from boredom that she couldn't resist.

She nudged her foot against the door, pushing it backwards until she could see inside.

The room was some kind of chapel, with an arched stained glass window set into the back wall; in front of it a tall wooden pulpit and a stone altar. Several rows of pews faced it.

She would probably have shrugged and gone back out if it wasn't for the single candle burning on top of the pulpit. The candlestick had slipped and fallen to lie resting on top of a thick book that could have been a bible. As the wax melted down the fire crept closer and closer to the brittle paper of the old book.

Kaede didn't stop to think. She marched up between the two rows of pews and plucked the candle up in her hands, blowing the flame out with one sharp breath. With a satisfied nod she put it back on the pulpit and turned around.

A grainy brown filled her vision and she screamed as a sack dropped over her face and pulled tight. She coughed as dust got into her mouth and the smell of wicker filled her nose.

'Get off me!' she screamed, but her protests were severed as a punch slammed into her stomach, bending her double, cutting off her breath. Winded, she gasped for air, but strong arms wrapped around her shoulders, pulling her hands behind her back and looping rope over her wrists. She struggled to get free, but she found hard wood pressed into her face as her attacker shoved her down against one of the pews.

'If you're going to rape me, use a condom,' she gasped, but her attacker just chuckled.

'Don't get excited. I have standards, you know,' said a voice she didn't recognise. 'Now shut up and don't make this any more difficult than it has to be.'

More ropes were tied around her ankles, then she was pulled back up and dragged across the room. She felt the ropes on her wrists tugging, and then her assailant stepped away, his musky sweat smell no longer in her face.

'Take a look around,' her attacker said.

'I can't see anything,' she gasped. 'Are you him? Are you that bird thing?'

'I'm me.'

He ripped the sacking off her head and she gasped as cool air filled her lungs. Condensation from the oppressive heat of the bag dribbled down her face.

She was lying on her side on the front pew, her face pressed to a wooden seat that smelled of old oil and slightly newer sweat. Her attacker was somewhere behind her, out of sight. With her hands bound behind her back she was unable to lift her head, but part of her was afraid to look anyway, so she just stared straight ahead at the altar in front of her.

'They are coming,' he said.

'Who?'

'Those who will end us all.'

'Um, okay. Any more details you can give me?'

'They will come from the forests, and they will kill every last one of us ... unless an offering of peace is made.'

Scared though she was, half of her felt like this might be some stupid prank. It definitely wasn't Ogiwara or Mishima, and the voice didn't belong to any of the other people she had seen. Maybe there were other students here that they hadn't noticed, and a group of them had decided to have a little fun with her.

'Look, if you're after a virgin, you're about three years too late.'

'The frequency with which you have spread your legs is of no importance.'

'Why me? Why not one of those big band guys or one of the boys?'

'A question of logistics.'

'Meaning you're a fucking weed and you couldn't capture any of them?'

'Logistics,' her attacker said again.

'Wimp.'

A hard hand closed over her shoulder, twisting her onto her back. She looked up into a pale face with thin, bloodless lips and over-large eyes, framed with two curtains of jet black hair.

'You!'

'You say that as if you know me,' Bee said. 'Sharing a bed with my hypersexual bandmate does not bring our relationship any closer than captor-captive.'

'Thank God for that. So what are you going to do with me, you weird freak?'

'I have observed, and I have determined that you are the best candidate among all of us that are left. I will therefore use you to save the rest of us.'

'Go fuck yourself!'

She tried to kick out at him, but her ankles were too tightly bound together, and she succeeded only in slipping off the bench and landing hard on the thinly carpeted floor.

'Had I possessed such urges I would have had plenty of opportunity to do just that while on the road,' he said with a thin smile. 'Life in a band can become a little … claustrophobic. Thankfully, my more illustrious bandmates spent enough time sowing the seeds of our success to leave me time to prepare for every possible situation, including such dire ones as this.'

'You're crazy.'

Bee rolled his huge eyes. 'Oh, come up with another cliché, please.'

'You're insane!'

Bee threw his head back and gave a tittering, birdlike laugh. 'Oh no, my dear. This entire situation is insane. I'm the one sane cog around which the wheel is turning.'

Kaede glared at him, a thousand insults on her tongue, but nothing would do any good. All she could hope for was a chance to slip her bonds and escape before he did something really crazy.

'I'LL STRING that motherfucker up when I find him,' Dai said, as Jun and Ken followed in his wake, their arms laden with rope they had found in a maintenance building near the south exit of the complex, behind one of the dormitories. Akane followed at the rear, carrying a bag of crampons Dai said they would need to get down into the forest. As they walked, Jun glanced up at the sky, grimacing at the clouds rolling in from the west. It looked like the forecast was right—more snow was on the way. Already the temperatures were dropping, and even if O-Remo was still alive down in the snow, he wouldn't be for much longer once the sun went down.

Of Forbes or the young man from the pub they had seen no sign. Dai was practically spitting fire, while the rest of them had settled into a dumb numbness at the severity of their situation. Knowing that there was something down there in the woods didn't make things any easier to deal with, but that the owner of the complex appeared not to care less about the fate of one of his guests lent everything a rather absurd air. Jun felt more and more like he'd stepped through a television screen on to the set of a Korean drama.

'That bastard,' Dai said. 'I'll cut his throat with a guitar string. In fact, I'll use one of Bee's bass strings. It'll take a lot longer.'

'Where the hell is Bee?' Ken said.

Dai just shrugged. 'Dead under a foot of snow for all we know.'

Jun looked back at Akane as he trailed after the others. She gave him a small smile. He wondered if she was still thinking about what they'd talked about, that it was better to stay here than go back. Trading a futureless but safe life for Akane's smile and a bit of danger … it wasn't a tough decision.

'Okay, we can secure the rope to one of these support posts,' Dai said, as they reached the lookout. 'Two of us go down for him, two of us stay up here and keep a lookout and an eye on the ropes. Who's coming down with me?'

Jun raised a hand without hesitation, then stared at it as if it had a mind of its own. Akane gave a little gasp, but Jun shook his head. 'I want to help, really.'

Ken looked pained, like he wanted to go down but didn't want to at the same time. Dai had clearly decided he was expedition leader, while Akane, by default of being a girl, had been nominated to stand watch via unspoken agreement.

'We don't have time to debate it,' Dai said. 'Get your crampons and your gloves on, kid.'

Ken held up a small ice axe and a thing that looked like a thick red marker pen. 'Take these. Bears have skulls as strong as iron so the axe probably won't be much use unless you can go for its neck, but the flare will scare it off.'

Jun gulped. The bellowing roar they had heard had sounded like the kind of bear that would face down a tank. Still, any weapons were better than nothing.

'You ready, kid?'

Jun clipped the end of his rope to the brace he had belted around himself and flexed a foot in the little metal crampon he had tied around his snow boots. He nodded. 'Ready.'

'Okay, let's go. Ken, be ready to haul on the rope if necessary.'

With the ropes tied around one of the lookout's support pillars, Dai began feeding it out through his hands as he climbed down through the disturbed snow. As Jun started to follow him, he understood why Dai had insisted on the crampons. He had expected soft, slushy snow, but the lack of sunlight and the deepening cold had made the surface crusty and hard like ice. It was easy to grip with the metal spikes underneath their boots, but without them they could slip down the slope at any time.

The lookout, with Ken and Akane standing beside it, became smaller and smaller as they descended, feeding the rope out as they went. Jun didn't like to look down any more than he had to, so he kept his eyes on Akane as much as possible. Every few steps she would lift a hand and give a brief wave.

Beside him, Dai was working the rope like an experienced climber; step, feed, check brace, step, feed, over and over again, while Jun jerked and tugged on the rope, his feet slipping and stumbling beneath him. 'You've done this before, I take it?' he said, alarmed at how his voice echoed out across the still valley.

'Grew up in Aomori prefecture,' Dai said with a smile. 'They get a lot of snow up there. The ski runs are crap though, so we spent most of our time snowshoeing and exploring in the hills. Good fun. Sucks if someone slips and hurts themselves. Getting a helicopter out costs a fortune.'

They reached the bottom of the initial slope, coming to rest in a deep gash in the hill where the avalanche had hollowed out a bowl, continued on over a flatter ridge and then begun descending again.

'Ropes are out,' Dai said. 'We walk from here.'

The sky was barely visible through the snowy branches overhead, just a darkening grey smudge that looked laden with snow. As Jun looked up, he saw a few errant flakes drifting down.

Dai was making his way across the flatter part of the ridge, following the trail of disturbed snow. Jun hurried after him, wincing each time the snow shifted underfoot, as if at any point it might give way and bury him up to his neck.

'There he is!' Dai hissed, pointing over the ridge. 'Oh my.'

As Jun reached Dai's shoulder he looked downslope and saw O-Remo lying among the disturbed snow under the trees, his hands outstretched, his legs spread behind him. Jun's eyes widened as O-Remo lifted his head, groaned, then reached out and pulled himself forward a few inches.

'He's still alive,' Dai said.

When they reached him, it was clear that O-Remo was clinging on to life by a thread. His face was ashen and a trail of blood showed his progress up through the trees from the base of the avalanche. As Jun stared at the twisted, bloody lump that was O-Remo's lower leg, he couldn't believe the singer had made it so far on his own.

Dai climbed down to him and squatted down. He pulled a

rucksack off his back and began rifling through it as O-Remo groaned on the snow beside him. Jun shook his own shock away and went over to help, unsure what Dai was planning.

'This'll do,' Dai said, pulling a roll of tape from the bag. 'Kid, get me a couple of sticks, about the same length.'

'Sure.' Jun turned and made his way off into the trees, looking for some loose branches. The hillside rose high above him, but as he climbed past a large stump it opened out, the slope easing off and arcing around towards a glittering pool of water, partly covered with ice, just visible through the trees.

Jun paused a moment, drinking in the beauty of the silent, snow-covered forest. He took a deep breath and looked around, trying to push the growing feeling of helplessness out of his mind. Then his eyes fell on the lake through the trees and what optimism he had begun to feel was crushed by its own damning avalanche.

Something stood down by the lake, its massive head lowered. It was clearly a bear, but it was enormous, far bigger than any bear he had ever seen on TV, its coat jet black, thick and shaggy, its head swinging lethargically from side to side as if searching for a scent.

Jun started to back away. He had no idea how good its eyesight was, but its familiarity with the terrain would allow it to run him down in seconds.

The trees around him were between ten and fifteen feet apart, at a consistency with having been planted, or pruned over time by a combination of man and nature. Yet, as he watched, the huge creature shifted its movement and eased itself between two of the trees, their boughs shifting and creaking, showering the bear with snow.

No bear on earth was fifteen to twenty feet wide at the shoulder. The thing was a behemoth, as big as a truck.

It was all Jun could do not to cry out. He began to back away, his eyes not leaving the monstrous bear by the lake. Behind him he could hear Dai speaking softly to O-Remo, and even though the drummer's voice was barely louder than his own breathing, Jun could only pray that the other man would come to his senses and shut up before he caused the death of them all.

'Sticks?' Dai asked.

Jun gave a slow shake of the head. 'Get him moving or we're all dead,' he whispered. 'There's a bear down by the lake and it's massive.'

Dai dropped into a crouch. 'How far?'

'Less than half a kilometre.'

Dai gave a resigned nod. He passed Jun the flare. 'That thing comes near, you point this end at it and pull the cord. If you're lucky you'll hit it in the face and burn the motherfucker's eyes out, but even if you don't, you should scare it off. The better you hit it, the longer we'll have before it comes back again.' He squatted down again. 'Right, let's get him up.'

'What about—' Jun started, as Dai pulled a strip of tape away and stuck it over O-Remo's mouth.

'He'll be quiet,' he said. 'Now, get hold of his arms. Three, two, one … lift!'

O-Remo's face contorted with pain as they lifted him up out of the snow, Dai taking most of the weight with his large shoulders.

'Get him on to my back. He's not heavy. I can carry him back to the ropes.'

Jun glanced back at the forest but there was no sign of the bear. The shadows were starting to lengthen in the trees though, and they had perhaps only half an hour before the gloom made it impossible to tell one shape from another.

O-Remo was groaning and jerking like a bird caught on an electric fence as Jun helped Dai haul O-Remo up onto his shoulders, wrapping O-Remo's arms around Dai's neck. Dai straightened up and leaned forward, lifting O-Remo's feet off the ground.

O-Remo's face was a sheen of sweat already taking on a frosted look as the cold air froze it to his skin. Jun carried the gear as Dai trudged a few weary steps up the slope, grimacing each time his crampons broke the surface, leaving him embedded up to his knees. Each time O-Remo's bad leg touched down on the snow the singer gave a spastic jerk, but there was nothing either Dai or Jun could do to ease his pain. Jun stared at the trail of blood on the snow and wondered if they wouldn't be better off leaving him to his fate.

'Kid, see how far the rope will reach,' Dai gasped, his forward motion slowing to a crawl as the slope began to steepen. 'I can't carry him much longer. We'll have to tie him, climb up ourselves and then haul him up.'

'What about the bear?'

Dai gave him a sour look. 'Please stop talking about it. Things are bad enough already.'

With one fearful glance back into the shadows lengthening beneath the trees, Jun moved on ahead, digging his way back to where the ropes had run out of length. Further up the hillside, he could just about make out Ken and Akane in the shadows around the lookout. *Please don't shout out,* he begged silently. Dai had warned them about keeping their voices down so as not to risk triggering any further avalanches, but seeing O-Remo alive might excite them.

Dai groaned as he reached the ends of the ropes and set O-Remo down in the snow. The singer's eyes bulged, a low moan coming from behind the tape, which he had partially chewed through.

'Quiet,' Dai hissed, without any hint of sympathy. 'Tie his hands,' he said to Jun. Make it tight, properly constricting tight. He's not got much blood left to lose, but he could lose his life if he slips out of the knots.'

Jun nodded. He hooked the end of a rope around O-Remo's left wrist, pulling it tight. Then he repeated the process with the other rope. The singer's skin felt hard to the touch, almost as if he was dead already. Only when O-Remo's fingers suddenly closed over Jun's hand, making him jerk back, did he realise the singer was still clinging on.

'Karrrriiiiinnnn...' O-Remo muttered through the hole in the tape.

'Shut up,' Dai said. 'Come on, kid, let's get up there.'

Discarding all of the gear they no longer needed, Dai and Jun left O-Remo behind and began hauling themselves back up the steep slope towards the lookout. As they came within a few metres, two of the shadows eased into clarity and Jun saw Ken and Akane standing there, knee deep in the snow around the support pillars.

'We've got him,' Dai gasped. 'He's tied to the ropes. Get pulling, it's his only chance.'

'There's a bear down there,' Jun added.

Akane stared at him. 'You saw the thing that made that noise?'

Jun nodded. He wanted to describe what he had seen to her, but his mouth was dry, his throat tight.

Ken, his arms fresh, was doing most of the pulling. Akane was tugging on the other rope as Dai stood a few feet further down the slope in front of her. Jun took a place at Ken's shoulder, taking the weight off the rope as the guitarist pulled. He couldn't see O-Remo among what were deep shadows now, but there was no sign of the huge bear either.

It hadn't felt so far when they were climbing up, but as they pulled and pulled with no sign of O-Remo, Jun began to wonder if the singer hadn't slipped off the ropes after all, and all they were pulling up was an accumulation of ice and snow.

'There!' Ken shouted, lifting one hand to point as a shape appeared out of the gloom about twenty metres down the slope. 'Hang on, O-Remo!'

'Quiet!' Dai hissed, just as the rope jerked in Jun's hands. He hauled at it but it was immovable, as if it had caught on a rock.

'It's hooked over a low branch,' Dai said. 'Fuck it. We'll have to go down and get him. I'll go. Jun, cover me with that flare in case that creature shows up.'

Jun nodded. He felt Akane give his arm a reassuring squeeze as he stepped forward. Dai was already several steps ahead of him, moving towards O-Remo, who was lying in the snow a short distance beyond where the rope had got snagged on a broken tree branch.

Dai reached the tree and began to untangle the rope from the branch, then the snow lifted up in front of him, a huge drift rising out of the earth that showered him with crystalline shards of ice as he looked up into the huge, opening maw of something from a nightmare. Akane screamed. Dai was gone with one swipe of the creature's huge, chest-sized paw, barrelling away downslope as chunks of bone and flesh left a gory plume on the snow. The creature, twenty feet tall, turned away and dropped out of sight after him, knocking the rope loose from the branch with one massive thigh.

Ken was screaming as he hauled O-Remo up to the base of the lookout, the singer's inert body dragged through the bloody leftovers of his friend. Jun's hands were shaking so much he dropped the flare on the ground, bent down and picked it up, dropped it again.

The third time he picked it up, he glanced back to see Akane staring down into the forest as Ken hauled O-Remo up on to the path.

'It was waiting for us,' she said, her voice barely more than a whisper. 'It was there all the time, Jun.'

He couldn't answer her. There would be time later to consider the implications of what had happened if they survived. 'Move,' he said, pushing her away.

Ken was dragging O-Remo up the path towards the Grand Mansion. Even though the singer was slightly built, Ken wasn't half the size of Dai and each step brought a gasp of near exhaustion. Jun stuffed the useless flare into his pocket and hurried after him, pushing his anger towards O-Remo out of his mind. Dai was dead because of the stupid drug addict singer and his crazy actions. It didn't matter that O-Remo was the singer in his favorite band. Dai was his favorite drummer, and more—he had begun to like Dai as a person. And that person was now a meal for some freakishly large bear.

Despite his anger, he couldn't leave someone to die. He grabbed one of O-Remo's arms and together with Ken they half carried, half dragged the singer until the Grand Mansion was in sight. Akane followed behind them, keeping a watch out for the bear.

'Hurry,' Ken gasped, lifting O-Remo up and over the fence at the back of the staff quarters. 'Akane, find someone who knows medical care. Quickly now.'

As the girl ran off, Ken and Jun dragged O-Remo towards the nearest door. Jun's ears were playing tricks on him, and every rustle of the wind sounded like the scraping of claws or the growl of a huge, terrifying beast.

He expected the door to be locked, but the latch opened easily when he pressed it, and a moment later he and Ken were lifting O-Remo up onto a bare wooden table in the centre of a silent, deserted mock-British pub, with dark Guinness and Bass signs over the bar, a huge, widescreen TV against one wall, and a stuffed stag's head protruding from a shield on the wall above a cold fireplace at the end of an eating area.

O-Remo seemed to have passed out. He was moaning, but even when Ken pulled the tape off his mouth he didn't cry out, he just continued that low, barely audible moan with his eyes squeezed tightly shut.

Across the tabletop Ken's eyes met Jun's.

'What just happened out there?' Ken said quietly, and Jun knew from the other man's eyes that he wasn't talking to Jun but to himself. And Jun was thankful, because he didn't have an answer.

29

AS DARKNESS FALLS

AKANE'S MIND was a whirlwind of emotions as she pushed through the door into the Grand Mansion, searching for someone—anyone —who might help them. Mika, sitting at the reception desk, looked up and screamed as Akane ran over, her hands cupping her face as she saw the disheveled, bloody schoolgirl.

Akane's words came in a series of breathless gasps. 'Hurt ... a creature in the woods ... killed Dai ... need help.'

Mika immediately began to cry. 'I don't know what to do!'

Akane aimed a slap at her face, hoping to snap her out of it, but the girl jerked away and Akane's fingers only brushed her cheek. Instead she grabbed Mika's arm and pulled her forward.

'Look, you didn't see what I just saw. I saw a bear the size of a small truck rip a man's body open. We have another man who's going to die unless we get him some medical care. Help me. Please.'

Staring at her openmouthed, Mika nodded. She reached down and pulled up a metal box from under the desk. 'This is our medical kit. This is all we have onsite.'

The box was the size of a microwave oven. Akane's vain hope that there might be a doctor at British Heights evaporated. Whatever O-Remo needed, they would have to do it themselves.

Without a word, she grabbed the box and headed for the door. As she reached it, she paused, suddenly terrified that the creature they had seen would have followed them into the complex. It had been lying in wait. It had shown a level of intelligence that a door couldn't protect against, but indoors was safer than out. Instead, she hurried down the corridor and went through the door onto the covered walkway leading along the east wing. At least here she felt less exposed, but when she reached the end she paused, squatting down and peering around the corner as if expecting sniper fire. The gap between the east wing and the shop and the pub was empty, so she darted across and down the steps to the pub door. The latch didn't move, so she hollered, 'Let me in!', and Jun's face appeared in a small window at head height. A moment later the door opened and she slipped inside.

'This is all they had,' she said, handing him the box after he had pulled a bolt back across the door. 'How is he?'

'In a word?' Jun sighed. 'Fucked.'

'But he's still alive. Unlike … unlike…'

She couldn't finish. As a flood of tears burst out of her, she felt Jun's arms wrapping around her back. She squeezed her eyes shut, trying to get the horrifying image of the creature's claws, ripping through Dai's chest like it was made of sponge, out of her mind. Was it worse? Could it possibly be worse than what she had seen that day when she pushed open the garage door and found … and found … found…

(please leave me alone)

He had been looking up at her father, his eyes hopeless and lost, her best friend, her Jun, the boy whose name she had written in her elementary school notebooks with a large red heart encircling it, the little boy whose hand she had dreamed of holding as they walked through a beautiful field while butterflies fluttered around them and the sun warmed their faces. He had been the only one she could ever dream of being with, and then she had found him there, and his face and the pale, dead face of her father became forever entwined.

Yet, something had happened. As the snow fell around them, isolating them from the outside world, she had felt her nightmares being wiped clean. Jun, so long shunned and avoided, had changed. He was still Jun, but he was no longer that little boy. He was a young man, one with whom she could fall in love if only she could sever the ties to her dark memories. It was possible. The snow and the isolation made it possible.

And now this.

'Come on,' Jun was saying. 'We have to do what we can for O-Remo. Dwelling on what happened back there isn't going to help anyone.'

She nodded, and let him lead her inside. The overhead lights were on, but they only filled the room with a dim twilight glow that was probably supposed to be reminiscent of a British pub. O-Remo was lying on a table Ken had dragged into the middle of the room. Ken was sawing at the singer's bloody trousers with a steak knife, revealing a bloody gash just below O-Remo's knee. Akane saw an off-white colour that could have been bone in behind the ripped and lacerated flesh.

'He's a lucky bastard,' Ken said, his voice strained. 'I don't even know that it's broken. If we can stop the bleeding maybe he has a chance.'

Around O-Remo's lower thigh Ken had tied a strip of cloth. Jun opened up the first aid box while Akane went behind the bar to look for some towels to wipe away the blood.

'Bring some spirits,' Ken said, his voice rising, near hysterical. 'Whiskey or brandy will do. I remember this time Dai … we were drunk, we were messing around backstage before a gig … he cut open his arm and all we had to hand to sterilise it was a bottle of Suntory … cleaned up perfect. What a gig, that. What a … gig.'

Akane took a bottle off a shelf and went back to them. She set it and a handful of tea towels down on the table and went back for some water, finding a plastic bowl behind the bar and filling it up from a tap. When she returned, Ken was dabbing a towel on O-Remo's wounds as the singer groaned. Jun was digging through the medical kit for something that might help.

'We need antibiotics, perhaps something to help him sleep,' Ken said. 'I don't know. Dai … Dai was the one who understood this kind of stuff.'

He sniffed. Akane put a hand on his arm in a gesture she hoped was reassuring, but she felt as hopeless as he looked. How long before that thing came up here looking for them? The snowy paradise where she had begun to forget the horrors of her past seemed so far away.

'These?' Jun said, holding up a pack of pills. 'Painkiller.'

Ken took them off him, glanced at the label, then nodded. 'See if you can get a couple down his throat.'

Jun lifted O-Remo while Akane pushed two of the tablets into his mouth and then poured a little water down his throat until he swallowed them. As O-Remo gasped, his eyes briefly opening before closing again, she could only think how none of them really knew what they were doing. The receptionist, Mika, was perhaps as clueless as they were, and hadn't seemed willing to help. And of the others there was no sign. Part of her wished that the monster had got them too.

As O-Remo drifted off into an uneasy sleep, Ken did his best to clean the wound and bind it using tape, band-aids, and bandages from the medical kit. When it was secured as best as possible, they added a splint from O-Remo's knee down to his ankle, using two wooden chair legs tied with more tape and another bandage. It was rough and would likely do nothing to help, but there was little else they could do.

Darkness had fallen outside by the time O-Remo was sleeping fitfully, his head resting on Ken's bunched-up jacket, Jun's jacket over his chest and Akane's over his legs. The shock had got to all of them so no one had really noticed the falling temperatures, but as soon as they could relax for a moment Akane found herself shivering.

'There's no heating,' Jun said. He flicked up a light switch and the lights went off and on. 'We have light, but that's it.'

'Let's get that fire lit,' Ken said, pointing at the fireplace beneath the looming stag's head. 'Akane, see if you can find some matches or something behind the bar. We'll also need some paper to get it started.'

Akane went off looking for matches as Ken and Jun started to break up some of the chairs to use as wood. At first they seemed tentative about destroying British Heights property despite everything that had happened, but soon they were smashing the chairs with casual abandon until they had a large enough pile of wood. Behind the bar Akane found a box of cigarette lighters and a couple of old boxes.

In the grate, the embers were still warm from a fire the previous night. It was almost too easy to get a fire going, and soon the three of them were sitting around it, warming their hands, with O-Remo's table pulled as close as possible.

A clock on the wall above them said six o'clock. None of them had eaten since breakfast, but Akane had found a few bags of snacks behind the bar, which they passed among themselves. Ken had also helped himself to a couple of beers, although Akane felt he was showing considerable restraint.

'What do we do now?' Jun asked.

Ken shook his head. 'If you have any ideas, I'm open to suggestions.'

'Mr. Forbes said a helicopter would come,' Akane said. 'I've not seen or heard it. If only we could get a message out.'

Ken shivered despite the warmth of the fire. 'What the fuck is going on with this place? I mean, seriously? What the fuck was that thing out there?'

'There are two of them,' Jun said quietly. 'That wasn't the one I saw. That one had been waiting for us. Waiting for the right moment. What was that about?'

Akane shivered. 'Why didn't it take him?' she asked, nodding at O-Remo. 'It could have taken him anytime. Why did it take Dai?'

Ken stared into the flames. Akane watched them dancing in his eyes, then turned towards Jun, who was staring down at his hands.

'It thought he was already dead,' Jun said. 'It wasn't killing because it was hungry. It was killing because it was a killer.'

Akane reached out to take his hand, but her fingers closed over something plastic. She looked down and saw Jun holding the unused flare canister in his hands, turning it over and over.

'It wasn't your fault,' she said. 'It wouldn't have made any difference if you used that thing or not. It would have probably just made it mad.'

He turned to face her. 'I'm scared,' he said.

Behind them, O-Remo moaned. Ken got up and went over to the singer, dabbed a wet towel on his forehead and administered some more of the painkillers. 'He's lost so much blood,' he said. 'He probably needs a transfusion, but unless we can get him out of here he might not last the night.'

'What can we do?' Akane asked.

Ken went over to the window, wiped away the condensation, and peered out. 'It's snowing again. Not as hard as yesterday, but they'll be another foot of it by tomorrow morning. With one or more of those things out there, I'm really not keen to try moving. I'm pretty sure that door wouldn't keep it out, but I'm not sure there's anywhere safer.'

'Maybe the Grand Mansion,' Jun said. 'The doors are thicker, but we'd have to move O-Remo.'

Ken shook his head. 'Who knows what damage we might cause? Plus, if the heating's off in here, the heating might be off in there, too. I vote we stay put. We have heat here and we're pretty secure. We've got water and a bit of food.'

Akane stared at O-Remo for a long time. Ken was right, of course. He might die in the night, but at least he was stable, and with the jackets and the fire, he was warm. If they moved him it might do more harm than good.

'I vote we stay,' she said.

Jun nodded. 'Okay, it's agreed. 'What about the others? Perhaps one of us should go and look for them.'

'You really want to go out there?'

'No, but—'

Ken sighed. 'It's time for another beer. Why don't you two join me? Takes the edge off things, you know.'

Akane started to protest that she was underage, then stopped. It might help them sleep. 'I'll have whatever's going,' she said with a weary smile.

MIKA's second shift of the day finished at nine p.m., but for the last hour she had hardly been in a state to work. She had got the fire in the reception area going, but in such an open space it offered scant heat unless she sat close enough to choke on the smoke. Instead, she sat in the office behind the reception area with a blanket over her knees to ward off the cold, while the news played on the TV in front of her.

Chained to her desk by a sense of duty, Mika had put out of her mind the high school girl who had come running for the first aid kit, preferring to stay near the phones in case the lines opened up or the Wi-Fi came back on. Two days ago she had been smartly dressed and welcoming new guests with a cheerful smile. Now she was alone in a freezing building, her hair was a mess, and a couple of hours ago a girl had come running in from the snow, covered in someone else's blood.

And now the news was talking about the mangled, dismembered bodies of high school students being found at the foot of the landslide, and the smashed remains of an all-terrain vehicle.

She switched off the TV and looked up at the clock. Nine fifteen. She was starving, cold, and tired. She had seen no one other than the girl in several hours, and she was terrified that everyone had gone and left her. Alone in the ornate halls of British Heights, the antiquated artifacts brought from England gave her the creeps, as if she were the sole living person in a closed-down museum. What she wanted more than anything right now was her bed.

She got up and went over to the main doors, looking out at the snow falling on the courtyard. The floodlights were on, illuminating the bus and the two vans nearly buried in snow where they were parked up in the corner. In the morning some of the guests had cleared a path down the centre, and it was now filling in with snow. It led straight down the middle with a branch curving off towards the pub, the shop, and the staff quarters just beyond.

She shivered. The covered walkway along the east wing would be freer of snow, but it was darker, more foreboding. Cutting straight across the courtyard was the quickest route, and while the light from the floodlights wasn't great, it was enough to guide her without any need to go near any creepy shadows until she was almost at the staff quarters. Plus, she could see lights on in the pub windows, so perhaps the others were in there. She gave a weak smile. A bit of company would be almost as welcome as her bed.

Finally giving up on the protocol drummed in by her training sessions, she took one of the jackets that could be lent to guests off a hook in a little cupboard beside the main door and pulled it over her head. It was a poncho-type made of thick material, with a hood. Feeling like an extra from a *Harry Potter* movie, she opened the door and stepped out into the snow.

She skipped down the steps and headed out across the courtyard, happy for the open space and the lights to chase away the shadows.

She was almost halfway across when she remembered that earlier there had only been one van, not two.

―――――

JUN JERKED his head around at the sound of someone rattling the latch. Akane was sleeping beside him, her head propped up on a pile of chair cushions, a couple of tablecloths draped over her. Ken, several beers deep, had taken a break from telling Jun tales from the band's early days to check on O-Remo. The singer didn't look any better, but nor did he look any worse.

'Who's that?' Ken whispered.

Jun climbed stiffly to his feet. 'I'll check.'

The door rattled again. 'Let me in!' came a woman's voice.

Away from the fire, the room was much colder. Jun shivered as he pulled back the bolt and opened the door just wide enough for the stranger to slip inside. She was wearing a ski jacket and a woolly hat, so until she pulled it off Jun didn't recognise her. As she shook out her hair and turned towards him, he started at the strikingly beautiful face, the large oval eyes that reminded him somewhat uneasily of Akane.

'Karin,' Ken muttered, putting down the cloth he had just used to mop O-Remo's brow. 'What the fuck are you doing here?'

'I want to see him.'

Ken took one step towards her and slapped her across the face, hard enough to make her stagger. Jun caught her before she fell.

'You fucking whore! Dai is dead because of you!'

She looked shocked for a moment, before recovering her composure. 'He dragged me out there! It wasn't my fault!'

'The fuck it wasn't.'

Ken lifted his hand to strike her again, but Jun stepped between them. 'Enough,' he said, staring Ken down. 'This isn't helping anything.'

Ken glowered for a moment before turning away. Out of the corner of his eye, Jun noticed Akane had sat up and was watching them.

'I'm sorry,' Karin whispered again.

'We should throw you out there for whatever it was that killed Dai,' Ken muttered, but he made no more move towards her. 'What the fuck are you doing up here anyway?'

'Rutherford … he's my … fiancé.'

Ken stared at her, then shook his head. 'Everything about you disgusts me,' he said. 'You could have helped him once, but you were too busy whoring yourself out to the highest contractor to care.'

'No one could have helped him but himself. He didn't want my help.'

'You didn't have to leave him like that.'

Jun's ears were burning. He couldn't stop himself from asking, as Akane came over to stand beside him: 'Left him like what?'

'At the altar,' Karin said quietly. 'He had a good heart. I ... didn't. I couldn't do it to him.'

'You broke his heart,' Ken said.

Karin laid a hand on O-Remo's forehead, stroking it gently. 'I broke mine too.'

O-REMO WAS SLEEPING AGAIN. In front of the fire, Jun lay on his side with Akane pressed against him. Her eyes were closed, but he was sure she was listening. Ken was sitting with his back against an overturned table, a bottle of beer in his hand. Karin sat beside him, almost close enough to touch. Resigned to the hopelessness of their situation, Ken's anger had quickly died away. Along with the others, he now sat in near silence as Karin recounted tales of her relationship with O-Remo, and her life before and after.

'I don't expect people to understand,' she said, her voice barely audible over the crackling of the fire. 'I don't expect people to care, but being in the public eye is what I am. And when I lost everything, all I could think of was to find a way back. That's how I ended up here, on the arm of a billionaire.'

Ken rolled his eyes as if it was an excuse he'd heard a thousand times before. Akane glanced up at Jun, who said nothing, and just kept his eyes on the fire.

'Where's Rutherford now?' Akane asked.

'Sleeping. He was driving me crazy so I dropped some pills in his coffee.'

'Taking advantage of people again?'

'I don't like him,' she said. 'I just want his money. As soon as I've been married long enough to claim enough to finance a new album, I'll divorce him.'

Ken shook his head, his nose wrinkled in disgust. 'You're like a snake, Karin,' he said. 'Dai and me knew it when you first started sniffing around. We tried to tell him, but he just wouldn't listen.'

'Come on, Ken, cast the first stone if you're without sin, and all that. Like the rest of you weren't taking advantage of people wherever you could? I saw Dai with that girl earlier. Just showing her around the area, was he? Don't give me your high and mighty crap. Rutherford gets plenty of what *he* wants, believe me.'

'We were only ever having a good time,' Ken said. 'What you're doing is calculated.'

Karin shook her head. 'You think I'm going to steal his livelihood or something? This place is just a toy for Rutherford. Barely more than a blip where his interests are concerned. He has factories overseas that are making him the real money.'

'Well, lucky for you, isn't it?'

Akane raised a hand. 'Do you think he knows about the things in the woods? That thing that killed Dai wasn't natural. It was like it had been bred like that or something.'

Karin shrugged. 'I doubt it,' she said. 'There's only that legend, about the bird guy. That's just a story, too.'

Ken shook his head. 'O-Remo didn't seem to think so, and Dai says he saw something too. And whatever it was, it stole my guitar.'

Karin shrugged. 'Probably just some crazy local. People are wacko out here in the countryside. I've been up here a few months and you get all sorts of people wandering in. It's just another story to bring in the tourists.'

Jun smiled. 'You know what sucks most?' he said. 'I've been up at this bastard place for two days now and I'm yet to sleep in a proper bed. When I signed up I didn't think we'd be camping every night.'

Akane shifted against him. She pulled his arm down across her chest and nestled in against him. 'It could be worse,' she said. 'It could always be worse.'

Ken glanced over his shoulder towards the windows, where snow was pattering silently against the frames. 'It could,' he said.

PROFESSOR KUROU HAD OPENED a bottle of one of Forbes's most precious wines, a 2004 Neblac Creek Vintage, to toast the bears' first success. The cameras hidden in the trees had caught everything, and he had played back the whole episode of the rescue numerous times from several angles. It had caused him a little concern that the bears hadn't shown any interest in the injured man, but they were designed to catch mobile prey, as the contract specified. Once a target had been disabled it could be discarded, and the injured man had clearly been perceived as already dealt with.

The other bears had now been alerted to the area, and two had already followed the trail up to British Heights. There was little that Kurou could do now, except stay safe and keep watch. Briefly engaging the Internet, he had learned that a rescue helicopter had been scheduled for tomorrow morning, providing the snow cleared enough to make a landing safe. Perhaps it would arrive to find no one left alive, who could tell? The contractor would be delighted to learn of the success of the prototypes, although capturing them again would prove a little difficult.

Kurou could deal with such problems at a later date, though. For now, he put his feet up on his desk, lifted a crystal glass full of wine so crimson it could have been blood, and gave a little salute.

'To you, my friends,' he said, taking a sip and scowling at the taste.

The phone rang, startling him. For a moment he wondered if the systems had come back on, then realised it was the satellite phone, the only way that British Heights could still be contacted. It was his private line. Even Forbes didn't know the number.

The Professor kicked out one misshapen foot and switched on the hands-free speaker. 'Mr. Forbes, are you there?' came a man's voice in heavily-accented English.

Kurou smiled. 'Mr. Park, how nice to hear from you,' he said, in a perfect representation of an English gentleman's voice. 'This is Mr. Forbes. How may I assist you this evening?'

PART THREE
HUNTED

30

DISCOVERIES AND PLANS

OGIWARA GROANED AND ROLLED OVER. Something heavy rolled off him and smashed on the floor. As the scent of whiskey filled his nose he leaned forward and vomited all over the broken bottle, before rolling backwards and squeezing his eyes shut.

He waited for the nausea to pass, but had no such luck; as he tried to concentrate on breathing slowly he coughed, starting it off again, vomiting what was left in his stomach up over the duvet pulled up over his chest. Shoving it away, he sat up, closed his eyes against the dizziness, then opened them again on to the wreckage of the King's Bedroom.

He remembered now. Bored and unable to find the others, they had gone back to the snooker room—which they had found unlocked—grabbed as much booze as they could carry and gone on a whiskey-fueled mission of destruction. Mirrors were smashed, tables and chairs overturned, antique bookcases pulled over and their contents kicked around the room. Antique vases had become baseballs as Ogiwara used a whiskey bottle as a bat.

He needed water, so he stumbled out of the bed and staggered into the bathroom. He ran the tap and splashed freezing water over his face. He felt like he'd descended the seven levels of Hell with a red-hot firebrand jammed up his butt.

'You sleep all right?'

Ogiwara spun at the sound of the voice, gasping in terror at the bear-human creature peering at him from the bathtub. He scrabbled for something to throw, then he realised it was Mishima, sitting in the tub with a bearskin rug draped over him, the long-dead animal's glassy eyes at his shoulder.

'What are you doing?'

'You took the bed, remember? I didn't want to sleep in the other room, I was too scared.'

Ogiwara grabbed an ornate hand mirror that had somehow escaped the previous night's destruction and flung it at Mishima, who ducked back behind the bearskin rug just in time. The mirror thudded into the tough hide and bounced away without breaking.

'Get up, you idiot. I'm hungry.'

They made their way out into the corridor, both rubbing their heads against thumping hangovers. Ogiwara felt like someone had punched him in the stomach, and his throat was sore and parched.

'Do you think we'll get in trouble?' Mishima asked.

'For what?'

'For, you know, causing all that damage?'

'From who? They fucking deserved it. Making all our friends sick, locking us in the snooker room, leaving us up here—'

'I thought Matsumoto locked us in the snooker room?'

'He did.'

'But you said—'

'Just shut up about what I said. I feel like shit. I don't know what I said.'

Ogiwara went out into the corridor with Mishima trailing behind him. From the stains down the front of his shirt, it was clear Mishima had been sick at some point too. Whether he remembered was another matter.

Ogiwara peered out of the window at a grey dawn. Snow was falling again, not as heavily as it had the first night but still enough to leave no hint of sun. The courtyard, which had been partially cleared the night before, was once more a sheet of white.

'I'm fucking hungry,' Ogiwara said. 'Let's find something to eat.'

They went down the main stairs to the reception, but it was deserted. The embers of a fire still smoked in the grate. As his hangover began to loosen its grip on him, he realised for the first time just how cold it was. He could understand the heating systems being off in the snooker room, but here in the main building? He glanced back at Mishima descending the stairs behind him, his arms wrapped tightly around himself.

'What happened to the heating? I'm freezing my tits off.'

'It's like everyone's gone.'

Ogiwara clenched a fist. 'Honestly, if they've all bunked off down this stupid mountain and left us here I'll burn this place down.'

Mishima laughed. 'Pretty difficult unless it stops snowing.'

'Just shut up.'

Ogiwara went down the corridor to the dining room. Like the reception, it was empty, but the door was unlocked so he went inside and headed straight for the kitchens. Mishima protested as Ogiwara began rooting through cupboards, but he quickly shut up when bowls of leftover food found their way into his hands.

They sat together at the end of one of the trestle tables and ate a breakfast of cold roast beef, rice balls, and cold corn soup.

'Best food I've had since my mama's tit,' Ogiwara said.

They went back to the reception area. Ogiwara tried the phones but the lines were dead, and the computer was password-protected so he couldn't check the Internet. In the office behind the desk they found a TV, but Ogiwara couldn't be bothered to wait for the news to come on so he curled up on a sofa and began watching a morning drama on NHK. He was just starting to get into the story when Mishima, who had wandered off down the corridor in a sleepy daze, came hurrying in.

There are lights on in the pub,' he said. 'I think someone's in there.'

Ogiwara jumped up. 'Did you see anyone?'

'No, but why else would there be lights on? This place is deserted. Perhaps they're hiding out in there. Perhaps they know something we don't.'

Ogiwara scowled. 'Let's go,' he said. 'Damn, I'm going to kick up a shit storm if that idiot Matsumoto is in there. I'm going to batter him like an old golf ball.'

Mishima sniggered. Ogiwara took the lead, taking a pair of the centre's snow boots and a jacket from the storage room next to the door.

Outside, the snow was beginning to ease as the sun pushed its way through the clouds. There had been about a foot of fresh snowfall, but because the others had dug much of the courtyard clear the previous day there was an obvious path across the open space to the pub.

'You go first,' Ogiwara said, pushing Mishima towards the steps. 'I don't want to get my feet wet.'

Mishima looked about to protest, but Ogiwara gave him a hard glare, so the smaller boy just shrugged and started down the steps. Ogiwara followed behind, stepping in the holes where Mishima had stepped first.

They were just passing the snow-covered bus and the band's knackered old van, when Mishima cried out and pitched forward into the snow, landing on his face. He flapped like a drowning fish for a few seconds before managing to roll over and sit up.

'What happened?'

Mishima shook snow out of his hair. 'I tripped over a rock or something.'

'Where?'

Mishima pointed. 'Just there.'

Ogiwara stuck out a foot and nudged something hard under the snow. A funny feeling came over him, a compulsion to see what was under the snow.

This was the car park. There shouldn't be any rocks out here.

Perhaps that stupid band unloaded some of their gear, then just left it here, he thought, reaching a hand into the snow, feeling for what was there. It was something hard, something round, about the size of a football.

Mishima started screaming first, probably because Ogiwara had picked up the woman's head from behind, and now her dead eyes were looking down at where Mishima still sat in the snow. Ogiwara, feeling the thick lumps of frozen hair in his hands, dropped it again. It landed in the snow, shifted in a disturbed patch of slush, and turned upwards to face them. The frozen, dead eyes of Mika the receptionist stared up at him.

'Oh, fuck!'

Ogiwara stumbled backwards and fell over the rest of her, or at least pieces, buried and frozen in the snow. Mishima was still screaming as Ogiwara pushed himself up and began running for the pub.

'What happened to her? What happened?' Mishima screamed behind him as Ogiwara slammed against the pub door and found it locked.

'Let me in, you bastards!' he shouted, thumping and kicking the wooden door.

'All right, all right,' came a muffled voice from inside. 'Get away from the door and I'll open it.'

Barely able to hear over the thundering roar of his heart, Ogiwara stepped back, pushing Mishima, who was still screaming, back with him. A click sounded from inside and then the door swung inwards. Matsumoto's face appeared.

'There's a dead girl out here!' Mishima shouted, and then they were pushing through the door to the inside.

OGIWARA AND MISHIMA sat near the fire, the flames flickering in the grate, shivering even though it wasn't that cold. Akane, Jun, and Ken sat at one of the bench tables, while Karin dabbed at O-Remo's brow with a cloth. Ogiwara and Mishima hadn't taken the story about the bears too well, but after discovering the body of Mika the receptionist, they were at least easy to convince.

'So what do we do now?' Karin asked, not looking up from O-Remo's pale, sleeping face.

'What happened to the helicopter your boyfriend promised?' Ken said. 'Was that yet another lie?'

Karin, Jun noted, refused to take the bait for another argument. Instead she just said, 'There's no way to communicate with anyone. We just have to wait and see.'

'We have to get organised,' Jun said. 'We have to act like no one's coming for us, because, for all we know, they might not be. We have to get ourselves sorted out with food and weapons, water, and in some kind of secure location in case one of those things get hungry. Then we have to plot a way to get off this mountain.'

Ken smiled. 'Do you play a lot of computer games, Jun?'

'He doesn't have any friends,' Ogiwara quipped. 'He plays games when his dick's too sore to toss himself off.' Mishima snorted with laughter, but the others just sighed or rolled their eyes.

Jun gave Ogiwara a steely glare, then looked back at Ken. 'It's just common sense stuff,' he said. 'I don't think we can stay here. That door won't stop a twenty foot bear if it really wants to get in.'

'Where then?' Ken said. 'The Grand Mansion? It's pretty solid. We could hide out on the second floor perhaps. We'd also have easy access from there to the kitchens. And there's bedding.'

Ogiwara and Mishima exchanged a glance. 'You'll need to tidy up a bit,' Ogiwara said.

Jun ignored him. He shook his head. 'No, I don't think so. The walls are good, but the doors are too wide. And the corridors. If one of those things broke in it would be unstoppable.'

'There's that building by the main entrance,' Akane said. 'The Fort, it was called. It had walls like a castle and huge doors.'

'It was all fake,' Ogiwara said. 'That isn't going to help us, is it? This whole fucking place is a damn toon town.'

Karin shook her head. 'No, Jun's right. Those walls are thick and those doors are strong. It would take a lot to break through them. Rutherford wanted everything to be as authentic as possible when he built this place. He borrowed British castle designs out of the British Museum and used them to recreate the Fort as accurately as possible.'

'He just borrowed them?' Akane said.

Karin shrugged. 'For a hefty donation, I imagine.'

Ken snorted. 'Amazing the things you can learn while lying on your back,' he said.

Karin glared at him. 'Yeah. You should try it sometime. You might be of more use.'

Before Ken could reply, Ogiwara's eyes lit up. 'I thought I recognised you! You're Karin Kobayashi, aren't you? Mishima downloaded a bunch of your DVDs off the Internet. He tosses off over them all the time.'

'Do not!'

'And he has all those shit Girls Chorus CDs just so he can spank one off over the cover pictures!'

'Shut up! No, I don't!'

Jun grabbed a piece of broken chair leg from the floor at his feet and hurled it towards the fire. It scissored through the air, missing Ogiwara's face by no more than a couple of inches, before landing in the fire and sending a shower of sparks up into the air.

'You seem to have recovered pretty quickly from finding a dead girl's corpse out in the snow,' he said. 'Perhaps you should pay attention so that next time it isn't you.'

Ogiwara met Jun's stare, and Jun wondered if Ogiwara would start something with the others present. The way he felt, Jun could happily use Ogiwara's face as a punching bag for a good few minutes, but whether he'd have a chance against the captain of the school judo team was something he wouldn't know until perhaps it was too late.

'I hope you sleep with your mouth closed,' Ogiwara said. 'Otherwise someone might just take a dump down your throat.'

Jun jumped up from the chair, but Akane put a hand on his arm. 'Leave it.'

'We should have left them out there in the snow.'

'Shut up!' They all looked at Karin. 'You pathetic jerks, just can it! We're in serious trouble here and we don't have time for your playground bullshit.'

Jun met Ogiwara's gaze for a moment, then turned away. Ken was looking at Karin with a newfound level of respect.

'The food is all in the kitchens,' she said. 'We should take as much as we need with us. The Fort has guest rooms on the second floor. There will be plenty of bedding. I don't know if the heating will be on in there, but there will be enough blankets if we need to hole up for a few days.'

'So first we need to ransack the kitchens,' Ken said. 'We need to take as much as we can to the Fort in case we can't get out again.'

'What about him?' Mishima said, pointing at O-Remo. 'Is he going to die or what? How do we get him over there?'

O-Remo had survived the night, but he'd lost so much blood that he drifted in and out of consciousness almost from one minute to the next. He couldn't even sit up, let alone walk.

'We'll carry him, Ken said. 'We're not leaving him here. One of these tabletops will make a decent stretcher.'

Ogiwara rolled his eyes. 'Good luck to whoever gets that job,' he said. In that snow it'll take hours. You'll be like a sitting duck waiting for those Godzilla-bears to take potshots at you with their little furry popguns.'

Ken gave a grim smile. 'Two strong judo lads like yourselves, I'm surprised you haven't volunteered.'

Ogiwara's eyes widened. 'Don't be ridiculous.'

'If you want to be part of this plan, you play your part. Jun and I will go to the kitchens and bring what we can carry. Karin and Akane will try to find Forbes and the others and bring them to the Fort.' He winked. 'You have the easy part. You get to go straight there.'

Ogiwara punched a fist against the ground. 'Go bone yourself,' he muttered, not looking up.

'Is that a yes?'

After a hugely dramatic sigh, Ogiwara nodded. 'All right, we'll do it. But you'd better not forget it. You owe us.'

Ken smiled. 'I won't.'

31

PROFESSOR CROW MAKES ARRANGEMENTS

Karin had disappeared again. Forbes was getting so sick of the stupid whore. If it hadn't been for the way she kept him content he would seriously consider replacing her. If his business took him back to China he would dump her and take up where he left off, but in the Japan Alps women were hard to come by. Forbes had urges just like every other man, and with his money there was no excuse. It came down to logistics, was all.

The girl was the least of his problems, though. Something had to be done about the creatures that had got out, and Professor Crow was the man to deal with that. The Professor too, though, was being elusive.

Forbes descended into the control centre beneath the Grand Mansion and slammed a fist against the steel door.

'Let me in!'

No answer came from the other side. He was about to begin entering his emergency override code when he heard the sound of clacking footfalls on the steps above him. He looked up to see Professor Crow descending towards him, a steaming cup of coffee held in one deformed hand.

'Where the hell have you been?'

The Professor cackled. 'Just brewed myself a latte. Thirsty work this, sire.'

'Open this damn door!'

'At once.'

The Professor's free hand moved like a rabid spider over the keypad, too fast for Forbes to follow. The door was only to be locked when Professor Crow was off duty, but with no other way in, Forbes wondered if he hadn't given his precocious underling too much power.

As the door swung open, Forbes barged in first, planted his hands on his hips and turned in a circle as he surveyed the monitor screens. 'Where are they?' he shouted.

'Which of the players in our little game do you seek? Our hunters or our hunted?'

'Don't patronise me, you ugly bastard. The bears, where are the bears?'

The Professor smiled. 'Love a good game of hide and seek, so they do. I've lost tracking signals on two. Two of the others are circling the complex, one on either side, while the last two are still in the forest, out of harm's way for now.'

'Have you made plans for their recapture?'

The Professor smiled. 'Of course.' His beak clacked together in a gesture of glee.

'Details, damn you!'

'A recapture squad will be flying in tonight, to a private airport in Toyama prefecture. They will be moved by road to Hakuba down in the valley, from where they will advance on foot unless the road is clear. Unfortunately, the heightened media presence in the valley and the collapse of the road has made this operation rather difficult. Secrecy and discretion is key, of course, but when you're trying to move the equivalent of two military units through a heavily populated area without any suspicion being aroused, it becomes something of a logistics headache.'

Forbes sighed. Despite the possible headaches, he knew the Professor could handle it. 'It should never have come to this,' he said.

'Sometimes things happen for a reason, sire,' the Professor said. 'It has given us a chance to road test our prototypes, and so far they've more than surpassed our expectations. Mr. Park will be so pleased.'

'Has he been informed of the situation?'

Professor Crow smiled. 'He's paying for the cleanup. He's delighted that we had a chance to test his acquisition in less controlled circumstances.'

Forbes felt a bloom of anger. He balled a fist and slammed it into the Professor's ugly, grinning face with all his might. The Professor squawked like the hideous monstrosity he was and fell back against his desk.

'He should never have known about this! You stupid idiot, Crow!'

Crow peered up at him, his face twisted at an angle that made

Forbes want to kick it. The Professor looked like a hawk that had been disturbed as it ripped apart its prey.

'He was, actually, rather pleased,' the Professor said, pushing himself to his feet and wiping blood off his chin. 'I've also made arrangements to have you taken off the complex. You are too important to risk, sire. A helicopter will arrive for you within the hour. It will be unable to land due to the snow, so will hover over the courtyard, where a ladder will be lowered for you. It will take you to the same private airport in Toyama, where you will be taken out of the country. I think that will be for the best, don't you? The Chinese government will protect you in the event that this goes public and there's a media fallout. After all, you know how much they hate the Japanese, and your charity work has done so much good.'

Forbes looked up at the monitors. On one, he saw a group of people moving about inside the pub. The light was bad and the feed too grainy to make them out, but he was sure at least one of them had the slight build of a woman.

'Is she with them?' he whispered, shaking his head. 'Has she turned against me?'

Crow gave another squawk. 'It would appear that Ms Kobayashi is something of a floater, sire. Such a wonderful cunt, perhaps, but one with a devious brain attached.'

'Crow…'

'Sire, while you might feel a little aggrieved about your investment, I assure you that the quality of cunt is of a similar standard the world over. She can be easily replaced. Not that I have any experience, but one observes…'

Forbes glared at him. 'Just make sure this mess is sorted out. I want there to be nothing to link this back to my other holdings.'

The Professor nodded. 'All will be well, sire. Now, one suggests that perhaps you should return to your rooms and prepare what you need for your journey.' A beady black eye closed in a slow wink. 'But watch out for bears.'

As Forbes headed back up the stairs, leaving the Professor to do whatever it was he did to keep things running smoothly, he wondered if he could have done things differently. The Professor was a genius, but he was also a loose cannon, one now firing at a group of extremely dangerous enemies.

As Forbes disappeared up the stairs, Kurou closed the door and locked it from the inside. He took a rag from a drawer and wiped the blood off his face. It wasn't the first time Forbes had struck him, but his master's doughy fists rarely did much damage. They'd managed to split a little webbing on one side of his eye, but it was a minor wound. More hurt was Kurou's pride. Rutherford didn't seem to understand just how little control he had. Kurou would show him. It was time for the fireworks display of the century … and perhaps a little shifting of power.

32

THE HELICOPTER ARRIVES

'YOU KNOW what we have to do if one of those motherfuckers shows up, don't you?' Ogiwara said as he stumped through the snow, holding the front end of the tabletop behind his back. Mishima had the other end, and was struggling to keep up with Ogiwara's pace. On the tabletop, O-Remo had been ingloriously secured using a roll of packing tape, and then covered over with several tablecloths to keep him warm. He groaned with every jerk of the tabletop, head lulling back and forth.

'What?'

'We stand this bitch up in the snow like a giant diet pancake on a plate, and then we run like we have firecrackers up our butts.'

Mishima didn't laugh. 'Do you think they're watching us now?'

'Be quiet or I'll whip your ass.'

'There could be one nearby. Remember what Matsumoto said about how that one just came out of the ground and ripped that guy's face off?'

'Matsumoto's a clown.'

'Well, you saw that woman. Or the bits of her, at any rate.'

'But I didn't see the bear, douchebag. Being a pussy can do funny things to your mind. Probably Matsumoto and those other dickheads were scared and exaggerated. Look, I'm not saying that there's not something buttcrack dangerous out there, but it's probably just a regular bear. Like, one with mange or something. All the ticks are sending it out of its mind.'

Mishima gave a nervous laugh. 'Yeah, probably.'

'Come on, let's hurry up and get this injured prick to that fort place. Then we can relax. Perhaps we can think up a plan to get that porn star chick to let us spit roast her or something.' He scowled.

'We'll probably have to give you plastic surgery first. I wonder where I'll find a knife?'

'Can we rest a minute? This thing's heavy.'

'Don't be such a pussy. I told you at club you were slacking off with the press-ups. Believe me now, don't you?'

'I'm sorry…'

It had stopped snowing, but in places some of the drifts came up to their thighs. As they trudged through the snow, the Fort came up on their left. Two storeys high, it looked like a giant honeycomb crossed with a British castle. It was about a hundred metres long, and built in a curve that followed the angle of the road. There was a large central entrance built into the wall with a ten-foot high fortified door and a mock portcullis attached to the wall above it. On either side of the entrance, five hexagonal buttresses arced away to form a gentle semi-circle. Each had two windows, a small one on the ground floor and a larger one above. The entire building was a slate grey colour. Battlements like a robot's teeth were a finishing touch.

Bored of following the road, Ogiwara started to cut across a wide open area dotted with trees, angling directly towards the door. About halfway across what he supposed was a lawn, he stopped near a lump in the snow and set the tabletop down.

'Please almighty God tell me that's not one of those things,' Mishima spluttered, pointing at the shape under the snow.

'It's not one of those things,' Ogiwara said. 'I can see a circle of metal poking out.'

He went over and wiped the snow off the top surface to reveal an antique cannon, its barrel pointing straight at Mishima.

'Wow, that's awesome. I wonder where it came from?'

'Same place as the rest of this junk,' Ogiwara said. 'Some secondhand shop in the UK.' He tapped the barrel, but it was fixed hard, concreted into the fittings. 'A shame it doesn't work, or we could line it up with Matsumoto's head and blow it into space with the rest of the junk humanity has no use for.'

'Are you still going to get him?' Mishima asked.

'Of course I am. Just biding my … what's that?'

They both looked up at the sound of a dull *duk-duk-duk* coming from just out of sight beyond the Fort. Ogiwara cupped a hand over his brow and peered up at the murky sky just as a helicopter appeared from the south, arced to the right and then headed straight for the Grand Mansion back down the road.

'Did you see that?' Mishima shouted. 'We're saved!'

'Of course I saw it! Come on! This is our chance to get out of this forsaken hellhole!'

Ogiwara began running as quickly as he could back through the snow towards the Grand Mansion.

'What about this guy?' Mishima called from behind him.

'Leave him! The guy's as good as dead anyway.'

Ogiwara didn't wait to see if Mishima obeyed him or not. Mishima was a dumb clown, and he could stay with the dying guy if he wanted. All Ogiwara wanted to do was get on that helicopter and out of this frozen shithole, back to the warmth and comfort of Saitama. Mountains and English study camps, he had discovered, really weren't his thing.

'My God, what a mess.'

Karin stared at the wreckage of the Queen's Bedroom with her eyes wide. Beside her, Akane just shook her head.

'Ogiwara. I guess it had to have been.'

'That guy's a real idiot,' Karin said. 'Jun seems nice.' She sighed. 'He reminds me of my first boyfriend, back before everything went so wrong.'

Akane smiled. 'The funny thing is that until we got here, Ogiwara was technically my boyfriend. Jun was ... an acquaintance.'

'Well, it seems like you made a good decision in switching them over.'

'Maybe. Jun and me ... we have *history*. Not all of it good, unfortunately.'

Karin smiled. 'I'm the absolute last person who could ever give relationship advice, I'm afraid. Look at me. I'm a professional gold-digger. I have no soul, if you believe what the newspapers say.'

Akane cocked her head. 'Do you regret it?'

'What? Anything in particular?'

'Any of it.'

Karin looked thoughtful for a moment. She rubbed her chin and frowned, and Akane could only marvel at how pretty she looked.

'I guess ... there are things I would take back if could. I would have treated my first boyfriend better. I wouldn't have let O-Remo down. I wouldn't have let my manager ... exploit me. But every decision I made, I made it because it was the one I thought was best at the time. Whether it was or not, that's not for me to decide. I thought it was the right one, so I made it. Does that make sense?'

Akane nodded. 'A little.'

'People think I'm a money-grabbing whore, and they might be right. But when you've stood up on those stages in front of twenty thousand people and every single one of them has *adored* you ... it's hard to turn your back on that. Fame is as addictive as any drug. I guess that's why I ended up with O-Remo.'

'Yet you jilted him.'

'I didn't want to, believe me. I loved him, for what it's worth. He was the only person I'd ever met who truly understood me. The only thing was that our drugs didn't mix. His drug was detrimental to me, and mine to him. For both of us—for our careers—I let him go. In retrospect I wish I hadn't, but I did what I had to do at the time because I was thinking about myself. I was selfish.'

'There's not a person alive who isn't,' Akane said. 'I love Jun with all my heart, but until I came here I couldn't look at him without thinking about something bad from my past. When we came here I realised that I'd stopped seeing Jun. Whenever I looked at him, I'd been seeing something else. Coming up here was like a cloud lifting off of me.' She sniffed. 'Part of me never wants to leave. I'm terrified that if we go down off this mountain—despite everything that's happened—that cloud will descend on me again. Only it'll be twice as bad the next time because I'll be able to remember how wonderful stuff was when it wasn't there.'

Karin pulled Akane forward into a hug. 'Come on,' she said. 'We can talk more about this later if you like. We'd better try to find Rutherford.'

Ever watchful for the bear, they had searched Forbes's private apartment and the bottom floor of the Grand Mansion, but there had been no sign of him or anyone else. They had gone upstairs to check the museum rooms just on the off chance, but all they had found were the signs of Ogiwara's passing.

'This complex is huge,' Karin said. Forbes rarely goes anywhere other than his apartment or the reception office that I ever see. There are other rooms that are his and his alone. This is only one of his investments. I think he runs the others from here, but if I'm truthful about it, I never really cared. I tried to avoid him as much as possible, spending my time relaxing in the pool or up in the teahouse near the Fort.'

'I bet this place is so peaceful,' Akane said.

Karin laughed. 'Yeah, you picked the wrong time to come. Usually it's lovely. A little too quiet, perhaps, but you certainly get some thinking space.'

Akane frowned. A funny sound she hadn't noticed before seemed to be coming from outside the window.

They rushed over and peered out.

'What the hell...?'

A small helicopter was hovering over the courtyard, a rope ladder dangling from its underside. It looked straight out of an American TV police drama, small and bug-shaped, not obviously a mountain rescue team or a military helicopter. In fact, besides the pilot and co-pilot, there was only room for one or two other people.

Forbes had promised that a helicopter would come for them as soon as it could brave the weather conditions, yet this helicopter was far too small for everyone who was stranded here.

Two figures appeared in the alleyway between the pub and the dining hall. The young man from the pub led the way through the snow, with Rutherford Forbes behind him, carrying a small suitcase in one hand.

'That bastard, he's abandoning us,' Karin spat, slamming a hand against the window pane. 'Of all the things to do.'

The young man reached the helicopter and took hold of the rope ladder, keeping it steady as Forbes started up. One of the pilots leaned out of the cab and reached down for the suitcase.

Karin screamed. Akane took a moment to understand why, then something huge and brown and terrifying was bounding out of the alleyway, reaching the helicopter in two massive strides. Massive claws closed over the ladder halfway up, the creature's weight and forward momentum pulling the helicopter sideways. One blade hit the ground and shattered; another cut the young man in half. Forbes had fallen into the snow and was cowering with his hands over his head as the bear jerked down on the rope ladder and the helicopter bounced off the ground. It spun away, its tail snapping off, its engine exploding out of the undercarriage to send a bloom of fire spreading out across the snow.

KEN WAS JUST AHEAD of Jun as they turned out on to the covered walkway, their arms laden with bags of food. Immediately Jun heard the sound of a helicopter and looked up to see a small private one hovering over the courtyard, a rope ladder dangling beneath it. The young man from the pub ran out across the snow and took hold of it, holding it steady for Rutherford Forbes, following behind. Forbes, struggling with a suitcase, began to climb up.

A roar from the alley beside the pub seemed to mute the sound of the beating wings. Jun gasped as a bear bigger than anything he could have imagined leapt out of the alley and reached the helicopter in two massive bounds. Its front paws caught the rope ladder and its weight pulled the helicopter down on its side. Jun winced as he saw the young man cut up in its blades, then fire was spreading out across the snow as its engine exploded.

One of the pilots fell out of the cockpit and began to crawl away, his face covered with blood. The massive, shaggy creature walked calmly after him, then made a strangely human reverse ripping motion across the man's back. Jun turned away as the man's body split apart—

—and saw Ken running across the snow towards Forbes, who was crawling in the direction of the bus.

'Ken! What are you doing?'

Ken didn't answer. He grabbed Forbes by the shoulders and hauled him towards the bus. The bear, finished with the pilot, swung its huge head back towards them. Its eyes seemed to glow red like hot coals. Its chest-sized mouth fell open and a growl as loud as a car engine escaped its throat.

What was Ken doing? It was suicide going out there. He was trying to rescue Forbes, but he had no chance. Then, as Ken dropped out of sight, Jun understood.

He'd dragged Forbes under the school bus, hoping the bear wouldn't be able to get at them.

The massive beast roared and slammed its paws against the side of the bus, denting the metal and smashing one of the windows. A plume of snow showered it. The bus shook, its wheels bouncing in the snow. The bear slammed against it again, this time using its shoulder, and the bus bucked.

The beast was almost as tall as the bus at its shoulder, and about half as long. A couple more shoves and the bus would topple over, and then Ken and Forbes would be at the creature's mercy.

Jun looked down, surprised to find he had taken several steps along the east wing's covered walkway. Halfway along, an arch opened on to a snow-covered set of steps that led down to the courtyard. Jun, feeling numb all over, his heart thumping, turned down them, reaching into his pocket.

Out of the corner of his eye he could see the pieces of the young man and the two dead pilots—one ripped apart by the bear and the other killed in the crash.

The bear loomed tall in front of him, standing on its powerful hind legs, swinging its arms in tandem towards the side of the bus, which rocked again under the force of the blow. Jun tried to stop his hands from shaking as he lifted the flare and pointed it upwards, aware that he would get one shot only, that if he missed the creature would rip him apart.

'Hey!' he screamed. 'Hey, you!'

The bear's enormous head swung towards him. It was the size of a coffee table, its mouth filled with row upon row of thick, curved teeth. Small crimson eyes watched him from behind a shag of fur as its lips drew back in a snarl, making him gag beneath its putrid breath.

'You hungry?' he shouted, pointing the flare at its neck through fear of aiming too high. As it lifted a massive paw to swat him away, he pulled the cord and the flare burst out of its casing.

He had been right. Its momentum took the flare higher than

where he aimed, straight into the creature's face. The bear roared as flames ignited its fur and it fell away into the snow, swatting at its eyes.

'Go!' Jun shouted at Ken, and together they pulled Forbes out from under the school bus and dragged him away towards the pub. The creature was reeling in the snow somewhere on the other side of the bus as they reached the entrance. Ken barely paused, shoving Forbes into the door even as he twisted the handle. Jun came up behind and jerked the door shut, sliding the bolt across but wondering what use it would be against an animal capable of grounding a helicopter.

'Thank you, thank you,' Forbes gasped as they pressed back against the inside wall of the pub. Jun didn't dare risk a look out, although he was pretty sure the creature had been blinded. A roar rang out across the courtyard as if in confirmation.

'You tried to run, you bastard,' Ken said. 'You said there would be a helicopter. You didn't say it would be single fucking occupancy.'

Forbes just glanced back and forth from Ken to Jun, his mouth hung open in surrender as blood streamed from a cut on his head.

'That wasn't supposed to happen,' he said.

33

WIRES AND REVELATIONS

Ogiwara stared openmouthed as the monstrous bear pulled the helicopter into the ground, throwing it over onto its side in a judo move as good as any he'd ever pulled off at club practice. The thing was as big as the band's van, a huge, powerful ball of teeth and muscle. Whatever freak of genetics had led to the birth of this creature, it was terrifying and awe-inspiring at the same time.

The helicopter's engine exploded. Ogiwara couldn't see what happened to the pilots but a moment later the bear began to ram the side of his school bus, as if trying to get at something inside or underneath it.

He had seen how fast it had moved, and from the way it had dispatched the helicopter and was now rattling the bus, he could tell it was immensely strong. He was no more than fifty metres away. If it saw him, he was dead.

He turned and ran.

Mishima knew that Ogiwara was a bully who thrived on pushing other kids around. That was how he had come to captain the judo club. He considered Ogiwara a friend, but it was a tentative friendship, one that could be broken at a moment's notice if Ogiwara so wished. Mishima just liked to have someone make decisions for him; it made life easier.

Now, though, as Ogiwara ran off back towards the Grand Mansion, Mishima looked down at the man lying on the stretcher and wondered what he should do. They were only a stone's throw from the entrance to the Fort, where they would be safe. Ogiwara had told him to follow when he ran off after the helicopter, but he couldn't just leave this man out here in the snow, not when there were bears around, could he?

Mishima frowned. Then, making perhaps the first free-thinking decision of his life, he went around to the front of the tabletop and lifted it up. With a grunt of exertion he began dragging it towards the door to the Fort.

THERE WAS ONLY SO fast Ogiwara could run through the snow. After the second night's dump the air had warmed a little despite a sun hidden by clouds, and the snow had thickened. They had been moving slowly when heading for the Fort with the sick guy, but now he was trying to run through knee-deep sludge. Within a few seconds his legs and hips were aching, and after only twenty or so steps he was forced to stop for a rest. As he leaned on his knees to get his breath back, he saw Mishima tugging at the door of the Fort.

Ogiwara took a few more slow steps. Catching on with the trail they had made while carrying the sick guy, he was able to use the old foot holes to increase his speed a bit. It was obvious that the door of the Fort was stuck, because Mishima was grunting with exertion as he tried to pull it open. Ogiwara had just reached the cannon where he had turned back before, when movement to the right caught his eye.

'No—'

The bear came bounding across the open snow, closing on Mishima in a matter of seconds. Mishima turned and had time to raise a hand, then the creature's massive teeth crunched down over his body. There was a faint cry, then the bear was ragging Mishima like a dog with a toy, blood and guts and gore flying in all directions.

Instinct took over. Ogiwara dropped to the ground, ducking down behind the cannon. He inched forward, hands parting the snow to reveal a tiny crawl space underneath the ancient military weapon, a wet patch of mud between the wheels that had been encased in lumps of concrete. Snow all around made a natural igloo, and he squeezed in against the underside of the gun as the sound of crunching bones came from a short distance away.

Not the same one.

The bear had come running from a different direction, meaning there was more than one.

A low growl sounded from right above him. The tiny crawl space went suddenly dark, and Ogiwara clamped a hand over his mouth to stop himself crying out. Something huge and shaggy walked across in front of the cannon. For a moment Ogiwara was certain it had seen him and would turn back, then the air lightened as it moved on.

For a long time, Ogiwara didn't dare to breathe. He lay still, listening to the silence, waiting for the creature to return.

Finally, the numbness that was starting to creep into his legs from where they were pressed against the snow forced him to move. He shifted forwards a few inches, bent into a crawl and peered up out of his hiding place.

The huge beast's passage was obvious from the wide gash in the otherwise pristine snow. It had carried straight on, heading across the buried road and into another car park, then climbed up an embankment and disappeared through the snow-covered tennis courts at the back of the Grand Mansion.

Ogiwara didn't wait. He leapt up and stumbled through the snow towards the Fort. All that remained of Mishima was a bloody mess of chewed up muscle and bone, but Ogiwara barely looked at it as he pushed though the gap Mishima had made in the door and then pulled it shut behind him.

Breathing hard, he sat down on the floor, his hands and legs shaking. He rubbed his eyes, determined not to be a pussy and cry. He'd not cried since his dad had taken the belt to him for the first time when he was five years old and he had no intention of crying now. Mishima might be dead, but he was still alive, and he was safely inside the most secure part of the whole complex, with thick walls and a fortified door behind him.

And a dying guy taped to a tabletop.

O-Remo groaned and turned his head, his eyes briefly fluttering open and then closing again.

Ogiwara understood now. He had thought Mishima was still trying to open the door, but his friend had already taken the dying guy inside and had come back out looking for him.

'You stupid bastard,' he muttered, wiping a bit of grit from his eye. 'You should have saved yourself.'

O-Remo groaned again. His eyes opened and his mouth worked slowly. 'Karin?' he gasped.

'Do I look like a chick?' Ogiwara said. 'I mean, do I?'

'Karin…'

'I don't know where she is.'

'Karin?'

Ogiwara leaned his head back against the cool stone of the wall and closed his eyes.

Bᴇᴇ, watching through the windows of the gym, nodded slowly as the bear took down the helicopter and then began trying to knock over the bus. He felt a momentary concern that it would turn its assault on the van containing the treasure trove of expensive equipment he had spent the past decade accumulating, then the schoolboy appeared from nowhere and blasted it in the face with a distress flare. Bee raised an eyebrow at the boy's nerve, but it was a futile gesture. Soon the complex would be overrun and only his plans would be able to prevent the deaths of all of them.

He turned away from the window. In the middle of the room, Kaede was tied to a chair placed exactly over the centre line of an indoor soccer court. Precision was key. It was precision that would win out in the end.

He had stripped her naked and painted her from head to toe in stripes of white and red. He smiled. She looked like a tablecloth he had seen for sale in a one hundred yen shop just last week. Tasteless, cheap.

A wet tea towel was wrapped around her mouth. For a long time she had tried to argue with him, offering him every sexual favour under the sun to the point where he'd almost said yes just to shut her up. He hadn't fed or watered her, and didn't intend to. If he kept her weak she wouldn't struggle.

It was how it had to be. He had dreamed of this, and now everything was falling into place.

The girl's eyes followed him as he walked. She didn't look so much afraid as angry. She narrowed her eyes and wrinkled her nose as if trying to communicate without words.

'Soon, soon,' he told her. 'Soon we will find out if you little life has any worth at all. Are you looking forward to that?'

She made a muffled sound that could have been a swear word. Bee just smiled.

AKANE SCREAMED. She clutched Karin to her as they watched the events in the courtyard below. She felt a momentary sense of pride as Jun ran out and set the flare off in the bear's face, then relief as Jun and Ken made it to the pub with Rutherford Forbes in tow. Then her relief turned back to terror as the huge bear, its fur burning, reeled in the snow, rolled over on its back like a dog at play, then leapt up and bounded towards the main entrance to the Grand Mansion.

She felt the thud as it crashed into the main doors. The air filled with a huge roar, and then everything went silent.

Akane let go of Karin. The two women looked at each other,

neither wanting to speak. Karin pointed a finger at the floor. Akane gave a little shrug.

The stairs to the lower floor were right behind them. Designed like a ballroom staircase, two sets of stairs on either side of a wide landing arced downwards, joined in the middle and then doubled back to slant down to the floor below.

It was easily wide enough for the bear to come up, Akane knew. That it hadn't was what worried her.

'What is it doing?' she whispered into Karin's ear.

Karin just shook her head. Akane remembered the way the bear had rose up out of the snow from where it had been hiding and then ambushed Dai. Did it know they were up here? Could it smell them? Was it waiting for them to come down?'

She had seen it burning. Was it possible it was dead? Wouldn't it have made a lot more noise if it was in its death throes?

'What are we going to do?' she whispered, but Karin had already taken a few tentative steps towards the stairs.

'I can smell it,' she said. 'I think it's dead.'

Facing them from the wall above the staircase was a huge framed painting. Karin went over to the top of the stairs and stared at the reflection in the glass. After a moment she nodded and started down. Akane, not wanting to be left behind, hurried after her.

Karin reached the turn of the stairs and squatted down, peering through the banisters at the reception area below. As Akane squatted down beside her, Karin pointed.

'It's dead,' she said. 'Look.'

The bear lay in front of the fireplace, as large as a dead mammoth. Fire licked at its face, at the hollows where its eyes had been. Most of its head had been seared free of hair, and the fire had spread to the carpet, chewing hungrily at the thick pile as it make its way towards the stairs.

'All this lacquerware,' Karin muttered. 'This place could go up in minutes. She started to stand up and turn away, but Akane took hold of her arm and pulled her back down. She pointed. 'Look!' she said, feeling her heart pushing up into her throat. 'Can you se it?'

'What?'

'There. Poking out of its head. *Wires.*'

'ANY CHANCE that you could tell us what the fuck you were planning to do?' Ken said, shoving Forbes back towards the bar. 'You were supposed to be getting us out of here, then we end up getting attacked by that thing and you try to do a runner, leaving us behind. Just what the fuck is going on here?'

Forbes lifted a hand to protest, but Ken slammed a fist into the older man's jaw. Forbes moaned and crumpled to the floor. As he tried to get up, Ken aimed a kick at his face, but Jun pulled the guitarist back. 'That's enough,' he said. 'Listen to what he has to say.'

Ken scowled, but nodded. He pulled Forbes up and pushed him back against the bar, holding him by the front of the shirt. 'Talk, damn you, and make sure I can understand it.'

Forbes's face was a mess of blood and bruises, but his eyes were desperate and hopeless. 'We made them,' he whispered.

'What? What did you say?'

'They're cybernetic.'

Ken let go and Forbes fell to the floor again. Jun helped him up as Ken slammed a fist down on the bar top.

'They're part animal, part machine. Genetically engineered. British Heights sits on top of a research laboratory.' Forbes started to laugh. 'We're all going to die, you know that, don't you?'

'I was slowly coming to that conclusion.'

'What are they for?' Jun asked.

Forbes laughed again. 'For sale,' he said. 'They were built on a commission.'

'For who?'

'For a rather secretive government. One that has a particularly sensitive border, and is keen to prevent asylum seekers getting out of the country. To save on the long-term costs of policing their mostly forested border with military personnel, they decided to create a visible deterrent. A legend and an aberration at the same time. It just so happened that my company's genetic engineering work in other fields attracted their attention. They submitted a proposal for a product, and like any good company, we designed a prototype and put it into testing.'

'The bears,' Ken said, shaking his head. 'What have you done here?'

'They weren't supposed to get out.'

'How many are there?'

'Prototypes? Just six.'

'*Just six?*' Ken slapped a hand against his forehead. 'You mean there are six of those things out there?'

'Forbes nodded. 'Somewhere, yes.'

'And we're trapped up here.'

Forbes nodded. 'For the time being, yes.'

34

JUN GETS CHASED

'WE HAVE to get to Karin and Akane,' Ken said. 'Then we have to get to the Fort, as per the original plan. Those boys should be there by now.'

'I'll go,' Jun said, standing up. 'Look after him.'

Ken glowered. 'I know how I'd like to look after him, but I'll be good. Be careful, Jun.'

Forbes pointed. 'Go behind the bar and down through the hatch to the drinks cellar. There's a route through to the dining hall kitchens. It's where we store food in January and February.'

'How many more secret routes are there?' Ken said.

'A few. Bring Karin back safely and I'll help you.'

Jun didn't see that Forbes was in any position to make bargains, but Karin was with Akane, so it served his purpose. He went back through the bar, and sure enough, found a trapdoor in the floor which led down into a cold, brick-walled storage room. Another door at the back led into a dark passage lit with a single dim emergency light. At the end, a wooden ladder led up to another trapdoor.

He found himself in a utility room full of washing machines and cleaning equipment. A door led through into the kitchen washrooms, and from there Jun found himself back in the dining hall. First he went to the windows and peered out at the courtyard, looking for the bear, but there was no sign of it. When he went through the entrance doors into the main corridor of the Grand Mansion he felt a warm draft coming from the reception area.

The whole entrance hallway was a burning inferno.

Akane and Karin had come in here to look for Forbes. Jun began to shout for them, but his voice was quickly lost over the roar of the fire. With one eye on the flames that were beginning to lick at the ceiling, he crept as close as he could, trying to see if they were in the reception area.

'Oh, wow.'

The burning ruin of the bear he had hit with the distress flare lay in front of the reception desk, fierce flames striping the hide off its metal-clad back. While he could see a metal exoskeleton, he smelt burning flesh too. Whatever kind of hybrid robot monster this was, he had killed it.

He heard a hiss from above him and a sprinkler system came on, but it was weak, its pipes partly frozen up, perhaps. As an icy spray soaked him, Jun leapt backwards, turning back towards the dining hall. There was another staircase there heading to the upper floor, but as he started towards it the glass doors to the east covered walkway exploded as another of the bears came raging through.

It swung its massive head towards him, its jaws opening into a vicious snarl. Jun clamped hands over his ears as it let out a deafening roar, then it bounded forward, huge shoulders knocking ornamental tables aside, pulling pictures and light fittings off the wall.

There was a door to his left. Jun grabbed the handle and jerked it, knowing if it was locked he was dead.

It opened on to a classroom decked out with tall British hardwood tables and high-backed chairs. Jun leapt at the nearest shadowy space as he heard the door snap off its hinges behind him. The warm, pungent scent of rotting flesh made him gag, and he glanced back to see the creature trying to squeeze through the gap, its jaws snapping at his legs.

The doorframe began to break away from the wall. Jun scrabbled backwards, looking for a way out, and spotted a second door leading back out into the corridor on the other side of a wide teaching blackboard. He jumped up and skirted around towards it, the bear stretching towards him. One huge paw broke through the wall and swung for him. A few more seconds and the creature would burst into the room.

He had to time his exit right. Too soon and it would pull back out into the corridor and run him down. Too late and it would snatch him where he stood.

'Come on!' he screamed at it with tears in his eyes, from the smoke and the overwhelming fear that had wrapped around him like a suffocating plastic sack. 'Come *on!*'

It roared one more time, and its other front leg broke through.

Jun bolted for the second door, praying it was open. For a moment his heart seemed to fill his throat as the door handle slipped through his fingers, then he leaned his weight on it and felt it turn beneath him, stiff from disuse. He pulled it open and swung around it, just as a huge paw broke through the middle of the wood.

Jun bolted through the smoke down the corridor towards the dining hall. He heard the creature roar behind him and felt the reverberations in the walls. He didn't dare look back.

Just before the door to the dining hall, a small staircase rose up to the second floor. Jun raced up it, not looking back. Only when he reached the top did he dare pause long enough to catch his breath.

The upper floor was filled with smoke. Jun put a sleeve over his mouth, but it didn't make much difference. Instead, he began opening doors and looking into rooms for any sign of Akane and Karin.

Jun knew Ogiwara had ransacked the bedrooms, but he was more interested in open windows or another sign that Karin and Akane had tried to escape. They'd said they were planning to search the Grand Mansion first, but they might have been quicker than he expected. They could already be in the staff quarters, safe for now at least.

He opened the door to the King's Bedroom and looked back out at the corridor. The smoke was thickening, and flames were licking at the banisters of the main staircase. There was no sign of the bear, so Jun ran to the windows, pulling one wide. He leaned out, gasping in a lungful of deliciously clean air.

'Where are you?' he shouted, gripping the window frames in anger.

'Jun!' came a voice from above him, startling him so much he almost tumbled out. He looked up to see Akane and Karin peering down at him. A moment later something huge and red billowed down towards him, making him jump back. It was one of the curtains he had taken down to cover Akane on their first night. It had been torn in half, the ends tied to make a crude rope.

'Grab it! We'll pull you up!'

'How did you get up there?'

'Just grab it!'

A deep growl sounded from the stairway behind him. Jun turned to see a huge, hairy shape climbing up the centre of the burning stairway. As flames danced across its coat, the bear seemed oblivious to its predicament, its eyes fixed only on its prey.

'Grab it!'

Jun wrapped his arms around the curtain-rope and leapt out of the window as the bear charged. For a moment he was airborne, swinging out over the steps of the entrance below, then he slammed into the wall beside the window. As the bear's head appeared beside him, he felt himself rising up. Its paw smashed into stone where his feet had been a moment before.

Akane and Karin hauled him up and over a low stone balustrade on to the roof. He stared at them openmouthed, but they both seemed unharmed.

'Run!' Akane shouted, as the bear's claws scrabbled at the edge of the balustrade.

Running wasn't easy through the thick snow, but Jun struggled along at the rear as Karin took the lead ahead of Akane. They headed east towards the far end of the building, where Jun saw a small room sticking up like a rooftop observatory.

Karin didn't even pause. As she reached it, she lifted a lump of stone Jun hadn't noticed her carrying and slammed it against the window. The stone actually bounced back, but Karin retrieved it and tried again. Akane came up behind her and Jun saw she was also carrying a lump of rock. It had white paint on one side as if they'd broken away pieces of the balustrade.

'Come on, Jun!' Akane shouted. She tossed something at him: a broken piece of roof tile.

Taking it in turns to slam their objects against the glass, Jun barely had time to notice what was inside as cracks slowly began to appear. With one last grunt of exertion, Karin slammed her rock against it and a small hole appeared. A few seconds of furious attack later and they had made a gap large enough to climb through. Why this odd little room would have bulletproof glass, Jun couldn't say, but as he climbed in behind Karin and Akane he marvelled at what appeared to be a miniature apartment, cut off from the rest of the complex, complete with kitchen unit, dining table and chairs, and a set of stairs leading down, he presumed, to a bedroom. Perhaps this was Forbes's secret retreat, he began to wonder, just as Akane tugged on his arm.

'This is it,' she said, her voice hollow. 'This is where he lives.'

'Who?'

Karin, too, looked ashen-faced. Akane lifted a hand at a painting on the wall. It was of a bird with dark features sitting on a tree branch, the mutilated corpse of a mouse caught in its talons.

'The man O-Remo saw,' she whispered. 'The one they call Professor Crow.'

35

THE PROFESSOR PLANS AN ESCAPE

KUROU GLARED AT THE SCREEN, his nose-beak cocking to the side and pinching at the air. 'No, no, no, no!' he shouted, banging a clawed hand down on the tabletop. 'You can't get away! You can't!'

The helicopter was a crumpled, burning mess of metal. Three people were dead, but the one whose blood was supposed to be staining the pristine snow had escaped, dragged away by two of those stupid, interfering guests. One of them had even had the audacity to set fire to one of the creatures. The flames had shorted out its systems and it lay burning inside the entrance to the Grand Mansion.

A second bear was now on fire. Caught up in the bloodlust of a hunt, the stupid things were showing none of the intelligence Kurou had hoped to have bred into them, and while they were making an unholy mess, the body count was distressingly low.

He ordered the bear to retreat, but whether it would listen, he couldn't be sure. Some did, some didn't. They weren't designed to be controlled, merely to be released into a localised area and left to their own devices. The organic part of each creature required regular sustenance, while the mechanical part had a thirty-year shelf-life in the absence of any servicing. Or so he had thought.

He tutted and shook his head. He had tried to press Forbes into more live trials, but the stupid Englishman had been too cautious. *Test them in a controlled environment,* he had always insisted. That's why he had captured elderly hikers and thrown them into the enclosures. But it was a waste of time; this was a real life trial, and for all its faults it would be invaluable to Mr. Park when he was delivered his shipment.

Forbes, though, was proving to be an irritation. His use was over;

it was time for the companies in his name to be turned over to his rightful heir. After all, Kurou had masterminded everything. All Forbes had ever done was put up the cash.

Looking over the monitors again, Kurou saw the second bear had given up the chase and retreated back out into the snow. The sprinkler systems were losing their battle with the fire in the Grand Mansion, and it had already caused thousands of dollars worth of damage to the interior. Kurou smiled; he would just charge the repairs to Forbes's expense account.

He checked the radar systems again, looking for the other bears, frowning at the way they seemed to be meandering aimlessly about. It was perhaps time for a little more testosterone.

Since the day his mother had sold him to Rutherford Forbes for the price of a first-class bus ticket to Shanghai, Kurou had found it difficult to trust women. That it had been infinitely easier to build and breed female bears was irrelevant, the five female prototypes paled in comparison to his one special favorite.

The male.

Lolo.

The others had numbers, but Lolo was the name Kurou had given to the first robot he had ever built, the one Rutherford Forbes had broken with his big clumsy foot on that very first day, and then kicked aside like a piece of trash. Kurou wasn't a resentful type, but there was a case for a grudge right there.

No, females were overly emotional in all shapes and forms, and a partially computerised brain made little difference. The female bears were headstrong, confrontational, and resistant to his attempts at controlling them.

Lolo, however, was another matter.

Down in the forest, waiting patiently for instructions, the huge bear was larger and more powerful. The females were prototypes in every sense of the word, but Lolo was a representation of the future.

'It's time,' Kurou whispered, fingers racing over the controls as he connected with Lolo's radio frequency. 'Let's put on a good show now.'

Somewhere deep in the forest, he could sense Lolo leaning forward off his haunches, dropping into that bear waddle and striding quickly up through the trees in the direction of British Heights.

'The games are just beginning, my little rats,' Kurou whispered, tapping one claw against the radar screen. 'You've had your little fun in my maze, but it's time to start closing off the exits.'

Lolo, are you there?

The huge, shaggy head lifted, ears pricking up. The instructions seemed so close, so clear, as if his master was calling him from outside his cage like he often did. Lolo swung his head from side to side, but the forest floor was empty. Keen eyes detected no motion, sharp ears no sound.

Lolo.

He grunted, looking up towards the grey sky peeking between the trees, but it wasn't coming from there either. He understood now. The sound was coming from inside his head.

It's time, Lolo. Are you hungry? There are lots of good things for you to eat. Head north, up the hillside. I'm looking forward to seeing you soon.

Lolo grunted again. He pushed himself up to his feet, feeling the trees bend aside as he began to move. Some of them snapped, their trunks splintering and their snow-covered leaves making a whooshing sound as they fell, sometimes to the snowy ground, sometimes into the waiting boughs of other nearby trees.

Lolo's powerful legs pushed him forwards through the forest with increasing urgency. His master was waiting, and Lolo was hungry.

KUROU GLARED at the TV station he was streaming on one of his monitor screens. The rescue operation around the landslip was getting dangerously close to the buried entrance to the underground facility. They would find it by tomorrow, and then Forbes's secrets would be exposed.

The prototypes, of course, could be destroyed. Kurou could detonate them at any time, leaving just a twisted tangle of metal and flesh, something that would fascinate the rescue workers but not necessarily incriminate Forbes's enterprises. Kurou was too good, too careful. Bribes in certain areas of government would help turn eyes away, but if it got out into the international media there could be big problems.

In general, he had learned that the world didn't care about what went on within other borders unless it was detrimental to their own survival or deductive from their economic gain. No one cared what a secretive Asian state was doing to its people, because a country squeezed up into a climatically worthless part of the world and developed on dull, valueless rock was of little consequence.

With a rusty, fading military that survived on handouts and ran on third grade oil, no one worried about a few threats. If the same state were to suddenly be in possession of cutting edge military technology, then that was another matter.

Kurou had big plans for his *de facto* company. He dreamed of world domination as much as the next man, but unlike most of the brainless masses, he had the knowhow to achieve it. Getting derailed at the first hurdle was something he was keen to avoid.

He dialled a number on his satellite phone.

'I need a transport,' he squawked into the receiver. 'The back entrance, the one by the lake. Road is safest as they'll be watching the skies soon once they discover the base.' He ran a finger over the figures on his computer screen, calculating how much space he would need to remove all the embryos and infants in production, then barked a series of numbers into the phone. 'Prepare a safe route to Niigata. We go by container ship to Vladivostok, and once there we'll go to ground until the client is ready to receive his shipment. Pay off who you need to pay off. As always, the fees are arbitrary. Use your discretion.'

A single word came back at him: 'When?'

Kurou paused. Every minute that he stayed at British Heights put the delivery at risk, but he so wanted to see the results of his experiment.

'Tomorrow,' he whispered, his voice coming out as a snakelike hiss.

36

O-REMO REMEMBERS THE BEST SHOW

THROUGH THE LITTLE lattice window beside the pub door, Ken watched the events over at the Grand Mansion. He saw the flames destroying the entrance, then Karin climbing up on to the roof with a curtain tied around her waist, which she used to haul Akane up beside her. A few minutes after that, a second bear appeared and rushed inside the building. Ken listened with tears in his eyes to it destroying the inside of the Grand Mansion, then Jun suddenly appeared at a front window on the second floor. Karin and Akane helped him up to the roof, then the three of them disappeared from sight.

'Can they get back down from up there?' he asked, turning to Forbes, who was sitting on a stool in front of the fire, his head in his hands. 'Can they get down from the roof?'

Forbes nodded. 'Yes, yes. There's a fire escape. There are also ... other ways down.'

Ken looked back out of the window. The second bear appeared through the entrance, a few tendrils of smoke drifting up from its coat. It rolled in the snow of the courtyard and then disappeared around the side of the west wing.

Everything seemed hopeless. One way or another, they were all going to die. The bears would smash the buildings to pieces one by one until all the humans were caught. There was no way to protect themselves, and no way to get off the mountain.

Fire...

The flare had worked for Jun. Just a simple flare, it had set alight one of the bears, and as it hadn't come back out of the Grand Mansion, Ken could assume it was dead, or decommissioned, whatever the correct term for a destroyed half-animal, half-robot abomination might be.

'Do you have more rescue equipment?'

'What?'

'Flares, that sort of thing.'

Forbes waved a dismissive hand. 'In the Fort. There's ski gear in one of the rooms. A lot of tour groups like to take daily skiing trips, but we always give our instructors flares and emergency beacons. We've got a room of ski gear.'

'How many flares?'

'Jesus, I don't know. I'm the owner. I don't do the inventory and other crap like that.'

Ken stood up. He marched over to Forbes, grabbed the man by the collar and pulled him up. 'Come on,' he said. 'You can help me look.'

'Where's Karin?'

Ken remembered the way Karin had shimmied up an outcropping buttress like an experienced climber. Obviously condition training for girl bands went to some extremes.

'She can take care of herself, and those two kids with a bit of luck. We'll go check on the boys and the friend of mine whom you abandoned.'

'I hope that scoundrel dies!'

Ken slowly lifted a fist. 'I'll turn your words on you, old man, if you so much as dare say that again.' For a moment he stared at Forbes, wanting nothing more to slam the old prick's head into the fire and set it alight. 'Come on,' he said. 'Let's get moving before any more bears show up. Is there a secret way over to the Fort?'

Forbes shook his head. 'Not from here.'

'Let's get going then.'

Ken figured they were just as likely to die regardless of which exit they took, so he opted for the front door. He slipped out first, dragging Forbes by one arm until he figured the English businessman would follow on his own, headed down the alley between the shop and the pub, then down another between the back of the pub and the staff residential buildings behind it. From there they had no choice but to head out across the main access road. Ken counted down from three and then ran as best he could through the snow, hoping Forbes would follow. A few seconds later he reached the cover of the nearest dormitory building and ducked into the entrance. Forbes, huffing and puffing like he'd never done a day's exercise in his life, came barging in behind him.

There were four more dormitories, then a stretch of open space between themselves and the Fort.

'We move one at a time,' he said. 'Any sign of one of the bears and we get inside and hide, and hope to Buddha that it doesn't see us.'

Forbes just nodded breathlessly.

'Okay, move!'

Ken ducked out of the building, running low along a clear space beneath its eaves. At the end of the building he paused and looked around. A short section of open space and a fence poking up out of the snow separated it from the next building along. As Forbes came up behind him, Ken stepped out, hurdled over the fence and went into the next building, ducking straight down out of sight. A moment later Forbes followed him in.

'Can't we rest a minute?' he said, puffing out his rosy cheeks.

'The Fort is the only building that looks strong enough to keep those bears out,' Ken said. 'You're welcome to stay here.'

Forbes shook his head. 'I didn't expect any of this, you know. British Heights was a perfectly legitimate operation. Thousands of students have passed through our doors.'

'Lucky them,' Ken said. 'Unfortunately, I'm keen to leave again.'

He saw no more sign of the bears as they moved from one dormitory to the next. Finally, all they were left with was a hundred-metre stretch of open snow up to the entrance of the Fort.

'Look.' Ken pointed at a cleared path in the snow. One of them has been through here.' The trail led from the front entrance to the Fort back across the road and through a visitor car park towards the tennis courts.

'If we follow it, we'll be able to move quicker,' Ken said.

Forbes just nodded, his breathing coming in ragged gasps. 'I'm ready,' he said.

Ken took a deep breath and started out across the snow. It was sun-warmed and thick like mud, making his thighs ache as he frog-walked through it, constantly turning his head to look for bears. When he reached the open trail he paused for Forbes to catch up.

'Can't keep going,' Forbes muttered, dropping to his knees. 'Need to … rest.'

'Get up,' Ken said, anger creeping into his voice. 'You think I'm going to just leave you here, you bastard? You're facing justice for this.'

He reached out and hauled Forbes up, but as he turned back towards the Fort something caught his eye.

In the woods behind the last dormitory, something was moving in the direction of the Grand Mansion, something huge and terrible, far bigger than any of the others, as black as the shadows beneath the trees.

'M01,' Forbes muttered. 'Oh, Heaven on Earth protect us.'

'What?'

'Male Number One. The one that deformed bastard calls Lolo.'

Ken didn't waste time replying. He grabbed Forbes and dragged him towards the Fort, even as a roar filled the air from the direction of the tennis courts. As they broke into a run across the brown grass exposed by the bear's trail, he glanced back to see another bear appear from behind the snowdrifts against the side of the tennis courts and turn towards them. With a thunderous roar, it broke into a bounding run.

'Open the fucking door!' Ken screamed as he approached, running as hard as he could. He could almost feel the thing bearing down on them. 'Open the door right fucking now!'

He didn't want to see the bloody remains of a person on the ground in front of the door, but he did. He stopped in his tracks and stared down at what had once been a schoolboy, chewed up and spat out by one of the creatures the man running after him had designed.

'You evil bastard,' he shouted at Forbes, even as the bear came racing towards them. 'You sick, evil bastard...'

Hands closed over his shoulders and hauled him backwards. He stumbled, then saw the wall of the Fort rising up around him, the door pulled open. 'Get inside!' Ogiwara shouted, shoving Ken back through the door.

Ken stumbled to the floor and rolled over, looking up as Ogiwara dragged Forbes inside after him. The older man crashed into the wall, grunted and fell over. Ken caught a glimpse of the bear still racing towards them as Ogiwara worked to close the door. He jumped up and slammed his shoulder against it as Ogiwara pulled across a huge bolt.

The reverberation of the bear striking the outside of the door knocked them both off their feet. It howled in rage and the door shook as huge paws smote it, but the heavy Medieval-style beams in their metal frame held.

'Mishima got crunched,' Ogiwara said, but there was no hint of amusement in his voice. 'Your friend is in a room down the hall. Think that door will keep the bitch out?'

None of them spoke. No sound came from outside, so Ken peered out of a small portal window beside the door. The bear had gone. Then, as his eyes searched the road and beyond, he saw it disappearing back into the forest.

'It's gone,' he said. 'For now, at any rate.'

'Thank fuck for that.'

'Where's O-Remo?'

'This way.'

Ogiwara led them through a set of double doors into a room that reminded Ken of a hotel corridor. Ogiwara went into the first room and Ken saw O-Remo lying in a comfortable double bed, a thick duvet covering everything except his face. Ogiwara had found a kerosene stove heater from somewhere and the room was far warmer than the corridor outside.

'There wasn't anything else I could do except make him comfortable,' Ogiwara said. 'I don't know if he's going to die or what, but he's still alive at the moment.'

'Thank you.'

Ken leaned down and pressed a hand to O-Remo's brow. To his surprise, the singer's eyes popped open and O-Remo's pale face broke into a wide smile. 'Where's Karin?' he said, his voice strained and weak.

'She's on her way.'

O-Remo's eyes closed again. 'Good. Wake me when she comes.'

Someone behind Ken cleared his throat. 'If he can hang on until tomorrow there might be another helicopter—'

Ken spun, his fist crunching into Forbes's face. The old man groaned and staggered backwards, but Ogiwara caught him and turned him towards the door.

'Just get out of here, you old clown, or we'll put you out as food for that thing.'

He shoved Forbes out into the corridor and closed the door again, turning a key in the lock.

'Thanks.'

A hand closed over Ken's arm. O-Remo's fingers dug into his jacket, and Ken looked down at the stricken singer.

'Do you remember that time?' O-Remo said, the smile still on his face, but his eyes closed. 'Do you remember that time?'

'What time?'

'The … the show at … Metal Garden in Osaka.'

Ken smiled fondly. 'Yeah, I remember it.' They had been sandwiched between Slipknot and Metallica on the final night of the three-day open air festival.

'That was it, Ken,' O-Remo gasped. 'That was the best one … of all of them. You remember what we said before we went on stage?'

Ken felt a tear in his eye. 'No prisoners.'

'Yeah … and we took none, did we? We took none.'

'No, we didn't.'

Ken glanced at Ogiwara, who was standing by the door with his arms crossed and his head down, lost in his own misery.

'We ascended that night, didn't we, Ken? We weren't just … a band. We were … gods.'

Ken smiled. The crowd had been baying for blood that night, a hostile mix of dysfunctional Japanese kids and Western soldiers from off the military bases. They had stepped up on to that stage with their amps turned up to max, their guitars tuned, and with battle in their hearts. They had come to fight, and they had conquered.

'The best one,' Ken said, wiping away a tear. 'Hell fucking yeah. That was the best one.'

'Yeah…' O-Remo gave a slight nod, his smile slowly fading away. Ken stared helplessly as O-Remo took one last breath and then was still. He stared at his bandmate for a few more seconds, then he sank to his knees and lowered his head on to O-Remo's chest.

And then there were two.

37

UNDERGROUND LAIRS

KARIN HAD ALREADY HEADED down a staircase at the back of the apartment. Akane turned to Jun and gave his hand a little squeeze. 'Are you scared?' she said, and from her tone he could tell that she was genuinely asking, not simply confirming he felt the same way she did.

'I'm not sure if I've ever been more scared,' he said. 'I'm trying to be brave, trying to hold myself together with every second that passes. I feel like if I let up my intensity for just one moment I'll fall apart.'

'Are you being brave for me, or for yourself?'

The shock must be frying her brain, he thought. 'Both,' he answered. 'I'm trying to be brave for myself so that I can be brave enough to protect you.'

'When you faced that bear and shot it with the flare, how did you feel?'

'You saw?' When she nodded, he said, 'Like I was going to die. I didn't just feel it, I *knew* it.' She nodded thoughtfully again, rubbing her chin. 'And you?' he asked.

Akane shrugged. 'That's just it,' she said. 'I don't feel anything at all. I feel like this is all just one long dream and that any moment I'll wake up.'

'You won't,' he said, a little harsher than he intended. 'Come on, let's get moving before that thing comes back.'

Jun went after Karin, with Akane coming up behind him. The first flight of stairs was gaudily decorated with framed 1950s movie posters and plastic pot plants standing on wooden tables, but from the second landing down it reverted into prefabricated concrete blandness, lit at each turn by a single naked bulb hanging from the ceiling. From below them came Karin's echoing footfalls. Jun wondered why they didn't just stay here; in this concrete tube they were quite safe, even if it did make him feel like a prisoner descending towards some hellish torture chamber.

Karin's footfalls had stopped. Jun turned another landing and found her standing at the beginning of a corridor that stretched away into the gloom.

'I don't think we're in British Heights anymore,' she said as they crowded in behind her. 'Any guesses where this goes?'

'Only one way to find out,' Akane said, taking the lead and heading down the corridor. Jun shared a glance with Karin, then they both hurried after the girl, who was already disappearing into the gloom.

They reached a corner and turned right. Jun guessed they were somewhere under the courtyard, but he couldn't be sure. They saw no other routes to the surface, although several doors led off the corridor. Jun tried a few as they passed. Most were locked, but a couple opened into blank concrete rooms like prison cells, while another contained just a couple of mops and a bucket standing in one corner. He had the distinct impression that this part of whatever underground complex they were in wasn't used very much.

'How far does this place go on for?' Karin asked.

Jun shrugged. 'I really wish we could turn back, but for some reason I feel safer down here.'

The corridor made a couple more turns, and seemed to be angling downhill. They reached a set of steps leading down into darkness. Akane stopped halfway down and turned to look back up at them.

'What do we do now?'

Jun reached into his pocket and pulled out a cell phone. He pressed a button and a flashlight lit up the steps below them.

'It's useful for something at least,' he said. 'I'll go first if you like.'

The corridor stretching away from the bottom of the stairs was similar to the first, only without any power. Jun saw lights embedded into the dull concrete walls, but none were working.

'What's that smell?' Akane said.

Jun had noticed it too. It smelled distinctly like rotting meat. He wrinkled his nose. 'Wow, that's something else. My god.'

The corridor ended at a large steel door with two heavy bolts pulled across it. Jun passed the phone to Karin while he began to pull one back.

'Do you really think that's a good idea?' Akane asked. 'It looks like that's designed to keep something out.'

'Only one way to find out what's going on here,' Jun said, as the first bolt slid out of the heavy locking mechanism. The second groaned in its fittings but came away with less resistance. Jun took a step back and pulled the door open.

Bright lights blinded him. He cried out and flinched away, covering his eyes with his sleeve. As they began to adjust, he peered around his arm into the room in front of them.

'Wow,' Karin said.

Jun stepped through the door onto a metal walkway some thirty metres above the floor of a massive cavern carved out of rock. Lit with huge floodlights set into the cavern roof, it was a complete microcosm of a forest, complete with pine trees, rocks, and even a small stream flowing through the centre.

The cavern appeared to have been tunneled out of a natural cave. Parts of the roof were smooth and water-worn, while others had the rough-hewn lines of drilling and boring equipment. Perhaps forty metres high, it stretched for several hundred metres, like a giant road tunnel. At intervals of fifty metres or so, it was partitioned by tall wire fences. More wire mesh like netting had been strung across the cavern from one side to the other, but below the walkway it had been ripped and damaged.

Jun spun at the sound of someone retching, and saw Karin on her knees, vomiting over the edge of the walkway. As it passed through the remains of the wire mesh, little sparks fizzed and jumped.

'There's the source of the smell,' Akane said, pointing.

The remains of a man who had been wearing grey work overalls lay beside the door. Jun could only tell it was a man from the pieces of beard on what was left of his face. His body ended just below the waist, the other half of him nowhere to be seen. Bloody handprints covered the back of the door.

A cloud of flies bloomed up from the corpse as Karin found her feet and took a step back. Jun stepped out across the walkway to give the women more room.

'I guess we found where those bears came from,' Karin said. 'I can't believe it.'

'What are they for?'

Jun told them what he knew. Both Karin and Akane stared at him as he recounted what Forbes had told him and Ken.

'This is insane,' Karin said. 'I had no idea. I thought his companies were legitimate. I mean, I didn't expect him to be a saint, but developing something like that...'

Akane shrugged. 'It's no worse than building any weapon though, is it? The only difference is that we're in the firing line.'

'I say we go back,' Karin said. 'Maybe that bear's gone and we can get back out the way we came.'

'No.'

Jun and Karin looked at Akane. 'We've come this far,' the girl said. 'Wherever those bears are now, they're not here. They're up above us somewhere, hunting. We might have a chance to stop this.'

Before Jun or Karin could answer, she pushed past them and started running across the catwalk towards a door in the wall of the cavern on the far side.

KUROU STARED at the video screen in amazement. How had they got into the facility? He could see them down there on a grainy video feed, running across Catwalk Three, which crossed the rear enclosure where Lolo had been kept. They were heading for the development laboratory and the incubation rooms. If they found some way to disconnect the power again they could jeopardise the entire shipment.

Kurou raised his hands in the air like a man praying for divine intervention, and squawked at the top of his lungs. Then, pushing himself back from the desk, he got up and headed for the door.

He would have to put an end to them himself.

RUTHERFORD FORBES RUBBED at a fresh bruise on his cheek as he ran down the long main corridor on the ground floor of the Fort. What had those idiots expected, that he would just sit around and wait for them to finish their moment of grief before getting stuck into him again? He wasn't some chump they could just push around; he was one of the richest men in the world. It was time they learned a thing or two about him. You didn't push Rutherford Forbes around and get away with it.

Once he had seen the end of these idiotic people, he would find Professor Crow and deal with him. The Professor's behaviour had become too unpredictable. In truth, the Professor's work was done; he had created the prototypes from which other scientists could work. The ugly bastard was a genius, but he wasn't the only one. Forbes would find others, and next time he would keep a tighter rein on them.

But first, it was time for a little payback.

He went through a set of stairs at the end of the corridor and took another corridor heading left. It was just another row of guest rooms and conference suites, but at the end was a small service door. He pulled a master key from his pocket, opened the door, and headed down a dark staircase.

At the bottom he reached up into the dark and pulled a string cord from memory. Overhead strip lights stuttered into life, illuminating a large subterranean hanger containing a huge snowplow and several smaller snow-clearing machines. The plow's regular driver had taken the sick students down in the snowmobile, but Forbes knew the basic controls. In his younger days he had always made a point of understanding as many of the lackey jobs as he could, because there would always be a time when the skills came in handy.

With an average of four metres of snowfall per season, he had needed an impressive vehicle to clear the roads around the complex. Forbes could do nothing about the landslide, of course, but his intention wasn't to clear the snow.

He climbed up over the huge wheels and into the cab. Locking the door, he felt safe even from the bears, although he would have to hope that their sensors recognised the vehicle for what it was rather than as prey. Crow had instilled them with size and weight approximators to ensure they didn't go chasing after every rabbit or young deer that came across their path. They were designed to hunt and kill humans only.

The engine burst into life with a huge roar, and Forbes grinned as the headlights illuminated a large garage door. A remote control was resting on the dashboard. Forbes jabbed a fat finger at a button and the garage door creaked as it began to rise.

38

THE KING OF ALL BEASTS

Bee stepped away from the window, a wide grin on his face. 'He comes!' he said, turning back to Kaede. 'The greatest of all bears is approaching!'

She shook her head. 'Let me out of here, you crazy prick! Can't you see the smoke? The building's on fire!'

Bee just threw back his head and laughed. 'Stop making excuses, you silly girl. These events have been preordained.'

He went over to the wall and adjusted the angle of one of the computer tablets he had set up, so that the live webcam was pointing directly at the chair in the centre of the room where Kaede was tied. The whole world would get to watch how he tamed the giant beast, with only a minor time lag. He was still rather annoyed that the Wi-Fi wasn't working, but the stream would be sent off into cyberspace to connect whenever British Heights's servers were ready. It didn't matter when. He had all of eternity to show his mastery of nature to the world.

Ignoring the smoke, he went out through the gym door and pulled open one of the corridor windows that looked out on to the courtyard below. He was aware of the flames licking at some of the windows, but it was mostly smoke and very little fire. He had opened the high windows in the gym, so they were safe for the time being.

Here he comes, Bee thought. *The* kaiju *himself. The king.*

The enormous bear passed through the entrance to the courtyard, his shanks pressing against the stone lions that topped each gate post. He was larger than a male African elephant, making the other bears look tiny, insignificant.

Bee had read about him on the Internet. Roaming the woods of the North Korea-China border, he was considered quasi-mythical, a legend. As a child he had watched endless TV reruns of *Monster Hunter*, and was fascinated by legendary beasts of all kinds, from those considered real like Nessie and the Sasquatch to those created by film studios like Godzilla and King Kong. From the first time he had read about Lolo, Bee had longed to learn more.

Of course, he'd quickly become suspicious of the accounts of Lolo's life, because all of the evidence littered across the net seemed to be coming from the same source. As someone who built websites in his spare time while the band was on the road, it hadn't been difficult to trace the source information to the same IP address, and then attach a GPS tracking location, to find out exactly where every original claim of the legend of Lolo, the giant black bear, had come from.

Right here, in British Heights.

Bee hadn't expected to find anything other than a crackpot computer nerd making up stories and posting them online, so things had proven a little more exciting. Now, of course, he had to give something back. He had to show the world how the beast was tamed.

'Hey!' he screamed, waving his hands out of the window. 'Over here, beast!'

The bear ignored him. It sauntered up to the wreckage of the helicopter and sniffed around it, then started chewing something half buried under the snow. Bee shouted and waved his hands some more, but Lolo was more interested in breaking open the cockpit of the helicopter with its huge paws so that it could get at the meat inside.

Bee looked around for something he could use to attract its attention. Against the opposite wall was an ornate dressing table holding several large porcelain vases. He chose the biggest one, hefted it in his hands and carried it back to the window. It had to weigh at least ten kilograms, and he was terrified of overbalancing as he leaned out, but he didn't want to just drop it. Instead, he slammed it down against a small ledge just below the window.

As the vase broke into pieces, the bear grunted and looked up towards him. Bee waved his hands frantically and finally it took notice. It sat back on its haunches and gave a bellowing roar, then began moving quickly towards the building in a lolloping run.

Bee had expected it to go in through the door, and up the stairs, but instead it rushed straight towards him, leaping against the wall and creating its own footholds by smashing into the rock with its paws. He gasped and fell backwards as one huge paw swung in through the window, tearing it out of its frame. A roar rattled the building, and then Lolo's head appeared, teeth bared in a vicious snarl.

Bee ran backwards into the gym as Lolo smashed his way in through the opening, his massive bulk filling the corridor. In the gym, Kaede was screaming behind her gag. Bee glanced at the three computer tablets set up around the room and hoped that the stream would be clear. Retreating to a rear staircase leading down to the lower floor, he ducked down and waited to see what would happen as Lolo broke through the double doors into the gym.

'See the beast tamed,' Bee whispered, wishing he had thought to set up some kind of microphone to allow him to provide a running commentary on this momentous event. 'Watch the creature fall, as so many others have done, to the charms of a beautiful lady.'

That, to Bee, Kaede was about as beautiful as the dirty prostitutes who littered the ends of shopping arcades after nightfall in every major population centre in Japan, was irrelevant. He wasn't expecting the beast to fuck her, only to fall in love with her, placating its anger. The moment would be beautiful, perfect, and the world would be watching.

Lolo growled and sauntered up to Kaede, looming over her like a great dark raincloud. Kaede struggled in her bonds, shaking her head back and forth, kicking out her heels. His huge shaggy head lowered until he was looking right into her eyes. He sniffed at her. Bee, crouched by the top of the back staircase, barely dared to breathe. *I hope you're all watching,* he thought. *This is a moment that will go down in history.*

Lolo lifted his head. For a moment his eyes seemed to meet Bee's, and Bee shivered at the darkness he saw in those crimson orbs, a lifetime of killing and anger about to be absolved. 'Let love into your animal heart,' Bee whispered.

The bear's lips stretched back in a snarl, then he bit down on Kaede, his teeth sinking into her back and stomach. Soundlessly her legs kicked as the bear lifted the girl and the chair into the air, then they fell back to the ground as Lolo chewed Kaede's upper half down into his stomach.

Bee stared openmouthed. Lolo kicked the remains of the girl aside and lifted his head, eyes narrowing as his lips drew back in a snarl.

Bee pushed off the floor and flung himself down the steps, trusting to luck. He bounced off the concrete halfway down and rolled to his feet, his hands battered by the hard steps as they searched for a grip. His body exploded with pain, but his legs were still working, so he shoved through a door out into the smoke-filled recreation room on the bottom floor. Not pausing to see if Lolo could get down the tight concrete corridor or not, Bee ran through the smoke and through the door into the swimming pool changing rooms, and then through another door into the pool area itself.

The fire that was slowly engulfing the rest of the Grand Mansion hadn't yet reached the gym and the pool on the lower floor of the west wing. With the heating off, the swimming pool had partially iced over. Bee ran past it, heading for the back of the complex, looking for another way out.

Behind him came a huge crash, followed by a thundering roar. Lolo had broken through into the changing rooms.

Bee had just seconds before the bear was on him. Near the wall was a small blue cubicle, its door hanging open to reveal cleaning equipment. He climbed inside, sat down on an upturned bucket, and pulled the door shut.

The air in the pool room was freezing, leaving the pool covered in a thin layer of ice, but it wasn't the cold that was making his teeth chatter. He clamped a hand over his mouth and squeezed until his cheeks hurt, trying not to think about the way Lolo's jaws had separated Kaede's torso from her legs like a knife slicing through a square of tofu. She hadn't even cried out.

She wasn't good enough, he thought. *She wasn't good enough for the king of all beasts. She was some dirty high school slut, when what he wants is a princess. A starlet…*

The cubicle shook beneath the force of Lolo's roar. Bee squeezed his eyes shut and ducked his head into his knees, hoping it wouldn't hurt when the teeth came for him. The ground trembled as Lolo broke into the pool room, several light-fittings detaching from the roof and crashing down onto the poolside.

Lolo roared again, and Bee heard the monster turn towards him, nose searching for the scent of his prey's fear. Tears pressed into Bee's eyes and tried to hold the sobs down, but he had never felt terror so strong, so complete.

Then there was a huge splintering sound, and a wave of freezing water splashed over Bee from above, soaking him through. Lolo roared again, but this time it was in anger and frustration. There was the sound of scrabbling limbs, then the crush and crack of breaking glass and masonry.

Bee sat still, trying not to shiver as the cold permeated every cell of his body. Nothing came from behind him but silence.

Lolo was gone.

Slowly Bee stood up, knocking water that had pooled in his lap onto the floor, and pushed the door of the cleaning cubicle open.

Most of the wall where windows had looked out on to the courtyard was gone. The pool's ice had shattered and it had lost a couple of feet of water.

Making a direct line towards where Bee had been hiding, Lolo had stepped on to the ice.

Bee shook his head. Too close, too close. He wouldn't make the same mistake again, trying to sell Lolo short with some cheap slut. The next time would be different.

With one eye on the empty courtyard through the gaping hole in the pool room wall, Bee crept around the pool and back to the changing rooms, hoping first to find a towel and a change of clothes, then to find someone a little more appropriate to tame the greatest forest creature of them all.

39

A BATTLE UNDERGROUND

'Leave me alone.'

'But where are you going? You can't be going out there, surely. It's suicide.'

Ken shook his head. 'I don't care. I'm done with this.'

Ogiwara grabbed his shoulder and tried to turn him away from the door. 'Stay here or you'll end up like the rest of them!'

Ken looked up from the floor. Every movement felt like a huge drag on his energy. Before O-Remo's death he had felt the fight, but now it was gone. One by one they would be picked off, and they would die. It was better to go on his own terms.

'Look after yourself, Ogiwara,' he said. 'Make sure you bolt the door when I'm gone.'

'You crazy bastard, you can't go out there!'

Ken pushed him away. He could feel the strength in the boy's arms, but Ogiwara didn't resist. In his eyes was understanding. The boy could hold him back all he wanted, but in his mind Ken was already dead.

'Bolt the door,' he said, then he pulled it open and stepped outside.

Ogiwara stared at him for a few moments through the crack in the door, then shook his head. 'Good luck,' he said, then shoved the door shut. Ken heard the bolts being drawn back across.

He turned to look out across the snowy landscape of British Hills. He took in a deep breath of clear highland air, and it didn't feel so bad. He felt a constricting feeling in his throat, but as he soaked up the atmosphere he began to feel relaxed, for the first time in forever, it seemed.

He didn't need to look at the bloody body parts on the ground or the trail in the snow where the bears had been. He looked at the pristine forest and the beautiful replicas of Medieval British buildings, their eaves and overhanging roofs draped in snow. He saw the red telephone box outside the quaint little teahouse, and he smiled at the serenity of it all.

Then he began to trudge across the snow, back towards the courtyard.

He saw several trails where the bears had passed, but no sign of the creatures themselves. The wreckage of the helicopter was still there, the bodies of the pilots, Mika the receptionist, and the young man from the pub poking up through drifts of snow blown by the buffeting wind, their dead faces and limbs draped with a layer of white.

The Grand Mansion was burning, flames flickering behind the windows on the upper floor, and the fire had now spread to the dining hall. In the west wing, there was a hole in the glass wall of the swimming pool room, and the tracks of some great bear in the snow, crossing the courtyard and heading down between two of the dormitory buildings into the forest.

Ken went up to their van, fingers running over the faded logo on the side. Plastic Black Butterfly, his life. With a dead singer and drummer and a missing—presumed dead—bass player, the final nails had been driven into the coffin of his dreams.

He pulled open the back and began to unload his gear. It was time for one last, mournful sonata, before the harsh, murderous arms of the world closed in around him.

———

'WHAT ARE WE LOOKING FOR?' Jun asked as he pushed through yet another door into yet another storage room. 'I mean, shouldn't we just get out of here in case one of those things comes back?'

Akane shook her head. 'I think we'll know what we're after when we see it.'

'Here,' Karin said, peering through a small window beside a closed door. 'This is it.'

'It's got a keypad lock. How do we get in?'

Karin lifted a piece of metal pipe she had picked up off the floor near the enclosures and slammed it down onto the keypad. Sparks flew and the door fizzed as it popped open.

'Primitive security,' she muttered. 'I doubt they expected anyone to ever get inside.'

Akane went first with Jun and Karin at her shoulder. She took a few steps into the room and stopped, letting out a small gasp.

'That's not good,' Jun muttered.

The room was filled with dozens of glass incubators, each with a tiny bear cub inside, attached to a series of wires and pipes. Jun went up to the closest one and peered in through the glass. The creature, about the size of his palm, was already fitted with metal plates and inserts that pulsed and shifted as it breathed through a mask attached to a pipe. Moving across the room, he found larger ones in a different section, and through a glass wall saw several others in cages. Some had their fur shaved off, and the metal parts of their bodies visible through their skin.

'That sick bastard,' Karin said. 'You think they bred these or snatched them from the forest?'

'Bred, I think,' Jun said. 'I don't know how, but we know why. What do we do about them?'

'We destroy them,' Akane said quietly.

Jun looked back towards her and gasped. She had opened one of the incubators and was cradling a tiny bear in her hands.

'What are you doing? Put that back—'

Akane turned towards him. 'These are not animals,' she said. 'These are someone's twisted idea of the future.' She lifted the animal over her head. 'We don't need this.'

It was Karin who cried out as Akane threw the thing to the ground. It made a tiny yelp that reminded Jun of a puppy, then it lay still. Akane stamped on it, her foot coming away in a mass of metal and blood.

'This is fucking sorcery,' Akane said. 'Scientists shouldn't be doing this. We have to destroy them. We have to destroy them all.'

'How?' Karin asked.

'There's nothing that will burn down here,' Jun said.

'The power,' Akane said. 'They're all attached to computerised feeding systems and regulators. All we have to do is switch them off.'

The others followed her over to a computer mainframe against one wall. She began to frantically press buttons, stabbing at them in frustration. 'One of these must turn those things off—'

'This might help,' Jun said, lifting up a heavy metal chair. As Akane stepped away, he slammed it down on the computer console, battering it like a hated enemy, letting his anger pour out. Sparks flew and wires broke. From somewhere behind him came a sharp hiss.

'What's that?' Akane said.

Jun turned around. Karin had gone to the far door to look through at the cages. 'You just released the locking mechanisms,' she said. 'The cages have opened!'

'The bears?'

'They're out!'

Something the size of a large dog slammed against the door

separating the incubation room from the cages. A second creature crashed into the glass, creating a hairline crack down the centre.

Jun grabbed Akane's arm. 'I think now it's time we got out of here.'

He turned towards the door just as Karin screamed. He saw something feathery blur across the room and then sharp claws raked across his face. He fell to his knees as blood dripped down onto his hands.

'You stupid meddling fools!' screeched the intruder. Jun looked up to see a monstrous creature with the body of a man but a deformed, birdlike face. Arms and legs ended in twisted limbs that resembled talons.

Karin threw her length of pipe at him, but Professor Crow caught it in one deft hand, and swung it towards Akane's head in the same fluid motion. Jun jerked her out of the way and it crunched harmlessly against a computer terminal. Crow screeched again, but Akane stood up and screeched right back in his face. Her absurd mockery made Crow hesitate, and in that moment Akane leapt at him, grabbing him round the neck and shoving him back against the wall.

He slashed at her face, but Jun pulled her back before Crow could get to her eyes. 'Open the door!' he shouted at Karin, as behind him another young bear slammed into the crack-riddled window.

Crow leapt forward at Karin, but she ducked and jerked the door open at the same time. A young bear, its face and body glinting with metal inserts, rushed out of the door, straight into Crow's path. Jaws snapped at Crow's face but he threw the creature aside.

'Come on!' Jun shouted, pulling Akane towards the door. They tumbled out into the corridor as a bear came after them, growling and snarling like a wild dog.

'Where's Karin?' Akane shouted, kicking out at the creature as it snapped at her legs.

'I'm here!' Karin shouted, running out of the door. One of the bears followed her as she ran away up the corridor. 'Get yourselves out!' she shouted at them. 'I'll find you!' Then she was gone, turning down a branch in the corridor, several of the dog-sized bears in pursuit.

Jun kicked the small but vicious creature away and pulled Akane after him, back in the direction of the enclosures. 'We need to outrun them,' he gasped. 'You sure they can't survive away from their life support systems yet?'

Almost as if predicted, the nearest of the bears suddenly let out a low squeal. It squatted back on its haunches, took a sudden deep breath, and keeled over on its side. Its legs twitched a few times, then it was still.

There were a couple of others following behind it, but one keeled over before it reached them, and Jun slammed a door into the face of the third. He pushed through another door and they found themselves back out by the large enclosures.

'We made a wrong turn,' Akane said. 'That's the door we came in on up there.' She pointed. About fifty metres deeper into the cave they could see the first catwalk. The catwalk they stood on stretched across to the other side of the cave, but then turned at a right angle and joined up with a third catwalk further along. There was no way back to the door without retracing their steps.

'There's a ladder down over there,' Jun said. 'If the bears got out somewhere, perhaps we can get out the same way.'

They started off across the catwalk, but Jun suddenly stumbled as sharp claws dug into his neck. As a deafening squawking ripped through his eardrums, he turned back to see Crow bearing down on him.

'You bastards let my children out, you'll pay for this!' Crow screeched, shoving Jun away towards the edge of the catwalk. The metal barrier at hip-height dug into Jun's back, and he knew he was only a single hard shove away from a date with the electrified netting below.

Crow cuffed him across the side of the face and Jun staggered to his knees as talons shredded the jacket on his back. Jun tried to throw a punch, but Crow easily blocked it and shoved him backwards again. Jun's lower back hit the metal barrier and this time he toppled over. He stuck out a hand and caught hold of one of the lower rungs in the side barrier, the metal cutting into his palm, but his legs and his other hand flapped uselessly in the air as Crow swung himself over the rail, taloned feet stretching to push Jun off.

'Hey, you ugly bastard!'

Crow looked up. Akane was clutching something in her hand. She held it up in front of Crow's face.

The monstrous thing squealed in terror, hands letting go of the catwalk, coming up to cover his eyes. Akane reached forward and shoved him; his feet lost their balance. For a moment Crow hung in the air, hands clutching his face, then he plummeted towards the ground, bouncing up off the electrified mesh in a hail of sparks. He twisted and bounced again, then fell through a hole torn in the mesh and disappeared into the trees below. They heard a thud as he struck the ground.

With Akane's help Jun climbed back on to the catwalk. 'What … what did you do?' he gasped.

'I showed him his own face,' she said, eyes downcast. She held up a woman's makeup mirror. 'Did you notice how there are no reflective surfaces anywhere? None. Everything is grey and dull, even the steel is unpolished. There was one mirror in his apartment, a tiny thing about two centimetres across that was sitting on the dinner table. That poor bastard despised the sight of himself.'

Jun nodded. He understood her feelings, but with the hideous creature's talons raking at his face he hadn't felt the same levels of sympathy. 'Come on,' he said. 'Let's get out of here.'

They headed across the catwalk and carefully descended the metal ladder rungs set into the rock surface. On the ground they found themselves in a mock forest, only the huge glowing floodlights in the ceiling above breaking the illusion. Crow had fallen into a part of an enclosure that was still fenced off, but from where they stood they could see where one huge beast had passed, ripping through each fence in turn.

'It's colder, isn't it?' Akane said. 'And the light's different somehow. Not so … artificial.'

The bears were long gone. As they stepped from one enclosure into another as the tunnel arced around in a curve, Jun understood why.

At the end, the whole tunnel wall had fallen in, and cold winter light shone down on them. Several catwalks and what looked like a guard building had been crushed in the rock fall, ripping through the fence nearest to the end.

'That avalanche,' Jun said. 'It must have cause this. The wall of the cave collapsed and they got out.'

They climbed up over the fallen rocks, hanging on to each other as the loose rubble groaned and shifted with every footfall. As they neared the top they found an increasing covering of snow, while the air temperature dropped dramatically.

The opening in the cave was about thirty feet high. A huge mound of snow almost covered it, perhaps the result of some secondary avalanche. They climbed up the side, the snow much more difficult to negotiate than the rocks as it crumbled and subsided underfoot. By the time they reached the top and looked out on to the forest they were both exhausted.

The sun had passed down behind the hills to the west, and the temperature was beginning to drop below freezing. Jun held Akane's arm as they climbed out on top of the huge snow bank and looked down into the chaotic mess caused by the avalanche.

'Jun, look!'

At the bottom of a gentle slope in front of them, something rectangular was lying on its back, half buried in the snow, surrounded by yellow police tape.

'It's the snowmobile they took the other students away in!'

Jun didn't want to look, but Akane was already wading through the snow towards the vehicle. Jun followed, trying not to look at the brownish stains on the snow just below the freshest layer which her boots had disturbed.

'They're not here,' she said as she reached the vehicle and stepped over the police tape to look inside. 'There's a lot of blood, but no bodies.'

Jun saw more circles of police tape in among the trees. He hoped Akane wasn't too optimistic. The distances from the upturned vehicle told him a story—that some of the students had survived the crash and tried to get away as the bears broke out. The secondary avalanche must have buried the cave entrance again, explaining why the rescuers had seemingly not discovered it. Only now, as the snow was beginning to settle, was it revealing itself again.

'Jun, the road.'

It disappeared into a slew of fallen rocks and snow, sawn off, but from where they stood they could see the rest of it, covered in tire tracks from the rescue workers, meandering off into the trees. All they had to do was follow it back to civilization. The rescue workers had perhaps finished for the day, but even if they had to trudge several miles, being on a road would spur them on. Jun nodded and started heading for it.

'No!'

He stopped and turned back. 'What?'

Akane hurried over to him. 'We can't, Jun. This isn't finished yet.'

'What the hell are you talking about?'

She shook her head, eyes wide in earnest. 'We can't leave the others. It could take hours to get back to the town. We know what those things are, and we can figure out how to stop them.'

'Akane, that's crazy! They'll kill us one by one!'

'No, Jun! We can't just leave!'

He looked back towards the cave entrance, just as the snow shifted and settled, slumping down to block the entrance. While they could probably dig their way back in, there was no telling how long it would be before another mini avalanche came crashing down. The road was their best choice now.

'Come on, Jun!'

He turned to see her climbing up the steep hedgerow beside the road, following a slightly wider line through the trees. He ran after her, planning to drag her back down and pull her with him if necessary, but she was already twenty metres away, climbing hard up through the snow.

As he reached the point where she had started up, he saw a little wooden sign poking up in the snow, covered with a faded map. He peered at it for a moment, noticing a house that represented British Heights in the middle of a tangle of forest nature trails.

Her footfalls had uncovered a set of steps. He started up after her, but now she had found the trail she was far ahead, marching as quickly as she could through the deep snow, back towards British Heights.

Jun took one last lingering look back towards the road that offered safety and salvation, then he groaned inwardly and hurried after her.

40

SWORDS AND SNOWPLOWS

KARIN, exhausted from the climb up the spiraling metal staircase in the dark, slammed her shoulder against the wooden door until it cracked. With a scream of frustration, she slammed against it one more time, and the lock finally gave way, sending her sprawling across a darkened room as the door burst open.

She looked up, letting her eyes adjust, listening for the sounds of pursuit from below. For the first few turns in the endlessly spiraling staircase she had heard the clang and crunch of the bears' feet on the rungs below, with the screeching of the one Forbes called Professor Crow creating a spine-tinging musical backdrop.

Then everything had gone silent.

She was in a hanger of some kind, a couple of snow-clearing vehicles standing in the dark beside her. The air was chilly and dry, as if the garage door had recently been opened. She got to her feet and stumbled across the room towards a shadowy cubbyhole in one corner. As she had suspected, she found a set of stairs leading up to the upper floor.

She emerged at the end of a corridor in the Fort. She'd spent a little time there over the last few months, mostly as a way of getting out of Rutherford's way. The Fort, with its long corridors and comfortable relaxation areas fitted with coffee machines and sofas, was a great place to sit with a book. There were often students wandering about, but a lot of the time she'd had one of the relaxation areas to herself. With its high, vaulted ceilings and tall windows looking out onto the forest, it was a comforting place where she could collect her thoughts, and analyse in her mind her reasons for being here.

Now, cold and silent, it seemed like a malevolent place filled with dread.

She crept down the corridor, unsure where she was going, and through a heavy wooden door at the end. She found herself in the main hall, a hexagonal space with stairs leading up to the upper floor and a concierge's desk in one corner for when there were parties of schoolchildren staying.

As she started up the stairs, she paused halfway where the stairs turned back on themselves, and reached up for an ornamental sword fitted across a metal shield on the wall. It was bolted into the stone, but when she jerked it the fitting came lose and it broke away. She hefted it in her hand, and touched the blade with her finger. It was as blunt as a fire poker but it was better than nothing. Just having it in her hand gave her comfort.

Upstairs was mostly classrooms and conference rooms. She looked into a few, but they were empty and deserted. From the windows she could see no sign of any of the bears, but the sun was starting to dip behind the distant hills and it would be only an hour or two before darkness fell. The heating was off, and unlike the tunnels below the complex, none of the lights worked. There would be nowhere safe from the bears after dark.

She carried on along the top floor, looking into rooms as she went. She wasn't sure what she would find, but they had planned to meet here. Perhaps Ken, O-Remo, and the two boys were here somewhere, hiding out. She wanted to call for them, but she didn't dare.

It was on the bottom floor, outside one of the last doors that she tried, that she felt a sudden shivery chill pass through her. Her hand paused on the handle, and for a moment she thought about just walking away, perhaps finding a closet or a cubbyhole somewhere to crawl into and wait until either rescue workers arrived or the bears chewed through the entire building to get to her.

Don't go in, a tiny voice whispered. Karin ignored it. She jerked the handle and stepped inside.

The sword clattered to the floor as a hand came up to cover her mouth. O-Remo lay on the bed, a blanket covering him up to his chest, his face cold and white.

Someone had closed his eyes. Karin reached out to touch his cheek. There was the tiniest residue of warmth beneath a creeping cold.

He's dead because of you, the voice whispered again. *He loved you. You pushed him away, rejected him, because of your selfishness. He was never perfect, but his heart was pure, innocent. You're nothing but a golddigging whore. He never deserved you, and you never deserved him.*

'I'm so sorry,' she whispered, squatting down beside the bed. 'What can I say? I did love you, Remo. I … always did.'

She rested her forehead against his chest, taking a lost comfort in him. When they had been together he had often held her in his arms while her career crashed and burned around her. He had taken his band to the greatest heights and seen them fade into the rearview mirror of his own career, but even when they were touring bars and live houses and playing to no more than fifty people at a time, he had always taken a pleasure out of what he did. The enjoyment was always there. He hadn't been celebrity hungry like she had; for a while the world had just hunted him. He had waved goodbye and moved on; she had forever been looking back.

And in that divergence they had lost each other.

The walls around her shuddered. Karin lifted her head, wondering if one of the bears had got into the Fort. From somewhere outside came the growl of an engine, and she stood up, wondering if rescue workers had arrived. She gave O-Remo one last smile, ran a finger down his cheek and then went out to find out what was going on, the old sword once more in her hand. As she pushed through the door into the corridor, something huge smashed into the main doors.

She could hear the sound of an engine, but it was trying to break inside. Was this some new kind of bear they hadn't seen before? She backed away, heading for the stairs to the upper floor, taking them two at a time.

Upstairs on the landing, she chose a door that was directly above the crunching, splintering cacophony below. She found herself in a classroom with a large bay window that looked out over the complex.

She ran to the window and pulled it open, letting in a cold afternoon wind. She shivered, pulling her jacket tighter around herself, and looked out.

Rutherford Forbes sat at the controls of a huge snowplow directly below her. With a twisted smile on his bruised face, he was trying to batter through the doors.

'Rutherford!' she shouted. 'Stop!'

If he heard her he showed no sign. He reversed a few feet, and then slammed forward into the door again. This time it gave way beneath the heavy snow shovel, but the whole plow bucked forwards, its front end punching into the Fort, the small cab smashing into the wall.

Forbes screamed as the glass shattered and the roof of the cab buckled and broke open. He tried to jerk the plow back into reverse, but its blade had got stuck on the inside wall of the Fort. 'Come on, you bastard!' he screamed over the groan of the engine and the whistling of the wind.

'Rutherford!' she shouted again, this time lifting the sword up by her shoulder like a javelin. The blade wasn't sharp but the point would do its business on his soft, fatty flesh. She looked down at him, thought about all the things he'd done, all the deaths he'd caused, and tensed her arm, ready to harpoon him like a diseased fish.

As the plow jerked, he glanced up at her. For a moment his eyes went wide, then he gasped in surprise. 'Karin! Karin, what are you doing?'

'You bastard, Rutherford. What did you do? Those things ... all those people dead...'

'It was just business, Karin! Jesus, you should know about that! Every time you put those wonderful lips of yours around some guy's dick it was the same thing!'

'I never *hurt* anyone!'

'Nor did I! The things weren't supposed to escape!'

Her fingers tensed over the sword handle. 'But they did! I should kill you, Rutherford!'

'Karin, don't be so stupid! Can't you see, you need me. You're nothing without me. Don't think I didn't know what you were up to. I knew from that first night that all you wanted was a way into my bank account. I played you just the way you tried to play me. I used you for whatever I wanted, and damn, I don't regret a minute of it. You were as good as in any one of those movies.'

'Shut up!'

'Oh, truth hurts, does it? The fact is, you bailed on that piece of trash singer because he wasn't any good for your career. He was some worthless lowlife who was only bringing you down. You jumped into my bed at the first opportunity because you wanted another shot and you needed someone to pay for it. Well, much as I think you're a disgusting little tramp, I'll do it. Put down that sword, Karin, and I'll do it. I'll marry you, and you can have all the money you want to put into your silly little media career. Just put that sword down.'

Karin shook her head, tears filling her eyes. 'He was worth ten of you, Rutherford,' she said slowly. 'He loved me, and he loved what he did. And he never ... meant anyone else any harm.'

She flung the sword as hard as she could, worried momentarily that it would be a total anticlimax and bounce off the cab of the snowplow, but the sword fell straight and true, finding the bull's eye at the back of Forbes's throat, impaling him like a knife-eater whose trick had gone wrong. He gurgled and blood pooled around the sword hilt protruding from his mouth, then he toppled out of the cab of the plow and landed in the snow.

For a moment Karin felt hollow, overcome with the guilt of murdering her fiancé, then the memories of everything she had seen overwhelmed her. She stepped away from the window, slid down to the floor, held her face in her hands and began to cry. She stayed that way for a long time, letting out not just the pain of now, but everything from her past, from the sweet loves she had lost to the shameless way she had got into her manager's bed and then lain on her back with a succession of strangers.

When she was done, she pushed herself to her feet, steeled herself, and headed for the door. It wasn't over yet. There were still lives to be saved.

41

DYING SONATAS

UNLOADING a Marshall Twin Head Stack in two feet of snow and without any help took Ken some time. Eventually he got it down onto the ground around the side of the van, facing the burning Grand Mansion. He connected it to a small generator which they used for occasional impromptu outdoor shows at the front of train stations or at campsites. Often the sight of a formerly arena-filling band busking outside of a train station would attract bigger crowds than they saw in many live houses, and they always sold a stack of CDs. Ken didn't dwell on how far they'd come down in the world, because right now he would be happy to play to an empty room if only he had his band around him. With two of them gone and the other missing, the only thing left was for him to play them one last lament.

His favorite guitar was in the room in the dormitory building, but he had several others. He selected a fine Gibson Flying V, the guitar he had used at the Metal Garden concert that O-Remo had remembered so fondly. It was only appropriate.

The flames biting at the windows on the upper floor of the Grand Mansion were his audience as he slung the strap over his shoulders and set the guitar to his favorite tuning, a sludgy dropped C which would rattle windows and shake bones. He thought about the best song to play, settling on the track that they often closed their shows with, *Consecrate my Heart in Blood*, a song that had reached the Top 20 of the Oricon Charts and brought them mainstream recognition, something they'd sneered about for years while spending the money the song had earned on beers, women, and computer games. It was a doom metal love song, an ode from a suicidal man to his dead wife. Apt, in so many ways.

As Ken started to strum out the first chords, he only wished he could sing, but he had the voice of a tone-deaf choirboy, so an instrumental would have to suffice.

'This is for you, guys,' he whispered, as the introduction came to an end and he stamped down on his overdrive pedal.

A sludgy roar filled the courtyard, the sound of his brutal, down-tuned chords echoing off the walls of the Grand Mansion. Ken gritted his teeth as he felt the music surge through him, filling in the cracks in his broken soul. His left hand worked the fretboard like a man wrestling with a snake, while the right attacked the strings with a ferocity he hadn't felt since the first club tours when all four of them were teenagers. In his last desperation, he sounded better than ever.

He looked up as an answering roar came from across the courtyard. A bear stepped into view between the end of the west wing and the first of the dormitory buildings. It bared its teeth and bounded forward.

This is it, Ken thought. *This is the end. This is where I play my last song.*

He closed his eyes, waiting for the beast to finish him, his fingers still working hard at the strings, letting the music flood through him.

Come on, he thought. *Where are you?*

He opened his eyes. The bear was standing in the middle of the courtyard, no more than ten metres from him, shaking its head from side to side, its eyes flicking back and forth as if lost. He'd seen fans like that in some of the club shows, veterans of the hardcore scene, their minds fried from the relentless brutality of the music, yet still enjoying it on a deeper, subconscious level.

The bear was rocking out.

Ken grimaced and attacked the guitar harder, segueing into one of their most brutal songs, *Eternal Laceration,* and the bear gave a short growl and sat back on its haunches. Ken couldn't be sure, but smoke appeared to be drifting out of one of its ears.

It's short-circuiting, he thought. *It's breaking down.*

He continued to hammer at the guitar. The bear climbed unsteadily back to its feet and stumbled away, repeatedly missing its footing and slipping to the ground, still shaking its head from side to side. Only when it made it to the break in the buildings from which it had come did it start into a slow run, disappearing around the back of the Grand Mansion.

Ken turned down his volume control and stopped playing, the silence immediately rushing in to fill the void where the sound had been. For a few moments it had looked like the bear would break down entirely, before it had taken control of its senses long enough to get away.

'It couldn't handle the frequency of the sound waves,' he muttered, giving a stunned shake of his head. 'God damn it, we can break them!'

He looked down at the guitar in his hands, and remembered how the bear had managed to get away.

But the guitar isn't enough. I need more bass.

AKANE'S PACE was killing Jun. He never seemed to be able to get within twenty metres of her, almost as if she thought he would try to turn her around. He had resigned himself to following her whim, however, whether it killed them eventually or not. Plus, the light was fading. A sign they had passed a few minutes before had given the distance to British Heights as one kilometre. He didn't know how far they had come, but he didn't like their chances of negotiating their way back in the dark.

The hillside had gradually flattened out, and although his thighs were aching, the snow was a lot shallower underneath the forest canopy and they made good speed. As they got closer, he saw the grey shape of what looked like the Fort through the trees, but in front of it—

'Akane! There's one of them! Stop!'

The grey shape lying in the snow looked like an upturned bowl. Like the bear that had killed Dai, this one was lying in wait for them, only the snow hadn't yet accumulated over it enough to form a proper disguise.

Jun started to run, trying to get to Akane, but almost as soon as he did, she started to run too, *away* from him, heading almost straight towards the shape lying in the snow.

'Akane!' he screamed again, but he had no chance, it was far too close. It would be on her before he could get anywhere near.

'*Akane!*'

IT DIDN'T LOOK that difficult to drive, but the snowplow's controls felt like iron bars set in concrete. As Forbes's dead eyes watched her from where he had fallen in the snow, Karin enacted every parody of a bad woman driver in the handbook, jerking the gears, stalling the engine, and slamming the vehicle forwards into the wall of the Fort, before reversing backwards into a tree.

Eventually she got the blade free from where it had caught on the entrance wall and managed to turn the vehicle round—crushing Forbes's body in the process—but driving it in the thick snow was difficult. Forbes had actually used the blade to clear a path from the back of the Fort around to the front door, but controlling it was yet another thing that she was unsure of, jerking it up and down, burying it in frozen soil and then lifting it too high to move the snow away.

Eventually she maneuvered the vehicle out on to the main road through the complex, and got the blade lowered to clear the snow. Wiping sweat off her brow that had formed despite the creeping cold as evening drew in, she turned down towards the courtyard where she hoped she might find the others.

She had gone no more than thirty feet when a figure stepped out from beneath the porch of the teahouse. It stepped out into the snow and began waving its arms over its head.

In the gloom it was difficult to see whether it was a man or a woman. With long black hair and wearing a white jacket, it could have been a girl, except the person's shoulders seemed a little too square. She moved the plow forward a short distance until the figure came up alongside.

'Karin! I'm so glad to see you!'

'Bee?'

He gave her a wide grin, the gaps between each of his teeth showing. With his huge dark eyes his face looked like a skull. She shivered. She had never liked Bee; even before he donned the sinister makeup he had worn on stage he had freaked her out. It wasn't just the odd way he looked, but what was behind his eyes. She was used to the way men looked at her. More often than not their eyes would run over her body like a digital scanner, and if they didn't she would see a steel in them that suggested it was a battle of wills to concentrate on her face. But with Bee, it was different. He'd never had any interest in screwing her. He looked right through her looks, right inside. Into her mind, her soul.

And she hated it.

'Quickly,' he said. 'Help me up.'

She started to reach out a hand, then pulled it back, something in his tone unnerving her. 'Where have you been, Bee?'

'Karin, I don't have time for this. Quickly.'

'Did you see any of the others?'

His eyes narrowed, his smile dropping away. With a reedy snarl that reminded her of Professor Crow, he grabbed a handle next to the steps up the cab and pulled himself up towards her, the other hand reaching out. She cried out and twisted away as his fingers closed over her hair, jerking her head around. He tried to slam her face into the dashboard, but she stuck out an elbow and caught him in the neck, knocking him sideways. He slipped on the icy footstep and fell back. Karin tried to kick out, but fingers made powerful from years of hitting a bass guitar closed over her ankle and gripped her tight. She aimed her heel at his face, but his grip was too strong.

'You fucking bitch,' he said. 'Don't you understand? I need your help. I need your help to tame him.'

'Tame who?'

'Lolo.'

She twisted her leg again, this time to the side, executing an old dance exercise. The sideways torsion made him lose his grip and she kicked out at his face, but he batted her leg away. Her ankle thumped against the metal frame of the cab and she winced in pain. Bee started to grab for her again when a growl came from behind him. He gasped, turning to look. A dark shape came bounding out of the gloom. Seeing he was distracted, Karin kicked out hard at the side of Bee's face. Her shoe caught him flush and he fell off the plow, straight into the path of the oncoming bear.

She didn't stay to watch. She pushed away and rolled out of the other side of the cab, sprinting away as fast as she could down the track she had cleared in the snow. Behind her came the sound of Bee's screams and crunching bones.

The Fort rose up in front of her, its doorway welcoming. Even though Forbes had broken it in, she might be able to find somewhere inside to hide. If she had to she could go back down into the tunnels.

Then a shadow moved across the doorway and made her plan redundant.

She veered off the path, running as best as she could. The chilled evening air had begun to harden the surface of the snow, making every step feel like she was punching through ice. Her legs felt heavy with fatigue, but adrenalin drove her on. Terrified that the bear inside the Fort would see her, she headed around the outside of the building and then cut straight into the forest, hoping to find somewhere to hide.

(I don't want to die)

She had barely reached the first trees when a roar came from behind her. She glanced back just long enough to see a shadowy bounding shape as it rushed across the snow. She stifled a scream and hurried forward, into the gloom under the trees. She could practically feel the breath that stank of Bee's blood, hot and tickly on her neck, and she closed her eyes, not wanting to feel its teeth

(please be quick please be quick don't make me suffer)

puncturing her skin and ripping through her body as it lacerated her muscles and crunched through her bones—

—then hands were pulling at her, and a girl's voice was telling her

(hurry hurry)

as she was dragged sideways into a small opening. Her feet felt hard concrete beneath them and someone was pulling her down into a cold, dark corner.

'We're safe here, Karin,' came Akane's soothing voice.

The bear roared, and the concrete shook around them as it slammed against the opening Akane had pulled her through. She tried to speak, but all she could do was let out a desperate scream.

'This is an old World War Two pillbox,' Jun's voice said, and she started, having not seen him in the dark crouching just inches away. 'We're stuck, but it can't get in. The opening is too small.'

As Karin's eyes adjusted to the gloom, she looked around her and saw Jun was right. They were in what resembled a giant egg made of concrete, with a slit less than two feet wide on one side for the entrance, a small sitting space inside and a long thin strip no more than six inches high through which to observe the forest. The pillbox walls were almost three feet thick, and as she watched the bear came around the front, one paw scrabbling at the outside of the slit, looking for a way in. Unable to fit its claws into the thin gap, it tried ramming its shoulder against the outside, but to no effect.

Karin felt Akane's hands wrap around her. 'We're safe here,' she said. 'Don't worry. We might freeze to death, but at least we won't get eaten.'

After a few minutes the bear gave one last frustrated growl, slammed the side of the pillbox with its paw, and then wandered off into the forest. The gloom was so deep now that within seconds it became nothing more than a shadow, melting into the darkness beneath the trees.

Crouched in the corner of the pillbox, Karin was in the middle with Akane on one side and Jun pressed against her on the other. As the adrenaline rush began to subside, she realised it wasn't just for comfort. The temperature was dropping quickly.

'Thank you,' she whispered.

'We got out through the hole in the cave that the avalanche caused,' Akane said. 'What happened to you?'

'The stairs I took came out inside the Fort,' Karin said. 'I found O-Remo dead … and I killed Rutherford.'

'Killed him?'

She nodded. 'He was trying to break down the Fort door with a snowplow. I told him to stop … I told him…'

The tears came rushing out, and once they started they wouldn't stop. They became more than just for what had happened to them, but for every failing in her life. From the moment she sold her soul for stardom, to the day she walked away from O-Remo and her dreams, to the first night she lay on her back beneath a sweaty

English billionaire in an attempt to get it all back. She cried and cried until the tears began to freeze on her cheeks.

As Akane held her close, Karin couldn't help feeling that it should be the other way round, that this brave young teenager should be finding comfort in her, the thirty-something former media starlet who had seen and done it all. As the tears finally began to subside, she told them about Forbes and then Bee, and in turn they told her what had happened down in the caves.

'We can't stay here,' Jun said at last. 'We might be safe from the bears but we'll freeze to death in a couple of hours. We're all soaking, and the temperatures are subzero already.'

'The Fort is the nearest place,' Karin said. 'I saw a bear inside, though. Perhaps if we could avoid it long enough we could shelter in the basement. It wouldn't be much warmer, but at least it would be dry, and we might be able to find some blankets or something.'

'We have to find a way to kill those bears,' Akane said. 'It's them or us. Sooner or later.'

'How?'

'You said Forbes had a snowplow?'

'I abandoned it when Bee attacked me. It's big enough to stop one, but it's not very fast.'

'It's better than nothing,' Akane said. 'If we can get to it, at least we can try to find the others.'

'The bears could be anywhere,' Jun said. 'We basically have no choice. If we can get to the back wall of the Fort, we can try to either get inside or get that snowplow.'

'Split up,' Akane said. She looked at both of them in turn, and though Karin couldn't see her eyes, she could sense the desperation in her voice. 'We can't risk it getting two or more of us at once. We have to be brave, and we have to be prepared to sacrifice ourselves so the others can make it. We have to stop them. There's nothing else that's important right now.'

'No—' Jun started to say, but Akane put a hand over his mouth.

'It's the only way.'

He sighed. 'Okay. If we have no other choice. Let's get this over with.'

The Fort was just a grey smudge behind the dark stalks of the trees. Jun gave a slow count of three under his breath, then they broke from the pillbox one by one, running as quickly as they could through the snow towards the back of the Fort. Karin stared straight ahead, refusing to look at the shadows of Jun and Akane on either side of her, terrified of seeing a bear's monstrous shape come looming out of the dark to drag one of them away. As the wall of the Fort came up in front of her and she pressed her hands against its cold stone, she gasped with relief as she saw the others make it.

Jun was ahead of her, Akane just behind. Staying low and close to the wall, they made their way around the Fort until they were on the front side of the building with the broken doors of the main entrance just in front of them.

'There's the plow,' Jun whispered, as they crowded in behind him and ducked down behind a stand of snow-covered bushes. 'What do you think? Go for it or head inside and try to find somewhere to hole up for the night?'

'The plow,' Akane said. 'Let's take the bastards on.'

Karin was about to reply when Jun put up a hand. 'Listen,' he said. 'Can you hear that?'

'What–'

'Shh!'

They all fell silent. For a moment, all Karin could hear was the gentle sighing of the wind and the light pitter-patter of freshly falling snow, then she heard it, a low drone over the top of everything mixed with a tinkling sound, like the breaking of icicles over the hum of a distance engine.

'What is it?' she whispered.

'I don't believe it,' Jun said. 'It's music.'

42

THE FINAL CONCERTO

Like the Pied Piper, Ken had known how to make them come. Standing on top of his van with the guitar strapped on and a cable snaking down to the amp below, he played a series of finger-picking pieces to get their attention, to draw them in. On the ground below him he had set up Bee's huge bass cabinet and plugged in the bassist's favorite instrument, a heavy six-string that could play almost low enough to slip into sound waves only dogs could hear.

As the dark set in and the evening brought subzero temperatures with it, he tried not to let his teeth chatter as his arms shook with cold. His fingers routinely missed simple notes, and he prayed the bears would come while he still had the strength to play the bass strings. So far there had been no sign of them, although he had heard them roaring from time to time, further out across the complex or back in the forest. He had seen no one else alive.

The Grand Mansion was still burning. The flames had spread to the dining hall and to the rooms on the second floor of the west wing, which was now a raging inferno. While Ken felt a sense of sorrow at the building's demise, he was grateful for the occasional gusts of warm air on his face.

A growl on the road leading out of the courtyard announced the arrival of the first of the bears. It snarled and snapped as it came through between the gateposts and circled around the van like a fighting dog looking for an opening.

He heard another roar as a second bear came through the space between the burning west wing and the first of the dormitories, completely heedless of the fire raging alongside it. It snarled as it reached the other, circling in the opposite direction as if they were pack animals trying to cut off his line of retreat.

'Come on, where's the others?' he muttered, willing his freezing fingers to play on. He couldn't wait too long. If they rushed him before he got a chance to take up the bass, his whole plan would fail.

A third bear came into view, appearing out of the dark below the courtyard. It was covered in snow as if it had been chasing something. It joined the others in their slow, wary circling of the van.

Six, Forbes had said. Jun had killed one with the flare, but where were the other two?

Something slammed into the van, knocking him forward. He slipped and fell off, lucky to land in a drift of snow which stopped the guitar from crushing his ribs. He pushed forwards and fell back out into the section he had cleared, just as the van shuddered again and a roar split the night. A moment later a fourth bear appeared around the side of the van, its maw bloody with gore as if it had just finished feeding.

The other three bears stopped their stalking and began to snarl. The spell was broken. The bass stood on its stand a few feet away, but Ken didn't have time to reach it. If he let go of the guitar he would be dead.

As the first bear charged, he rolled on to his back, depressing the distortion pedal with his shoulder, stabbing at the strings at the same time.

A droning guitar roar burst out of his Marshall and the bear fell back, wailing. It knocked into a second, but the other two kept their distance, snapping and snarling, waiting for a chance to get closer. His fingers were aching as he hit the strings as best he could, but the guitar alone wasn't enough. All he could do was hold them off. If only——

A low crunching hum came from further away, on the other side of the van. The twin beams of headlights illuminated the group of bears and then a massive snowplow rumbled into view. The three people in the partially crushed cab were just silhouettes, but as Ken watched a slender figure jumped out and ran across to him.

'Akane!'

Close behind her came Jun. One of the bears darted forwards, but Ken smashed at the guitar and the creature jerked away as a thundering dropped C chord echoed across the courtyard.

'The sound is messing with their radio signals!' Ken shouted. 'I just can't make enough of it!'

'I can play bass,' Akane said, almost nonchalantly, grabbing up the instrument and hitting a heavy note as a bear lunged forward. She stared at the beast as it recoiled, a fearless gleam in her eyes. 'It's easy. Any clown can do it.'

She started to pound out a droning rhythm, stretching to reach the heaviest fifth and sixth strings. The other bears whined and drew back. One of them snapped at Akane, but Karin revved the snowplow and the front blade slammed into it, knocking it over. Another turned on her, but its attack was slow and lethargic, as if it too was struggling to decide what course of action to take.

'More sound!' Ken screamed. 'Jun, ever wanted to sing with your hero?'

Jun had already made that decision. He pulled a microphone out of the back of the van and plugged it into a spare input on Ken's guitar effects pedal. He looked at Ken, and behind the desperation in Jun's face there was a shimmer of excitement. He gave a small, half-frozen smile.

'Play me something badass,' he said. 'I know them all.'

Whether it worked or not, Ken no longer cared. He wanted one last chance to rock out. He started playing the intro riff to his favorite song, *One Against All*, which, rather conveniently, was about the last man standing in a war. Akane began to play a simplified rendition of the bass riff, then Jun began to roar the words, holding the mike with both hands, his body arched over the way O-Remo would have done. It was fitting, Ken thought.

'War, gimme more, come on here, I'll fight you all;
Down to the soil, soles of my feet, you'll have to cut me up, piece by piece;
One little man, on solid ground, against them all, I'm still standing tall;
One … Against … Allllll!'

As a bear keeled over, Karin revved the snowplow and crunched the blade into its neck. Another was standing motionless, its head swaying from side to side. As Ken watched, its feet fell out from under it. It collapsed on its side in the snow, a low whimpering coming from its throat.

One of the others attempted a final charge, but as Ken broke into a blisteringly heavy solo on his guitar's bass strings while Jun roared, it veered off course and slammed face first into the bus, keeling over on its side, smoke coming from a hole in its neck.

The last one looked like it wanted to leave, but as it turned towards the gap between the west wing and the dormitory, it stumbled sideways and rolled onto its back. As it lay there, belly facing up at the sky, it let out a hideous shriek that made Ken shiver. The sound seemed to last forever, an antithesis for their downturned sludge rock, a last desperate display of resistance.

As the sound died and the creature fell still, Ken let go of his guitar and shoved his hands into his pockets, desperate for warmth. One last open chord rang out across the courtyard as Jun and Akane also stopped playing and turned to look at him.

'Did we do it?' Jun croaked. 'Did we kill them?'

'It looks like it,' Akane said, her voice sounding surprisingly downcast.

Ken felt the sudden urge to high-five all of them, but when he looked up at Karin, the flames from the Grand Mansion inferno lighting up her face, his hope dispersed like snowflakes blown by the wind.

She was staring past them at the pub, a look of hopelessness on her face.

'Don't stop!' she screamed, and then the rest of her words were lost beneath an earsplitting roar.

Forbes had said there were six. Ken had forgotten one.

The king.

43

____

EXIT STRATEGIES

OGIWARA DIDN'T WANT to think about what was going on outside. He had hidden away in an upstairs bedroom for a while, watching the forest out of the window until it got too dark to see, but suddenly he heard a commotion from downstairs, the sound of an engine followed by a splintering crash. He lay there in the dark for a while, waiting and listening. He was tempted to just hide under the bed until morning, but his curiosity got the better of him.

A few minutes after everything had gone quiet, he sneaked out of the room, crept to the end of the corridor and peered through the door. It was empty, so he went through a door on the other side, into a classroom which had windows facing out on the main complex.

He was several rooms to the left of the main door, but he could clearly see something huge crouched in front of it. Then the road outside was illuminated by two circles of light, and he gasped, wondering what kind of a monstrosity was this. Then he realised—it wasn't a bear at all, but a snowplow.

He couldn't make out the driver in the shadows of the cab above the lights, but as he watched, it pulled into reverse and turned away from the building, moving in shaky jerks away towards the main road through the complex. Whoever was driving it was leaving him behind. He banged on the windows, then opened one and shouted out, but the driver obviously didn't hear him as the plow turned in the direction of the Grand Mansion.

I have to catch it, he thought. _It could be my only chance._

He rushed out of the room and down the corridor, taking the stairs two at a time. The Fort was dark and silent, with only the last twilight filtering in through the small downstairs windows guiding him as he ran towards the main entrance.

He was nearly there when something dark and huge stepped in through the open doorway, blocking out the light.

Ogiwara cried out and tried to turn, succeeding only in losing his footing. He was already trying to get up even as he struck the floor, bashing his knees and elbows as he landed on the hard surface. The bear growled, and Ogiwara broke into a run, fleeing for his life.

It was too close to escape by hiding in one of the rooms; it would see him. He had to find somewhere secure where it wouldn't be able to follow. He burst through the double doors at the end of the corridor and into another dim corridor lined with bedroom doors. He heard the double doors burst open behind him as the bear followed, but he didn't dare look back.

He reached the end of the corridor and found one door standing open, a set of steps leading down. He pulled the door shut behind him and started down in pitch blackness, terrified of what he was running into, but more scared of what was coming behind.

The stairs gave way to a concrete floor and he stopped for a moment, trying to figure out where he was. He turned on his heels as he heard the door breaking open above him. Could it get down those stairs? They had seemed tight, but how flexible—and how desperate—was that bear?

A tiny glow was coming from a door in the corner. It was the only thing he had to go on, so he ran towards it and found himself at the top of a spiraling metal staircase, lit by occasional LED emergency lights fitted into the ceiling.

This doorway was much tighter than the other, but he pulled the door shut anyway and started down. He had nowhere else to go, so he hurried as quickly as he could, descending into the earth. After a few flights he slowed down, confident the bear couldn't follow, but aware that his way out was blocked. It was down or nowhere.

On the next landing he saw something dark lying on the ground. As he reached it he bent down, his eyes adjusting to the gloom, and pulled back again with a gasp. A dead bear cub about the size of a dog lay on the ground. Unlike bear cubs he had seen on TV and in zoos, it was anything but cute, a monstrosity of teeth and lumps of metal poking out through its fur. He nudged it with his foot, but it didn't move.

A couple of landings later he found another, then several more as he continued to descend. All of them were dead, and they seemed to be getting smaller, as if the strongest had made it the furthest up the stairs, as if they had been chasing someone.

At the bottom of the stairs he stepped out into a dull concrete corridor. The bodies of several tiny bear cubs no bigger than his foot littered the ground.

'Ugly mothers, weren't you?' he said, nudging one with his foot, repulsed at the wires protruding from its body as if it had been involved in a collision with a steel brush.

This had to be the underground base that old man had been talking about. He carried on a little further, looking through doors into rooms, but the place had been trashed. He found several more dead bears, and a few dead maintenance workers, who, from the smell, had been dead a couple of days.

Then he stepped through a steel door out into something straight out of one of those crappy children's adventure novels that Mishima had liked to read.

'What the hell is this? *Journey to the Centre of the Earth*, my butt crack.'

A huge cave lit by massive spotlights stretched away from him, arcing around a bend out of sight. The cave floor was a mock forest, trees and rocks and streams. Several catwalks stretched across to the opposite cave wall, while various ladders and metal steps led down through a wire mesh that was stretched across everything.

'Help me!'

'What the fuck? Matsumoto?'

Jun's voice drifted up from behind a screen of vegetation almost directly below him. Ogiwara looked down. He couldn't see Matsumoto, but there was a hole in the wire mesh where a human could have fallen through.

'I fell. Help me, please.'

Ogiwara smiled. He would help him all right. He was a good sort; he'd help Matsumoto up, but not before he'd given him the pasting he'd been asking for. Fuck the bears, fuck British Heights, fuck all those other pricks whether they were alive or dead. This was personal.

'Hey, Jun,' he called back. 'It's Ogiwara. Don't worry, mate, I'll come down and get you.'

A set of metal steps led down from the edge of the catwalk. Ogiwara started down, reaching a steel gate about halfway that blocked the way through.

'It's locked,' Jun called. 'Pull the lever on the wall to your left to open it. I fell, and I couldn't get out. It only opens from the outside.'

'Sure, no problem.'

He yanked down the lever and heard a click. He pushed the door open and descended the last flight of steps to the spongy ground below, trying not to clench his fists, trying not to let that prick Matsumoto know what was coming until the first punch landed.

'Where are you, you … my, um, friend?'

'I'm over here. I fell in the bushes, but my leg is trapped under a rock. Can you move it for me? I can't get up.'

Ogiwara smiled. Perfect. The rock would hold Matsumoto still while he took a few clean shots. 'Of course,' he said. 'Just hang on a moment.'

He reached a screen of bamboo, and pushed it aside, wading through. There was Matsumoto, lying on the ground, waiting for his beating—

It wasn't Matsumoto.

Ogiwara screamed as the figure leapt at him, closing his eyes to block out the sight of the hideous, birdlike face that obscured the visage of a man. Sharp, twisted talons reached for his neck and the last thing he heard was a screeching, crowlike scream.

KUROU THREW the body of the student aside and headed up the stairs and through the door that the boy had conveniently unlocked for him. His body still tingled and ached from the electrified wire mesh, but it would fade with time. The backup generators had left the power too low to kill him, but until the boy had showed up he had been faced with a difficult and painful climb.

He went into the incubator room and stared with dismay at the ruins of his life's work. His plan had been destroyed, and Mr. Park, if he ever found out Kurou still lived, would be very disappointed indeed.

Taking a few personal objects and a computer tablet filled with contacts and important account information from a safe in the incubator room wall, Kurou headed back towards the enclosures. There was another way out that he knew of, but while he might have to walk as far as the nearest town he could arrange for someone to smuggle him out of the country. The big question was what to do now. Mr. Park's men would be on his trail, and with his distinctive face nowhere would be safe. Except of course, somewhere with closed boundaries.

He smiled. Britain was in upheaval right now, if Internet reports were to be believed. The last one he had read had mentioned that it had closed its borders to Europe and broken away from the European Confederation.

If he could find a way in, perhaps he could offer his services to the new government.

Smiling to himself, he headed for the secret way out that not even Forbes had known about.

44

___

LAST STAND IN THE SNOW

'LOLO!' Karin screamed, as the gigantic rampaging bear broke through the wall of the pub and stepped out into the open, bared its teeth and roared at them so loud that Jun thought his ears would burst.

The creature no longer looked like a bear at all. It was something out of a nightmare—a monstrous porcupine carved out of ice, a mess of silvery spines with an enormous snapping maw in the centre. Only as it took a few steps forward and several of its spines broke off did Jun realise what it was, a bear whose fur had turned into needles of ice, as if it had been submerged and then the water had frozen as the creature had tried to shake it out.

Lolo tingled like Christmas bells as he bounded towards them.

Ken started to play again, with Akane pounding away on the bass, but it seemed to have little impact on Lolo as he slammed into the van, knocking it sideways. Akane managed to jump clear, but Jun and Ken fell into the snow as the van toppled over. Jun felt a sudden heavy weight bearing down on him, and knew he would have been crushed were it not for the snow that cushioned him all around. As it was, he was still trapped from the waist down. He looked across at Ken who was similarly trapped, but on his back with the guitar pressed down on top of him. With desperation in his eyes, Ken hacked at the guitar with his one free hand, but no sound came.

The light from the burning Grand Mansion blinked out as something huge and glittering loomed over Jun. Easily the height of the bus, Lolo was the biggest creature he had ever seen, an abomination of science and biotechnology. It almost seemed honourable to die at the claws of such a creation, but Jun shut his eyes, not wanting to see the end when it came.

Be quick, his mind pleaded.

'Hey, you big bastard! Over here!'

Akane, no!

The girl was standing halfway across the courtyard, waving her arms above her head. Lolo growled and turned towards her, huge head lowering like a cat ready to pounce.

'You big ugly turkey!' Akane shouted. 'Come on! Over here!'

She turned and ran as Lolo bounded forward, faster than a speeding truck. Akane headed for the west wing, towards the broken wall of the swimming pool. Jun wanted to shout out to her, but it was no use. He could do nothing to stop the massive, terrifying beast as it bore down on her. As Lolo came up behind her, the bear lifted a huge paw and swatted Akane to the ground. His jowls stretched back, ready to rip her to shreds—

—then he was rolling forward as Karin slammed the snowplow into his back, the blade raised to push him forwards and down, using his momentum to shove him through the broken glass wall and into the swimming pool room from where Jun guessed he had got his covering of ice. The engine of the plow roared as Karin slammed the vehicle forward into the building. There was a splash as Lolo hit the water, then the plow broke through and drove onto his back as he fell under the water. Lolo thrashed, but the plow was jammed between the bear and the room's low ceiling; his huge limbs could only shake it back and forth. He let out one last defiant roar, then there was a crackle of electricity and the bear went still.

Ken had dragged himself out from the snow and he came over to dig Jun free. Over by the swimming pool room, Karin was climbing up out of the snow where she had jumped from the snowplow's cab, and was peering in through the opening towards Lolo's submerged body.

Jun pushed past Ken and ran straight to Akane. She lay on her back in the snow, but as he reached her he knew it was too late. Her body was lacerated by Lolo's claws, and her face was white and pale as her last strength drained away. As he knelt down beside her and pulled her up into his arms, she gave him a weak smile.

'Jun…'

'Akane … oh god, *why?* Please don't die. Please don't leave me.'

'It's all right, Jun,' she said. She tried to lift a hand, but it fell back in the snow. Jun took it and pressed it against his face.

'Akane,' he cried, unable to stop the tears. 'Why did you do it? Why?'

'Jun … it's okay,' she said. 'I never really wanted to leave. I'm happy to stay here forever now.' She coughed. 'Thank you, Jun.'

'What do you mean? What for?'

'For coming back to me. All those years, I lost my best friend … but you came back. You came back to me. I love you, Jun. I always loved you, and I always … will.'

'Akane…'

'Thank you,' she said again. 'Thank you for coming … back.'

Jun looked up at the sky and screamed as he felt her go limp in his arms. Ken's hand fell on his shoulder and nearby he could hear Karin crying. They had lost friends too, but it didn't matter. As he held Akane's body in his arms nothing mattered any longer, not British Heights, not the bears, not anything.

For a few brief days she had come back to him.

Now it was over, and she had gone.

EPILOGUE

ENDINGS AND BEGINNINGS

JUN HAD TO ADMIT IT, Ken and Karin made a good couple. As they walked down the aisle, arm in arm while a handful of close friends tossed confetti, they carried the look of shared happiness that only a closeness to suffering could give. They held each other with a tightness that suggested they never wanted to let go, that they were afraid to, even. Jun smiled as he tossed the little packet of tissue confetti over their heads. He was happy for them. In their collective grief they had discovered that they shared more in common than they had expected, and from the ashes of their lives they had found a budding flower of respect for each other that had bloomed into love.

They were the lucky ones.

***

LATER, as the reception drew to a close, Ken found Jun standing out on the balcony of the sixteenth floor hotel restaurant, looking out over a view of Tokyo. He patted the younger man on the back, and held out a glass of wine.

'I'm too young…'

'Yeah, whatever. Just drink it.'

'Thanks.'

'I guess there's no point telling you not to jump, because if you were planning to you would have done it by now.'

Jun smiled. 'I'm not going to jump.'

'What are you going to do?'

'You still looking for a vocalist for your new band?'

Ken smiled. 'You know I am.'

'Well, I'm interested. I have some other stuff to do too, though.'

'Like what?'

'I need to find him. Everything that happened … it was his fault.'

Ken sighed. The body of Professor Crow had never been found. They had found Ogiwara's body in the same area into which Jun said Crow had fallen, but of the one responsible for everything, there had been no sign.

'He's out there somewhere,' Jun said. 'Akane … would still be alive if it wasn't for him. As would all the others.'

'He was only partly to blame, Jun. Yeah, so he built them, but Forbes was the power behind everything.'

'But he's dead, and Crow is not.'

Ken sighed. He patted Jun on the shoulder. 'There are lessons to be learned from Akane,' he said. 'One of them is when it's time to let go.'

'He's still out there,' Jun whispered.

Ken nodded. He patted Jun on the shoulder one more time, then turned and headed back into the party. As he reached the door he paused. Unable to stop himself, he turned and looked back.

Jun was still there, staring out at the night sky.

*****

ACKNOWLEDGMENTS

The Eyes in the Dark was conceived while I was enjoying a school field trip at a rather wonderful study camp in Japan in December 2013. While my students enjoyed various British-themed classes I was left to wander around the lovely setting, taking pictures and breathing in the atmosphere of a Medieval British town high up in the mountains. While the camp will remain nameless, the setting provided the backdrop for this novel. If any of you can figure out where it is and happen to find yourselves in Japan, it's well worth a visit. And just in case you're worried, I saw no evidence of killer mutant bears or a crazy deformed scientist by the name of Crow.

That's not to say that they weren't out there somewhere...
C.W.